Janet Laurence began her career in advertising and public relations. In 1978 she moved to Somerset with her husband, and started Mrs Laurence's Cookery Courses, beginning with basic cookery techniques for teenagers and later introducing courses for the more advanced. She combined this with writing for the *Daily Telegraph*, eventually taking over Bon Viveur's weekly cookery column. Janet Laurence now divides her time between writing crime fiction and cookery books, and she makes regular trips to Brittany, where she and her husband have converted a set of ruined barns.

Janet Laurence's previous culinary whodunnits are also available from Headline, and have been widely praised:

'Exuberant tale of gastronomic homicide, full of intriguing inside-knowledge ... Engaging chefette, Darina Lisle, sleuths zestfully and there are even some helpful culinary hints along the way' *The Times*

'Filled with mouth-watering recipes as well as mystery' *Sunday Express*

Also by Janet Laurence

FICTION

A Deepe Coffyn
A Tasty Way to Die
Hotel Morgue
Recipe for Death
Death and the Epicure
Death at the Table
To Kill the Past

NON-FICTION

A Little French Cookbook
A Little Scandinavian Cookbook
A Little Coffee Cookbook
A Taste of Somerset Guide to Good Food and Drink
Just for Two
The Craft of Food and Cookery Writing

Death
à la Provençale

Janet Laurence

HEADLINE

First published in 1995
by Macmillan London Limited

First published in paperback in 1996
by HEADLINE BOOK PUBLISHING

10 9 8 7 6 5 4 3 2

ISBN 0 7472 5082 0

Printed and bound in Great Britain by
Cox & Wyman Ltd, Reading, Berks

HEADLINE BOOK PUBLISHING
A division of Hodder Headline PLC
338 Euston Road
London NW1 3BH

TO
DELLA & DAVID AND PAT & ANTHONY

with many thanks for memorable times in the
South of France – and apologies

ACKNOWLEDGEMENTS

Many thanks to Charles Carey, the Oil Merchant, for all his information on olive oil and its processing and for introducing me to some sensational oils. This book does not set out to be a primer on olive oil and for those interested in learning more about this marvellous product, there is *The Essential Olive Oil Companion* by Anne Dolamore, published by Macmillan. My thanks also go to Alan Pitt for much information on Lloyd's, and to John Paxton, Laurence Edgecombe and Patrick Moule. Both my husband and I owe Della and David Robson and Pat and Anthony Frodsham enormous gratitude for making a succession of visits to the Côte d'Azur truly memorable. I hope they will forgive me for the licence I have taken in writing this book to invent characters and incidents very different from their own experience.

If, despite the help I have had, there are inaccuracies in this book, they are my fault, nobody else's. Needless to say, but I will say it anyway, none of the characters or incidents in this book bears *any* relationship to real life except by the long arm of coincidence. Finally, many thanks to my husband, Keith, who has been, as always, such a help and support during the writing of this book.

Chapter One

The cake glistened golden in the sun. It dripped with goodness. Everything about it, its roundness, its luscious colour, the open crumbs gleaming with syrup, held the promise of sweetness and plenitude, a rich and luxurious satisfaction.

'Honey cake for honeymooners,' said Helen Mansard, placing it on the table.

She was a small woman in her late forties with a sweep of fair hair piled on top of her head, skin like a ripe peach and a neat but generously curved body. Her round face was given grace by large, bright blue, laughing eyes and a wide mouth with a lower lip as full as a slice of mango.

Darina sniffed the sweet aroma that floated up from the cake. 'It's as heady as wine,' she said. 'And we're drunk already!' She smiled at the man sitting beside her on the cushioned wooden bench. There was a relaxed air about her, a suggestion that marriage had proved a delightful surprise.

Darina Lisle was now Darina Pigram. The new surname wasn't an improvement but everything else about the wedded state was. Happiness radiated from her. It turned her straightforward good looks into beauty, glossing the long fair hair waving around her shoulders, softening the

1

impact of her shade-under-six-foot height and deflecting attention from the direct, uncompromising gaze of her grey eyes.

Darina looked again at the cake. Why should slipping a ring on her finger four days ago make everything shine with such a golden light? She had lived with William for a year before their wedding, she had thought she knew him through and through, that marriage would merely prove a formalization of their relationship. Instead it was as though familiar food had taken on new flavours.

'I thought honeymoons should be spent by the happy couple alone, preferably on some desert island!' Bernard Barrington Smythe, the fourth member of the luncheon party, replaced the wine goblets with fluted glasses and opened a bottle of champagne. He'd covered his balding head with a Panama to protect it from the sun. The hat cast a shadow over bushy sandy eyebrows that sheltered pale amber eyes like small plants growing along the edge of a cliff.

'I've always thought that a dreadful idea.' Helen cut the cake and placed slices on Provençal faience plates. 'The last thing you need as newlyweds is to be left on your own. All that stress and strain of getting married, all the exhaustion of writing thank-you letters and keeping the in-laws from each other's throats, the terrible business of sorting out the new home. I think the perfect honeymoon is one with lots of not-too hectic activity, preferably with a few friends thrown in.' She gave the newly wedded couple a sly smile that acknowledged her role in that day's honeymoon entertainment.

Bernard filled the glasses with care, twisting the bottle above each with a neat flourish that avoided drips, then sat back in his chair, his chubby body battling against the confinement of his white designer jeans and a chic shirt, a patchwork of striped and checked green and white cotton. He raised his glass. 'What she means is, we're incredibly honoured to have you with us today. Let's drink your health.'

Darina raised her glass and exchanged another smile with her husband.

'Husband.' She articulated the thought and laid her hand along his thigh. 'What a strange word it is. Anglo-Saxon, I suppose. It has a peasant flavour, a suggestion of a house bondsman.'

'If I remember aright, it's Old English and you can forget about the bondsman bit,' said Bernard.

'I didn't think you'd been to university,' broke in Helen.

He skewed a knowing look at her. 'There are other ways of accumulating information than incarcerating yourself in a learning institution. William, husband means master of the house. Don't stand for any nonsense, put your foot down now.'

The groom laughed. It was an easy, amused sound that said he was his own man. 'We're a partnership, no top dog about either of us.'

Darina felt muscles in his long leg twitch under her hand and slipped her fingers closer round his thigh as she attacked the cake with her free hand. 'This tastes of love,' she said with a sigh of satisfaction. 'If we are what we eat, we should have this regularly.'

'Every day,' William agreed.

'The way you two look at each other is scandalous.' Bernard put down his glass with mock force. 'Helen, don't give them any more or they'll be eating each other before our very eyes.'

'If they can't feel passionate on honeymoon, it's a poor look-out.' Helen slid another piece of cake on to William's plate.

The lunch party was in the South of France, in the hills near Grasse, where Helen Mansard had bought a Provençal farmhouse, a *mas*. Its square weight sat solid in olive groves, the warm brown of the earth and the whispering, silvery green of the trees providing a perfect setting for the grey stone. The courtyard where they were sitting was protected on two sides by buildings and on the other two by walls but a strategic gap in the southern aspect meant they were offered a view of the Mediterranean, intensely blue under the early March sun that the sheltered courtyard concentrated into enough warmth to enable them to eat outside.

One corner of the courtyard was occupied by a pristine swimming pool, the water lapping fondly at brilliant blue tiles. Round the edges of the pool, the landscaping had the raw look of recently completed planting, the profusion of small shrubs an eloquent testimony to generous expenditure.

All the property, in fact, had that sleek look achieved only through a hefty injection of cash. Newly pointed walls and smartly painted shutters, well-ordered paving and expensive plant containers (no doubt later in the season they would be bright with geraniums), and the attractive iroko garden furniture all suggested that Helen's cookery books were selling very nicely indeed.

Darina refused another slice of honey cake. 'Frankly, I can only say I'm stuffed, you've fed us too well.' Was it the fresh air and the sun that had made the food taste so good or had Helen worked some particular magic? The ingredients had been so simple: roasted red peppers with an anchovy dressing, eaten with crusty French bread, followed by a prodigal quantity of langoustines grilled over prunings from olive trees and served with a green salad, the dressing made from an olive oil that had married sweetness with a captivating citrus freshness. Cool white

Chablis had accompanied the meal and a vintage claret, a 1966 Margaux, had appeared with several ripe and full-bodied cheeses before the final blessing of the honey cake and champagne.

Helen had even managed to curb her tendency to insist on post-mortems after every course. They had spent no more than five minutes discussing the saltiness of the anchovy dressing and whether it was counter-balanced by the peppery power of the Italian estate-bottled olive oil; only ten on the composition of the mayonnaise served with the langoustines and the possible desirability of wrapping shellfish in lettuce leaves before their grilling. Now she seemed to have forgotten completely to ask their reaction to the honey cake.

Darina sighed, replete, feeling the relaxation that only perfectly flavoured and balanced food could bring. She sat back and let the peace and calm of the old farmhouse and its setting flow over her like silk.

Helen was so right about the stresses and strains of getting married. The wedding itself had been held in the Somerset village where Darina had grown up, the church service followed by a reception in a large local house lent for the occasion. It had rushed past her, as though the day had been speeded up like film, leaving her joyous but breathless. And, oh, how she wanted to forget everything that had led up to it, the pressures, the arguments, the hectic arrangements.

'We thought about going to the Seychelles for our honeymoon,' William was saying. 'But then we were offered an apartment in Antibes and we both agreed it was too good an opportunity to miss.' He, too, appeared totally relaxed.

'And it's lovely to have the chance of catching up with you, Helen,' added Darina.

Both Helen and Darina were cookery writers. Over the

last decade, Helen had made quite a name for herself. Prior to moving to France, she, too, had lived in Somerset. Although there were nearly twenty years between them, she and Darina had spent much time together, experimenting on each other, defining flavour, exploring different cuisines and discussing ways of stimulating the appetite. Then, two years ago, after a very successful television series – its accompanying book had headed the bestseller list for a gratifying number of weeks – Helen had abandoned England for the Mediterranean.

'What a spot you've found here,' said Darina enviously. 'Perfect for writing. All this peace!'

'Too perfect!' A caustic note burned its way through Helen's voice and the full mouth tightened. 'I spend most of my time inventing reasons why people shouldn't come and stay. Sometimes I think everyone I've met is planning to visit the South of France. The summer is one long series of distractions.'

'Helen gets distracted all too easily.' Bernard shifted back in his chair. The brim of his hat hid his expression.

Darina moved a little closer to William.

'You don't help,' snapped Helen suddenly. 'Turning the place into a factory.'

'Factory?' William looked easily around the bright courtyard.

'Helen, is this the new venture you mentioned? Stop being mysterious and tell us about it.'

Darina's friend looked sulky. 'It's Bernard's, really.' She glanced at the man at the opposite end of the table, his face unreadable under his Panama. 'Don't hang back, Bernard. Usually you can't wait to tell everyone about it.'

Bernard put his arms on the table, the lazy relaxation suddenly gone. 'You said you thought it was a good idea.

Great idea, was what you said. I thought you were behind it.'

For a brief moment Darina thought she saw panic in Helen's eyes, then her friend laughed, carelessly. 'Bernard you're such an idiot! Of course it's a great idea. You know how uptight I get when anything comes between me and a deadline. Now, tell Darina and William all about it, you can see they're dying to know just how clever you've been.' She reached across the table and gave his hand a quick squeeze.

'Well, here we sit, agog for details,' William prompted.

Helen turned up the voltage of her smile.

Bernard ducked his head in the gesture of a man modestly receiving undeserved rewards. 'As soon as I saw this place, I realized what Helen had found,' he began.

There was the sound of a tractor approaching the courtyard wall. 'Oh, God, what is happy Jacques up to now?'

'Not another row, please, Bernard! Remember, he's our neighbour.'

Bernard groaned and turned to Darina and William. 'You wonder about sheep being burned alive by the French or the lorries of Europe brought to a standstill? One confrontation with Jacques Duval explains it all.'

Helen's fingers beat irritably on the table. 'He's just your average French chauvinist.'

'Chauvinist? Too right, the word was invented for him.'

The tractor stopped, there was a mechanical grinding noise and over the wall drifted unspeakably mature farmyard odours.

'Hell's teeth!' Bernard leapt out of his chair and charged over to an old granite mill standing picturesquely in a corner of the courtyard and pulled himself up so he could peer over the wall. His short, overweight body poised itself perilously on the edge of the ancient mill; he'd lost his hat in the charge to the wall and the sun shone brilliantly off the polished bald patch, but the depth of his outrage stripped the scene of comic overtones.

Darina felt for his anguish but she couldn't help contrasting Bernard with her husband. William was tall, topping herself by several inches, and had a full head of dark hair. His aquiline features were handsome – she liked to think dashing was the best description. He had presence, and a very English charm that was compounded of intelligence, consideration and education.

Darina wondered exactly what had attracted Helen to Bernard. His drive and energy? It certainly wasn't his looks.

'*Monsieur.*' Bernard's indignant voice floated over to them. '*Que faîtes-vous?*'

A growl of French drifted over with the ripe, rank smell. Darina caught such words as *salaud, connard* and *salopard*.

'*Espèce de con!*' shouted Bernard back. Then his shoulders tensed as he controlled himself. '*C'est affreux, je proteste! Nous mangeons ici, dans notre cour. C'est impossible avec le parfum de votre fumier.*' Bernard's fluent French was seasoned with a strong English accent.

More unintelligible grunts and growls that finished with, '*Va donc, eh, imbécile!*'

The fat rolls of Bernard's neck purpled with anger. Shaking with rage he jumped down from his perch, stumbling as he hit the ground. 'I'll sort out that French cur,' he said, through gritted teeth.

Helen held out a pleading arm towards him. 'Darling, you'll only say something you'll regret. Why don't you come and have some coffee and tell Darina and William all about our plans?'

'Don't think you can sweet-talk me out of a showdown with that bastard. There's a bloody great pile of manure

8

against our wall and he says it's going to stay there! But', his voice softened suddenly, 'I don't want to spoil our lunch.' He returned to the table and surveyed the remains of their feast, his nose pinched in disgust. 'Come on, we can't stay here.'

Inside the house, the dark dazzled Darina's eyes. She had to wait until she was accustomed to the lack of sunlight before she could appreciate the big, open-plan living room with its enormous fireplace and plain plastered walls. Like the courtyard, this, too, looked recently renovated. Nothing pretentious but the heavy pieces of French furniture had not been found in a flea-market and there was a well-preserved sheen to everything. The kitchen area looked as though it had benefited from the services of a top designer and the equipment was all of the best.

Settled on one of the pair of large, comfortable sofas that were arranged in the centre of the room, Bernard pouring out the last of the champagne, William said, 'Tell us more about Frère Jacques. Is that his land on the other side of your wall?'

Bernard discarded the empty champagne bottle and placed Cognac and Armagnac on the huge, heavy, polished table. 'His land marches with Helen's; the western side of this house and the courtyard wall are the boundary, which then runs down the middle of the olive grove you can see beyond the courtyard.'

'Well, I don't know much about French law but there must be some regulation against causing a nuisance in that way.'

'Ah, I forgot, you're a policeman, aren't you?'

William shifted slightly on the sofa but said nothing.

'He's a detective, an inspector in the Avon and Somerset force,' Darina murmured.

'I don't know how many nuisances you've had to deal with in the West Country but I can tell you Jacques Duval would make any of them look like a dispute in the school playground.'

'He wasn't too bad until last summer,' Helen said quietly, placing a cafetière on the table then going off to fetch coffee-cups.

'No, I offended his *amour propre*, not to mention threatened his profits.' Satisfaction laced Bernard's tone. He arranged brandy glasses on the table beside the bottles and sat down, looking a little happier.

'What happened?' asked William.

'Well, that's just what we were going to tell you about when the manure arrived.' Helen poured coffee and started handing it around. 'Go on with your story, darling.' She gave Bernard a little smile that seemed intent on charming him back into the good humour that had characterized him when Darina and William first arrived for lunch.

'We've renovated the old mill and started producing olive oil,' Bernard said.

'Poor darling, old Jacques really has got to you. Usually it takes you ten minutes at least to work up to that bit of news.' Helen placed a cup of coffee in front of him and lightly kissed the top of his bald head.

Bernard reached up for her hand and pulled her down on to the sofa beside him. 'Was ever man more blessed?' He smiled at her.

Helen drew up her legs and settled herself comfortably. 'It was our oil that went into the dressing and baked the cake today. What's your verdict?' she asked Darina.

'Wonderful, such a fresh, sweet flavour.' Darina wasn't fooled by her diffidence. 'You don't mean you're using that old mill in the courtyard, do you?'

Helen laughed. 'You call that old, you haven't seen the

10

original press yet! I'd have loved to have restored them. They're traditional, full of history, and you can still see examples being used around here, but Bernard said if we were going to run a commercial venture, we needed modern equipment.'

'It sounds quite an undertaking,' commented William.

'Helen was pretty dismissive about the idea at first but there are all these olive trees on the property and such fruit as was picked just ended up at the local co-operative! Vintage olive oil is all the rage at the moment – as a food writer, you know that.' Bernard looked towards Darina. 'I told Helen to round up all her gourmet connections, the writers, epicurean wholesalers and retailers she's come across, and prepare to make a bit of a killing.'

'Bernard's thrown himself into it all, heart and soul,' Helen added. 'He'd bought all the equipment and researched the whole process before I knew he was more than toying with the idea.' Her smile was dulcet and her voice like cream.

'I'm into a new life, a second career.' Bernard relaxed against the sofa cushions and picked up the remains of his champagne. 'Here's to no more city, no more suits and no more ice and snow. Instead, sun, good living and Helen!' He raised her hand to his lips, then saluted her with his glass.

There was a tiny silence before Helen gave a short laugh and said, 'You haven't mentioned hard physical labour, cruel winter winds and the mistral.'

'What was your first career?' asked William.

'I was at Lloyd's, partner in both a members' agency and an underwriting agency. For thirty years I donned a sober suit and set off for the city. Now, at last, I can wear what I want.' Bernard looked complacently down at his colourful wardrobe.

'And you're moving down here?'

11

'Have moved, William! *Fait accompli!* Brought over my things last autumn just in time for getting to grips with the olive harvest.'

'He installed all the equipment last summer,' Helen said without expression.

'You've had it planned some time, then?' suggested Darina.

'As soon as Helen found this place.' Bernard beamed. 'Woke up one morning with a brainwave. I couldn't see myself just settling down here with nothing to do, not when Helen spends so much of her time locked away writing books.'

'I know exactly what you mean.' William grinned at him. 'I shall have to get myself some time-consuming hobby before I retire. I know Darina won't give up writing!'

'Ah, I hail a fellow sufferer from the author syndrome! Have a Cognac.' Bernard pushed a glass towards William and filled it before he could refuse. 'Darina can drive back, she hasn't had more than a glass of any of the wines I so lovingly chose for you both.'

'They were wonderful, truly,' Darina assured him. She sighed. 'We should have organized taxis instead of bringing the car.'

'You men are the end!' Helen threw a cushion at William. 'Don't tell me you don't love trying the recipes and even if we both gave up writing tomorrow, I don't suppose we'd see any more of you two. It's all an excuse to do exactly what you want.'

William slipped the cushion behind his back and took his bride's hand firmly in his. 'So you decided to set up your own venture,' he said to Bernard.

'I once dreamed of a vineyard in Bordeaux and my own vintage claret. Olive oil seemed a more than worthwhile substitute.' Bernard's tone became earnest. 'There's the

12

same dedication to quality, the same battle with the elements, the same dependence on traditional methods allied with modern techniques to produce a pure product that tastes wonderful. Plus olive oil is incredibly healthy. It's mono-unsaturated and can actually reduce cholesterol. We'll live for ever!'

The little silence that fell as he finished could have been respectful or dumbfounded.

'I don't know if it was fluke but the oil he's produced is marvellous. Somewhere between the sweetness of Spanish and the fire of Italian. It's got depth of flavour without being overpowering. I've got a flagon for you,' Helen said to Darina. 'We're getting some special tins printed for next year's vintage and I've invited all sorts of people out this spring and summer to interest them in it.' No hint now that she hated having her time invaded by visitors.

'We've done up the guest rooms and put in a couple more bathrooms. After sampling Helen's hospitality, they'll be seduced into stocking the oil or promoting it. It'll sell at vastly inflated prices and make our fortunes.'

'Watch that all your profits don't disappear in feeding and wining your guests.' William sipped his Cognac then looked at the glass with delight. 'I can't remember when I've drunk so well.'

'That's Bernard's cellar. When he said he brought out his things what he meant was he drove a large van at a very slow rate through France, across the Massif Central, down to Provence, nursing his precious bottles as though they were a baby that mustn't be woken up.' Helen laughed. 'But our clients are going to want to taste Provençal wine, not this overpriced Bordeaux and champagne muck.'

'I'm glad you treated us to the overpriced muck.' William sipped again at his Cognac with a contented sigh.

'Ah, the local wine has greatly improved over the last

few years, they won't suffer too much,' Bernard said. 'And, after all, we don't want the wine to overshadow the oil or the food, do we?'

'Do I gather your neighbour took exception to your project?' It was just like William not to lose sight of the incident that had marred the end of their meal but as Bernard's anger reappeared, Darina wished he hadn't brought the subject up again.

'That bastard has his own olive mill, producing oil of very little merit, and thinks I'm going to do him out of business.'

'So he could well see you as a threat?'

'But we're not going after the local market! Or processing other people's olives. If anything, we're going to increase his business. Once the publicity machine gets going, people are going to beat a path down here. They'll want to see his mill as well as ours and we'll be the South of France centre for olive oil.'

'Bernard's ambitions are boundless!' An edge was back in Helen's voice.

He stood up. 'Come and see what we've done.'

But once again the party was interrupted by the sound of an engine as a car drove up to the farmhouse and braked with a loud fanfare on its horn.

'Have you asked anyone?' Helen asked Bernard, craning her neck and trying to see out of the window from where she was sitting.

'Not a soul, today was reserved for our honeymooners.' Bernard headed for the front door. It opened before he could get there and a young man entered followed by a girl in her late teens. He was tall and thin, dressed in jeans and sweatshirt, with straight fair hair only slightly overlong and a face that was notable for the smoothness of its features.

'Hi, Mum! Guess who's here!' A wide smile displayed a set of very white teeth.

'Stephen, I didn't know you were coming down, what a wonderful surprise!' Helen flew across the room and flung her arms around her son.

The girl remained by the door, taking in the scene with bright brown eyes. Her short, stout body was not flattered by a bright pink sweater knitted in an intricate cable pattern. It ended just below her bottom, revealing thick legs covered in tight, polka-dotted leggings. On her feet were a pair of laced ankle boots. Long, dark brown hair that looked in need of a wash hung over square shoulders and half obscured her heavily made-up face.

'Look, darling, look who's arrived!' Helen turned to Bernard with her son's arm wrapped around her.

'Stephen, nice to see you.' Bernard bounced forward with an outstretched hand.

Stephen ignored it. His teeth gleamed in his smooth face and his mouth assumed a derisive twist as he said, 'Still here then, I see, Bernard.'

The shaggy eyebrows drew together.

Helen gave Stephen's arm a little squeeze. 'Darling, you know Bernard and I are living together. Now, don't be difficult as soon as you arrive. Come and sit down and have some coffee. And won't you introduce us?' She turned and held out a hand to the girl standing by the door. 'I'm Stephen's mother.'

'This is Terri,' Stephen said nonchalantly. 'She wanted to see the South of France and I said she could come along.'

'How lovely to meet you. Can you stay long?' It was hard to decide whether the enquiry was addressed to both or just the son.

'You and Bernard aren't running a hotel, are you?' Then the edginess disappeared from Stephen's voice as he added more warmly, 'I'm down here to suss out backgrounds for a new drama series. I told Terri you wouldn't mind if she stayed as well.'

15

'Stephen's in television, he's a producer,' Helen said proudly, introducing Darina and William.

Bernard went across to the girl. 'Hello, Terri, good to have you here, come and have a brandy. You can probably do with one after driving all that way with Stephen; if he's ever learned what a speed limit is, I'd be very surprised and as for acknowledging other drivers have rights, forget it. What's your other name?'

'God, Bernard, you are a nerd! As if names matter anything these days.' Stephen flung himself on to one of the sofas and poured out a large glass of Armagnac.

'It's Arden, Terri Arden.' She flipped a long length of lank hair back over her shoulder and looked Bernard over coolly. Her voice was very deep and slow. Slow not from affectation but as though her thought processes took time to translate into words. 'I'm a fashion designer and I'm working with Stephen.' The dignity of this claim was rather spoilt by her adding, 'Shall I get the bags?'

'You come and relax, we can look after your things later.' Bernard sat her down next to him, as far away from Stephen as he could manage, poured out a glass of Cognac and gave it to her. 'Helen, perhaps more coffee would be a good idea.'

In some imperceptible way he had taken charge. Darina transferred her attention from the newcomers and eyed Bernard Barrington Smythe curiously. There was more to him than appeared at first sight.

16

Chapter Two

It wasn't long before Bernard repeated his invitation to view the mill.

Darina and William agreed immediately. Stephen refused with a curl of his lip but Terri looked as though she could be interested.

Helen reached out a hand towards her. 'Come and sit here, beside me. You and Stephen must tell me all about what you are up to.'

The invitation appeared to cancel out any attractions offered by Bernard, and Terri slid clumsily over to the other sofa. The mill party left Helen sitting between her two unexpected guests, her hand firmly grasping her son's.

Outside the smell of manure lay on the air like scum on a lake.

Bernard brought out an ostentatious handkerchief and held it to his nose as he led the way across the courtyard to a large stone barn. 'This was the original mill but I've thrown out the old hopper and press.'

'What a pity – you could have started a museum,' commented Darina as she stepped inside. 'People are really interested in the past. Old recipes and traditional dishes have never been so popular.'

The mill was cool and dim. Peering through the gloom,

17

Darina could make out two small windows and a pair of glass doors that led out on to a stone platform but it wasn't possible to see much more before Bernard turned on the lights from a battery of control switches by the door and stood with his shoulders thrown back, his head high, a smile on his face that said this was his kingdom.

Darina had never visited an olive-oil mill before but from somewhere she had built up a mental picture of a small-scale peasant industry carried out on primitive machinery. Nothing had prepared her for this battery of shiny, stainless-steel equipment. It seemed to consist of a series of large cylinders, some on their side, others, more dumpy, standing erect, all with pipes leading from either end. The most reassuring items were a couple of huge steel pails that a giant might find useful for milking a gargantuan cow.

Bernard led them over to the French windows at the side of the mill and out on to the stone platform. 'The olives are brought here in these boxes.' He indicated a stack of empty shallow containers. 'They're unloaded into this hopper then carried up into the mill.' He waved an arm at a conveyor belt leading from the hopper to the top of the wall. 'A powerful fan blows leaves and twigs away, then the fruit goes through up there and comes down here.' Bernard nipped agilely back through the windows and showed his guests the metal chute leading down from the wall to another hopper. 'They're washed at the same time then loaded into this crusher.' He led them to a long, shallow trough standing about waist height. 'It reduces the olives to a paste.' Darina drew in an involuntary gasp as she saw the inside of the trough was composed of serried ranks of razor-sharp blades.

'Lose a finger in there without too much trouble,' said William, his face a blank.

'It's marvellous, means the fruit is chopped rather than

crushed and it's a much cleaner process, we don't have to filter out all the debris that the old mill produced,' enthused Bernard. 'Old Jacques's got nothing like it.'

'What about the stones, what happens to those?' asked Darina.

Bernard grinned. 'They're chopped as well, the whole shebang's reduced to a homogeneous paste.'

For a moment they all looked at the lethal piece of machinery then Darina asked, 'What happens after that?'

'The paste goes into here.' Bernard opened up one of the long barrel-like steel contraptions in the middle of the floor, displaying how it was interrupted along its length by curved arms that wound round a thin central, horizontal spindle. 'The paste gets mixed with water and then it's fed into here,' he opened another, similar-looking machine 'where the oil and water together are spun off by centrifugal force.' He moved on to where pipes connected up the machine with a sturdy upright steel container that had more pipes leading off in various directions. 'This separates the oil from the water and decants it into those.' He pointed towards the giant pails, each equipped with a lip.

'And then?' Darina asked.

'Then we bottle it or store it in those tanks up there.' Bernard pointed to the one traditional aspect of the whole mill, a large old wooden cupboard set against a back wall, topped by several oblong tanks painted green.

'It all seems very modern,' said Darina doubtfully, her vision of the centuries-old process of making olive oil fading before the slick procedure that had been described to them. She wished the mill was in operation. Perhaps if the progress of the olives could be followed through, it would all bear some relation to the unctuous, golden liquid she so loved to cook with.

Then she thought Bernard was looking disappointed by

19

her reaction. 'You make it sound an incredibly simple process,' she offered.

'It all looks rather like a small winery I went to once,' William commented. 'Not exactly the same machinery, of course, but the place looked very much like this.'

'The process is not dissimilar.' Bernard beamed at them; William had said the right thing. 'Perhaps the greatest difference is that no fermentation takes place. The oil is ready as soon as it has been separated from the water. It *is* simple, that's its beauty.'

'So why isn't everybody doing it?'

Bernard shrugged his shoulders. 'It's labour intensive. The trees need pruning and fertilizing; the picking all has to be done by hand. One mature tree will yield fifteen to twenty litres of oil in a good year. If it's been a rainy season, the olives will be plumper but not yield as much oil, the weather affects the quality. Likewise, if you pick the olives green, when the flavour is at its fruitiest and most powerful and can really catch the back of your throat, the yield won't be nearly as great as that from ripe black olives, when the flavour is much sweeter.'

'How many trees to a hectare?' William had had his attention caught.

'About a hundred and fifty mature trees.'

'So a hectare could yield up to three thousand litres?'

'I applaud your mental arithmetic!'

'And how many hectares does Helen own?'

Bernard looked cunning. 'Nearly twenty-five.'

'On that basis, you could produce something like 75,000 litres per annum?'

Bernard's expression became pained. 'They've got an incredible system here. The peasants get paid with half of what they pick. So if I want the full yield, I have to buy the damn things back.'

'Surely it comes to the same thing? And if you don't need your full crop, it can pay for the picking of your fruit.'

'But then they take the damn things and get Duval to press them.'

'Thereby keeping your rival in business?'

Bernard nodded. It was as if he couldn't trust himself to speak.

'But you could press them yourself for them, couldn't you?'

Bernard said nothing. The inference was obvious: he wasn't being offered the chance.

Darina thought it was time to get off olive yields. 'Can you do anything with the water left after the oil has been taken off? Use it for cooking?'

Bernard shook his head. 'No, Darina, it contains all the acid that was in the olives and getting rid of it is a problem. In the old days the farmers just used to pour it away, polluting the rivers and the land. Now, under European Union laws, it all has to be disposed of properly, which costs. All the health and hygiene regulations that the EU has brought in have sent most of the old mills out of business.' He grinned, a shark displaying his teeth at the sight of a tasty morsel. 'Old Frère Jacques still pours his water into the stream that runs through his farm. I've seen him at it. And I'm going to tell him that if he doesn't stop his dirty tricks and his other underhand practices, such as lacing his oil with cheap Spanish stuff, I shall report him.'

'I thought a lot of French oil was mixed with oil from other countries quite legitimately,' Darina commented. William was leaning against the crusher looking at their host with interest.

'Indeed, it is. Provence can't keep up with demand. But if you're selling your product like château-bottled wine, mixing it with inferior oil is like adding Algerian plonk to your vintage. It increases your profits and cheats the buyer.'

'I should watch it if I were you, Duval sounds a tricky character.'

'That's what Helen says, Bill. Helen's trying to get me to make friends with him. I adore that woman, I'd do anything for her, but she has no idea how to handle people. She won't realize that the only thing someone like Duval understands is force. I've got to put the fear of God into him and then he'll start seeing things my way.'

'What, exactly, has Jacques Duval done?' asked William curiously.

Bernard gave a deep sigh. 'The first salvo was unloading a pile of stone in the lane so we couldn't get out and nobody could reach us without climbing over them. It took days to get him to remove them. Then we had a series of wrong deliveries. Either things we hadn't ordered or the wrong amounts. When I changed our suppliers to ones he didn't use, the trouble stopped. He's bad-mouthed us to the local shopkeepers. Not that he got far with that, our trade's far too valuable! Oh, it's too boring to go through the whole catalogue. He's just taken every opportunity he can to make our lives miserable.' Bernard paused for a moment then added, 'It's interesting, though. The one thing he's never done is try to damage the trees in any way.'

Darina broke in quickly, 'It's all fascinating, Bernard. Will you be making any more oil this year? I'd love to see the mill in action.'

His face cleared. 'Probably one more batch. I'll check the trees tomorrow but I've already booked the pickers provisionally for four days from now and I'll be processing the day after that. I like the fruit to rest a day, I think it increases the yield. Longer than that, though, you risk fermentation setting in. Come along, it's not a particularly scenic process but we'd love to see you.'

'And after that you shut down until the next crop?'
William ran a finger idly along the stainless steel cylinder.
'It sounds a good life.'

'After that I shall be into the mammoth business of
pruning. Left to itself, the olive bears biennially. We have
to persuade it into fruiting properly every year.'

'Make sure you save lots of lovely twigs for barbecues.'

Bernard smiled at Darina. 'You enjoyed the langoustines,
then? I knew you would. Isn't Helen a marvellous cook? I
must have put on a stone since we got together. And
enjoyed every ounce of the way.' He patted his stomach
happily. 'Since we met everything in my life has got better
and better.'

'Does that go for your membership of Lloyd's as well?'

Bernard's tufted eyebrows drew together in a quick
frown and he held out a protesting hand. 'Dear boy, don't
mention the insurance business.'

'I take it you are a member yourself?'

'Still a Name, dear boy. Still a Name. And solvent! One
hasn't been there all those years without knowing which
syndicates to be on, you know.'

'Indeed.'

Bernard looked at William suspiciously but was
prevented from any further comment by a tentative knock
on the mill's half-open door.

'Bernard? Are you there?' In came what at first sight
Darina thought was a young girl, then she realized that the
long printed skirt and antique lace blouse had misled her.
The newcomer must be in her middle thirties at least, with
a thin face and dark hair that curled on to her neck. She
was pulling on a lock as she came into the mill, stretching
it out in a nervous gesture, her expression anxious.

'Anthea? Are you looking for Helen? You didn't try
the house?' There was nothing welcoming about either

Bernard's small movement backwards or his voice.

Anthea flushed, painful colour staining her neck and cheeks. 'I wanted some oil. I thought I saw you come into the mill so I didn't bother with the house.'

Darina thought of the length of time it had taken for Bernard to explain the procedure of making olive oil. Had the woman been waiting outside all that time? Why not come straight in? Or had she only just arrived, seen the open door and taken a chance? In which case, why not say so?

Bernard went over to the old cupboard on the other side of the building, reached for his watch chain, inserted a key into the lock of the door, and swung it open. He took out a glass flagon and handed it over without a word.

Anthea's colour darkened. She undid the thongs of a leather draw bag, scrabbled inside, found a leather purse and took out a banknote. 'I think this should cover it,' she said in a voice that shook.

Bernard thrust the oil at her. 'Don't be stupid,' he said roughly.

Anthea clutched at the bottle and dropped the note on the floor.

William bent and retrieved it. He handed it back to her with a smile. 'You obviously like the oil as much as we do,' he said lightly. 'We've just had a marvellous meal here.'

Anthea gave a small, uncertain smile.

Bernard squared his shoulders, took a visible breath and performed the introductions. 'Anthea Pemberton, a neighbour of ours,' he said. 'Darina and William Pigram, friends of Helen's.' It was the minimum he could have got away with but it seemed to put new heart into Anthea.

'Are you living here or just down for a holiday?' she asked Darina.

'We're on honeymoon. But by the time we go back we'll be wishing we had a house here, it's all so lovely.'

'Anthea, did you want anything else?' Bernard broke in.

Again that painful flush. 'I just . . . I mean . . . I wondered . . . that is, did you get my letter?' she ended in a rush of words.

For a moment Bernard was silent, it was as if he was wondering what to say, then he struck his forehead with a gesture that would have done credit to Irving. 'Of course, your letter! Forgive me, Anthea.' He put an arm round her shoulders and guided her out of the barn. 'I'll ring you about it this evening, promise,' he was saying as the printed skirt brushed against the old wood of the door and they went out into the sunlight.

Darina and William avoided looking at each other.

Bernard returned almost immediately. 'Poor girl has her problems,' he said gaily. 'I'm a bit of a dutch uncle to her. Now, where were we?'

'You've given us a first-rate tour and now I think we should be on our way.' William slipped his arm around Darina. 'You and Helen have other guests.'

Gloom descended on Bernard again. 'You'd be doing me a favour if you stayed around a bit longer. Stephen's not the most friendly of souls, as I expect you know.'

'I haven't met him before,' murmured Darina.

'Jealous, that's the trouble. He and Sasha have enjoyed Helen's undiluted attention ever since she broke up with their father, when they were small kids.'

'But she's had other boyfriends,' Darina said.

'There was the one Sasha tried to seduce, the one whose car Stephen borrowed without permission and smashed up, and no doubt they've seen off several others one way or another. You've no idea what those two can do when they really try. It's only because Helen moved down here and they've embarked on careers of their own that I've stood a chance.'

'Tough luck,' said William and applied a gentle pressure

to Darina's shoulders, moving her out into the courtyard. 'Let's hope Stephen's location work doesn't take too long,' he added brightly. 'Now we really must find our hostess and thank her for this wonderful lunch. Perhaps before we go back you'll come down to Antibes and let us return your hospitality?'

Bernard's face brightened again. 'Most kind, dear boy, we'll be there. I always like a trip to the fleshpots.'

Darina drove down the small, rutted lane, past the ramshackle entrance to Jacques Duval's mill, and on to a properly surfaced road. All too soon they had left behind the peace of the olive groves and modern civilization pressed around them.

'I can't believe the amount of traffic,' Darina said as they reached the dual carriageway. 'I thought we were meant to be away from it all here.'

'Not these days.' William roused himself. 'More and more people have moved down to the South of France in the last twenty years or so, chasing the sun like us. Building the motorway speeded up the process and now the Côte d'Azur has lost its charm.'

'I think it's wonderful. All right, there is a lot of development,' Darina looked at a new scar in the hills that was being filled with small, shrimp-pink villas, 'but the centre of Antibes is lovely, all traditional French.'

'You should have seen it before. I remember coming with my parents when I was about fourteen. Even along the coast there was real country and when you went inland, you found little *auberges* with chickens running around.'

'Don't turn maudlin on me! You shouldn't have drunk so much at lunchtime. I love Antibes, you can see the French living their ordinary lives, shopping at all the places you expect. Marvellous fishmongers, butchers, wonderful

26

cheese shops and delicatessens, and as for that covered market, we've got to go back there tomorrow morning.'

William gave a small groan. 'Today's lunch will do me for several days to come.' Then he brightened as he saw a road sign. 'Mougins! There's a restaurant I want to take you to up there. You'll love their food!'

'How long before you've recovered your appetite?'

There was no answer. After a few more miles, Darina asked thoughtfully, 'Do you think Bernard can be right about his neighbour, that Jacques Duval? Can he really be doing all those things to his oil?'

William stirred himself again. 'Don't see why not.'

'But the French are so fanatical about food and taste.'

'Doesn't stop them ignoring Common Market regulations if it suits them.'

'But what about diluting his olive oil with inferior stuff?'

'Every country has its rogues. He probably doesn't see anything wrong in it. If the public wants to buy his product, that's their look-out.'

'And if they buy it without tasting, more fool them?'

'Precisely.' William put his head back and closed his eyes again. A moment later he added, 'Bet if Bernard does try tangling with Frère Jacques, he'll come off very much the worse.' Then a small snore escaped his half-open mouth.

Darina concentrated on finding her way back to Antibes without a navigator.

The apartment they'd been lent was high in a block above the main part of the town and offered a panoramic view of the Mediterranean. Look one way along the coast and you could see the sprawl of Nice, look the other and there was tree-clad Cap d'Antibes with its large villas and lighthouse that swept the whole area at night-time with broad rays. Floodlit permanently was the old fort that stood directly below the apartment, beside the yacht basin.

The yachts might smack of conspicuous consumption, so might some of the shops and developments, but the hinterland where they had been today had offered small medieval towns and real countryside with little farms like Helen's and her neighbour's. Even if they were all hugger-mugger together, Darina thought she much preferred it to a tourist paradise like the Seychelles. And when the shopping was such a delight, she didn't mind doing a little self-catering.

Not when it was such a joy being with William.

She found the right turning off the main road and drove the little hired Renault into the underground garage of their apartment block complex, manoeuvring it carefully into their limited space, pleased she wasn't driving anything larger. She switched off the ignition and turned to look at her husband, still with his mouth open, still whiffling the odd light snore. Not the most romantic of sights but she wouldn't have swapped it for anything.

In the few days since their wedding William had appeared to relax. Had he been so unsure of her before? It was as though the fact that she'd demonstrated her commitment to him through the marriage vows had given him a new confidence. At this moment, sitting in the small car in a dim garage, Darina couldn't imagine why she had hesitated so long or why the lead up to their wedding had been so fraught. It all seemed so simple now.

She released her safety belt, leaned over and kissed him. Two arms enfolded her, tightening around her back.

'Mmmm,' she said in satisfaction, 'do you want to stay down here for the night or go upstairs?'

'Why settle for gear levers sticking in all the wrong places when there's a comfortable bed within two minutes' reach?' His smile was warm and lazy.

Hand in hand they found the lift and pressed the button

for their floor. Still hand in hand, they managed to unfasten the apartment's safety locks. Once inside, not bothering to relock the door, William drew Darina closely into his arms.

The telephone rang. Reluctantly he drew back.

'It can't be for us,' Darina said, moving closer to him again.

'Well, I did give the number to one or two people,' her husband confessed and picked up the receiver. 'Hello? Who? . . . Of course, Geoffrey said you might ring . . . Yes, having a wonderful time . . . What, tomorrow? . . . Yeah, that sounds great, we'd love to!'

Would they? Darina wondered just what he'd let them in for.

Chapter Three

'Do you mind being social?' asked William, knotting his university tie round the collar of a striped blue and white shirt.

'As long as we are together, I don't mind anything,' came in muffled tones as Darina fought her way into a loose-line cream jersey dress. Her head emerged out of the round neckline and she gave her husband a sparkling smile. She added a floating voile shirt in shades of beige and ochre, left it unfastened over the dress, topped it with a cinnamon silk waistcoat, then found a long necklace of chunky amber beads. 'Just remind me who we're having lunch with.'

William shrugged his shoulders into a dark blue blazer. 'Roland Tait's an old city friend of my uncle's, he's into venture capital. According to Uncle Geoffrey, Tait bought a villa down here last autumn and is now dividing his time between the South of France and London. Apparently Geoffrey mentioned after some board meeting that we'd be out here and Tait insisted on having our telephone number.' He came up behind Darina and slipped his arms underneath the floating material of the shirt, cupping a hand round each swelling breast through the soft, smooth fabric of her dress as she sat on the dressing-table stool brushing her hair. He buried his face in the springing waves

31

of pale gold. 'I just hope lunch doesn't go on too long.'

Darina leant back against his chest, feeling the rapidity of his heartbeats echo through her. She met her reflection in the mirror and gave a small, secretive smile. 'If you don't let me finish my hair and face, we'll be late,' she said severely, gently removing his hands. 'What's his wife's name, and is it going to be just us or will there be others?'

In the mirror she saw William drop on to the end of the bed and sit watching her.

'I don't know,' he said, leaning back on his hands, his grey eyes filled with love. 'I know nothing about Tait's marital state and I have no idea what sort of affair it is. I just hope it's going to be more relaxed than yesterday.'

Darina put down the hairbrush and picked up a lipstick. 'It was all right until that wretched manure got unloaded under our noses, then everything started going downhill.' She slicked lipstick on to her mouth and moved her lower lip over the upper to blend out the colour.

'If you go on doing that, I warn you I'll have to remove the whole lot.' William gave an exaggerated groan, then his eyes grew thoughtful. 'How long have Bernard and Helen been an item?'

'Let's see. I know Helen met him some time before she bought the farm down here. I seem to remember it was at a London party. I don't think she took him seriously for ages. She said he had all the bounce of a rubber ball and the undiscardability of a boomerang.' Darina gave a strangled gurgle of laughter.

'Yes, he's a determined character. So, eventually he succeeded in making her his own. Are they going to get married?'

'Helen hasn't said anything.' Darina blotted her lipstick and reached for a glosser. 'She used to talk, though, about the security of marriage, the joys of always having a man around. She comes over as such an uncomplicated soul but inside she's a bundle of nerves, especially when she's got a cookery project on. She needs someone like Bernard, someone who isn't concerned with his own image, who can support her and give her confidence.'

'That was how he struck you, was it? Someone unconcerned with his own image? I wonder if you're right. And what about that Anthea woman who turned up at the mill?'

'Darling,' Darina laughed, 'don't start detecting on our honeymoon! We're not here to sort out other people.'

'Look who's talking! Who's the one who always sticks her nose into anything odd she comes across?' William got to his feet in a swift movement. 'You look sensational, you know that? Come on, we'll be late.'

'Just a minute, turn round, yes, that blazer needs a quick brush.' Darina smartened up the dark material. 'There, you look marvellous, too.' She opened a drawer, found a long beige voile scarf and wound it loosely round her neck without bothering to check her image. 'Now, who's going to drive?'

'I'll take us there, you bring us back.'

'Rat!'

Lunch certainly wasn't going to be a quiet, intimate affair today, Darina thought as an Italian maid showed them into a room filled with people.

'You must be William and Darina. How lovely you were able to join us.' The woman who had come up to greet them was around forty and looking good on it. She had an expensive gloss compounded of subtly highlighted hair, a tanned skin, liberal amounts of gold jewellery and an Italian-chic silk shirt in an equestrian design that was worn with perfectly cut white trousers that minimized her generous size. Her social poise was flawless.

'I'm Maura Russell. We're so delighted you could come, it's lovely to meet new people. I don't know where Roland's got to but let me get you a drink and introduce you around. What would you like?' She gave a small wave to a manservant and he came over to take their orders.

Darina asked for a mineral water, William a kir. 'Would you like it with crème de pêche rather than cassis?' Maura asked. 'It's a little different and we like it.'

'I'll try anything,' said William.

'Are you really here on honeymoon?' Their hostess surveyed them both with twinkling eyes the colour of her citrine earrings. At their nod, she broke into a wide smile. 'Romance is alive! I must find Roland – ah, there he is, come with me.'

Darina let William follow on Maura's heels and kept close behind him as they were led through the happily talking throng of an unusually eclectic group of people. Some were as smartly dressed as Maura and others were more casual – several, indeed, seemed to have taken no particular note of what they had put on. Both English and French were being spoken.

She caught odd phrases as they worked their way through: 'We're here for another couple of weeks and then it's back to depressing old Britain and the money mills . . .'

'Saw Robert and Lisa the other day, he's broken and she's desperate. Thank God we're managing to keep afloat at the moment but we dread the postman . . .'

'Got the sweetest shirt in M and S in Nice the other day. Who says French fashion is everything? . . .'

'*Tu n'as pas visité Bruno's à Lorgues? Mais c'est formidable, incroyable! . . .*'

'Björn, where have you been? And don't say working, I won't believe you. I've been waiting for that call you promised me for weeks.'

Darina stumbled into William's back as he stopped. A man had detached himself from a group of three standing beside a large window and was coming towards them.

'Roland, darling, it's true, marriage is not a thing of the past! Look, here are Darina and William, on honeymoon.' Beneath Maura's laughter was a hint of pique that Roland either missed or ignored.

'Great you could make it,' he said heartily. 'William, I'm hoping you'll persuade Geoffrey and Honor to visit me. Perhaps when Maura's cousin, the Earl, is with us. I'm sure Lord Doubleday thinks I've bought some run-down farmhouse, that I'm pigging it down here.'

Darina glanced round the room. 'Pigging it' was an inappropriate phrase. The house looked as though it had been recently built but in a traditional style. The enormous, double-height room had natural stone walls and a wooden gallery running across one end. Well chosen French antiques provided a background to the collection of modern paintings and sculptures with which the room was liberally decorated.

'And look at that *vue panoramique*,' their host continued. 'Isn't that *vaut le voyage*, as Michelin would put it?' Perched on an outcrop of rock, the house had an eagle's eye view of mountains, trees and the sea that rivalled the one Darina and William had been offered the previous day. But grey clouds sabotaged the sun. The landscape had lost its hard edges, its colours today were selected from a palette of soft blue-greens, greys and browns. All was quietness and space, no sign here of the frantic bustle of the coastal region. Again Darina felt a sense of peace.

Below the giant window, the ground fell sharply away. On a lower terrace she could see a swimming pool with a large, gaily decorated pavilion furnished with a long wooden table and chairs.

'I'm sorry it's not warm enough today to eat outside. In the summer I shall be living out there.'

'I', thought Darina, not 'we'? 'It's the most heavenly place,' she said. 'I don't see how you can bring yourself to go back to dingy old London.'

Their host had grey eyes, lit with a fascinating but steely iridescence, that gazed intently at her. He was not quite as tall as she was. She had the impression that that annoyed him, that he preferred to look down at women. She completed her rapid assessment: middle fifties, lithe, with dark hair and a deeply tanned face that combined a hint of arrogance with a sparkle that gave it charm. His clothes were lighthearted: a colourful shirt of blue, apricot and terracotta stripes tucked into toning terracotta trousers, and a blue silk scarf tied round his neck, pirate style.

'Leaving gets harder each time,' he said with a smile. 'We're out here for three weeks this visit then I have to get back for a board meeting before going off to the States for a week or so followed by a trip to Switzerland, but I should be back here after that.'

Again that 'I'. Darina glanced at Maura but her confident smile hadn't wavered.

'A busy schedule. And I don't suppose you leave work behind when you're here?' suggested William.

Roland's eyes focused more keenly and Darina could have sworn his nose sharpened. 'Work anywhere these days. As long as you've got a telephone, and a fax modem in your laptop, the world's yours.'

'I know all about laptops. My wife is a cookery writer and hers goes everywhere with her.'

'Even on honeymoon?' asked Maura incredulously.

'You better believe it,' William said grimly as the barman came up and offered them their drinks.

'I'm not going to work really,' Darina put in hastily.

36

'But I hope we'll visit some interesting restaurants and one always finds new ingredients and ideas and the laptop makes note-taking so easy.'

'It sounds just like you, Roland.' Maura gave a sigh. 'Perhaps romance is dead, after all.' She tucked her arm into William's. 'I bet you don't take your work everywhere!'

'No?' Darina gave her a quizzical look. 'He's a detective, his mind never stops working and my charms wouldn't stop William from poking his nose into any crime he came across.'

He held up his drink in a gesture of surrender. 'Not on honeymoon, darling, I promise you.'

Roland placed a hand on Darina's arm. 'I think you and I are the only sensible ones here,' he said lightly. 'We refuse to make rash promises and hold ourselves ready for all eventualities. Maura is too idealistic, she seeks perfection, total commitment.'

Maura seemed not in the least put out. 'A little idealism doesn't come amiss these days and someone has to keep reminding you there are other things in life besides business! Now, we shouldn't monopolize you lovely people. Come and meet some friends.'

At luncheon, Darina found herself separated from William.

Two large round tables had been arranged in a dining room that was almost as spacious as the living room. Each table seated some sixteen people and Maura efficiently directed the company as they milled around finding their places.

Darina soon discovered her name and watched William seat himself at the other table; no nonsense about newly married couples being allowed to sit together. He was between a smartly dressed middle-aged woman and a quietly attractive girl of about her own age.

A craggy man in his middle thirties with a thatch of fair hair appeared on her left and helped her to sit down. 'Hi,' he said, seating himself and holding out a hand. 'Björn Björnson.' He looked deep into her eyes. 'You have the most beautiful cheekbones I have ever seen. How do you come here?'

Darina laughed, he was so obvious and yet managed to be charming with it. 'I'm on my honeymoon.'

'Oh, that is terrible news! Tell me which is your husband, I have to kill him. I cannot have discovered the nearest thing to a Valkyrie outside of Scandinavia only to find someone has beaten me to her.'

'Pay no attention to him,' said the man on her right. 'He is only a crazy Swedish sculptor who tries to make away with all our women.'

'John, you malign me,' Björn said sorrowfully. 'I observe the sanctity of all happily married women but you can't blame me for wanting to bring a little warmth and laughter into the lives of those less blissfully situated. How am I to know if this gorgeous creature isn't in need of a little solace unless I enquire?'

'Are you really a sculptor?' asked Darina.

'We forgive him his outrageous behaviour because of his art,' said the man on her other side, the man called John.

'What sort of sculpture?' she asked, gazing at bright blue eyes that somehow appeared serious although the rest of his bony face was smiling.

'Busts, mostly. And I would, most seriously, love to do one of you. Your cheekbones, the whole of your face, it is poetry. Do you stay long?'

'Two weeks. Do you live here?'

'For five years now. I love the light and the sun. That and the beautiful women. I would hate to live anywhere else. In Sweden, where I come from, for so much of the

38

year we live in darkness. I hate the dark, I love the sun and light. Your hair is all light.' He put out a hand and ran a finger gently through the lock that hung over Darina's left shoulder, then had to draw back as the company was served the first course, a beautifully arranged curl of sole stuffed with salmon mousse and surrounded with a sea of watercress sauce.

'What do you say to the girls who have dark hair?' Darina asked demurely.

He laughed. 'That they are like the night and I long to be enfolded in its depths.'

'And redheads?'

Björn shook his head. 'Allow me some secrets.'

'Do many foreigners come here to live?' Darina asked, looking round the table and wondering how many nationalities were represented.

'Yes, from all over. But mainly the English, the Germans and some from Scandinavia. We have a very pleasant time of it.'

'The idea is to escape the cold and the damp,' said the man on Darina's right.

'This is John's first visit,' said Björn. 'Here for ... is it two months? Well, we are trying to persuade him to make it an annual event. And to stay longer.'

'Alas, my business can't be transported about quite as easily as yours, Björn. I would be very happy if it could.'

Darina sneaked a look at her neighbour's place card. John Rickwood, it said. 'What is your business?'

'Oil. I run a small exploration company.'

'Our host seems to think he can run a business anywhere.'

'He may be able to. I have an office with staff who need to be kept up to scratch.'

'But you've managed this visit?'

'I'm seeing how it goes. I keep in close touch, and Nice

airport is so near, it's easy to fly back for essential meetings.'

'What a lovely life.' Darina sighed. 'Being able to fly down to this beautiful part of the world, enjoying the sunshine while England shivers. And Roland says all you need is a fax modem and a telephone.'

'The fax and the telephone!' Björn said scornfully. 'Always pressure, always worry. You work too fast so you make mistakes. You make mistakes, you get heartburn. In life you need to cut yourself off, think about things other than business. I am sure Jules would agree with me.' He directed a look over at the other table, towards the girl sitting beside William, who was now deep in conversation with her.

John Rickwood's severe and rather mournful face softened as he followed Björn's gaze. 'Yes,' he said. 'She's always saying I should forget business. She'd like me to retire.'

'Then retire! You are rich, you have enough money, even with starting a new family.'

'How did you know that? We've only just found out ourselves.' The man sounded disconcerted, more than that, put out.

'Easy, my friend, Jules has just told me. It is a secret?'

'No,' conceded John.

'I am sorry. Jules is so happy, I think she just has to tell people and, after all, she and I have known each other for so long. But I will not mention it myself.'

John suddenly smiled and warmth flooded his face. 'I'm sorry, Björn, I sometimes forget she had a life before I came along, and that she spent so much time here when she was single. Of course she should tell people. We're both of us absolutely delighted.' He turned his attention to Darina and began to question her about herself.

Men who were interested in women as individuals were

rare in Darina's experience: usually she found they preferred to respond to questioning about themselves. This man was different. Skilfully he drew from her details of her career and marriage and then she was telling him about the lunch they had enjoyed the previous day.

'It's so nice to be able to catch up with old friends and see where they've moved to. I never think it's the same when you don't know what sort of house they've got and can't picture them in the kitchen. And William and I both enjoyed meeting Bernard. Do you know them?'

His air of quiet reserve returned, a turning in on himself as though he no longer wished to pursue a subject. 'Jules is a great admirer of Helen Mansard, she has a number of her cookery books. But I am afraid I don't know Bernard.' He hesitated as though wondering whether to add something else. It could have been the clearing of the first course that caused him to change his mind.

Clean plates were laid in front of them and they were served with fillet of beef, wild mushrooms, rösti potatoes and a green salad. Then Darina noticed her neighbour's plate bore a portion of wild mushroom risotto instead of the meat. 'You're a vegetarian?'

He seemed happy with the change of subject. 'So's my wife. That's how we met, actually, sharing the watercress garnish at some pretentious dinner party with enormous steaks and almost no vegetables.'

Darina found herself even more interested in John Rickwood. She tried to assess his age, late fifties? 'Have you been one long? I meet lots of younger vegetarians, but . . .' She hesitated, wondering if she was being tactless.

He came to her rescue. 'Not so many my age, is that what you want to say?' His mouth twisted in grim amusement and Darina decided he wouldn't have to try hard to turn into a difficult companion. 'Mine isn't a

41

philosophical commitment, I just don't like the taste of meat. Jules is quite different, the sight of a roast really upsets her.' He hesitated again then decided this time to continue. 'I have always liked hunting. You know how keen the French are on *la chasse*? They'll go after anything and, left to myself, I'd be joining in. The owner of the villa we're renting is a keen shot. He's left me his guns and several introductions for a day's shooting but Jules would find that outrageous; to kill birds for the pot is bad enough, to have fun doing it is the ultimate sin.'

Darina looked across the room at the girl sitting beside William, smiling gently at him as he talked. She looked some twenty-five years younger than John. 'Is this going to be your first child?' she asked.

'No, I was married before. It didn't work out and we were divorced long before I met Jules but I have a daughter just turned twenty. It's a difficult age and Pat finds her a bit of a trial. I do what I can but it doesn't seem to help much.'

'How will she adjust to the idea of a half-brother or -sister?'

'I like your choice of words. I think the news will be a shock – sharing me with a new wife was bad enough. But Jules handles her beautifully and eventually I think it'll be all right.'

His voice was controlled, almost contemplative, but Darina thought she could see beneath the surface. She remembered Stephen Mansard's attitude towards Bernard Barrington Smythe, who hadn't official stepfather status and certainly wasn't going to father a half-brother or -sister for him to share his mother with.

The lunch drifted pleasantly on into the late afternoon. A lavish cheese board was followed by Grand Marnier ice cream served with out-of-season strawberries and crisp little biscuits. Then Roland announced that coffee and liqueurs would be served in the living room. 'Come and meet my wife,' said John Rickwood as the guests rose. He took Darina over to where Jules and William were still talking.

'I've been looking forward to meeting you.' Jules gave Darina a small, neat smile. 'I heard so much about you over lunch.'

'And I was treated to a most interesting account of your activities in the oil world, sir.' William shook John Rickwood's hand.

'We, I regret to say, have been talking about ourselves. Now, what does that say about us all?' John darted a mock serious look at Darina.

She laughed. 'That we're selfish and lucky to be married to such generous people.'

They moved together into the other room.

Maura brought over coffee. 'If there was a trophy for the two most devoted couples in the room, there's no doubt you lot would win it.'

'If you're not devoted on honeymoon or with a baby on the way, what hope would there be for the future?' asked John Rickwood. 'But you manage to keep Roland looking very happy.'

Maura looked over to where Roland Tait was laughing with an older woman. Her face was unreadable. 'What makes you think it's me?' She picked up her tray with sugar and cream and returned to her coffee-pouring activities without waiting for an answer.

'Poor Maura,' said Jules Rickwood gently. 'She tries so hard but Roland is never going to marry her.'

43

Chapter Four

'Come and have a drink with us,' said Jules as the luncheon party broke up. 'We're on the Cap, not far from where you're staying.'

'Yes,' John Rickwood added, 'Jules has been complaining I'm not allowing her to do any entertaining.' He put his arm round his wife.

'John would like to wrap me in cotton wool and keep me in a box. I'm only three months' pregnant – what he's going to be like later on, I dread to think!' Jules said, her back straight and uncompromising, but her eyes, an uncertain shade somewhere between hazel and grey, were laughing. Darina admired the feathery cut of her short brown hair and the crêpe wool trouser suit she was wearing – Armani, for sure – that made the most of her slender figure.

'I know, you hate any fuss. But you just have to humour a father-to-be more mature than most.' His fingers gave her right shoulder a small caress as he looked back at Darina. 'Do come. How about six o'clock tomorrow?'

It was all arranged and William took down the directions to the villa the Rickwoods were renting.

'I'm not sure I like all this sharing you,' said William, as he

45

drove along a narrow road the following night, Darina scrutinizing the names of the villas they passed, searching for the right one.

She knew how he felt. 'You'd like to wrap me in cotton wool and keep me to yourself?'

He gave a wry smile. 'Protective, isn't he? I felt his eyes on me and Jules several times during that lunch. Since he was sitting next to the most beautiful woman in the room I thought it was rude as well as unnecessary. And wasn't he the greased lightning as soon as we all rose? Brought you over immediately and it wasn't so that we could be reunited.'

'Well, he is a good deal older than she is and you are very attractive,' murmured Darina. 'But he certainly wasn't inattentive during lunch and I enjoyed his company.'

'Beneath that soft exterior, Jules Rickwood seems to have some remarkably strong ideas. You know she's a vegetarian?'

'So's John.'

'Really? He looks such a roast-every-Sunday man. Still, I'd back Jules to convert even such a no-nonsense chap as Rickwood.'

Darina was just about to say that, on the contrary, vegetarianism had been the matchmaker when she caught sight of a discreet name plate they'd almost missed, 'Hey, here we are!'

William stopped the car, backed it up a little, then drove in through hospitably open high gates and up a short drive. A pink stucco villa of some size stood importantly in the middle of neatly tended shrub beds surrounded by billiard-table-smooth lawns.

William straightened his tie as they got out of the car. 'Should we have dressed?' he murmured, slipping a hand beneath Darina's elbow.

The front door was opened by a manservant whose style

was so polished that to call him urbane would have been a monstrous understatement. Unable to look at her husband, Darina followed the butler through to a room furnished with an over-abundance of antiques that breathed exquisite taste and a large bank balance. High french windows opened on to a wide terrace and more lawn, which swept down towards the sea, the water sparkling under the setting sun. Any slight chill in the evening air was offset by a blazing fire in the marble fireplace.

Mr and Mrs Pigram were announced in tones of crystallized honey; Jules and John rose from their chairs and came forward. Discarded on a small polished table lay a piece of half-completed tapestry and what looked like a company report.

'I hope we're not too early?' Darina asked as the butler shimmered out of the room and she and William went forward.

'Not at all. I was waiting for you to get John to abandon his work. Even for the few weeks we're here, he won't leave it behind.' There was no mistaking the edge to Jules's soft voice.

John Rickwood paid no attention. All quiet charm, he sat them down on an eighteenth-century straight-backed sofa and asked if champagne would be acceptable.

'I'd find it difficult to concentrate on business in these surroundings,' William said. Darina watched their host busy opening a bottle at a gilt-encrusted side table liberally organized with a range of alcoholic and non-alcoholic drinks, ice buckets and glasses. How had he persuaded the butler to let him loose amongst it all?

'You don't find the décor restful?' Jules firmly closed the business report, placed it at the back of the table and looked at William with eyes that were suddenly sharp and gave her neat face the look of an alert hamster.

'Restful?' He considered the question, carefully studying

47

the skilfully assembled and arranged collection of museum-standard furniture and pictures.

'I love it,' Darina said quickly. 'Stunningly beautiful, of course, but also comfortable. I would find it difficult *not* to relax here.' She controlled her desire to change her position on the period piece, conscious of her husband sitting stiffly in the other corner.

'It's all Jules's work,' John Rickwood said complacently, bringing over glasses of champagne on a silver tray. He'd certainly taken lessons from the butler, decided Darina.

'But I thought you said you were renting?' William took a glass.

'That's how we knew about this place. Jules is an interior designer.'

'Was,' his wife corrected him. 'Since I married John, I haven't had time for a career.'

'Am I that demanding?' Her husband gave her a glass of what had to be freshly squeezed orange juice. 'You know I didn't want you to give up everything.'

Jules smiled at him, a warm, wifely smile. 'I enjoy looking after you.' She turned to Darina. 'We've a house in Gloucestershire as well as the flat in London and John has to entertain a lot. I want to make sure everything's done just right. He has such high standards.'

'Not higher than yours,' he protested, sitting himself down.

It was as if he hadn't spoken. 'And now there's the baby coming.' There was just a touch of complacency in Jules's voice as she glanced down at her flat abdomen.

'You don't miss your work?' Darina noted William's admiring look at the girl with a slight sinking of her heart.

'It's funny, when I was working, I couldn't imagine giving it all up. Now I wonder how I could have been so, so . . .' she searched for the right word.

48

'Dedicated,' her husband supplied. 'Jules is brilliant,' he told them. 'Well, you can see that from this house.'

'I've done several places round Nice and Cannes over the last few years – I love it down here.' Jules glowed with gentle intensity. 'When the Steinbaums heard we were looking for a place, they insisted we took this while they were in Africa. They said it would do the staff good to have something to do.'

On cue, a maid entered the room with two plates of elegant mouthfuls. She handed them round, placed the plates on a low marble table in front of Darina and William and left.

'Jules had a bit of a job persuading me it was a good idea but I'm actually enjoying myself.' John looked slightly surprised. 'It's certainly helping get through the winter. As the years move on, I find the cold and damp of England more and more depressing. Now, that's enough about us, what have you two been doing?'

'A mixture of exploring the locality and meeting people,' said William, sipping the wine appreciatively and helping himself to a roll of smoked salmon stuffed with crab mousse. 'It must be the most sociable honeymoon on record.'

'Ah, life here is very social – that's part of its charm. I've not been one for partying before but Jules knows so many people. Half of them she's designed houses for.'

'Sometimes it gets a bit much,' Jules put in. 'And there are people one would rather not meet.' There was a pointed emphasis to the remark that left Darina wondering who it was she meant.

'We do have time for ourselves,' said her husband. 'Have you managed any sightseeing yet?'

'We went to the Napoleon Museum the other day, by

49

the lighthouse. Have you seen it, it's practically on your doorstep?' William asked.

John Rickwood's face lit up. 'One of the first things we did, too. Have you been to Golfe Juan, just around the corner, to see where he landed from Elba?'

'Napoleon is a great hero of John's,' murmured Jules.

'There was an aura about that man even his defeat at the hands of the allies couldn't dispel. And for him even to imagine that he could triumph again, against all the odds!' John shook his head in admiration.

Darina saw a large, illustrated work on Napoleon on top of a pile of books on the table in front of them. She reached for it – and knocked over her champagne glass. The remains of the wine fizzed over the surface of the marble.

'Oh, I'm so sorry,' she gasped, grabbing the books out of the way of the impending flood.

William dug in a pocket for his handkerchief but John was there before him. 'No disaster,' he said, wiping up the spilt champagne with a large square of fine linen. Darina, moving more items around the table to assist the mopping up process, found her attention riveted on John's right hand. The top joints of the third and fourth fingers were missing.

He noticed her gaze. 'An old accident,' he said easily, while she flushed with embarrassment. 'There, that's fine now. No harm done, the glass hasn't even cracked. Let me refill it for you.'

'John's got all the grit and determination of a Napoleon,' said Jules. 'He survived weeks in the Arctic once.'

'Darling, they don't want to hear about that! And it was Labrador, not the Arctic.'

'It sounds fascinating. What happened?' William leant forward with every appearance of deep interest.

There was silence.

'If you don't tell them, I will,' insisted Jules.

John gave a brief laugh, 'There's no need to make a great song and dance about it. It was nothing very much. Many years ago I was prospecting some promising mineral rights with my partner. Our little plane ran into a storm and crashed. I survived, minus two finger joints, Philip didn't. That's about it!' There was a note of finality in his voice.

'That can only be a fraction of the story,' William started, then found himself interrupted by the telephone.

'Henri will take it,' said Jules as John rose.

'No, it'll be the office. My assistant usually rings about this time,' he explained as he left the room.

'I don't know why he doesn't like talking about the crash,' Jules said, as the door closed after him. 'He was so incredibly brave.'

'Brave people quite often dislike talking about their exploits,' said William.

'Do they?' Jules looked at him with her head held slightly to one side while she considered what was obviously a novel thought. For an instant she looked more like twenty than thirty. Then she gave a little nod, as though the suggestion fitted in with what she knew about her husband. 'When I first met John, he seemed such a, well, such a committed businessman. If he hadn't been a vegetarian, I don't think I'd have been at all interested in him. Then someone told me about the crash and, suddenly, I saw him in a different light.' Jules's face was lit with enthusiasm. 'Anyone who could survive that sort of experience had to be really special. I mean, it takes courage, doesn't it? And grit. All the things I knew I wanted in the father of my children. I was dying to hear all the details but would he tell me?' The question was rhetorical. 'So I went to the library and searched for newspaper reports on his rescue. Took me ages.'

51

Had she, indeed? A determined character was Jules, thought Darina. And was there something a touch cold-blooded about the way she had decided that John Rickwood would make a good father? Darina gave the magnificent room they were sitting in another quick glance. Had she also been ambitious for this sort of lifestyle? A house in Gloucestershire and a flat in London, she'd said. And Björn had described John as rich enough to retire even with a second family on the way. How much money had Jules had before she married him?

'How was John rescued in the end?' asked practical William.

'Sheer luck, really,' said Jules, her face still alight. 'He broke his leg when they crashed and could hardly move. If there hadn't been some sort of army survival exercise going on in the area, he'd probably have died. As it was, his escape really hit the headlines. I wish I'd been old enough to read about it at the time – as it was, I wasn't even born. In that dusty library on a funny micro-fiche, it all seemed too incredible. It made me realize what a very special person he is.'

The very special person entered the room as she spoke. He looked acutely embarrassed. 'Sorry about that,' he said quickly. 'Penalty of running a company and wanting to escape to the sun, I'm afraid.'

'No problems, I hope?'

'None of any concern, William, thanks. Now, how are the drinks?' He went over to the baroque side table and drew the bottle of champagne out of the cooler. 'Let me top up your glasses. And do tuck into those small eats. Maria will be upset if they're not eaten. Have you been to any good restaurants yet?'

Halfway through William detailing the couple of Antibes places they'd so far tried, the doorbell sounded.

Jules lifted an enquiring eyebrow at her husband. It was almost a repeat of what had happened at Helen's lunch party and Darina wondered if there was something about William and herself that attracted unexpected guests. John shook his head and both Rickwoods looked expectantly towards the salon's large double doors.

The butler entered, closing the doors behind him with a look of conspicuous uninterest on his face. 'A young person—' he managed to invest the phrase with overtones of sleaze. 'A young person', he repeated, correcting his intonation, 'has called to see you, sir and madame. She wouldn't give a name—' Before he could get further, the doors were thrust open and a young girl pushed her way past the impassive butler and stumped aggressively across the room. She came to a halt in front of John Rickwood.

'Tell him to sod off, Dad.'

'Theresa!' John appeared stunned, then he stepped forward and gave the girl a quick embrace. 'Lovely to see you, darling. How did you get here?' He drew back with a frown. 'There's nothing wrong, is there?'

For a split second, Darina caught a fleeting look of some powerful emotion impossible to interpret crossing Jules's face. Then it was gone.

'Thank you, Henri,' Jules said to the butler with her normal calm. 'Miss Theresa likes to spring surprises. I'm sorry she didn't introduce herself properly.'

The butler inclined his head a millimetre and eased himself out of the room. The set of his shoulders spoke volumes.

'Terri, come and sit down and tell us what's finally made you accept our invitation.' Jules placed her arm around the girl's shoulders and gave her a brief hug that Theresa woodenly resisted. 'And let me introduce Darina and William Pigram – they've come for drinks.'

'We've already met, I think,' Darina said, holding out her hand to the girl. 'The other afternoon, when you arrived with Stephen?'

The girl stood with her weight awkwardly poised on one leg, seemingly with no intention of sitting down. The long, untidy black hair obviously hadn't been washed since her appearance at the olive farm. The sulky face with its dark, kohl-rimmed eyes and pale, full mouth looked uninterested in either Darina or William. Today she had on striped leggings that might have been borrowed from some Renaissance youth and should only have been worn by the slenderest of legs. They were topped by a large white shirt that billowed over the ample hips and was gathered across the large breasts. Over it was thrown an emerald satin bomber jacket liberally decorated with chrome studding. Another stud winked in her right nostril.

'Would you like a glass of champagne?' asked her father.

Some of the belligerence began to fade. She dropped her gaze and shifted her weight from one foot to the other. 'Mum said I shouldn't bother, you'd never help me. But I thought I'd come anyway. After all, you did ask me.'

A glance passed between her father and his wife. Jules held out her hand again. 'Come and sit down and tell us all about it, Terri.'

The girl ignored the hand and helped herself to several of the little canapés, swallowing them like a lizard would flies; she took another handful then flung herself into a Louis Quatorze armchair, her weight causing a creaking of the wood. Jules briefly closed her eyes.

'It's this shop Emms and me have found.' The slow voice Darina remembered had given way to a faster, abrupt way of speaking.

'Shop?' interjected her father sharply. He gave his daughter a glass of champagne and sat himself back in his chair.

54

Terri crammed some canapés into her mouth, picked up the rest of the champagne, drank thirstily, then put the nearly empty glass down on a side table. Her voice came in short, jerky phrases. 'It's perfect, just the right distance down the King's Road. Everything's up for sale, all the fittings, stock, everything. It's just our thing. We've worked it all out. The clothes aren't much but they'd bring in something while we got our own stuff made up. Then we'd really start moving.'

The aggression had disappeared, so had the sulky expression.

Her father held up a hand. 'Darling, don't go so fast. Who is Emms and what is this shop all about?'

Terri turned to him, her voice resentful now. 'I've mentioned Emms a thousand times. She's my best friend, we met at design college.'

'Did she drop out as well?' Jules asked in a quiet little voice.

Terri flushed. 'It was all crap. We couldn't see the point of it. We know what we want to do.'

'Which is run this shop?' the quiet voice asked with utter reasonableness.

Terri rose, scooped up more of the small eats and returned to her chair, aggression once more in every line of her body. 'It's the start of our careers. Emms and me are going to design our own clothes. We'll make them up ourselves to begin with, in the evenings, then, as the money comes in, we'll get outworkers. They'll go like a bomb,' she added, speaking through a mouthful of food and staring at her father with intense eyes. 'We've already sold some. We just need this shop.'

John Rickwood glanced towards Darina and William. 'Can we leave discussing this until later? We'll talk about it over supper. Where are your things?'

Terri stared truculently at him. 'I knew you wouldn't

want to treat me seriously!' Her voice shook slightly.

'It's not that,' her father protested.

'You have to understand you can't just walk in and take over whenever you feel like it,' said Jules gently. 'We're in the middle of entertaining guests.'

'So an actual daughter doesn't mean very much,' Terri burst out. She fumbled in one of the bomber jacket's generous provision of pockets, drew out a small tin box and, with unsteady fingers, started to stuff a cigarette paper with vegetable matter. Coarse shreds fell onto the floor.

'Not here, Terri!' Jules's voice was stern but controlled.

For a moment her gaze locked with the girl's. Terri looked at her father; he said nothing. Then she blinked rapidly, stuffed everything back into the tin and returned it to her pocket. 'I can't stay,' she muttered. 'My friend's picking me up in half an hour.'

'A friend!' exclaimed John in disgust. 'I suppose it's too much to hope he's more suitable than your last! Who is he and where are you staying?' Jules put out a soothing hand towards him. Darina and William picked up the book on Napoleon and began turning the pages.

Terri was back in the sulks. 'Stephen's perfectly respectable, he's in television and you don't have to worry, we're staying with his mother.' She stared at Jules. 'And she's someone even you approve of. You've got her books.' As Jules said nothing, Terri added, 'Helen Mansard.'

The effect was not what she must have been expecting. Her father put down his glass with a bang. 'You're not staying with Bernard Barrington Smythe?'

His daughter stared back at him. She said nothing.

'Terri, you can't!' Jules sounded outraged.

'Why not? He's not a junkie, hasn't got a criminal record!'

Darina and William glanced at each other, got up and

strolled through the open french windows on to the terrace. The sun was setting over the sea in a drunken splurge of golds and reds, gilding the gently ruffling water.

Darina sighed. 'Doesn't it look beautiful?'

William placed his arm around her shoulder and drew her against him. His voice muffled by her hair, he said, 'What a little liar you are. That room comfortable, indeed, somewhere you can relax!'

'I was only compensating for your bad manners.'

They stood together for a moment or so, then William said, 'Do you think they'd notice if we just eased ourselves round the house and left?'

'We could always ask the butler to present our apologies.'

Odd fragments of the increasingly heated conversation carried to them. John's voice, steady but angry, 'Lloyd's . . . your stepmother's losses . . . you must see . . .'

Terri's furious voice, 'It's always money with you . . . you've never really cared . . .'

Jules saying in reasonable tones, 'Terri, we only ever hear from you when you want money. You must see, with your record . . .'

Terri again, her voice rising hysterically, 'Oh, you're so bloody perfect! I suppose you've never done anything wrong!'

'Terri, you'll apologize to your stepmother, how dare you talk to her like that?'

William's arm gently guided Darina round the side of the house. When they reached the car he said, 'I don't think we'll bother the butler.'

'We can't just disappear.' Darina was shocked and delighted at the same time. She ran across to the front door and lightly knocked.

As she'd expected, the door was opened almost

immediately. She left a brief message and returned to the car.

They drove out of the gates.

'Let's find a nice restaurant and forget all about it,' William said. Then he added, 'Promise me our daughter won't grow up like that?'

Darina felt the sharp stab of an emotion she didn't want to analyse. 'Perhaps,' she said thoughtfully, 'if Terri's mother and father hadn't separated, she would be different.'

'You're not making excuses for her?'

Darina saw again the awkward girl handling her father and stepmother so badly. 'We don't know any of the background.'

William gave a grunt of laughter. 'Thank heavens! Come on, let's forget all about the Rickwoods and enjoy ourselves for the rest of the evening.'

Darina was only too happy to agree. But as they rejoined the main road she asked, 'Why do you think Terri doesn't use her father's name?'

She got no reply.

Chapter Five

Two days later, Darina and William were shopping in the little village of Tourettes-sur-Loup.

Darina was inspecting a range of cheeses and trying to decide how many she would be justified in buying when she realized Anthea Pemberton was standing next to her.

Without thinking, Darina greeted her. The other woman looked confused. 'We met at Helen Mansard's the other day, with Bernard, in the mill, Darina and William Pigram. William's over there looking at some wine.' Darina wished she had waited for Anthea to recognize her before she'd said anything. 'This is all such a treat for us,' she continued. 'We love food and wine and being offered such choice without having to hurry is a holiday in itself.' She gave the woman her best smile.

At last there was a response. As a diver might adjust from murky depths to daylight, Anthea's blank face gradually cleared. 'Yes, I remember, I'm sorry. Are you enjoying yourselves?'

The banal query was offered without real interest and Darina subdued an inward sigh. Then Anthea made a visible effort. 'Of course you are, you're on honeymoon! You must think me an idiot. My mind was miles away, I was thinking of something else.'

Totally absorbed in a question of deep importance, Darina would have said. 'I'm so pleased we met you. Now you can advise me which of these cheeses I should try.'

Anthea looked disproportionately pleased to have her opinion sought. Eagerly she began to describe various of the local cheeses. 'Are you buying just for yourselves? And when are you going to eat them?'

Darina laughed and explained she and William were going on a drive round the Gorges du Loup. She'd packed a small picnic and thought some cheese would make a perfect addition.

Anthea guided her towards a *tomme* and a *vignottes*. 'It's not really local but it's so delicious and this one looks perfectly ripe.'

'Ah, you're obviously interested in food as well.'

Anthea flushed the way she had the other day, as though the comment was unbearably personal. Again she pulled herself together. 'I run art courses at my house – it's between here and Vence. They're residential and I have to do quite a bit of cooking.'

'How interesting,' Darina enthused, wondering how such a shy and awkward woman managed to deal with quantities of guests. 'What sort of people come on your courses?'

To her it sounded an inane question, the only one she could think of to keep the conversation going, but Anthea treated it with careful consideration. 'All sorts, mainly amateurs, of course. But sometimes I take artists and writers desperate for somewhere quiet and away from it all to work seriously in sympathetic surroundings. There is such inspiration here.'

At last a genuine spark lit Anthea's face. Darina remembered the Swedish sculptor, Björn Björnson's enthusiasm for life in Provence. 'Are you an artist yourself?' she asked.

Something glowed in the speckled brown eyes but there was a deprecating twist to her mouth. 'I wouldn't call myself an artist exactly. I'm a potter.' She gave a hesitant smile. 'The shop a few doors from here sells some of my work.'

'Great, we'll go and have a look as soon as we've done our buying.'

Anthea immediately looked worried but it was her turn to be served and a few minutes later she threw Darina a brief goodbye and scurried out of the shop looking anxiously at her watch.

Darina bought pieces of the two cheeses and the bottle of red wine William had selected. Then, telling him about her conversation with Anthea, she found a nearby gift shop. Particularly prominent were items based on the local violet industry but at the back they found a display of pottery.

'What do you think?' asked Darina as they gazed at plates, bowls and mugs.

'Rather like the woman herself, undistinguished but no doubt serves a purpose.'

'Darling! That's not at all nice!'

'Did you want me to be nice or honest?'

William was obviously anxious to be off on their expedition but as Darina turned away, the shopkeeper advanced offering assistance. Darina summoned her sketchy French. '*C'est les oeuvres de Madame Pemberton?* she enquired, indicating the pottery.

'*Madame Pemberton?*' the woman repeated, looking puzzled. Then her face cleared. '*Mais non,*' and with a stream of rapid French she led them across the shop to a display they had missed. With a wave of her hand the shopkeeper indicated the few items that decorated the shelf.

'She's saying that this is all she has at the moment of Madame Pemberton's work,' William translated.

'Apparently it sells very well and she has been promised some more in a few days.'

'Well!' said Darina with a touch of triumph. 'What do you think of Anthea now?'

'I'm suitably chastened.'

On the shelf were a bowl, a jug and a large plate; their flowing lines had a surety of style and something more, a generosity of curve that promised anything served in these vessels would be well worth consuming. But the glaze was their most outstanding feature: a soft grey streaked with blue, it was hazy, luminous, suggesting depths and a mysterious obscurity of design.

'Anthea said she was no artist but these are wonderful!'

William agreed they were.

'We've got to buy one.'

He agreed they should in the tones of a man to whom anything that meant they could get on was acceptable.

'You'll love it,' Darina promised, picking up the jug, thinking how wonderful it would look holding white roses or narcissi. Perfect for milk, too, or custard.

Not long afterwards they were back in the square, a bright sun shining through the leaves of trees, Darina clutching the jug wrapped in a piece of paper.

'Why not a coffee?' suggested William, relieving her of the plastic bag containing the cheese and wine.

'I thought you wanted to get on!'

'Well, I do, but a cup of coffee first would be nice.'

Interpreting this to mean that consuming something was worthwhile where dallying in gift shops was a waste of time, Darina followed him across both the square and the busy road that led from Vence to Grasse and into a café/bar.

They settled themselves at a table by a long picture window that allowed them to enjoy the warmth of the sun without suffering from the brisk breeze that blew outside and gave them a view of the road and square, a ringside seat to the comings and goings of Tourettes-sur-Loup.

It was not, however, the village scene that drew Darina's attention. At the back of the café she spied Anthea. Not only Anthea: sitting opposite her, with his back to the window, was a figure that looked exactly like Bernard. Darina half rose in her seat to wave at them, noticed the aggressive angle of the man's back and the stark unhappiness on Anthea's face, and sat down again without drawing attention to herself. 'If we hadn't already ordered, I'd suggest leaving,' she said quietly to William, who was watching the passing parade out of the window with enjoyment.

'What?'

She made an unobtrusive gesture towards the table at the back. 'Something tells me they would rather not be disturbed.'

William observed the couple without comment while the coffee arrived. 'I shouldn't jump to any conclusions,' he said, raising his cup. 'They probably met here by accident. Helen's farm isn't all that far away.'

'No,' said Darina thoughtfully. 'Helen lives towards Grasse and Anthea's just told me she lives near Vence, in the opposite direction. Tourettes is conveniently placed between the two of them.'

'Now, now!' warned William. 'Enjoy your coffee, look into my eyes and tell me you love me.'

Darina gave a gurgle of laughter, proceeded to do exactly that and forgot about the other couple. Until a movement caught the corner of her eye. Bernard had risen and was poised over the table, his hands supporting himself as he leaned towards Anthea. It was impossible to hear what he was saying but his whole body was rigid with some suppressed emotion. Then he swung away from the table and strode out.

He passed close by, his face suffused with anger, but

Darina and William could have been invaders from Mars and he wouldn't have noticed them. Darina looked back towards Anthea, still sitting at the little table, and something inside her went cold as she saw Anthea's face contorted into an unrecognizable mask. It was only for a moment, then the woman dropped her gaze to the coffee cup sitting on the table in front of her and the lines of eyes and mouth resumed their more normal droop.

The blare of a car horn made Darina glance at the road outside. Bernard was crossing heedless of the traffic, causing chaos as brakes were hastily stamped on and vehicles swerved to avoid him, drivers shouting imprecations after his uncaring back. A moment later he had reached his car, parked not far from theirs in the village square. With squealing tyres, he drove it relentlessly out on to the road and towards Grasse, leaving more chaos in his wake.

Darina looked back to where Anthea was sitting. She hadn't seemed to register the noise outside and her eyes still stared at her cup. Then her mouth firmed to a thin line. She fished out a purse from the bag on the chair beside her, dropped some money on the table, picked up her things and walked out of the café, her expression resolute, her attention never wavering to right or left.

The Gorge, its precipitate slopes plunging starkly down towards the river Loup at the bottom that ran busily through its twists and turns, enthralled Darina and William. They picnicked at a sheltered spot, enjoying the sun. Then explored a tiny village perched on the side of a dizzying cliff face and bought cakes of olive-oil soap, Darina drinking in the subtle perfume. She ignored the essential oils also on sale, their aromas cloying and insistent.

'Why is it,' she asked as they started walking back to

their car, 'that the essence of some products is pure heaven whilst that of others is dreadful? Rose, for instance. In the garden it smells marvellous, in a bottle it's disastrous. Is it something to do with the methods used?'

'More to do with personal taste, don't you think? There's obviously a market for attar of rose, or whatever they call it. Not everybody thinks its aroma is disastrous. It's the same, surely, with food. Aren't there people who hate olive oil and would far rather have corn or sunflower? Take tripe – haven't you told me it's one of the few foods you can't stand, yet ten thousand Frenchmen will tell you you're wrong? And what about religious objections to food?'

'Ah, now that's something completely different. There are valid reasons for food taboos. Or were at one time.'

'Like placing a ban on the eating of people in case it's your turn for the pot, you mean?'

'Be serious!'

'I am being serious. It's like murder – and incest for that matter. All of our strongest taboos are basically protective devices. All of them threaten the continuation of the human race. They are nothing to do with hygiene or profound philosophical truths.'

'That's far too simplistic, you can't forget moral issues,' Darina protested.

Arguing happily over the reasons for cultural development, they found their car and resumed their exploration.

Much later that afternoon, as the sun was losing its warmth, Darina was at the wheel. As they regained the main road, she turned towards Grasse. 'Would you object if we called in on Helen and Bernard?' she asked.

Her husband gave a small groan. 'Your curiosity over this morning's incident has to be satisfied, I suppose.'

'Nothing like that, darling! Whatever Bernard is up to is

nothing to do with me. No. Remember what he said the other day about processing a last picking of olives? I'm dying to see the mill in action. In any case, Helen forgot to hand over that bottle of olive oil she promised me. We could fix a day for them to come and lunch with us as well.' She started to drive in the direction of Helen's farm. 'And don't give me that sort of look!'

William apologized for looking anything but suitably enchanted with his wife.

When they arrived at La Chenais, Darina parked the car on the rough ground in front of the old wooden shed that had been converted into a garage. Inside the open doors stood a battered Citroën, last seen driving incontinently out of Tourettes square that morning. No sign of the BMW that had also been there when they'd arrived for lunch the other day or of Stephen's big Volvo.

Darina used the iron knocker. No one came to the door. The square stone house sat quietly, its shutters closed to protect the interior from the sun.

Darina knocked again, louder. William leant against their car, looking resigned and patient. Across from Jacques Duval's farm came the faint noise of a tractor.

Darina said, 'Helen can't be home, I'm going round to the mill.'

She went round the side of the house, through to the courtyard. The table where they'd sat eating lunch the other day was empty, its surface undecorated by cloth or utensil.

Darina looked again at the old mill stones standing in the corner, their turning mechanism rusted and useless, then listened. Through the musical chatter of cicadas from the olive groves she could hear a mechanical sound, the rattle of some sort of machinery.

She walked towards the mill. 'Bernard? It's Darina, are you there?'

The sun outside had been so bright it was difficult to see the interior of the mill. The rattle of machinery was louder now. It was the olive cutter, its razor sharp little blades happily winking backwards and forwards, reducing olives to paste. Behind the freshness of the olive smell was another, metallic aroma, that caught at the back of Darina's throat.

'Bernard?' she called again.

Her eyes adjusting to the light, she saw him bending over one of the big pails.

At least, that's what she thought until she realized the figure was far too still. Then she noticed his hands.

'William!' she screamed, her voice high and uneven as she rushed towards the pail.

He arrived too late to help her drag the dead weight of Bernard's body out of the pail of oil.

Dead weight indeed. It hadn't taken more than one heart-stopping glance at the bloated, dark face swimming in the golden oil, the eyes bulging as though they would break free of their sockets, to convince her of that.

But still she hauled at his body, something insisting she couldn't leave him there, the oil lapping at his ears, his eyes, invading his nostrils and mouth.

With a final heave she dragged him out of the pail and he fell with a heavy thump on to the concrete floor. The body lay bent unnaturally at an acute and rigid angle. Oil oozed from the shoulders of Bernard's blue denim overalls, poured in a pool from his swollen features, dripped from the sandy hair that was sticky and dark with it, clinging together in clumps around the bald scalp that shone like a well-dressed salad.

Oil, too, now decorated the front of Darina's sweatshirt and trousers and her hands were wet with it.

William crouched down and felt for a pulse. Darina knew it was a hopeless exercise. She closed her eyes and gratefully inhaled the clean fresh odour of aftershave that wafted gently up from her husband and briefly blunted the smell of death and gore that pervaded the atmosphere.

'Dead.' William straightened up and reached out for his wife, pulling her against his leather jacket. 'I'm sorry, darling.'

'His fingers,' groaned Darina, screwing her eyes shut and burying her face in his warmly breathing chest, her body trembling.

For a moment they stood like that until she felt her control return. With a small sigh she pulled herself away from William's grasp, hardly noticing the oily marks she'd made on his jacket. His hands were reluctant to let her go. 'Are you all right?' he asked, his eyes searching her face.

She nodded. 'What happened?' she whispered. 'Was there an accident?' Reluctantly, she forced herself to look towards the machine that still worked away in the background, saw that the guard wasn't in place, then drew a shuddering breath as she realized the tiled wall behind it was spattered with dark gobbets.

William bent again over Bernard's body, studying the stubby fingers that were even shorter now, mangled and gory. From the chuntering olive cutter it seemed to Darina that the smell of blood rose stronger than ever. 'How could he get his hands caught in that machine?' An all too vivid picture rose in her mind of Bernard somehow trapping his fingers in that lethally sharp piece of equipment, pulling them free and, blinded by pain and shock, tripping and falling into the pail. Drowned in oil, like poor Clarence in that butt of Malmsey. But Clarence hadn't fallen, he'd been pushed.

'Turn it off!' She heard her voice come out in a harsh whisper.

William made no move towards the switches beside the

entrance door. Instead he bent again over the body. His fingers gently parted the sticky fringe of hair at the back of the anointed head and Darina inhaled sharply as she glimpsed the broken skin.

'I'm afraid this doesn't look as though it was an accident.' His voice was grim. 'We shouldn't touch anything else.'

Darina felt a jolt of shock run through her. Her mind screamed for the implications of that open graze on the back of Bernard's head to be some other kind of accident, anything but what William was suggesting. The restlessly insistent noise of the cutting machine became too much. She strode towards the wall.

'Don't!' William's voice was sharp, the voice of the policeman. He was beside her in an instant, his hand grasping her arm, gently but firmly restraining her from reaching for the switch. 'We've got to leave everything as it is. You must see that.'

She gave a sobbing gasp and he gathered her to his chest again. He pressed his head against hers, his hands caressing her back. 'I'm sorry, my darling, but you do understand, don't you?'

She did, all too well.

With a sigh she drew away and prepared to leave the mill that had become a morgue. Then she heard Helen's voice calling, 'Bernard? Are you there?' and the tap of her heels on the courtyard flagstones.

Chapter Six

William and Darina tried to prevent Helen going into the mill but she insisted.

Clutching Darina's hand, she approached the awkwardly bent body and stopped a few feet away. It seemed she didn't notice the swollen face and mutilated fingers at first for there was a pause before Darina heard a horrified intake of breath. The hand holding hers tightened convulsively, then Helen pulled it away and flung herself down beside the body. 'Bernard!' she cried, pulling at his overalls, opening the front and thrusting her hand inside. She put her head down, as though she wanted to listen for a heartbeat.

Darina hurried over and took her by the shoulders. 'Leave him, Helen, there's nothing you can do.'

'Don't,' Helen moaned, shaking herself free. 'He can't be dead.' Once again she felt inside the overalls.

'I'm afraid he is.' Darina stepped back and glanced at William.

'You shouldn't be touching him,' he said, and put a hand on Helen's shoulder.

Slowly she drew back from feeling Bernard's chest and sat on her heels, thrusting her hands deep into her side pockets as though she couldn't trust them to behave. Her gaze fell again on Bernard's hands, she bit her lip and gagged. She brought a clumsy fist to her mouth, rose from the floor and rushed outside.

Darina found her heaving uncontrollably against the old mill stones, one hand clutching the edge of the pan as though without its support she would sink to the ground.

'Oh,' she groaned as Darina held her shaking body. 'Tell me it isn't true.'

Gently Darina led her into the house. She took Helen, unsteady and blindly moaning, to the downstairs cloakroom and helped her rinse her mouth and splash her face with fresh water then wash her hands. Afterwards she washed off the oil that still lubricated her own hands.

Back in the living room, William had been phoning the police. 'They'll be here shortly,' he said, as Darina sat Helen down on the sofa, went to the stove and put on the kettle.

'Why did I go out?' Helen groaned, when Darina returned with a cup of hot sweet tea.

'When did you leave the house?' From somewhere William had found a piece of paper and a pencil. Darina recognized with a sinking heart that he was going to take notes.

'I don't know, ten o'clock?' Helen looked at the cup of tea as though unable to recognize what it was. She ran a distracted hand over her forehead. 'No, it was later. Bernard was in a terrible mood, complaining we never saw each other, that I was always either out or working.' Wisps of hair were falling down from her French pleat. Her eye make-up was smudged, traces of mascara stained her cheeks. Her suit, a smart beige light wool two-piece worn over a white silk sweater, was stained with oil and splashed with water. Huddled into the cushions as though she was a dog seeking to burrow out a refuge for itself, Helen looked rumpled and vulnerable.

'Where did you go?' Helen stiffened as though she

recognized an implicit threat in the quiet question.

'Into Nice, to do some shopping.' Her voice was jerky, defensive.

'What sort of shopping?'

'What does it matter?' Helen burst out, panic, aggression and petulance all in her voice. 'How can you think of anything but that, that *thing* out there. I can't call it Bernard – it's not him, not him at all.'

Darina sat down beside her and picked up her hand. It was cold and trembled. She gently rubbed it between both her warm ones. 'Darling, Helen's upset, surely you don't have to put her through this?'

'The French police are going to want to know all her movements.'

'So can't you leave the questioning to them?'

'If I know the details, I may be able to help.'

'Help? Why should I need help?' Helen's panic came through clearly now. 'I told you, I went into Nice, I don't know anything about what happened here.'

'Did you meet anyone in Nice?'

Helen stared at him. 'Meet anyone? I don't understand, why are you asking all these questions?' Her hands went up to her hair, moving among the drooping bits like a housewife picking up discarded underwear, her fingers trembling as she removed pins then used one as a comb, automatically tidying and reorganizing the pleat.

'William, can't you leave it? Won't Helen sound more natural if she hasn't been grilled before the police arrive?'

William shot her a sharp glance.

Fighting down her disquiet, Darina turned to her friend. 'Helen, you don't have to answer anyone without a lawyer. Not William or the French police. Who's the British consul here? Shouldn't we ring him?' She looked coldly towards her husband. 'Wouldn't that help Helen a great deal more than asking her what she's been doing today?'

He put down the paper and pencil. 'Would you like me to do that?' he asked Helen gently.

Slow tears began to fall down her face, she put her head in her hands and her body seemed to crumple. 'I don't know what to do,' she wailed. Suddenly she rose and rushed upstairs, high heels stumbling on the polished wood.

'Now see what you've done!' Darina said.

'You know exactly what the problem is,' he retorted.

'All I know is Helen is my friend.'

'And I'm a policeman.'

Darina rose from the sofa and walked angrily across the room. 'Not here you're not. We're in France, remember? On our honeymoon!' She stopped by a big window that looked across the courtyard, through the gap in the courtyard wall to the Mediterranean. The sunny lunch they'd eaten with Helen and Bernard the other day seemed to belong to another world. 'You think she's guilty, don't you?' Darina's voice jerked out the words. She wheeled round and faced him.

The light fell directly across William's face. His expression of remote reserve chilled her. 'I have no evidence to show either guilt or innocence,' he said.

'But you think she *could* be!' For Darina it was enough.

He surprised her. 'Don't you?'

'She's my friend!'

He rose and came over to her, enveloping her in his arms, holding her close against his body. 'Darling, friendship's a lovely thing but you can't allow it to blind you.'

'Friendship's nothing if you can allow such easy doubt.' Darina's body remained rigid in his clasp. 'Anyway, how could Helen have forced Bernard's hands into that machine?' she challenged. 'Because that's what the murderer must have done.'

'She certainly doesn't look capable,' he acknowledged. 'But surely you'd be the first to admit most cooks are strong? It's all that chopping of meat,' he added with a misguided attempt at lightness. Darina pulled away from his arms. 'My darling, I'm not saying she's guilty, I'm just pointing out what the French police are almost certainly going to suggest. You know the statistics, how many times it's the victim's nearest and dearest who is the murderer. We can't help Helen unless we know the truth.'

'She had nothing to do with Bernard's death,' Darina said obdurately, and returned his gaze with a stubborn defiance. The sigh he gave seemed to her to be loaded with a weary patience that hit her with a physical force.

Darina turned abruptly and ran up the stairs to find Helen.

She found her in the main bedroom, on her knees in front of an old chest. Papers littered the floor.

For a moment Darina stood in the door and watched in astonishment as Helen took out another pile of documents and sifted through them, pieces of paper slipping and slithering from her hands on to the floor.

'What are you doing?'

A whole clump of paperwork fell to the floor. Helen grabbed at it and started her sifting through once again.

Darina came forward. 'What on earth are you looking for?'

'Bernard said he'd made a will.' Helen sounded distracted and her hands dived back into the bottom of the chest.

After one amazed glance at her friend, Darina knelt on the floor beside her.

The papers were the usual collection that one gathers going through life: insurance certificates, share certificates, letters from brokers and bankers, statements of account from various sources, bills, receipts, demands from the

Inland Revenue and a wide variety of correspondence from all parts of the world. Once it might all have been in order, now it would take some considerable time to sort out. Darina started gathering them together, noting with some dismay that her hands were trembling.

'Leave this,' she said brusquely. 'The police will be here soon.'

Helen's hair was coming down again. 'I don't understand,' she said, shuffling through the little piles Darina had created, reducing them to instant confusion. 'I'm sure he said he'd made a will. I must know . . .' Her voice died as though her energies were needed for something other than speaking but she stopped her hopeless trawling through the papers.

'Let me help you up.' Darina slipped a hand underneath Helen's arm and tried to raise her.

But the arm was snatched away as Helen started to hug herself, her face dissolving like a snowman's in a thaw. 'Oh, Darina,' she wailed, 'what am I going to do?' Tears started down her face.

Darina was disarmed and held Helen in a warm embrace, 'It's all right,' she soothed. 'I know it's ghastly. We've just got to take one thing at a time.' For a fleeting instant she remembered her husband, the detective, waiting downstairs. 'First of all, we've got to clear all this up.' She released Helen's stiff body and made another attempt to pile together the various papers. 'What's it going to look like to the police if you're trying to find Bernard's will when they get here?'

Helen dragged a hand across her face, smudging more of her mascara. 'Oh, God, Darina, I can't think any more. They can't arrest me for that. I mean, they can't arrest me for anything, can they? I wasn't here.'

'Where were you?' Darina started to shift papers back

76

into the chest. All that Helen had left in it was a scattering of ancient photographs in the bottom. Bernard looked cheerfully up at her as she placed certificates, statements and letters back as neatly as she could, obliterating the young man in army uniform, a somewhat older Bernard snapped at the wheel of an expensive sports car, Bernard at the helm of a yacht, Bernard with a series of attractive girls. She couldn't obliterate her mental picture of him in the mill so easily.

Helen sat collapsed against the end of the bed, watching Darina with dull eyes, still hugging her arms across her chest.

Darina retrieved the last of the paper, added it to the chaos in the chest and closed the lid. 'There,' she said as cheerfully as she could. 'That looks better. Now, where were you today?' She wouldn't admit, even to herself, that William might be justified in his suspicions but there was no doubt that, as he'd said, Helen was going to have to account for her actions to the French police and it might be just as well for her to start by telling Darina.

'I went into Nice, shopping.' Helen listlessly repeated her previous statement.

'What did you buy?'

Helen's eyes glanced away. 'Not very much, I couldn't find what I wanted.'

'But you bought something?'

She nodded. 'Some nuts. I put them on the kitchen counter as I came in. They must still be there.'

'You set off about ten thirty, you said? Then you must have spent something like five hours in Nice – and all you bought was nuts?'

Resentment flared in the dull eyes for a brief moment, resentment and something else that Darina couldn't or wouldn't identify. 'So what? I wanted to buy a new dress.

I went into shop after shop but I couldn't find anything I liked. So eventually I called it a day. Haven't you ever done anything like that?'

Darina looked at the figure of her friend slumped on the floor, her clothes pulled awry, the hair falling around her blotched face, the mouth mutinous. Yes, of course she had had failed shopping expeditions; perhaps it would have been more strange if Helen had been able to account for every minute of her day. 'Let's get you tidied up,' she said gently, stretching out a hand to help the woman off the floor.

'I can manage.' Awkwardly Helen got herself upright and went into the connecting bathroom. She closed the door behind her in a way that said she wanted to be left on her own.

Darina was left looking at the quietly luxurious room that Helen had shared with Bernard, at the beams that ran across the ceiling and down the attic-style walls, the deep pile carpet and polished chintz-covered sofa. Had it been Bernard who'd chosen the military prints that were so effectively arranged on the wall? What about the antique bed in the shape of a shell, so different from the kingsize version with padded headboard in Helen's previous house? Which of them had chosen that? And just how much was Helen going to miss Bernard?

Darina sighed to herself and moved over to one of the dormer windows. It overlooked the courtyard. There she could see William standing purposefully in front of the entrance to the mill. He appeared to be inspecting the interior. From her vantage point, his tall figure was foreshortened, the width of his shoulders exaggerated. She saw him peering into the building, careful not to venture in, not to contaminate the evidence any further than it had already been. His concentration appeared total. Her husband, the detective. On his honeymoon. From behind her Darina heard the flush of the lavatory, then the running of a tap.

There came the strident blare of a car siren. Darina watched while William walked quickly across the courtyard, back into the house. A few minutes later he reappeared with two other men, one with nondescript features and dressed in uniform, the other in plain clothes and dark, with an aggressively hawklike nose; both were considerably shorter than her husband.

William led them towards the mill, talking. But when he would have led them in, the man in plain clothes stuck out an arm to bar his path and said something. Then both the Frenchmen disappeared inside the mill and William was left outside, his hands jammed inside his trouser pockets, his shoulders mutinous. It wasn't long, though, before he appeared to have been called inside as well, for, with a darting swiftness, he also disappeared from view.

The bathroom door opened and Helen reappeared, her hair in place, her face made up. She appeared calm and composed. 'Did I hear a car?' she asked.

'Two police officers have gone into the mill with William.' But a movement in the courtyard caught Darina's eye. 'They've just come out again. They're walking back to the house and it looks as though one of them is using a mobile phone.'

'We'd better go downstairs,' said Helen. She appeared to have regained control of herself, the only trace of the agitated and distressed woman who had sought refuge in her bedroom that Darina could see was a slight trembling of her hand as she took hold of the door handle.

Downstairs, Helen was greeted courteously by the dark officer in plain clothes. The uniformed officer had disappeared outside. Through the window, Darina could see him sitting in the police car talking on his phone.

The investigation into Bernard Barrington Smythe's death had begun.

Chapter Seven

Terri Rickwood, who had chosen to be known as Arden, sat in the sun at a café on the Antibes front. A light breeze wisped high clouds across a brilliant blue sky and a small boat with one white and one brown sail idled along on a corrugated sea.

Like her life at the moment, Terri reflected bitterly. She needed an outside force to provide the impetus that would allow her to achieve great things. She slumped further down in her seat and stared gloomily at the remains of a *citron pressé* and a plate of pastry crumbs. She was twenty and, unless her father coughed up the money she needed for the shop, she couldn't see a future for herself. So absorbed was she in her own thoughts, she didn't see Stephen until he sat down beside her.

'Hey, cheer up, things can't be that bad!'

She managed a small smile. Stephen always had the power to raise her spirits.

'The old man still refusing to stump up?'

'Fucking butler said he'd gone out and didn't know when he'd be back.'

'Bad luck!' Stephen said perfunctorily. 'I said you should ring.'

Terri was back in her gloom. 'Then he could have put

me off. If I just turn up, he has to speak to me.'

Stephen called the waiter and ordered a whisky. Terri said she'd have another *citron pressé*. 'You should cut down on the hard stuff, it's not even four o'clock,' she said.

'Look who's talking! I suppose you're going to tell me you haven't had a smoke all day, or stuffed yourself with pastries?'

Terri made a face at him. She reached down beside her chair and hauled up a green satin rucksack that matched her bomber jacket. From it she took the small tin containing her smoking equipment. She rolled a cigarette in silence then offered it to Stephen.

He shook his head. 'Not now.'

She placed it between her lips, struck a match, lit the joint and then sat back, inhaling deeply.

'How much of that stuff have you got?' asked Stephen abruptly.

She was jolted by his tone. 'Not much!' she said defensively.

'Well, I'd get rid of it. We may be in for a sticky time.'

Terri put back her head and took another long inhalation. Already she could feel some of her tension beginning to ease. 'What do you mean?'

Her eyes took him in as he sat waiting for their drinks to arrive. She knew his face so well now. The smoothness of its contours never failed to fascinate her. No angles, no hard bones, only the nose jutted out, everything else was soft, fluid. Yet there was nothing feminine about Stephen. What was it that gave his face that strength? The ice of his eyes, so pale they almost weren't blue at all, or the thin line of his mouth? Then she noticed the frantic pulsing of the corner of his left eyelid.

Terri removed the cigarette from her mouth and handed it across the table. 'Come on, it'll do you good, relax you.'

He gave her a long look then took the joint and smoked it for a couple of minutes before handing it back. 'So what have you done with your day?' he asked.

She gave a small shrug to her shoulders. 'Walked around town, looked at the shops.'

'Did you have lunch?'

She shook her head. 'Wasn't hungry.'

His eyes had lost some of their ice. 'Come off it, you're always hungry. I asked you if you needed any cash.'

'I'm not a schoolgirl!' Terri said huffily. 'I pay my own way. Anyway, I had some sort of pear tart just now.' Its smooth, fresh sweetness still lingered on her tongue. She felt an overpowering urge for another but knew Stephen would prevent her ordering anything like that. 'I tell you, they could do with some of my clothes down here. The gear I saw is all too straight for words.' She adjusted the loosely knitted cotton sweater that hung off one shoulder and glanced complacently down at her tiger-patterned leggings. Who said fatties couldn't be fashionable? She was really sorry her father hadn't seen them. They might have made him laugh. If only she'd managed to catch him on his own, she could have convinced him she knew what she was doing and he'd have written out the cheque that would mean Emms and she could open the shop.

Terri arrested her nice little dream. Her father would never behave as fathers should, by now she knew that.

'They want me to leave you and go and stay with them,' she said abruptly.

Stephen's half-closed eyes flicked open. 'They've never met me.' His tone was matter of fact.

'It's not you, it's Bernard.'

Stephen reached across the table for the cigarette and took another deep drag. 'What's Bernard got to do with anything?' There was a strange, dreamy edge to his voice

83

that Terri put down to the effects of the dope.

'Jules says he's responsible for all the money she's lost through Lloyd's. She and Dad threw a real wobbly when they heard I was staying with him.'

'You're not staying with him, you're staying with my mother.' Again, that dreamy, detached quality.

'He and your mother seem pretty close.'

Stephen took another deep drag and handed back the last little bit of the joint.

The look in his pale eyes gave Terri a jolt – it was so different from his voice. Nothing dreamy or dispassionate about the way his gaze burnt the air between them. 'I've seen to Bernard,' he said. 'We don't have to worry about him any more.'

There were times Terri felt she didn't know Stephen at all.

The waiter brought their drinks. Stephen added water to his whisky and drank half of the glass without pause. Terri sipped at the lively flavour of the slightly sweetened lemon. 'What about you?' she asked. 'Find any locations?'

'Nothing really interesting,' he said carelessly, his gaze now fixed on the sea.

'How much longer is it going to take?'

Stephen seemed to gather his thoughts from some remote corner of his psyche and looked at Terri as though he really saw her. 'Probably not much more than another few days. Come with me tomorrow, I've got some interesting houses to see. Unless you want to try your father again?'

'No point,' said Terri bitterly. 'He's not going to give me the money, not with Jules taking the attitude she does.'

Stephen appeared to accept this.

'But Bernard seems nice,' she added.

Stephen followed her line of thought exactly. 'If I was casting him in a play, I'd choose an actor who could look straightforward on the outside while suggesting inner corruption.'

Terri thought about the kindly way Bernard had poured her drinks and chatted to her as though he understood how terrified she could sometimes be at meeting new people, wondering what they were going to think of her size and the fact that she wasn't beautiful. And though Bernard was confident, he didn't appear to have Jules's terrifying sense of certainty in her own opinions that her father seemed to accept so easily. That implacable sense of what was right and what was wrong.

'You don't see beyond that blunt little nose of yours, do you?' Stephen commented, his gentle tone removing any sting from the words.

'You're very fond of your mother, aren't you?' Terri said, almost as though she was realizing it for the first time.

'There's nobody like Mum,' he answered simply. 'And she needs me to protect her.'

'What from?'

'Nerds like Bernard. For an intelligent, beautiful woman she has the most terrible taste in men.'

'Everybody says what a ruthless businessman Dad is but he allows Jules to twist him round her little finger.' Terri sipped some more of her lemon drink. She was completely relaxed now: she could feel her bones floating in her body like eels in jelly. Her mind was an engine running on standby, able to start up at any time. She could hear its little wheels gearing up as she asked, 'What's your father like?'

Stephen turned the whisky glass round on the white table, studying the pattern of condensation on the outside as though he, too, was engaging the wheels of his brain. 'He's taken a lot from my sister and me,' he said at last. 'He's an accountant and I suppose that means our lives are pretty different from his. It's always balancing the books with him, making sure the figures add up right, whether it's your career or love life or the company annual accounts. I suppose', he added reflectively, 'it's no wonder Mum went off him and told him to get out.'

'Sounds amazing she ever married him.'

'She was very young.'

Was he excusing her action or explaining her conduct? 'Ma always says if she'd known what an impossible bastard Dad would turn into, she would never have married him,' she said dreamily. Her father's conduct no longer seemed very important. He'd left them so long ago, the hurt and the pain had become absorbed into her very soul. But the guilt remained. That and the love. Terri looked across at Stephen, sitting with his eyes half-closed, seemingly absorbed in the pigeons wandering between the tables, searching for crumbs. Was she in love with him?

They'd met at a party, of course. One of those huge, rowdy, uncontrollable raves when you needed to watch everything you drank or ate, unless you weren't bothered about what went down you, that is. Even after her bust, Terri still used pot, especially at parties like that, but she really didn't want to have anything to do with the hard stuff. Not when she'd seen what it could do to you. Relaxation was one thing, bad trips and the desperate need to score were something else. It was difficult enough wanting food the whole time.

They'd ended up back in his grotty flat and her size didn't seem to bother him – he said fat girls made the best love.

Then he'd offered her a job organizing the clothes for a short film he was shooting that was going to open all sorts of doors for him.

Was it being around Stephen that had persuaded her college had nothing more to offer? She'd felt a professional, even though he hadn't paid her.

86

It was getting chilly now. If they were staying at the café any longer, they should move inside. But lethargy had taken hold of Terri and she continued to sit without even the energy to take her jacket out of her rucksack. Stephen, too, seemed oblivious of the increasing chill.

Funny how neither Stephen nor she saw eye to eye with a step-parent. Not that Bernard was exactly a stepfather but Stephen didn't like him any more than she liked Jules. It was a mystery how her father could believe they were friends. At least Helen didn't make that mistake with Stephen and Bernard. But then, it was so obvious: staying at the olive farm was like waiting for World War Three to break out.

Terri studied Stephen's face. The half-shut eyes made it seem oddly naked, stripped of expression, almost sinister.

Suddenly the eyes were wide open. 'We'd better go back and face the music,' Stephen said. He made no effort to get up.

Terri giggled, light-headed with pot. 'I'll play any tune you want.' Underneath the sense of euphoria, though, she knew she was disappointed. Why hadn't he suggested they go off for a meal somewhere? Helen's food was lovely but it would be so much nicer just to be the two of them instead of having to act as a wall for everyone's verbal squash playing.

Stephen stood up. Terri tangled with her rucksack, finally slipping a strap over her shoulder while he fished money out of the pocket of his jeans and flung it on the table. She had to hurry to keep up with his quick stride to where he'd parked his car.

'Is there a party?' Terri was still giggling as they drove up to the old farmhouse. 'I should have brought my harp.'

Cars were everywhere. Police cars, ordinary cars, an

ambulance, all parked anywhere they could find a place. All at once sobriety threatened. 'Has there been an accident?'

Stephen said nothing, just the way he'd said nothing on the drive back from Antibes while Terri wished she'd insisted he smoked a whole joint. He jerked to a stop, yanked on the brake and was out of the car.

Terri followed more slowly, half inclined to hitch a lift back to the Cap. Even Jules might be preferable to what could be waiting inside.

Chapter Eight

After the police arrived, the afternoon became a blur in Darina's mind. She could remember giving an account of how she and William had discovered Bernard's body, and the way the French detective patiently questioned Helen. William translated for both of them – the detective didn't appear to have much English. She had no trouble remembering the polite way Helen's bald account of her ineffective shopping expedition to Nice was received.

But when exactly the teams of men arrived to start the forensic examination of the scene of death, she couldn't have said. It just seemed that at some stage Helen's home had been taken over by officials. Had it been England, Darina would have offered to make tea or coffee; here it seemed inappropriate. It was as if a barrier more tangible than a difference in language had been erected between the English and the French. An interpreter arrived to take over from William and she could see his frustration mounting at having no role to play in a situation that was so familiar.

The French detective disappeared outside to direct the various specialists who were still arriving. The inside of the mill was flooded with light but nothing could be seen of what was going on there. Darina knew, though, what must be happening. She knew that the pathologist would pronounce what was obvious to everybody, that poor Bernard was dead; that the scene would be photographed and videoed; that everything was being fingerprinted and minutely examined for traces of the murderer. She knew all this though none of it could be seen, and that William would know even more and was hating not being allowed to be part of it.

Behind the courtyard, in the gathering dusk, Darina could see the silvery-grey of the olive trees. They'd been there for so many years, seen so much; even now their serenity seemed undisturbed, their purity unsullied by the outrage that had taken place. Had they ever witnessed anything quite so horrific before?

Darina wanted to leave this place. She wanted to return to her honeymoon, for them to be able to focus on themselves again. But she knew it was hopeless. Helen needed her and William was engrossed in everything that was happening.

Then another car arrived.

Until he surged into the room, Darina had forgotten about Helen's son, Stephen. Forgotten, also, that Terri, the stout girl who had so unexpectedly turned out to be John Rickwood's daughter, was staying in Helen's house with her son.

Stephen looked around, at the uniformed officer standing stolidly to one side, at William studying the scene outside the window, a hand irritably tapping at the frame, at herself perched on a corner of the low table trying to distract Helen, and lastly at his mother, once again slumped in a corner of one of the sofas. 'What's happened? Are you all right, Mum? Why are the police here?'

Helen rose and rushed towards him. 'Stephen, darling, it's dreadful, Bernard's dead!'

'Dead?' The word was jerked out as his arms closed automatically about his mother.

'He's been murdered!'

Before she could say more, the French detective was back in the living room. Had he been summoned by the uniformed officer? Darina couldn't have said. All her attention had been focused on the scene between mother and son and noting how Terri had hung back with a curious expression on her face. She looked frightened but also like a child who has been told a longed-for treat has been cancelled.

Finally Darina and William felt they could leave. Helen had Stephen for comfort. The British consul had arrived and taken charge of Helen's interests. There was nothing more for Darina and William to do.

Helen hardly reacted when Darina said they were leaving. 'But we'll only be on the end of the telephone. You've got our number. If there's anything we can do, just ring, it doesn't take much more than half an hour to get here.'

'She'll be all right,' Stephen said shortly. 'I'm with her.'

Terri said nothing. She was sitting on the other side of Helen, holding her hand. It seemed as though she was seeking comfort rather than giving it but Helen looked happy to have her there.

The last thing the French detective said as William and Darina left was not to leave the area without telling the police where they were going.

'It's as though he thinks we're as much under suspicion as anyone else,' said Darina, as William drove away.

'We are,' said her husband briefly.

'You can't be serious!' Darina stared at him but it was too dark for her to see his expression.

'He's read all the books that say how often it's the murderer that finds the body.'

'But that's ridiculous! We only met Bernard the other day. Why should we want to kill him?'

'At the moment he doesn't know.'

'So that's why he doesn't want you to help him?'

There was a ruefulness in his voice as he said, 'I can understand. If I were in his shoes, I don't think I'd want me to assist in any investigation either.'

How contrary is the human spirit. An hour or so earlier Darina would have sworn she'd be delighted to hear that her husband wasn't going to be allowed to pursue his profession in France. Now she became indignant.

'Can't you get the British police to ring him and put him straight?'

'You really want a busman's honeymoon?' His voice sounded genuinely amused.

'I think Helen's going to need all the help she can get and you on the investigating team would be the best protection she could have.'

'Even though I believe she's the prime suspect?'

Darina swallowed hard. 'Is that because she would have discovered the body if we hadn't arrived out of the blue?'

'I would like to know what she thought she was doing trying to shop for clothes in Nice over the luncheon period.'

Darina thought for a moment. 'You mean the shops would be closed? I know most of them are in Antibes but surely not in Nice!'

'It's something that needs checking but I'm willing to bet quite a large sum of money the chic places Helen would shop in will be. The sensible shopping expedition in France starts in the early morning or after a long lunch hour.'

'You don't really think Helen could have murdered Bernard?' Darina asked in a small voice.

William's right hand left the steering wheel and closed on hers for a brief moment. 'I know she's your friend, darling, but I can't help my training.'

Darina sat silent. It was hard for her to think, so many emotions had been crammed into the last few hours. The horror of finding Bernard, the stress of trying to help Helen, the peculiarly disorienting process of discovering her husband couldn't forget his profession even on honeymoon. Yet through it all some instinct stronger than reason made her say, 'Helen couldn't have killed him. Nothing will make me believe that.'

'I hope you're right,' he said soberly.

Back in their small apartment, high above the sparkling lights of Antibes, William rang England and spoke to his boss. He put down the receiver, depressed. 'He says there's no way he can get me assigned to the case. The only hope would have been if Garnier, that's the chap who was in charge this afternoon, asked for me. And he's not going to do that.' He walked back to where Darina was sitting. 'It's so senseless. They'll have to liaise with the UK to find out about Bernard's background. I speak French, I could help so much.'

'And it's not as if you are involved with anything else at the moment,' Darina said sweetly.

He gave her a sharp look then grinned and threw himself on to the sofa beside her, taking her hand. 'I'm sorry, sweet. I should be thinking of you. What a rotten thing to happen on our honeymoon.'

Before Darina could say anything more, the telephone rang.

William leapt up to take the call. Then his face fell. 'Oh, it's you.' Immediately aware of his gaffe, he attempted to repair the damage, his voice now warm and welcoming. 'No, I'm delighted you called, really. Does it mean you can take on the commission? That's great! Yes, tomorrow morning will be fine. Just tell me where to find you and we'll be there. Ten o'clock? Right, see you then.'

He replaced the receiver and swung round to Darina, his face alive with delight and apprehension. 'I don't know what you're going to say to this, my darling, but Björn Björnson is going to sculpt you. It's my wedding present to myself!' Having a bust made of herself sounded an incredible experience to Darina. 'Björn Björnson? Isn't he very expensive? I sat next to him at Roland's lunch. I got the impression he's very fashionable and charges the earth.'

'He's not that expensive, at least the price he quoted to me didn't sound extortionate, and I've just had some luck on the stock market.'

Darina looked at her husband. They hadn't discussed finances before they married. He knew she had a house in Chelsea and an income mostly made up from her earnings as a cookery writer. She thought he had his salary as a police officer.

'Stock market? Have I married a man with independent means?'

'Grandfather Pigram left each of us a small trust fund. Advised by an old schoolfriend who entered stockbroking, I've done quite well with mine.'

'Have you, indeed? Don't you think I should have been told about all this unexpected wealth?'

'What, and have you marry me for my money?'

'How much exactly are you worth?'

He gave her a cheerful grin. 'Don't get excited, it doesn't amount to much more than thirty or forty thousand.'

'Good heavens, that seems a lot to me! Especially when I get the quarterly bills for Chelsea!'

'Well, to most of the people we've been meeting down here it's small change.'

'And how much is Björn Björnson going to charge for immortalizing my features?'

He smiled and shook his head. 'I'm not going to tell you. As I said, a recent investment has come good and what better way to spend it?'

She was constantly getting new insights into William. 'Do you have to spend it?'

'Ah, you think I'm the sort of person who goes around with burning pockets? Don't worry, normally I would plough profits back into the portfolio. But this is something I want. Didn't you see that head of Maura the other day on the table in Roland's hall? A beautiful bronze? I noticed it as soon as we came in. When I realized it was of our hostess, I asked Roland who'd done it.'

Darina hadn't seen the bust but she found it incredibly flattering that William wanted her immortalized and told him so.

'I'm glad the idea appeals, I think we deserve something pleasant after today.'

Darina shivered. 'I could do with a drink.'

'Of course you could! Whisky?'

'Please.'

William poured generous measures into two glasses and brought them over to the sofa. 'I'm sorry if you thought I'd forgotten we were on honeymoon.' So he'd noticed! 'I hadn't, not for a moment, but I can't forget either that I'm a policeman.'

'And a detective?'

'Quite.'

'Any more, I suppose, than I could come away without my laptop.'

He gave her a small smile over the top of the glass.

Darina took a deep breath. 'I really think you should be involved.'

William set down his glass and started playing absent-mindedly with an executive toy on the glass coffee-table, an intricate affair of interlocked chrome circles. 'What worries me is the violence. The way his hands were forced into the chopping mechanism. Somebody not only wanted Bernard dead, they hated him.'

'Surely the two go together?'

'Not necessarily. He could have been standing in someone's way and they might have wanted him removed without actually hating him.'

'Helen didn't hate Bernard, she was living with him.'

'That's a *non sequitur*.'

'What a cynic you are!'

'Think about that lunch we had with them. Did they seem to you a happy couple?'

'Well, they did seem a little tense. But lots of married people are like that from time to time. We don't know what's been going on between them.'

'Exactly!'

Darina said nothing, she was trying to tell herself that Helen's extraordinary behaviour in her bedroom had been the result of shock, that it had nothing to do with her relationship with Bernard.

William turned to her with resolution. 'I'm not investigating his death, we're here on honeymoon and we're not going to be involved in this tragedy any more than necessary. Let's try and forget it for the rest of the evening.'

Chapter Nine

Björn Björnson lived in a handsome villa not far from Roland's.

Björn himself opened the door to Darina and William, welcomed them warmly and took them through a large room furnished with severely simple furniture, out through patio windows that gave on to a paved courtyard surrounded by aromatic shrubs. Then they were led through a stone arch and past an attractive swimming pool to a long low stone barn perched above a series of narrow terraces that tumbled down the hillside. But no view of the Mediterranean: the aspect was north east.

The barn was Björn's studio. Skylights remorselessly illuminated a disciplined, whitewashed space. Tools and turntables were lined up neatly. Work in progress was hidden under damp cloths. Bins and tubs were tidied away underneath wide working surfaces either side of a stainless steel double sink. A long run of cupboards topped with a white working surface was kept clean of any clutter. At one end of the long barn was a divan loaded with cushions covered in bright, Provençal prints; beside it stood two comfortable rattan chairs, also furnished with the Provençal cushions, and a low table.

'Take a seat,' Björn said as they entered. 'I'll make us

coffee.' He moved over to an expensive, Italian-looking coffee machine at the other end of the long studio and started adding grounds to small containers, then screwing them into the machine.

The lightly lecherous man Darina remembered from the lunch was not on show that day. His craggy face had lit with genuine pleasure as he opened the door to them both. His long, bony body, lithe as a sailor's, was clad in a grey smock worn over jeans and a red polo neck. The thick, muddy-blond hair was neatly trimmed at a length just long enough to qualify as artistic.

'I was so delighted to be able to accept the commission,' he said, getting out heavy green porcelain coffee cups from a wall cupboard. 'Immediately I met Darina, I wanted to sculpt her, cheekbones, nose, neck.' He turned round as though to remind himself of her charms. 'They are quite unusual, such a beautiful strength. But when you spoke to me the other day,' he said to William, 'I couldn't, I had too much work, too many deadlines.'

Darina wandered along a shelf holding a collection of clay heads, studying the unknown faces sculpted with power and liveliness. One or two she recognized as walkers of the corridors of power. Others looked, from the strength of their features, as though they might belong there as well. There were female faces, some with strength and others with beauty, a few with both. Björn didn't seem to be in the business of obviously flattering his sitters but Darina thought they would all have been pleased with the result. She found a model for Maura's head and stood looking at it. Björn had caught the sensuousness of her face, its generous amplitude that could well slip into blowsiness if she didn't watch her calorie intake. And something else, a determination that Darina didn't remember from meeting her. Did she work at hiding it? How had Björn discovered it?

'You are interested in my work?' Björn brought over a cup of espresso coffee.

Darina thanked him and, looking at the row of clay heads, added, 'I think they're marvellous. It's hard to believe that I'm going to be up there with them.'

Björn took another cup to where William was sitting in one of the rattan chairs, then sat down with one for himself. 'You sound a little apprehensive.'

Darina ran a gentle finger down Maura's nose. 'You seem to see so much.'

'That worries you?'

She gave a small laugh. 'Don't we all have our private areas?'

'And you'd rather not let me in there, hmm?'

William put down his cup of coffee on the table. 'There's nothing mean or devious in Darina, nothing that isn't lovely, intelligent and generous. That's why I want you to do her head. I know she'll always be beautiful but I want her captured just as she looks now.'

Darina felt the bones in her body give way and she leant against the cupboards for support. She had never heard her husband talk of her like that before.

Björn looked at them both and smiled. It was a genuine, warm smile, not his readily produced social version. 'I think I'm more pleased than ever that I can do this for you.'

'So what happened that you were able to fit us in?' asked William.

Björn shrugged broad shoulders. 'Suddenly I get a commission cancelled.'

'Do people often do that?'

'No, not at all. I do not work that way. When something is commissioned it is commissioned, if you understand me?' There was a granite note to his voice that was unmistakable.

'Can you make them compensate in some way?'

'Ask them for money? No doubt I could try but they are,

were, friends. And they are hard on their luck. Anyway,' the bright blue eyes warmed again as he produced a cheerful smile, 'now I can say that it is good luck for me because I can capture the beautiful Mrs Pigram. You are here how long?'

'Another ten days,' said William.

Darina arrived at the end of the line of heads and found one that she felt might not have pleased its owner. Then wondered if being cast in bronze would have made it look less mean. She moved from viewing the right profile to study it full face. From that angle the sharp nose acquired a neatness that looked almost pleasant above the thin-lipped but wide mouth. The blank eyes didn't look quite so narrow either.

'Sir Robert Bright,' Björn, said, regarding her unobtrusively.

'Another of the South of France residents?'

He nodded. 'A retired mover and shaker in the City of London. His company asked him what he'd like for a leaving present. He said his head done by me. I think it was some kind of a joke.'

'Joke?'

'He said people had always been asking for his head and now they'd have to pay for the privilege of giving it to him.'

'Was he pleased with the result?'

Björn's face crinkled engagingly. 'At first he is very pleased because I make sure the head is placed correctly when he sees it. Then he walks all round and perhaps he is not quite so pleased. But it is a good head, it is very like him and everyone admires it so, yes, he is pleased. But now I think we must get to work on Mrs Pigram because we don't have so much time.'

Getting to work on Mrs Pigram appeared to consist of taking endless measurements of Darina's head while

William sat and watched. The distance between nose and mouth, between the eyes, between the eyes and the ears, between the ears over the head, between the ears around the head. At one stage Darina laughed and said it reminded her of measuring up a room to work out the amount of wallpaper and carpet that would be needed.

'Well, it is something like that. Until I have the basic skull, I can't work on what you are.'

'You mean what I look like?'

'More than that. To me there are always two parts to a person. First there is a collection of bones and muscle and skin. Those are the measurable bits, what you might call the technical part. Then there is the personal part. The character that subtly alters what nature has arranged. Every morning it is a little different because of what has happened the day before. So little you can't see any difference. But over the years, it all adds up and gives a quality that has a little to do with the bones nature gave you and a great deal more to do with the person that you are. That is what I try to capture.' Björn adjusted the set of his callipers to reflect the depth of Darina's forehead, measured the distance on his scale and entered the figure on a chart showing different views of a stylized head. 'You know how you can be shown a photograph of someone you've never met? Maybe two or three? And you think that you'll recognize them? And then you do meet and you say, but you're quite different, not what I expected at all?'

'Oh, yes,' cried Darina, 'that's often happened.'

'And do you know why?'

'I've always thought it was because the photographs caught an unusual expression, or the person had a mobile face that couldn't be frozen in one particular instant.'

Björn checked that he had taken all his necessary measurements and gave his callipers a twirl. 'Everyone is many people. To some they show one face and to another another. My task is to identify the different faces, put them all together and find the one that is truly them.'

Darina looked over towards the row of heads. 'I can see why you are so much in demand.'

'Now, that is all we can do today. Come through to the house and we will have a drink and you will tell me all about yourself.'

So they went back past the swimming pool and through the little walled garden, into the spacious house.

Björn settled them into a set of exceedingly comfortable chairs, left for a few minutes then came back with a bottle of champagne in a cooler. He took it over to a sideboard where a tray with glasses was waiting, opened the bottle and poured out some of the wine.

'Here is to your new marriage, may it be a long and happy one.' They all drank the toast.

'Now,' Björn said to Darina, 'tell me again what you do, what you are involved with.'

'Is this all part of the getting behind the face I present to the world?' Björn nodded, looking amused. 'I don't really like talking about myself but I suppose if William's going to get his money's worth, I'd better try.' And Darina proceeded to overcome her reluctance and describe her career in cookery, how she created dishes, demonstrated and wrote articles and books.

'And she's starting to get involved in other things as well,' added William when she dried up. 'She's just finished a series of television programmes and been taken on as a consultant with a food firm.' Darina blushed at the pride in his voice.

'You are a lucky man, William. I have no one to do my cooking – either I eat salads or I go out.'

'I refuse to feel sorry for you, anyone who wants can

learn to cook. William manages very well when I'm not there.'

'But it's better when you are,' hastily put in her husband.

'And I'm sure you've no lack of lovely ladies willing to cook for you when you want,' added Darina to their host.

'Ah, you believe my line the other day at lunch? It's all a front,' said Björn with a twinkle as he refilled their glasses.

'Oh, yes?' Darina placed a protesting hand over her glass as Björn tried to top it up. 'I don't think I've ever drunk so much champagne as over the last few days. First there was the wedding, then the lunch with Helen and Bernard . . .' She drew a quick breath as the dreadful picture of what they'd found in the mill the previous afternoon came back to her. For a while, talking with Björn, she had not exactly forgotten but had been able to push it to the back of her mind.

He looked at her with concern. 'There is something the matter?'

'I don't suppose you've heard about Bernard,' William said.

'What about Bernard?'

'He was killed yesterday.'

'Killed? A car accident?' There was an odd note in Björn's voice.

'I'm afraid not. He appears to have been murdered,' said William.

Björn stared at them out of eyes that suddenly seemed hooded. 'Murdered? Surely not?'

'I regret to say it's true. Darina and I found him yesterday afternoon.'

Björn put down his glass of champagne, rose and walked up to the end of the room, turned and walked back to them.

'Did you know him well?' asked William.

Björn squeezed the bridge of his nose between finger

and thumb and closed his eyes for a brief moment. 'Know Bernard well? Yes, I suppose you could say I did. It is a shocking thing.' He paused for a moment then added, delicately, 'Is it known who killed him?'

William shook his head.

Björn swung away again and walked over to the window, where he stood looking out at the terrace. Neither William nor Darina said anything. Eventually, without turning, Björn said, 'You must forgive me if I say that I cannot be sorry he is dead.'

There was a short pause. Then, 'People are rarely so honest,' William said. 'What had you against Bernard?'

For several minutes it seemed as though Björn wasn't going to answer. When he did start to speak, he appeared to have wandered on to quite a different subject. 'I first came down to the South of France ten years ago. I was just beginning to be known. A Swedish businessman commissioned a head of his wife and asked me down here to carry out the work. It was January. Behind me, in Sweden, I left days of darkness with only a few hours of daylight, almost no sun, and deep, deep cold. I arrived to bright, no, brilliant sunshine. I could walk outside without swathing myself from head to foot in heavy clothes.' He flung himself back into his chair. 'If you haven't experienced the Scandinavian winter, it is difficult to make you understand my feelings of release and happiness down here. Then and there I promised myself that, as soon as I could, I would come here to live.'

'How long did it take you?' Darina asked.

He gave her a brief, satisfied smile. 'Not long. The businessman and his wife were very happy with the bust I did. They moved in an international set and many of their friends saw my work and some of them gave me commissions. Soon I was able to raise my fee and later I found this place.' He glanced around the big room. 'It didn't look quite like this then, I have done considerable rebuilding. I travel, of course, much of my work is now done all round the world, but always I love coming back here. For me it is home.'

'We can understand how much the climate here must mean to you. The winters in England are not precisely warm or cheerful.'

'It's more than the weather, William. There is an earthiness, a beauty to life here that is precious. The French have no pretensions. Oh, I don't mean the Parisians who come down to their *résidences sécondaires*, I mean those who have always lived here and those entrepreneurs who have come here to work. Their attitude to life is so basic and so healthy. Next door there is a farm where they grow violets and other flowers. The whole family works, planting, cultivating, cutting, arranging in bunches and bouquets, taking to the market. It is a hard and simple life. They see my possessions, my pool, my large car, the way I live, yet they show no jealousy. Perhaps they are even amazed that these things are important to me. Perhaps soon I will have to recognize that life can be lived without them.' Björn's chin fell towards his chest and he brooded for several minutes. Then he lifted his head and his eyes were bright. 'But you are wondering what all this has to do with Bernard. I will tell you.

'About eight years ago, soon after I come to live here, I meet Bernard at the house of some friends. He does not live here then, he comes down to visit. Sometimes he stays at the Negresco in Nice, sometimes with friends. He knows so many people and as time goes by, even more. Many of us here,' Björn gave a little, deprecating shrug, 'we are not what you would call really rich but we are very comfortable. Bernard talks to us of Lloyd's. Of this great insurance

105

market, its copper-bottomed, worldwide reputation. How he is a members' agent and can help us make our money work better if we become Names and allow him to place us on leading underwriting syndicates.'

Björn gave a shrug. 'I say to him that I have always believed you have to be very rich to be accepted as a Name. He says I have enough. One is not allowed to include one's house in the amount one needs to prove to the committee of Lloyd's one has enough capital to qualify for membership but banker's guarantees can be used and these can be supported by the value of one's property.

'I ask Bernard what happens if there are disasters and I am asked to pay up under this "unlimited liability" we have to accept. "Dear boy," he says to me,' – Björn's voice took on Bernard's plummiest tones – ' "Dear boy, life is always a gamble but the odds on a large call on your funds are about the same as on you falling under a bus tomorrow.' So, when the Committee give me my interview and explain to me about the last pair of cufflinks I have to be prepared to lose, I cannot take the matter too seriously.'

'You never expected to lose money?' William sounded sceptical.

Björn flushed slightly. 'I am no idiot. Of course I didn't expect to gain profits all the time. The first few years I am lucky and, as I have been recommended, I put the money aside, altogether some eight thousand pounds, to provide a . . . a sinking fund against the bad years.' He paused as though considering what next to tell them. 'Then one year I receive a tiny, tiny cheque. Still, I tell myself it is not a loss. But three years ago, the losses start and I am being asked for much, much money. Last time it was for two hundred thousand pounds.'

Darina gasped.

Björn smiled grimly at her. 'You, too, think that is a lot

of money? I have already paid much more than that and I am trying now to raise enough money without selling this house. If I am asked for another such sum, it will be disastrous.'

'Did you ask Bernard what had happened?' enquired William, placing his empty champagne glass on the table by the side of his chair, his eyes watchful.

'Of course. Bernard is very sorry. He says there are unfortunate disasters; a major oil platform in the North Sea, hurricane Hugo in America. It is exceptional and the market should soon adjust and we shall be in profit again. So I pay and others here pay. But as we are asked for more and more money we begin to ask questions of others, to try and find out exactly what is happening.'

'And?' asked Darina as he paused again.

Björn frowned. 'I find it difficult to understand. John Rickwood tried to explain it to me the other day, Jules is also involved you see. He says that in underwriting, high-risk business has part of the risk passed on so that if disaster does occur, many will bear the loss.'

William nodded. 'I think I know what you're going to say. You and others have been caught in what is being called a spiral. Reinsurance has been concentrated amongst a few syndicates rather than spread not only among many syndicates but also between different insurance markets. As long as there wasn't a disaster, the syndicates earned high premiums but the risks of such a practice are enormous. It's like passing the parcel; when the music stops, disaster strikes for the one holding it.'

'According to John, our syndicates (all Bernard's members seem to be on the same ones) owed us a duty not to behave in this way. Jules says that now she will not pay, that it is a matter of principle.' He gave a twisted smile. 'Jules is very strong on principle. John was going to talk to

Bernard because he was not only a members' agent but also the managing agent of one of the syndicates. John feels we definitely have a case against this syndicate and could perhaps sue Bernard.'

William looked sceptical. 'Do you know if they met?'

Björn's expression shut down and he shrugged his shoulders. 'I am not sure what happened.'

'What a terrible position for you,' said Darina, looking around her and thinking how dreadful she would feel if she had to give up this lovely house and the studio that was so beautifully organized.

She received a bleak smile. 'I am not so badly off as some. Sir Robert Bright, whose head you looked at in the studio, had to sell their house last year. It was magnificent. Now he and Lila live in a small apartment in Antibes. And there are others in equally difficult positions. I at least have my work and I can earn more money. For the retired, it is the end of the line.'

'You make it sound a grim prospect,' said William.

Björn gave a short laugh. 'What's money, after all? If one has health and a place to live, one shouldn't complain, there are thousands worse off. But when one hears of Bernard, who has brought all this on us, enjoying himself living a life of luxury with his rich girlfriend, while we are all so desperately worried we shall lose everything, is it surprising if we resent his comfort? Would like to, how do you put it, stick it to him?' The grimace Björn gave made him ugly in a peculiarly unpleasant way. For a moment it was as if another man inhabited his skin, someone avaricious with at least a touch of cruelty. Then he gave a small wave of his hand, a dismissive gesture, and his features reverted to their previous disarming pleasantness. 'Now Bernard is no more and I cannot be sorry. So, let us think about my work with the beautiful Darina. I shall try not to take up too much of your precious honeymoon but I will need two or three sessions with her. Then you will have to wait some time before I can deliver the finished bronze but no more sittings will be necessary. Would the day after tomorrow at ten be convenient?'

William looked towards Darina, who nodded. He stood up. 'That should be fine. Now, we mustn't clutter up your day. Thank you for the champagne and the coffee, both were delicious.' Then, as Björn was showing them out, he added, 'By the way, what were you doing yesterday?'

For a moment Björn was startled, then he laughed. 'Never forgetting your profession, Monsieur l'Inspecteur? I may not be sorry Bernard is dead but I have nothing to worry about from your enquiry. I was here. In a meeting with my financial adviser.'

As they drove away, Darina said, 'Björn seemed such a playboy when we met at that lunch but today he appeared so serious. And I'm not just referring to after we broke the news of Bernard's death.'

'Today he was a professional, the other day he was off duty. Do you mind if we go straight back to Antibes? I'd like to do some telephoning.'

'What sort of telephoning? We were going to explore.'

'No need to sound like that. I thought we'd ring Roland and Maura and see if they could come to lunch tomorrow.'

Darina slipped him a sideways glance. 'Why do I get the impression this is not a purely social invitation?'

William slowed the car as they came up to a roundabout. His gaze was fixed on the road as he changed gear and filtered through the traffic. 'Well, we do owe them and Roland does seem to know an amazing number of people down here.'

'You mean you're going to pump him for background?

That you are going to get mixed up in Bernard's murder?'
All at once Darina felt a slow anger begin to build in her.
William was going to concern himself in this investigation
after all, without even asking her if she minded! Helen
Mansard's possible plight as a primary murder suspect
slipped to the back of her mind and she forgot she'd said
he ought to be involved.

'Haven't you been told the case is nothing to do with
you?' she suggested, tight-lipped.

'I'm in a far better position to discover who had cause
to murder Bernard than the French police. Or even
whoever they send out from Scotland Yard to liaise with
them. We have an *entrée* into the world Bernard and Helen
have been moving in down here that is unique.'

'What about all the official angles you've always been so
quick to point out to me? Like the forensic evidence and
all the details police investigations so painstakingly put
together that solve killings? Haven't you always told me
unofficial investigations merely complicate the picture for
the professionals?'

'I am a professional.' William began to sound heated.
'You don't understand.'

'Oh, I understand all right. I understand that you've
always told me to keep out of police business, that solving
crimes should be left to those in charge of the investigation,
that they can be relied upon to come up with the answer.
It's not enough that I'm married to a policeman, he can't
forget that he's one even on his honeymoon!'

William negotiated the narrow streets of Valbonne and
turned on to the Antibes road. 'Do you really mean that?'
he said at last.

'About not wanting you to spoil our honeymoon?'

'No, about being married to a policeman?'

'You're not getting all sensitive about your job, are you?

110

For heaven's sake, William, can't you see things from my point of view?'

'But you're usually the one who wants to get involved in solving murder. And Helen is your friend.'

'Yesterday you seemed to think she was the prime suspect.'

'Today I think that is what the French police are going to believe but that there could be other possibilities worth exploring.'

'Then tell them that and let us get on with our honeymoon!'

'Is that really what you want to do?'

Darina opened her mouth, then closed it again, hasty words evaporating as she thought of Helen, distraught and bereft, Bernard lying with his mutilated fingers, his face swollen and distorted, his body lifeless. She swallowed. 'We can't just enjoy ourselves, can we? Not now. Anyway, nothing I say will make any difference, will it?'

Chapter Ten

Anthea Pemberton was washing salad in her large kitchen. The kitchen was at the back of the house; from the window you had a view right down the rock face that plunged to the river Var far below.

The drawback about the kitchen was that it was too far from the front door; you couldn't hear cars approaching up the drive, had no warning of visitors. Many times Anthea told herself she should get in the habit of locking the front door – the days had gone when you could safely leave it open. Too often, though, she forgot. Now she started round in fright as she heard someone entering the kitchen.

Then she relaxed. 'Björn, I wasn't expecting you, I thought you had work to do today!'

The tall figure dropped a quick kiss on her cheek. 'You're right, I can't stop long.'

'Have some coffee,' she said, moving to pick up the kettle from the stove. 'Or would you prefer a drink?'

'Have you brandy?'

'I think so.' She went and opened a large cupboard in the corner of the kitchen, rummaged around its chaotic contents and found a bottle. She placed it on the table with a couple of glasses and looked at it doubtfully. 'It's what I use for cooking. I don't know if you'd think it good enough for drinking.'

113

He picked up the bottle and glanced at the label. 'It'll do and it's not for me.' He took one of the glasses and poured a generous slug. Then he pulled out a chair from the table and held out the glass of brandy. 'Sit down and take this.'

She obeyed with a sick feeling of apprehension. 'What's happened?' She held the glass between both hands, resting it on the table as though it might dissolve if she didn't keep a grip on it, her mind skittering violently over possible disasters. There was a terrible churning in her stomach.

Björn drew out another chair from the table and sat so he could face her. He put his right hand gently but firmly over hers. 'Bernard is dead, Anthea. Someone killed him yesterday.'

She sat looking at him and for a single instant all she felt was relief that it wasn't what she had expected to hear. Then horror twisted and turned inside her as she took in what it was Björn had actually said. The colour drained out of her thin face, turning it to a clay mask. All feeling ceased. It was like being turned to stone: blood no longer ran in her veins, her brain was incapable of thought, incapable of reaction.

Time stopped. At some stage she became aware of Björn's concerned face. Abruptly she freed her hand, raised the glass of brandy and drank; its coarse fire burnt down her throat and she coughed, sending some of it the wrong way. She bent over, fighting for breath and spluttering hoarsely, brandy splashing down her lacy sweater.

Björn moved to pat her back but she stretched out a preventing hand, her eyes closed, her face contorted as she struggled to control the coughing. Then another sip of the brandy and this time it went down easily.

At last she could open her eyes and look at him. 'Tell me what happened.'

'I don't know any more. I was just told this morning. Apparently he was murdered.'

'Murdered?' The word came out on a harsh, rising note. He sat watching her with concern. 'So I was told.'

'Who told you?' Again that harshness.

He explained.

'I can't believe it,' she moaned. 'I saw him yesterday morning.'

Björn stared at her. 'You saw Bernard yesterday? Where?'

'Tourettes.' Her gaze dropped to the table. 'I . . . I asked him to meet me there.'

'Whatever for?'

'Don't look at me like that. I just wanted to talk to him, that's all.' Even to her own ears she sounded sulky, mulish, a child chided for unacceptable behaviour trying to excuse itself.

Björn sighed in exasperation. 'And did it do any good?'

Anthea shook her head. 'He wouldn't listen to me. He was angry that I was bothering him.' The little colour that had come to her cheeks faded again. 'God! I hated him then. I think I could have murdered him myself.'

He reached out and grasped her hand. 'Good, that's good, hang on to that.'

All at once her face crumpled. 'Oh, Bernard!' she wailed and tears started to flow.

He leaned across and held her, patting her back, '*Stackars lilla flicka*, poor little girl. There, there.' She felt the comforting pressure of his fingers across her back. Those flexible, powerful fingers could be so gentle at times. And they were so skilful – skilful and merciless and cruel. Anthea sometimes stared at his hands, wondering about the mind that directed all that expertise.

After a few minutes she drew back. She used a tea towel

115

to wipe away the tears. 'Thanks, Björn,' she said awkwardly. 'Thanks for coming and telling me.'

'I didn't want you to hear of it on the telephone or in the odd conversation, you know?' He watched her as she reached for more brandy.

The full meaning of what he had told her began to take effect. It was as though all life was draining from her. She sagged against the chair's ladder back, her eyes hopeless and unfocused.

'You say you met with Bernard yesterday morning?'

She sighed and gave a brief nod.

'And did anyone see you together?'

'What do you mean?'

'Don't you see? The police will want to know everything about Bernard and who he saw, especially yesterday. They will want to know who had reason to kill him.'

'And you think they might suspect me? Björn, you can't be serious!'

'You said yourself you would have liked to kill him. If they suspect you, they will turn over your life, like . . . like a prospector looking for gold. You can't allow that.'

The tone of his voice shook Anthea. She looked properly at him, and was chilled by his eyes. Bright, burning blue, fiery sapphires, cornflowers carved from ice – the images tumbled through her bruised mind.

'I repeat, did anybody see you with him?'

She tried to force herself to think back. But too much had happened in the last few minutes; her brain whirled, unable to process anything more. 'No, I'm sure not. Tourettes was as busy as ever but I didn't see anyone I knew. Anyone, that is, apart from the Pigrams.'

'The Pigrams?' His voice was sharp, jagged. '*Djävlar!*'

It didn't matter that she couldn't understand the imprecation, his tone said enough.

'But they don't matter! Anyway, I was on my own then, buying some things in the square. Darina said they were going to drive around the Gorges du Loup.'

'And where did you meet Bernard?'

'In the bar, we had coffee. Björn, it can't have mattered if anyone saw us together.' But in her mind's eye she saw again his angry departure, felt her murderous despair as he left her; left her without hope, without reason for living.

Anthea forced herself to be sensible. There was always a reason for living. And there was nothing that could connect her with Bernard's death. She said so to Björn.

'The question,' he said carefully, 'is whether you should go to the police and tell them that you saw Bernard that morning. Or wait to see if they come to you.'

Anthea began to feel a terrible coldness spread through her veins. 'Why should they come to me? Nobody knows we met that morning. Nobody,' she amended, 'except you.' She looked at him with the unspoken question in her eyes even though she was convinced she had nothing to fear from him.

He gave her a twisted smile. 'Oh, I shan't tell them, you needn't be anxious about that. But I don't like it that you met Darina and William. They could easily have seen you with Bernard. Perhaps it would be best if you contacted the police. You could have met Bernard there by accident. He won't have told Helen what he was going to do, after all.'

'I'm afraid,' Anthea said slowly, 'that if the Pigrams did see us together, they might not believe it was accidental. You see, I went to the mill the other afternoon and they were there as well. They heard Bernard promise to ring me about my letter.'

Björn put his head in his hands in a gesture of despair.

'Don't do that,' Anthea said sharply. 'How was I to know

Bernard would get himself killed? Anyway, it's nothing to do with you what I do or who I meet.'

He raised his head and looked at her and her eyes dropped their gaze. Her hands started to tremble. She wished, oh, how she wished, they had never met. But it was too late now.

Someone had introduced them at a pottery exhibition the previous summer.

That evening she had been feeling happy for the first time in a long while. At last something good had happened to her and life appeared to be opening out with a sweet promise. More than that, her pieces at the exhibition had attracted considerable attention: not only had she sold all of them, she had also received a number of valuable commissions.

Björn's perceptive comments had led to a discussion of pottery techniques, and her usual inhibitions had fallen away. She had talked about her work with unexpected fluency. Even when she found out who he was, he hadn't allowed her to feel awkward that she hadn't recognized him. And when she told him about the courses she ran, he'd seemed really interested. 'If you are ever short of someone to help those interested in sculpting, let me know. Perhaps I could help.'

'Oh, I couldn't ever ask you, you're far too distinguished. But, perhaps if you had time to come to dinner and chat with some of our guests? They would be thrilled.'

'I would like that very much. I would also like to see more of your work. I was too late to buy one of your bowls but perhaps you could make one for me?'

By now Anthea had felt bold enough to say, 'Only if you will show me some of your work.'

And that had been the start of it all.

Looking back, Anthea supposed that she could have said

118

no at the start. She hadn't been forced into agreeing with his suggestions. He hadn't held a pistol to her head. He'd made it all sound rather fun, exciting. And one thing had gradually led to another. Until now she was in so deep she could see no way out.

Unless she had the courage just to walk away?

In the light-filled kitchen, the smells of her slowly cooking cassoulet beginning to permeate the room, she looked into the face of the man sitting opposite and remembered the friendship Björn had given her over the last few weeks. They'd been the worst she'd ever experienced, and that was saying something – without him she would surely have collapsed.

'Are you sure you're going to be all right?' he asked her. 'Why not come back with me? You could help prepare the armature and base for Darina's head.'

It was the most generous offer he could make.

She gave a bleak smile. 'No, I'll be fine, honest.'

He scrutinized her face and appeared satisfied. He placed his hands on her shoulders, pulled her up towards him and planted a swift, soft kiss on her mouth. She had to force herself to remain still under his touch. Then he released her and left.

Anthea sank back again into the kitchen chair. The news he'd brought seared right through her brain and along her nervous system, down to her very toes.

She flung up her head and bellowed her distress; somehow the noise helped. She bellowed again, then the tears came and she collapsed over the table in pitiful weeping.

Chapter Eleven

Darina refused to be taken out for a meal after William had made his telephone call to Roland and Maura.

The fact that they had appeared only too eager to come to lunch the following day did not help her temper.

'Now we're here,' Darina said, 'it'll be much better to have lunch in the apartment.'

She then gave William salad.

William didn't like salad; he wasn't a rabbit, he always said. This afternoon he ate it without comment.

Then they went out for a walk, exploring the built-up streets around their apartment. The scenery offered little excitement and their conversation even less.

Gradually Darina began to feel guilty. Hadn't William always supported her whenever her career had meant she'd abandoned him to look after himself, even when it coincided with a difficult time in his own work? What was she doing, sulking when he had to suffer the frustration of being shut out of what should be his case?

On their return, she went to the excellent butcher in the little run of shops that abutted their apartment and bought calf's liver, William's favourite. To go with it, she fried onions and sautéd potatoes, his chosen accompaniments to almost any meat or even fish.

William made no comment on the food and conversation still failed to sparkle.

After supper he got out a large pad and started writing. Darina retaliated by switching on her laptop.

Its screen offered the notes she'd made on Bernard's olive oil mill. For a long time she stared at them. Then she looked across at William.

Before she could say anything, William discarded his notebook. 'There's a programme I want to watch on TV,' he announced, switching on the set.

It was a travel programme and Darina quickly realized she couldn't understand more than the odd word of its commentary.

After fifteen minutes of struggling with the French she announced she was going to bed.

At the door of the living room she paused, waiting for William to say he'd be along in a minute and to keep the bed warm for him.

His eyes remained glued to the screen. It was as if he hadn't heard her.

Darina made sure her eyes were closed when he came to bed and her breathing regular. William undressed in the bathroom and slipped quietly into bed. Soon came the whiffling sound that meant he was asleep.

It was a long time before sleep claimed Darina.

In the morning she awoke disoriented and heavy-headed and rolled over in bed, automatically feeling for William, but the other side of the mattress was empty.

She swung her long legs out of bed and looked down at the nightdress she was wearing. It was the first morning of her honeymoon that she had woken up with it not lying discarded on the floor.

Darina reached for her négligé, a flimsy affair of champagne-coloured silk and lace that matched her nightdress, and slipped it on. She went through to the living room and found William sitting in the same chair he had occupied the previous night. His notebook was open on its arm but he wasn't looking at it.

Darina went and knelt beside him. 'I'm so sorry,' she said. 'I've been a beast and a pig.'

He looked at her and his eyes came alive. 'I've been sitting here thinking exactly the same. I just assumed you'd go along with what I wanted. But it's our honeymoon. I had no right to allow my professional instincts to take over.'

'No, I was wrong! A half-witted baboon is less selfish and more intelligent than I was. This case involves both of us.'

'I should have discussed it with you. What was it we said the other day about being a partnership?'

William pulled Darina up on to his lap.

'I'm too large for this sort of activity,' she said, resting her head on his. 'The chair will collapse.'

'Nonsense.' He tightened his grasp around her silk-clad body.

'I'm usually the one insisting on barging into a murder investigation and you're the one telling me it should be left to the professionals. But you are a professional.'

'You're very loyal,' he said, settling her more comfortably on his knees. 'Shall I confess what's really been bugging me?'

'What's that?'

'That you don't think much of my job.'

'What do you mean? I think you're a wonderful detective.'

'Do you?' His voice was sceptical. 'Aren't you sometimes embarrassed, having to introduce me as a policeman? It's as bad as a dentist. Wouldn't you rather I was a successful businessman like Roland or an artist like Björn? Someone respected in the community?'

'But policemen are!'

'I wish I could believe you're as sure as you sound. I know my mother's deeply disappointed.'

Whatever Darina had been expecting, it wasn't this. Her relations with her mother-in-law were prickly, to put them at their best. She had been convinced Mrs Pigram believed her son could have done much better for himself than an over-tall cook who had no influential relations.

'She's been waiting for me to make up for the fact my father never made general. When I joined the Foreign Office, she saw herself as the mother of a future ambassador. She's never recovered from the shock of me giving up that chance to become a member of the fuzz.' William's voice was bitter. 'I think sometimes she actually searches the papers for derogatory mentions of the Force, that she gets some peculiar satisfaction from finding others share her view.'

Darina tightened her arms around her husband. 'I'm proud when I say what you do and you better believe it. And what's more, that French policeman's a fool. He should be delighted you were on the scene and could help him.'

William laughed. 'That's my girl, but I'm not so feeble-minded I can't understand Garnier's point of view. My position is suspect, we can't get away from that.'

'That's nonsense and you know it.'

William leant back so he could plant a light kiss on his wife's mouth. '*Tu as raison, ma chère.* And you, too, have a part to play. Between us we are ideally placed to help this investigation.'

'You agree I'm right, then?'

'I just said so.'

'You did? Well, I'll back you all the way. What's so funny?'

'Nothing, my darling. Except, you're hardly going into this investigation with an open mind, are you?'

'If you mean that I'm convinced Helen is innocent, right on, mate!'

'I can't afford the luxury of blind loyalty. I have to approach the problem believing anyone could be responsible.'

'Within the limits of what we saw, that is,' said Darina firmly.

'Which is?'

Darina swallowed hard then said as steadily as she could manage, 'Do you honestly think little Helen could have forced Bernard's fingers into that machine then hit him over the head? He wasn't all that big but she's minute. I doubt if I could do that to you and the difference in our sizes is much less than theirs.'

'Cooks are strong but I see your point. The trouble is, I can't stop thinking of something Björn said yesterday.'

'He said an awful lot. What particularly?'

'He talked about Bernard living with his rich girlfriend. Now, I know Helen is slightly more successful than you are—'

'Slightly!' Darina snorted. 'Thanks for the compliment, darling, but her reputation is streets ahead of mine.'

'OK, given that, what about her income? You're always complaining your earnings from books and even that television series aren't nearly what everyone thinks they must be. So, are Helen's earnings enough to pay for all we saw the other day? Not only the size of the property but what looked to me like a complete refurbishment, new bathrooms and kitchen, the swimming pool, all that furniture?' His arms tightened round her again. 'Don't just say I'm talking nonsense, think about it.'

Darina sighed. 'If my returns are anything to go by, not a chance!'

'But perhaps she sold a large house in England and

125

transferred the proceeds into the property out here?'

'No, Helen's hopeless with money. She told me once she'd never managed to get enough together to put a deposit down.' She leaned slightly away from William and looked at him. 'Are you suggesting Bernard bought the farm and paid for everything?'

'He told us himself that he'd equipped the mill.'

'He really must have thought they were as good as married.'

'Better!'

'How do you mean?'

'Remember Björn's tale of woe? All the money he was being asked to pay to settle his liabilities at Lloyd's? Well, Bernard was probably in the same boat. He was not only a members' agent, he was a Name himself. He could well have thought buying property in Helen's name was a neat way of making sure that the money didn't have to be paid to Lloyd's.'

'As long as no one knew where it had gone?'

'Exactly, my sweet. Otherwise Lloyd's could still make a claim on the money. There needs to be a five-year gap after any transferral before the funds are no longer at risk.'

'I didn't want to tell you before, but you know when Helen ran upstairs after we'd found Bernard's body? Well, she was knee deep in papers when I got there and said she was trying to find his will.'

'Her live-in lover is murdered and her first thought is of his *will*?'

'It does sound odd but she was distraught, really distraught. I thought it could be a displacement activity, something to distract her from what had actually happened.'

'Hmm, turning to housework or cooking I could understand, but looking for a will?'

Darina thrust away the picture of Helen desperately

126

shuffling through papers. 'But didn't Bernard say he hadn't lost much money?'

'Can one trust what he said?'

'And I don't know much about Lloyd's but I thought all the big losses had been sorted out and now was a good time to become a Name because it was all going to get profitable again?'

'That may or may not be so. But Lloyd's always declares its accounts three years in arrears. Many people, like Björn and those others he was talking about, still have to find very large sums.' William frowned. 'I don't know nearly enough about Bernard, about his dealings at Lloyd's, about the situation at the mill, his relationship with Helen or with heaven knows how many other people down here.'

'Then Helen isn't your only suspect?' Darina exclaimed.

'Having heard Björn, it seems to me that a number of other people could have very good cause to want Bernard dead.' He slipped a hand inside the silk négligé and caressed Darina's back. 'Wouldn't it be a good idea if we continued this discussion in bed? We ought to make up for last night's lost opportunities. After all, we are on our honeymoon.'

'Darling, look at the time! You shouldn't have invited people to lunch if you wanted to spend the morning in bed.' She slipped off his knees and made for the bathroom.

'We'll get something sent in,' William called after her. 'Or we'll take them out.'

The words were addressed to a closed door.

Down in the little shopping centre at the bottom of their apartment block, Darina bought escalopes of veal from the butcher who had produced the liver. As she paid for the meat, she noticed bottles of a local olive oil and bought one of those as well, and some tiny olives prepared in oil with herbs. At the greengrocer's she found tomatoes, potatoes, fresh spinach, garlic, salad and some fruit. Next door was the grocer's, where she finished her shopping with tins of anchovies in olive oil, grated Emmental, some ripe Camembert and Roquefort for the cheese board, *crème fraîche* and some full cream milk. Finally she bought a couple of *baguettes* from the *boulangerie*. The worst hazard of being a professional cook, especially one who published recipes, was the incredibly high expectations of guests. For a moment Darina wished she had agreed with William's suggestion and allowed him to take them all out to a meal. But she genuinely enjoyed feeding people. If only they wouldn't make such a fuss about the food itself.

Back in the little apartment kitchen, Darina made her preparations with a speed born of long practice and thought about the meal she and William had been served at Roland's and Maura's: an elaborate starter, beautifully presented; a conspicuously expensive main course; another elaborate and rich dish for pudding. Darina was willing to bet a considerable sum its high standard had been supplied by an outside caterer, a *traiteur*.

What was the menu they were being offered in return? Spinach soufflé with an anchovy sauce, escalopes of veal in an olive oil, garlic and tomato sauce, with *pommes dauphinoises* and a salad, and for pudding a simple *crème caramel* which the French would call *crème renversée*. Nothing elaborate, nothing unusual, nothing that would overload the stomach. It would have to do. Darina checked that William had laid the table with his usual skill and that the wines had been prepared.

With true French *politesse*, Roland and Maura arrived a couple of minutes after 12.30 p.m.

'This is good of you,' said Maura, giving Darina a kiss and handing over a large bunch of white roses elaborately wrapped in shiny Cellophane. 'You shouldn't be cooking on your honeymoon.'

'Darina gets itchy if she's kept away from the kitchen too long.' William's face was completely straight. 'Too many meals out and she begins to feel like a kept woman.'

'It's not a bad feeling,' said Maura amiably, passing into the living room as Darina shot William a furious glance. 'Not all of us want the chains of marriage.'

'Keeps the men on their toes, too, I should think,' William said, his joviality only slightly forced.

'Oh, Roland certainly keeps on his toes, thistledown-footed, that's what he is.'

'A tripper of the light fantastical,' he agreed urbanely, dropping a kiss on Darina's left cheek. 'Glad to see the bride still looks both beautiful and deliriously happy.' He followed up the first kiss with one on the other cheek. 'When in France, eh?'

'He always uses that as an excuse to obtain maximum value,' observed Maura.

'Then he should go to Brittany, the usual form there is four times, twice on each cheek,' said William, with determined good humour.

'Like this, you mean?' asked Roland, reaching for Darina again.

'Should be alternate cheeks,' said William, demonstrating on a pleased Maura. 'Now, what would you like to drink?'

Things were going rather more stickily than Darina had expected. Had Maura and Roland been so little in tune with each other at luncheon the other day? As Darina slipped into the kitchen to put the soufflé in the oven, she realized they hadn't seen much of Roland and Maura as a couple. Well, the host and hostess of a large party didn't spend much time together, did they? She remembered Jules's remark, that Roland was never going to marry Maura, however hard she tried. Just now Maura had given the impression she was the one who didn't want to be tied down.

Was it important to know which was the truth? Darina took a plate of *crudités* and *aïoli* back into the living room.

'How delicious,' Maura said as she picked out a stick of red pepper and loaded it with the garlic-flavoured mayonnaise. 'I bet you made this yourself.'

'Maura resents any time spent doing something she can buy already prepared,' announced Roland, settling himself in a chair with a large glass of the single malt whisky William had bought in duty-free before their flight to Nice.

'Long experience has taught me it's the cheapest and most sensible way,' Maura said, her voice betraying no hint of resentment. 'You'd be the first to complain if I served you up my effort at mayonnaise.' She stuck a piece of carrot into the *aïoli* and crunched her way through it. 'Roland is one of those people who insists everything is of the best. My pitiful attempts to provide what he liked in the early days were met with such scorn I quickly learned to rely on the expertise of others.'

'The lunch we had with you the other day was delicious,' said Darina quickly.

'I can always trust Maura to sort out the most expensive of the *traiteurs*,' drawled Roland, despatching the whisky with a speed that Darina knew would cause William great pain. He liked to think its peaty flavour was properly appreciated.

'Who is it gets his shoes hand-made at Lobbs?' asked Maura sharply.

Roland idly raised a foot and surveyed the deep shine on his leather brogues.

'Have you any idea what those shoes start at?' asked Maura.

'Never been able to contemplate that sort of investment, I'm afraid.' William glanced from Roland's foot to his own well-polished Church's shoes. 'I have to admit they have an air of their own, though.'

'An air worth fourteen hundred pounds?'

Darina heard herself draw a sharp intake of breath.

'It's the fit,' said Roland, without apology. 'Once experienced, the foot can't adapt to anything other. Like you and your silk underwear from Switzerland,' he added to Maura. He popped one of the olives in his mouth. 'These are my favourite,' he told Darina. 'Nothing to beat the Niçoise, a fine example of good things coming in little packages.'

Darina suddenly felt every ounce of her size.

The amply rounded Maura darted a look at Roland that spoke volumes and said to her hostess, 'How on earth do you keep your weight down? If I produced such delicious food, I'd be the size of a house.'

'Instead of just a bungalow with pretensions,' murmured Roland, attacking the *crudités* with gusto.

Who knew what started such internal sniping in a partnership? Incorrigibly quick to decide when she liked someone, Darina was sure it couldn't have been Maura. Then she remembered her own behaviour the previous day. She looked again at Roland, at the dark, witty face with its bony nose and deep creases either side of the mouth. She wasn't at all sure she liked him but he was a man of considerable personality and wickedly attractive.

Darina excused herself to finish the cooking of the escalopes. By the time she returned to the living room to announce they were ready to eat, conversation had moved on.

'*You* found him?' Maura was saying. 'How dreadful.'

'When did the news reach you?' William asked.

'Helen rang yesterday,' Roland said, his voice devoid of expression.

Darina stood in the doorway trying to decide what she should do. The way William was sitting with the middle finger of his left hand tracing the line of his chair arm with careful exactitude, told her he was watching for something important. But she could only hold up the soufflé for a few minutes – after that it would be ruined and with it her reputation as a cook.

Quietly Darina retreated to the kitchen and turned down the oven then came back and stood just outside the living-room door.

'Helen must be devastated.' Maura sounded embarrassed. 'I ought to ring her but it's so difficult to know what to say.'

'Darina's been in touch and, apart from the grilling she's getting from the French police, she seems to be bearing up. It's a terrible experience for her, though,' William said. 'I suppose you must have known Bernard well. Didn't he come down here often, even before he retired?'

There was the tiniest of silences then Roland spoke, his voice cool. 'We knew him quite well at one time. Forgive me, didn't I see our hostess ready to summon us to the table?'

So that was that. Darina entered the room trying not to feel too relieved her soufflé had been saved.

Seated in front of food, Roland began to quiz William on his chosen career. 'I'm more than grateful to chaps like you but, seriously, Bill, do you really think the forces of law and order stand a chance with the world as it is today?'

'Shouldn't your question, Roland, be do we stand a chance without policeman like William?' Maura suggested.

'You're saying exactly what I think,' Darina put in. 'The police force needs to attract men of the highest calibre, not only to fight crime but to increase its standing. It's time policemen were respected again.'

'I'd never have guessed that's what you are,' Maura declared. 'You look much more impressive. A diplomat, perhaps, or a captain of industry, like Roland.'

'Never!' Roland declared. 'Bill lacks the killer instinct.'

'Essential to a successful industrialist?'

'Yes, Bill. If you can't be ruthless when necessary, your company soon goes under.' He cocked his head and surveyed his host. 'Diplomat, though, yes, I could buy that.'

'Now I'd have thought Roland was a pirate,' Darina announced gaily. 'Only the eye patch is missing!'

But Maura hadn't finished. 'There are jobs, aren't there, that never really stop? I hate sitting next to psychiatrists at dinner parties, I'm always sure they're analysing everything I say. And you,' she turned to William, 'I bet your detective's training means you're always looking for clues. Like Sherlock Holmes.'

William laughed and disclaimed any such thing.

'It must have been ghastly finding Bernard but how fortunate it was you. I bet the French police are expecting you to solve the murder for them.' She looked at him with bright eyes. 'Who do you suspect?'

He shook his head. 'I'm as much under suspicion as anybody else, except I don't think they could find a motive for either Darina or myself to have murdered poor Bernard. Just as well because we have no alibi. We spent the day driving round the countryside but we can't prove that.' He looked across at Roland. 'I bet you and Maura don't have alibis either – innocent people rarely do.'

Maura shot Roland an enigmatic look. 'Yes, darling, just what were you doing that day? You left mid-morning saying you wanted to look at some property.'

'And so I did,' he replied easily, helping himself to the last of the spinach soufflé.

'No trouble about an alibi, then,' William said

133

triumphantly. 'You have a business acquaintance who can vouch for you, that's splendid. If, of course, the police should ever question you, I mean.' He managed to sound as though that was the remotest of possibilities.

Roland added more anchovy sauce to his plate. 'No, I'm afraid it wouldn't prove quite that simple. I never got to the estate agency, I had a puncture. I suppose someone might remember me by the side of the road but I suspect I may well have faded into the background.'

Darina thought Roland's ability to fade into the background would be on a par with that of a racehorse in a field of nags.

'And you, my dear,' Roland looked at Maura. 'You were out when I returned home mid-afternoon. Didn't come back until five o'clock. What were *you* up to?'

He had succeeded in deflecting the attention from his own activities. But Maura looked not in the slightest bit disconcerted. 'Shopping,' she said blandly. 'If you remember, you helped me in with a load of supplies.'

'Bought in the Vence supermarket. That can hardly have taken you long.'

Maura turned prettily to William. 'Wouldn't he make a marvellous inquisitor? But I bet you're as good.' She turned back to Roland. 'I ran over to Monte Carlo. I felt like a little expedition. Do you mind?' She stared at him in a most challenging way.

'You know I'm always saying you should enjoy yourself,' he said imperturbably. For a moment they looked at each other, Maura's eyes angry, Roland's inscrutable.

Then William rose, picked up a bottle of wine and started filling glasses. 'Well,' he said. 'It looks as though none of us has much of an alibi. But, then, perhaps that's as well. Police learn to distrust good alibis – so often, there's some very good reason for them.' He sat down again. 'Now,

134

Roland, give us an insider's look at the economy. Tell us we're over the worst, that industry is surging ahead and the "feel-good" factor's coming into play.'

For the rest of the meal he quizzed their guest. Soon Darina saw the thrust of his questions. And it was Roland who eventually brought Lloyd's into the conversation. 'I can tell you,' he said, 'I'm grateful I resisted Bernard's blandishments to increase my underwriting line. If I had, I'd really be in the shit. Sorry, hostess.'

'Your line?' queried Darina.

'A line represents the amount of insurance business you're prepared to underwrite,' explained her husband.

'It's related to your resources,' agreed his guest. 'I could have increased my exposure and in the good times it would have upped my profits. And I did consider it. Then I thought, why be greedy? Thank God I did. At times like these, it would only have inflated my losses. You referred to "poor Bernard" earlier, Bill. Let me tell you, those of us down here he put into Lloyd's have another epithet for him!'

'Are you badly burned?' asked William.

'Let's say there's a nasty smell of singeing.'

'No danger of you having to put that lovely house we saw the other day on the market, I hope?'

Roland gave him a straight look. 'No, Bill, no danger at all.' He turned to Darina. 'If ever your fortunes go down shit creek, sorry, that word again, well, there'd be a job waiting for you as my cook.'

'That's the great thing about being able to produce food, you can always get work.' Darina cleared the soufflé plates and fetched the main course.

Conversation drifted into other areas. Under the influence of the food and wine, the guests started to relax and the luncheon party suddenly achieved a life of its own.

Maura revealed an unexpected talent as a raconteuse and produced more and more ribald stories. The laughter grew and by the time coffee and what the French like to refer to as *digestifs*, Cognac and liqueurs, were served, murder and Lloyd's both seemed to have been forgotten.

At last Roland rose. 'Come on, woman, it's time we went home and left these two to resume their honeymoon. Can you drive or shall we call for a taxi?'

Maura smiled at him. 'Taxi, I think, darling.'

Roland drew out a small, palm-size electronic notebook from his pocket and flashed up a number. 'Mind if I borrow your telephone, Bill? We'll collect the car tomorrow.'

'And while we're waiting for the taxi to arrive, I insist on helping to clear away some of this mess.' Maura started stacking coffee cups and empty glasses on a tray.

She was so obviously determined that Darina made no protest.

Her guest might not be sober enough to drive but she retained enough of her faculties to prove an efficient helper in the kitchen, organizing dirty crockery and the clearing of the table quickly and unobtrusively. Almost too soon the doorbell went and the taxi driver announced he was waiting downstairs.

'Oh, Roland,' said William, assisting Maura into her jacket, 'do you by any chance have Robert Bright's new address?'

Out came the electronic notebook again. 'Sure! Have you got a piece of paper and a pencil?'

A moment later William and Darina were saying goodbye to their guests. 'I'll be sure to tell Geoffrey to make time to bring Honor down to see you.'

'And give our bell a ring when you collect your car.' Darina planted a kiss on Maura's cheek.

'Bit excessive that, wasn't it?' commented William, after they'd watched the lift doors close.

'I like Maura and she's getting a raw deal from Roland.'

'It's her choice. You heard her, she has her freedom.'

'But if she loves him?'

'How much humiliation can love take?'

'And remain uncorroded?'

'She looks in pretty good shape to me,' murmured William.

Darina flicked a tea towel at him.

William looked at the address he was holding. 'Haven't I seen a map of Antibes somewhere around this place?'

Darina pulled it out and William pored over the complex pattern of streets while she finished the last bit of clearing up.

'I've found it!' he announced. 'Not far from the Juan-les-Pins road. Come on, let's drive round there.'

Chapter Twelve

Sir Robert Bright's address was a neat apartment block on a steeply sloping street between Antibes proper and Juan-les-Pins, the much smaller commune, which drifted into the other side of the Cap.

'It looks smarter than our block,' said Darina, as William drove past looking for somewhere to park the car.

'Doesn't have our view.' He found a space a little way up the road and slipped the car in.

It was a residential area mainly occupied by apartment buildings. Gay blinds decorated balconies, many sporting miniature jungles of green plants. Darina got out of the car and looked down the hill. Beyond a jumble of roofs could just be seen the blue of the Mediterranean.

'If their previous house was anything like those others we've seen, this seems rather a comedown,' she commented.

'Mmm,' agreed William. He walked down to inspect the doorbells. 'Looks as though the Brights are on the ground floor,' he said. 'Good for the shopping but not much else.' He pressed a bell. 'Now, leave the talking to me.'

'Wouldn't dream of doing anything else!' Darina waited beside her husband and wondered just what sort of approach he was going to use.

It seemed she was doomed not to find out, at least that afternoon, for there was no answer.

William pushed the bell again but still there was no response.

He sighed. 'Come on, let's go home, our luck's not in this afternoon.'

Darina and William got out of the lift and found a chunky man with a lived-in face leaning against the wall outside their apartment door. Corduroy trousers, sweater over a casual shirt, a jacket held loosely over one shoulder all added up to an Englishman. A briefcase and a suitcase stood on the floor beside him.

'Mike!' William went forward eagerly. 'Can I guess why you're here?'

'Waiting for you, Willie, and hoping you'd be back before midnight! Just as well I was able to slip in the front door behind someone else or I'd be out in the cold. I thought the Côte d'Azur was supposed to be warm.'

'It's not the Caribbean! Come in.' He ushered the other man into the apartment. 'Darling, meet Inspector Mike Parker of the CID. Mike, this is Darina, the very new Mrs Pigram.'

'Honour to meet you.' Inspector Parker shook Darina's hand, his grip strong, his eyes assessing her warmly. 'Though why a girl like you wants to tie herself up to this old sod, I can't guess.' He turned to William. 'Trust you to find a corpse on your honeymoon!'

'Would you like a cup of tea or coffee?' offered Darina, discarding her jacket.

'Would I ever! Tea, please, strong as you can make it. All the rush to get here has given me a thirst you wouldn't believe. What a view!' He walked over to the window as though drawn by a magnet.

Armed with a cup of tea, Mike Parker finally agreed to be quizzed over his mission. 'As far as I can gather, my two qualifications for this little sojourn in the south are a mastery of the language, God bless my French mother, and acquaintance with you, little Willie.'

'You mean?'

Mike Parker leaned forward. 'As far as the French police are concerned, I'm arriving tomorrow, as is my colleague, Chris Spring. I don't think you know him, Willie. He's a good lad, coming along nicely, and says he knows enough of the lingo to get any girl where he wants her. But this evening the guv has suggested you give me all the information you have on the victim, his partner and anything else you think could be valuable. That is, as long as you don't have some heavy engagement.' Mike's tone was lewd.

'I really did get up *le nez de l'inspecteur*, then?'

'As far as he's concerned, I understand you and the fair bride can be considered *numero uno* in the suspect stakes.'

'Idiot,' commented William mildly. 'Did the French send you over any details of the investigation?'

Mike Parker shook his head. 'All that's coming tomorrow.' He went and collected his briefcase from where he'd left it sitting on the floor by the door, pulled out a set of papers and placed it on the coffee table in front of him.

'We've managed to get together some sort of profile of Barrington Smythe.' Mike picked up the top sheet of notes. 'Lloyd's members' agent and a syndicate managing agent, recently retired. The agency he was a partner in was badly affected by losses over the last year or so and what's left of it has merged with two others. Barrington Smythe himself is thought to be in a bad way financially, like so many of his members.' Mike glanced up. 'Certain justice in that, eh? But there's also the question of irregularities concerning the syndicate he managed. Accountants claim there's a shortfall in the reserves and reinsurance premiums are missing. At the moment expert opinion reckons that it will be difficult to assemble enough evidence for a case but that there seems little doubt something between three and four million pounds has been spirited away under the most dubious of circumstances. The educated bet is that it's now safely residing in the Cayman islands.'

'Three or four million?' Darina was disbelieving.

'According to our sources.'

'And it's gone into Barrington Smythe's pocket? Is that what you're saying?' asked William.

'His and, it's reckoned, one of the other underwriters'. He's now living happily in Switzerland and there's little hope he can be brought back to answer any of the burning questions.'

'What about Barrington Smythe's personal situation?'

'His first wife left him for another man after they'd been married four years. His second marriage lasted twenty-five years and ended in divorce two years ago. There were two children: a girl, now married and living in Henley-on-Thames, and a boy, still at university. Neither has spoken to their father for years.'

'Who was responsible for the break-up this time?' asked Darina.

'According to the constable sent to break the news of her former husband's death, the ex-Mrs Barrington Smythe said no news could give her greater pleasure. He'd deserted her, she said, after she'd given him the best years of her life, fallen for some floosy of a cook. The alimony had stopped coming about the time he left the country and her solicitor had failed to get it reinstated.'

Mike picked up another sheet of notes. 'The ex-Mrs Barrington Smythe is not at the moment considered to be a likely suspect. At the moment we think the murderer is probably based down here. But, of course, we know nothing of what he's been up to in France or who he's been associating with. That's where we're hoping you can help. The guv's sent you a note.' Mike dug down into his pile of paper, found and handed over a sealed envelope.

William tore it open and read the short message. 'I see I'm being asked to give you all the help I can but in a very unofficial capacity.'

'That's about the size of it.'

'Well, if I'm to disrupt our honeymoon, I want something in return.'

Mike looked uneasy.

'I want to be kept informed on the investigation.'

There was a shuffling of papers. 'I'll do what I can, Willie, but it may not be easy. Garnier was adamant on keeping you out of the picture.'

'It's the only deal on the table, Mike.'

The other detective gave him a long, hard look. 'You know what, Willie boy? Marriage suits you! OK, my head's on the line but I'll do what I can to pass on whatever the froggies have got and the French system of an examining magistrate in charge of the investigation could be a help.'

William grinned. 'You won't regret it, I promise.' He gave his hands a little rub and got up. 'Right! Before we start, how about jacking in what's left of that tea for a beer?'

'You're on, mate!'

'Where are you staying?' asked Darina, starting to collect cups and saucers.

'Haven't had time to make any arrangements yet. No doubt there's a convenient hostelry which can provide a bed for the night?'

'How about here? There's an extra bedroom and it wouldn't take a moment to make up a bed.'

'Hey, I can't disturb the love birds!'

'Stuff that, Mike, we wouldn't have offered if we didn't

143

mean it.' William brought over beer and glasses.

Mike ripped the ring opener off one of the beers and drank straight from the can, then he lowered it to the table. There was a pause.

After a little, Darina realized he was waiting her for to leave. Inwardly fuming, but reluctant to upset the deal William had achieved, she rose and muttered something about seeing to food.

William's hand shot out and closed about her wrist. 'Sit down, for heaven's sake, darling, you know just as much about the case as I do, if not more. Helen's your friend, after all. Right, Mike?'

'Sure,' he said, with a heartiness that rang hollow.

So, while William filled Mike in on what they knew, Darina sat quietly in a chair with an unaccustomed pleasure coursing through her.

It wasn't the first time she had been involved in a murder case, indeed, she and William had met during one, but always in the past William had done his best to make her keep out of police way. Never before had he behaved as though they could act as a partnership.

'Want to summarize your thoughts on the case so far?' Mike invited him when he'd finished detailing the facts they had on Bernard, Helen and their life down here.

William wandered over to the window and stood looking down at the fort while he spoke. 'The most obvious angle is Lloyd's. Over the last ten years Bernard Barrington Smythe recruited a number of well-to-do people he met here as members of his agency. To say they now hate his guts is to put it mildly.'

Mike fished out another sheet of paper. 'We've identified Sir Robert Bright, Björn Björnson and Roland Tait as Names living or staying down here at least some of the time. You met any of them?'

144

'Björnson and Tait. He, incidentally, came to lunch here today.'

'No!' Mike looked at William with respect. 'You really have managed to gain an *entrée* into the right circles.'

William gave him a small smile. 'There's another Name you can add to your list: Jules Rickwood. She and her husband are renting a very plush villa on the Cap and I understand she, too, is one of Bernard's Names suffering Lloyd's losses.'

Mike consulted his list. 'Ah, yes. Joined as Julia Medlicott, married John Rickwood a year ago.'

'She's an interior decorator,' put in Darina. 'From what she told us, she's been a frequent visitor down here for years. It occurred to me part of John Rickwood's charm for her might have been his wealth – she struck me as a lady who likes to live in certain style. But if she's been a member of Lloyd's for some years, it sounds as though she has money of her own.'

'She didn't strike me as a gold digger.' William threw up his hands in surrender at the look Darina gave him. 'All right, I know, my mind is open, I promise you.'

'What about her husband, Rickwood? If he's having to cough up for his wife's losses, he could have had a considerable grievance.'

'He seemed pretty straightforward,' said Darina, 'I liked him.' She wrinkled her nose at William as he threw her a derisive look. 'He's very much in love with his wife but he hardly struck me as the sort who'd kill in revenge for financial losses.'

'He has a reputation as an extremely successful businessman,' added William. 'I'm sure he'd like us to believe he could cope with any financial loss Jules might be suffering. The facts, of course, could be different.'

'What about Tait?'

'Talked as though his losses were copable with. But then, if he'd murdered Barrington Smythe, he would, wouldn't he?' William considered for a moment. 'He's certainly ruthless enough, I would have said. Neither he nor Maura could account satisfactorily for where they were the day Bernard was killed. No information on the time of death, I suppose?'

'Not until tomorrow.'

'Rigor mortis had set in, I can tell you that. So death must have occurred several hours before we arrived.'

'What about this sculptor chap, Björn Björnson?'

'He's admitted to hurting over Lloyd's losses but he's got a big reputation for his work and his potential earnings must be considerable. On the other hand, it was he who told us about Bright having to sell up and move.'

'Could be suspicious, you think?'

'It was gratuitous information and, yes, I do consider it could possibly be Mr Björnson's way of giving us something to think about.'

'So that's the Lloyd's angle. What about other possibilities, such as this woman Helen Mansard? Cookery writer, isn't she?'

'I'll let Darina tell you about her.' William came and sat down again.

She sketched in Helen's career and personal background as far as she knew it then added, 'I can't believe she'd kill anyone, let alone Bernard, but her account of what she'd been doing that day was unsatisfactory and I agree with what William said earlier, something was souring their relationship. Also, it's most unlikely she could have afforded to buy and do up that property herself.'

Mike was scribbling down notes as they talked. 'What about the woman you saw Barrington Smythe with in Tourettes the morning of the murder?'

146

'Anthea Pemberton? I'm afraid what William told you about her is all we know.'

'Runs art courses, you said?'

'So she told us. I know nothing about them but I agree with William that there was something odd about her behaviour when she came to the mill and she was definitely very upset when he left her in Tourettes that morning. I think they must have been involved together in some way.'

'Sexually?'

'I suppose so,' Darina said reluctantly. Anthea seemed such an unlikely *femme fatale*.

'So include her on our list of suspects.' Mike made another note.

'But would she have had the strength to hold Bernard's hands over that awful machine?' asked Darina. 'She seemed quite frail. I'm almost twice her size and I think I'd have had difficulty.'

'I should think potters have strong hands, like cooks, but you've got a point,' William mused. 'I can't see it could have happened by accident, the odd finger maybe, but not both hands. No, I think Darina's right and it's unlikely any woman could have inflicted those injuries. I think we should be looking for a man as prime suspect.'

'So, have you any other names to add to the list?' Mike sat with pencil poised above his notebook.

'Well,' William gazed down at the last of his beer, 'the afternoon we were at the mill, Helen Mansard's son arrived. There was very little love lost between him and Barrington Smythe and he's a large young man. He'd have had no difficulty in pinning Bernard down at all.'

'Oedipus complex?' Mike's pock-marked face and bent nose managed to give the query a distasteful flavour.

'No idea! I can only say that though he and Helen seemed ecstatic to see each other, Bernard looked far from happy

147

and it was no time before Stephen started needling him.'

Mike Parker made more notes. 'We haven't much on Barrington Smythe's background. Can you help us there?'

William contemplated locked hands for a moment. 'Gave the impression he knew what was what and was definitely fond of the best of everything but didn't produce any pedigree and something rang a little hollow. That mightn't have helped with some of the Names when the going got rough. I would have said Tait was a self-made man as well. His girlfriend, though, is very well connected.'

Darina looked at her husband in astonishment. Most of this had completely passed her by. Where had he picked it all up from? So often, though, men were like that. Meet anyone and five minutes later they knew exactly where they'd been to school, what their background was and no doubt which political party they supported. She had other ways of assessing people. Could class be of any importance in this case?

Looking up from his note-taking, Mike put forward another question. 'What about the nature of the crime, Willie? Any suggestion it was planned?'

'Difficult to be sure but on the surface it appears spur-of-the-moment stuff. We may find that someone knew Helen was going to Nice for the day and decided they could go along and bump Bernard off but I think it's much more likely they went to have a talk with him, found him on his own and got carried away with rage.'

'Rage at what?'

'Answer that question and you ring all the bells. One detail that could help considerably is that the murderer must have been liberally spattered with blood. It was all over the wall.'

Darina closed her eyes briefly but only saw more clearly the white tiles with their bloody dashes.

'No way he could have cleaned himself up?'

William shook his head. 'I wouldn't have thought so.'

Darina forced herself to concentrate on other matters. 'Björn said that John Rickwood was going to talk to Bernard,' she said.

'He did indeed.' Her husband looked at her slyly. 'I thought you said he wouldn't need to resort to murder to sort out his wife's losses?'

'That's right,' she agreed equably. 'And I don't think he would be carried away by rage, either. A very controlled chap, John Rickwood, I would have said.'

'He got quite upset with his daughter.'

Darina remembered the way John had exploded when Terri had said where she was staying. 'True.'

'That Terri's a big girl, too.'

'Are you suggesting she could have killed Bernard? Why on earth would she have wanted to do that?'

'She needs money and the other night it sounded as though her stepmother's losses could mean she wasn't going to get it.'

'But killing Bernard wouldn't give it to her, surely?'

'Any more than it would with any of the Lloyd's Names,' put in Mike.

'No, for all of them it would be a revenge killing. There are very few things people get so worked up about as losing large sums of money.'

'There's one other possibility,' Darina said suddenly. 'It's probably pretty remote but apparently there was no love lost between Bernard and his French neighbour – I think his name's Duval.'

'Thank you, darling! I should have mentioned him.' William turned to Mike. 'A cantankerous peasant, according to Bernard, who also makes olive oil, felt his business was being threatened and was making life unpleasant for his neighbours.'

'Didn't Bernard say he was contravening EU regulations

and he was going to tell him if he didn't stop making his and Helen's life a misery, he'd blow the whistle on him?'

'Add up resentment, jealousy and a belief your livelihood is at risk and you could have a dangerously simmering pot of emotion,' suggested William.

'We've all seen murders done for less,' Mike agreed, adding to his notes. 'Anything else you busy little bees have sucked up whilst sampling the honey?'

'Have a heart, we've only been down here a few days and we've had other things to concern ourselves with.'

'Course you have, Willie! And you've given me an amazing amount. Thanks, it's all going to be most helpful,' Mike said heartily. 'Now, if you're going to give me a bed for the night, you must let me take you both out for a meal.'

'You mean, you're not going to discuss how the case should be tackled?'

'Come on, Willie, you know it'll be up to the French to call the shots. Chris and I will only be bit players.'

'Don't try that with me, Mike, or I'll chuck you out to find your own accommodation.'

Darina watched until Mike's gaze fell. 'OK,' he said finally. 'I know when I'm beat. But I'm famished and we can talk just as well over a plate of nosh. Get your coats.'

Chapter Thirteen

Darina found that sitting for a sculptor was surprisingly hard work.

William dropped her off at Björn's studio and left her there. He said he had a few things he wanted to check out and would pick her up in a couple of hours' time.

Björn took her through to the studio, helped her off with her jacket and eyed the tumble of fair hair. 'I think it would be good to take most of that off your face. You brought the things I suggested?'

Darina fished out the various bits and pieces she used to fasten her abundant hair in various styles. 'I can fix it in a French pleat, or up on top of my head in a sort of cottage loaf, or perhaps a plait?'

Björn lifted the hair with both hands and moved it this way and that, studying the result with half-closed eyes. 'I think if we can lift these bits at the sides and fasten them on top, we will be able to see your bones and the shape of your head; then if we leave the rest tumbling down the back, it will give a little softness, what?'

After Darina had arranged her hair, he had her remove her knitted jacket and silk shirt and slip her bra straps off her shoulders. Then he tucked a warm wrap round her chest and placed her in a low-backed chair. She sat with her hands in her lap, shoulders down, neck long.

'Perfect! Now, remain like that and look at me.'

Björn had a clay head on a turntable tall enough for him to work standing up. Darina thought she could recognize something of herself in the head but the features were bland, lifeless.

'Now, while I work, we will talk. But you will keep quite still, please. Unless you really cannot and then you will tell me, yes?'

'Yes,' agreed Darina rather faintly. Suddenly it all seemed rather a responsibility, as though the success of his work depended on her ability to sit without moving.

For the next hour she watched the long, skilful fingers manipulating clay so that, slowly, very slowly, her head began to take shape. Björn worked quickly and while he worked, he talked. Amusingly, entertainingly; asking her questions, taking her answers and twisting them into something new. It was as though Björn could split himself into two people, each performing a quite different task at the same time. The long, craggy face reflected a constant succession of fleeting emotions. In repose his face appeared to be carved out of rock but in motion it proved to be constructed of something much more flexible. Meanwhile his eyes appeared to have no connection with the expression on his face. Their gaze darted from Darina's head to the head on the turntable before him. Occasionally they would narrow and for an instant his entire face would freeze, his chatter cease as he focused all his attention on his work. But only for an instant, then some part of himself would disengage from the sculpting process and be off, once again constructing the airy conceits of his conversation.

It was impressive – and unsettling.

Then Björn laid down the little flat spatula with which he had been working. 'Now I think it is time we had a coffee, no? You have been very good and I have been very good and we both deserve a rest.' He went over to his Italian coffee machine.

While Björn fussed with his toy, Darina studied the studio.

It was so neat, everything in its place and a place for everything. Darina was fiercely envious of the discipline that had kept all the working surfaces and shelves free of clutter. She looked at the long bank of cupboard doors that ran the length of the back wall – how she would love all that space. What did Björn keep in there? She couldn't imagine him hanging on to all the bits and pieces she found it so difficult to part with. Bags of clay ready to be mixed for sculpting, perhaps? No, she could see those beside the sink. Rolls of the wire that he had explained formed the base for each head? Supplies of charts ready to be filled in with measurements? There did seem, though, to be an awful lot of cupboards.

Darina switched her attention to the wall opposite. Between two windows, a small shelf held a number of bronze figurines, arranged with a typically Scandinavian appreciation of the value of space in design. She moved over to look more closely. Mostly nudes in a variety of poses, the figures were moulded with a grace and subtlety that was immediately attractive. Björn's talents obviously stretched beyond busts.

As he tended his coffee machine, Björn gossiped about other ex-patriots drawn to the Côte d'Azur. 'All some of them come for is the sun. There's an old English boy been here over twenty years who still knows hardly any French. He just shouts at everyone and expects them to understand. Then he complains they don't make any effort and asks where were they educated. This is for shopkeepers, eh? And workmen! And he can't understand why they don't sell English sausages or fruit cake.'

'He should have stayed at home!' laughed Darina.

Björn shrugged, 'He likes the sun, he hates what is happening to England, he could get a better deal on his property here. But he expects everything to be done his way.' He brought over a cup of black coffee. 'Now, you will excuse me for a moment?'

He disappeared into the small cloakroom he'd shown Darina when she arrived.

She sipped the excellent coffee and continued to study the figurines, admiring their energy and thinking about the Swede. Why wasn't he married? He was attractive, very attractive. He obviously liked women. Was he reluctant to make a commitment? But he was only a few years older than herself, mid-thirties, William's age. Plenty of time to find someone to spend the rest of his life with.

The telephone rang and after a moment's hesitation, Darina went over and answered it.

'Björn?' The female voice was agitated.

'He's popped out for a moment – do you want to wait or shall I take a message?' Darina offered.

'He said he'd be there!' complained the voice.

Björn emerged from the cloakroom. 'Here he is now.' Darina held out the receiver.

'Who is it?'

'I'm sorry, I don't know.'

'Hello? Ah, you got my message?' There was no change in Björn's voice but something about the way he turned slightly so that his back was towards Darina, suggested the conversation might be private. She wandered outside, arranging the wrap around her shoulders; the sun might be shining but the breeze was chilly.

Straggling through the stones of the studio terrace was a patchwork of plants, many of them herbs. Darina bent down and rubbed some thyme between her fingers and drank in the warm aroma. Björn's voice drifted into her ears like a tune absorbed without conscious effort. 'But it must be done . . . I'm waiting for you to play your part, you know our agreement and you know I need the money . . . Don't get upset!' Darina's attention was alerted as his voice rose sharply. 'Bernard's dead! Look,' there was a reining in of his tone, exasperation severely contained, 'look,' he continued more evenly, 'my part's done, now it's up to you.' There was a long pause then Darina heard, 'OK, then, I can wait for a few more days but that's all . . . so you'll ring me, eh?'

She walked without haste to the far end of the little terrace and stood looking at the view until Björn called her back into the studio.

'I'm sorry, a client,' he said as he arranged her again on the chair. 'Not everyone pays up when they should, I'm afraid.'

As Darina tried to compose her features again, she wondered why the voice of the caller had sounded familiar.

William arrived at the studio exactly at the time agreed. They had a short drink with Björn, discussing the morning's progress. William was offered a look at the head but he refused. 'No,' he said. 'I prefer to wait until it's finished.'

Then they were off.

'I thought we'd have lunch somewhere and then visit Jacques Duval's oil mill,' he said as they drove away.

'Sounds a great idea but why, particularly?'

'Several things. First, I'm interested to see if Bernard's operation could have been considered a threat. Second, I want to find out what sort of person Duval actually is. Finally, there's a definite possibility he knows whether anybody visited La Chenais that morning.'

'Surely the French police will have interviewed him? Won't Mike let you know what they found out?'

William was silent for a moment then said, 'I'm not

absolutely sure I trust Mike to give me all the details.'

'But he promised!'

'To get me off his back. Mike and I go back a long way. He's intelligent, great company and fiercely ambitious.'

'You mean, if it's a choice between keeping his promise to you and keeping in with the French police, you won't get much of a look in?'

'I hope I'm being unfair.'

'But couldn't you be helpful to him? If he's as ambitious as you say—'

'Oh, he'll make every bit of use of us, our information and contacts down here, that he can. I just think I'm going to have to work hard at getting much back from him in return.'

'You mean we're really going to try and solve the case?'

He looked surprised. 'Don't you want to? I know it's not much of a honeymoon activity but I thought you were interested. After all, you're pretty much a detective yourself now.'

Darina leaned over and gave his cheek a quick kiss. 'That's the nicest thing you've ever said to me.'

He shot her an amused glance. 'The nicest?'

'Well, one of the nicest.'

They found a small, modest restaurant for lunch and had the *menu touristique*, a three-course affair of deeply flavoured ratatouille, a succulent pork chop with sautéd potatoes and cheese or fruit tart. All for 55 francs.

'Why can't we give this sort of value in England?' asked William, finishing his glazed apple tart with a sigh of pleasure.

'Don't get me off on that subject! Tell me, what have you been up to this morning?'

William looked smug. 'Checking driving times.'

'To Bernard and Helen's?'

'Right, you clever little thing!'

'Flattery will not get you a cooked supper, not after this meal,' Darina said severely. 'What have you found?'

'It all depends on the traffic. I drove to Roland's and started from there. It took me just under half an hour but the road was almost clear. I checked Anthea's address last night and she's not far off the same road. I came back that way and found her house. It would take her about the same time to get to La Chenais. I didn't have time to check out the Cap but anyone driving from there would have the same options we do, the faster but longer road via Grasse or the more direct and slower road through Valbonne and Opio. Either way, I reckon it would take something like fifty minutes.'

'And from Björn's?'

'About twenty minutes.'

'So, John Rickwood would have required about two hours to get there, kill Bernard and return again, the others rather less.'

William nodded.

'Roland, according to what he said yesterday, could definitely be in the frame.'

'Right.'

'And we don't know whether any of the others has an alibi?'

'Not yet.'

Darina suddenly remembered the telephone call Björn had received that morning. She told William about it. 'There's nothing I can put my finger on, it was all too cryptic, only hearing one side of the conversation. But it definitely didn't sound as though it was a client.'

'You're sure? After all, he must be trying to get in every penny he can to meet his Lloyd's obligations.'

'Quite sure, you use a very different tone when you're

157

asking someone to pay you money they owe. Björn sounded as though he was talking to a partner in some enterprise.'

'And he said, "Bernard's dead and now it's up to you"?'

'Well, it wasn't exactly that.' Darina thought back carefully. 'It was, "Bernard's dead", as though if he was alive it could be a problem. Then he added, "My part's done, now it's up to you".' Darina fiddled with a piece of bread. 'When you arrived, Björn left me to put on my shirt and jacket while he opened the door. Before I came through, I tried to look in the cupboards. You remember that long run down the back of the studio?'

'And?'

She shook her head. 'They were all locked.'

'What did you expect to find?'

'I don't know,' she confessed. 'I was just puzzled what he could be keeping in them. They're so many and he's so organized. It's probably nothing, neat piles of the sculptor's trade paper or something like that. But why keep them locked?'

'Because they contain something valuable?'

'More valuable than those bronzes sitting on the open shelves? And the original clay heads? No, I think it's something that's got to be hidden.'

'His early works that he can't bear to throw away but can't bear anyone to see either? No, perhaps not. All right, what's your idea? I can see there is one.'

She looked across at him. His eyes were alive with interest. 'Suppose it was Helen on the phone? You said yourself there was something wrong between her and Bernard. Well, knowing Helen, it's more than likely to be another man. Suppose she's been sitting for Björn on the quiet?'

'But sculpting is his business! If anyone saw a head of

158

Helen in his studio, they'd just think Bernard had commissioned it.'

'But suppose it wasn't a head?'

'What do you mean?'

'There are some lovely female nudes among those figurines.'

'If I produced a theory like that, you'd tell me I was incurably cynical. And I thought you were convinced that Helen couldn't have killed him?'

'I am,' protested Darina. 'But that doesn't stop me recognizing her weaknesses and I'm quite willing to believe she could have been two-timing him.'

'Wouldn't you have recognized her voice?'

'I'm not sure,' Darina said slowly. 'The voice on the phone was agitated and it only spoke a few words. But it was familiar, I'm sure of that.'

'So what do you think they were talking about?'

Darina leaned forward. 'What if Björn killed Bernard so he and Helen could sell the house and the mill? Perhaps he wants her to get a move on because he needs the money to pay his Lloyd's losses?'

'Surely he'd realize she couldn't do that in a hurry, especially not at the moment?'

'But if he's desperate?'

William called for the bill. 'It's an interesting theory. And I suppose it could provide a more compelling motive for murder than revenge for losing large sums of money.' He glanced at the account, drew out his wallet and put some notes on the table. 'Come on, let's go and find Frère Jacques's olive mill.'

As she followed him out of the little restaurant, Darina thought William might *say* her theory was interesting but she knew that it didn't appeal to him as particularly likely.

Chapter Fourteen

To find Helen and La Chenais, Darina and William had been told to follow the signs from the main road for *'Moulin à huile'*.

As they once again bumped up the rough path to the two farms at the top, Darina wondered why, when she'd given them the directions, Helen hadn't mentioned that she was also producing olive oil. Had she wanted to leave Bernard the glory of breaking the news? Or had she wanted to block it out?

The Duval mill was just before Helen's property. Darina and William drove through a narrow gate into a small forecourt surrounded by a collection of rough-stone buildings. The property was unkempt. Walls lacked mortar, shutters looked in imminent danger of falling apart, roofs sagged and tiles were missing; rubbish and clutter were everywhere.

Several aged cars and vans were badly parked but William edged the Renault neatly in beside an open shed holding a pile of dry, fibrous material resembling coarse sawdust.

'At least he looks busy,' William commented as they got out and surveyed the scene.

They faced a large old building fronted by a high concrete

platform. On it stood an elevator taking up a consignment of olives. Dark purple, conker brown, coal black, with the odd blond and tan amongst them, the olives rattled happily up, supported by wooden slats attached at regular intervals to the webbing. From the top of the elevator a fan blew leaves and stalks back along a mesh sleeve to die in a sack behind the elevator. So far the mill wasn't too different from Bernard's.

People wandered around, hauling sacks, handling containers and chattering amongst themselves. A middle-aged Frenchman in blue overalls was weighing a consignment of olives; after marking up a label he placed the sack next to the elevator. By the scales stood a roughly written sign: *Les olives sourriés et noisiés sont refusées.*

'They don't seem to worry too much about the condition of anything else,' William commented as they went into the main building.

Inside, the contrast with Bernard's mill was dramatic. Little seemed to have been done to this interior for many years and the machinery looked basic and worn.

'Smell the oil!' Darina sniffed ecstatically at the rich, emollient aroma. Just inside the entrance sat an old farmer on a stool, his gaze fixed on the flow of oil that was slowly emerging from a filtering machine and decanting into a plastic container. He could have been watching liquid gold pour from a crucible. By his side was a similar container that looked as though it had already been filled.

Darina moved towards the part of the mill where the olives that had come up the elevator and been washed were now collecting in a hod. As she watched, a hefty young man threw a switch and the olives were sucked from the hod up into the base of a large mill. Another throw of a switch and two enormous round stones began to circle the pan, crushing the olives into a dark paste. A label was removed from the hod and hung on the mill.

Round and round went the stones in mesmerizing circles. Just so had the Romans crushed olives. Darina looked at the electric switch. That must have been the first revolution, electricity replacing animal power. Now other changes were following. Classical methods two thousand years old were suddenly being overthrown by technological miracles.

'Isn't it weird?'

Darina turned. Standing beside her was Terri, her gaze riveted on the revolving stones.

'I mean, a bottle of oil from all that gook?' Her expression was compounded of disbelief and awe.

'Are you interested in olive oil?'

'Bernard and Helen talk, I mean, talked, about it as though it was something religious. I mean, it's oil, right?'

'It is used in religious rites.'

Terri tore her gaze away from the paste, now an almost homogeneous brownish-mauve mass flecked with darker specks, and looked at Darina. Her previous aggression had given way to what seemed a genuine puzzlement. 'I mean, what's with this food thing? Ma's always on about what you should eat – junk food means a junk mind, all that sort of crap. And Jules is this vegetarian nut, won't eat anything animal, says it's all wrong. The body isn't some sort of shrine. I mean, if you're hungry, you're hungry, right?'

Today Terri was dressed in leggings speckled with tiny flowers. Over them she wore some sort of linen shift and over that a rose-patterned shirt left hanging open and billowing about her generous body. The lank hair had been washed and its newly clean silk was caught on the top of her head with a pink ribbon tied in a large bow. The pink matched the pink of the roses on her shirt. Apart from a ludicrously formal pair of black button boots, Darina considered it was the most attractive outfit she had yet seen Terri wearing.

'Did Bernard explain the olive oil process to you?'

'He showed us what he called his mill.' Terri glanced around at the age-darkened walls of the old building, its recesses stacked with the accumulation of centuries of oil production. 'Bit different from this!'

'Is that why you came? To see an old-fashioned mill in action?'

Terri shrugged her shoulders, the heavy breasts moving the large roses on her shirt as though a soft wind blew through a bush in full bloom. 'Stephen's terrified his mother's going to be arrested. He shouts at everybody, her, the lawyer, the police, me.' Her mouth quivered suddenly. 'I can't open my mouth without him jumping down it. Anybody would think I'd killed sodding Bernard.' Her lower lip stuck out in a sulky pout. But behind the childish resentment was real distress.

'It must be pretty dreadful for you all. How's Helen today? We thought we'd pop in after our visit here.'

Terri shuddered artistically. 'I wouldn't go near there! Helen isn't speaking. She just sits in a corner holding Steve's hand.'

Terri and Darina had to move slightly as the olive paste had its consistency assessed, then was transferred into an oblong hod, the label travelling down the production line with its olives.

'This mayn't be state of the art like Bernard's set-up but it's much more interesting,' said Darina as the young mechanic brought over the pad and spindle portion of a hydraulic press.

'I suppose this machine was state-of-the-art once,' said Terri. 'I mean, I don't suppose they used anything like this a hundred years ago, did they?'

Bravo, Terri, thought Darina. There was a mind in full working order inside the bolshie teenager outlook and extraordinary clothes.

164

They watched while olive paste was dispensed from the hod on to the woven plastic pads. 'Before electricity, the presses operated on a screw principle,' said Darina.

But Terri wasn't listening. Her attention had been caught by a small group of people clustered around a Frenchman dressed in worn working blues. His face was wrinkled and brown, like a well-oiled walnut, his eyes dark as the darkest olive. With economical gestures, he was indicating various of the machines and seemed to be giving an exposition of the olive-oil-making process. Every now and then he paused to receive and answer questions. At the back of the group was William.

The Frenchman, Darina realized, must be Jacques Duval. Followed by Terri, she drifted over to where William was standing and slipped her arm through his. He gave her hand a quick squeeze.

'Hi!' he said to Terri, who flashed him back a smile of gratifying strength.

The group began to break up and Duval turned away. William hurriedly detached himself from Darina and walked after him.

A few minutes later he was back with the farmer. 'I've explained to Monsieur that my wife is an avid foodie who would love to be shown his olive trees,' William said to Darina. 'And he has graciously agreed.'

'*Monsieur, vous êtes très gentil,*' Darina told the farmer. '*Ce sera un grand plaisir pour moi . . .*' Her command of French ground to a halt and she smiled at him with what she hoped was persuasive force.

Close to, Monsieur Duval didn't seem as old; his compact, muscled body belonged to a man in his fifties and the eyes were uncommonly shrewd. He looked up at Darina with a certain admiration.

'*Eh, bien,*' his gravelly voice said. '*Venez, venez!*' With

165

quick, short steps, somewhere between a shuffle and a walk, he led the way, William and Darina following and Terri tagging on behind. Round the back of the building they went, out into a grove of olive trees.

It was almost identical to Helen's. The leaves shivered in the slight wind, their silvery undersides offering grace notes to the duller dusty green, the gnarled trunks twisting and turning up into the quicksilver activity of the leaves. Yet Darina thought she saw a difference; maybe it was her imagination but the trees seemed sleeker than those of La Chenais, better tended perhaps? Were the trees more important to Duval than his buildings? There were nets slung between the trunks, like frail hammocks. The ground underneath the trees was covered with plastic sheeting. Several women were picking olives, flicking them with astonishing swiftness into the nets. On the ground were shallow wooden trays that other women were filling with fallen fruit; it looked backbreaking work.

Jacques Duval stopped beside a tree thicker and larger than the others. His hand stretched out to touch the trunk, lightly stroking the rough surface of the bark. He spoke in short sentences. Darina strained to understand the strongly accented French but quickly gave up and waited for William to translate.

'Monsieur says his family has farmed these olives for centuries. His mill produces oil for their own use and to sell. In addition, the mill processes the olives of others in the area.'

Darina looked across the olive grove to the line of poplars that divided the Duval property from Helen's and remembered the old stones in their rusty harness. 'Darling, ask Monsieur Duval why there are two mills next door to each other.'

As William translated, the Frenchman's wrinkled face

tightened and his eyes flashed as he looked across to the other property. '*Eeough!*' he exclaimed. Then the gravelly voice produced another clump of short phrases. Between each came a little pause as though the speaker needed to assemble the next piece of information before it was uttered. Eventually a pause lengthened into a stop that allowed William to translate.

'Monsieur Duval says once his family owned all the olive trees around here but when his grandfather died, French inheritance law meant the farm had to be split between his father and his uncle. They both wanted the mill and there was a bitter fight. Finally the uncle took the larger part of the olive trees and left Monsieur's father with the mill. He then set up another mill in competition but it didn't do well, the customers preferred to come to the old mill and in the early fifties the price of olive oil dropped while the cost of everything else rose. Then came the great frost of 1956 which destroyed production for several years and that was too much for the uncle. He had to sell the farm. Monsieur's father couldn't afford to buy the property and wept to see it pass out of the family. Much as he disliked his brother, he preferred to see him owning the olive trees rather than strangers. After the trees began producing fruit again, the new owners tried to carry on the mill but they weren't successful either.' William smiled gently as he said, 'Monsieur says they lacked the skill to make good oil.'

Darina wondered, this man sounded as though he had a deep relationship with his trees and oil. Could he possibly have been behaving in the way Bernard had suggested?

'*Et maintenant, Monsieur,*' Darina addressed the farmer. He turned towards her, her height dwarfing his short figure. '*Maintenant, la fermière, Mme Mansard, est-ce-que son huile est bon?*'

'You should hear Helen on about it,' broke in Terri in

167

disgust. 'Sheer boresville! Queen of the oil, no less.' She thrust her hands into her pockets, humped her shoulders and looked down the valley as though searching for something more interesting to devote her time to.

The miller's face darkened, his eyes narrowed. '*Ce n'est pas Madame, c'est le monsieur!*' He spat on the ground, a scornful, dismissive gesture. '*Cochon . . .*'

Darina didn't understand the rest of what the Frenchman said but gathered that, in his eyes, Bernard had not rated at all highly.

At last William was allowed to translate. 'Monsieur says the La Chenais oil is *pas mal*, which actually means it's quite good, but he considers Bernard's equipment is not the way to produce olive oil – it's too modern, too technical.'

Jacques Duval stood with his head cocked on one side, his bright eyes fixed on Darina's face as she listened. As soon as William stopped, the Frenchman once again said, '*Venez, venez,*' and set off with great rapidity towards the house behind the mill.

Once again they all followed.

Monsieur Duval's home was larger than Helen's farmhouse and had an impressive-looking tower at one end. The interior, however, left much to be desired. The room into which they were led was large but it was dark, with smoke-stained walls and ceiling. There was a huge open fireplace at one end, and by the sparse light from two small windows could be seen a long table, a fine old dresser, several battered cupboards and some uncomfortable-looking chairs. It all looked as though it had been there for many years and received rough treatment.

'*Asseyez-vous,*' the farmer ordered, jabbing a dark-stained finger towards the table. He disappeared out of another door but by the time the three of them had sat themselves on the benches running down either side of the table, he was back again carrying a *baguette* and a flask of oil. He put both on the table, drew a knife out of a back pocket and sawed off slices from the bread. He poured some of the oil on to three of the slices and then gave one to each of them.

'*Mangez, mangez,*' he commanded and stood watching intently as Darina and William ate the oil-soaked bread. '*Bien, eh? Bien?*'

Terri looked at the bread as though she'd been asked to eat turds.

'Try it,' Darina said. 'It's really good.' She finished her bread. '*C'est très bien, Monsieur.*' She cast about for something else to say, '*Elle est fraîche, un petit peu comme un citron?*'

His face broke into a satisfied smile. '*Vous avez raison, Madame. Encore?*' He held up the flask and the smile broke into a wide grin as Darina nodded enthusiastically.

Terri stuffed the anointed bread into her mouth, briefly chewed then swallowed it. An expression of pleased astonishment dawned on her face. 'Hey, not bad!' She held out her hand for another piece.

Jacques Duval was once again talking in stiff phrases, spitting them out like stones from an olive. William listened then translated, the Frenchman watching Darina's face.

'Helen gave him one of the first bottles of La Chenais oil. He says it is better than the oil the previous owner made but not as good as his and asks if you don't agree?' Without changing the tone of his voice William added, 'It would help matters if you can say that his is much better.'

Darina looked at the small, wizened man. '*Votre huile est meilleur, Monsieur, sans doute.*' The strict truth would have been to say that she couldn't detect much difference between the two oils as far as taste was concerned and that, judging by the flask sitting on the table, Bernard's oil was clearer than his but she hoped she would be forgiven the small inexactitude.

Jacques Duval gave a small decisive nod as much as to say he didn't expect any other verdict. Terri helped herself to another hunk of bread, doused it with oil, then rose from the table and started to wander round the room, pausing to look out of the window and then to examine the clutter on the dresser as though the constant stream of French was too incomprehensible for her and she couldn't be bothered with William's translations.

Darina remained at the table and accepted another piece of bread. William declined politely and said, '*C'est une tragédie, n'est-ce-pas, la mort de Monsieur Barrington Smythe*?'

He had opened floodgates.

Darina gathered from William's translation after the miller had finished his tirade that Jacques Duval wasn't prepared to commit himself as to whether Bernard's death had been a tragedy or not. There was no doubt that Monsieur had proved a neighbour of some unpleasantness and it was also certain that he himself had been greatly inconvenienced by all the police vehicles that had arrived at La Chenais. Customers hadn't been able to get to his mill either that afternoon or the next morning. It had all been a very great nuisance and he had certainly lost a lot of business.

No doubt, William had then suggested, there had been little traffic earlier on the day of Monsieur Barrington Smythe's death? But, then, perhaps Monsieur Duval had been too busy to notice how many cars had passed his mill?

Oof, as to that, well, he had begun his pruning of the trees; a large job Monsieur must understand, best started as soon as the olives had been picked. That big tree in front of the house, that was always the first to bear fruit, the first

170

to be picked bare and the first to be pruned. Well, up here, one could hardly help noticing cars coming up the lane, *hein*?

So, had there been many cars?

Darina, managing to understand the gist of William's query, held her breath.

Duval looked cunning. Monsieur must surely be a policeman to ask such a question and he had already given the French police such information as he had on the traffic to La Chenais that day.

William complimented Monsieur on his discernment. Yes, he was a member of the English police; Monsieur Barrington Smythe had been an Englishman, Monsieur Duval understood? Here was his, the Inspector Pigram's authority, perhaps Monsieur would like to inspect it? It would be a very great kindness if Monsieur Duval could repeat to him the details he had told the French police. He had to tell Monsieur, though, that there was nothing official about this approach. With an incredibly shifty look, William managed to convey that his request was, in fact, the very reverse of official and he brought out a 500-franc note, pushing it slightly towards the miller as he passed over the card.

Darina watched while the warrant card was carefully inspected, the likeness of the photograph assessed, then handed back. The note was equally carefully inspected. Duval looked across at William, who calmly returned the look and said nothing. The note was slowly folded and put in an inside pocket of the blue jacket.

Eh, bien, well then, here is what he had seen that morning. It had been one of great activity, of a surety. Monsieur Barrington Smythe had left the farm about ten-fifteen, in the little Deux Chevaux, then Madame had gone, in the big German car. About eleven Monsieur had returned. He had not appeared happy, *hein*? He had slammed the door of the car even harder than usual, Jacques Duval banged the table with the flat of his hand, making Darina jump.

Duval continued with his story. Shortly after Monsieur returned, he had had to come down from the tree and check a delivery. But after he'd climbed back up, a car had come up the lane and gone to La Chenais.

What kind of car?

Jaques Duval shrugged his bony shoulders. It was a large car, he said, a large black car. It had not stayed long. Some time afterwards another car came up the hill. This one was a Swedish car – he knows because his son has a friend with one. Some little time later it left again. Then it was time for the *déjeuner*.

William's attitude suddenly changed. All trace of shiftiness vanished and his voice became that of a righteous official.

Duval shifted his position on the bench uneasily then cried, '*Non, Monsieur, non, je vous assure.*'

It did no good. William continued implacably, then leant across the table, grabbed the other man by his blue jacket, reached inside and pulled out the 500–franc note. He waved it in front of the man's face, still talking rapid French.

Jacques Duval became more and more nervous and looked more and more stubborn. Finally William stopped talking and gazed at him with eyes as stern as a judge's.

The miller dropped his gaze. '*Mais, Monsieur, c'est vrai, c'est vrai.*'

Once again William launched into French and Darina wished with all her soul she could understand what was being said. At one point he indicated towards her then continued his harangue.

Finally Duval bowed his head and the obstinacy drained

out of him but when he spoke the phrases were jerky and reluctant.

After he finished, William appeared to query some of the information. Eventually he seemed satisfied and stood up. 'Come on,' he said to Darina. 'We've finished here.'

Darina rose and called to Terri that they were leaving. Then, in her halting French, she thanked Jacques Duval for his hospitality and for showing them the olives.

Darina and William left the big room with Terri trailing behind and William led the way, not to where their car was sitting but to the entrance of the mill where a large olive tree stood. There he stopped. Terri continued out on to the lane. 'Better return to the morgue,' she said. 'See if I can pry Steve away from his mother.' She gave them a casual wave.

Darina watched her short, thick figure stomp its way to La Chenais. From where they stood you couldn't see if cars stood outside the front door or in the garage.

'Stephen's car is Swedish,' she said thoughtfully to William. 'He drives a Volvo.'

'So he does.' William turned back to where they'd parked their car. 'OK, I've seen what I wanted to here, there's no doubt Duval had an excellent view of passing traffic. And the old fox was holding something back. Apparently, just before he came down from his tree for his *déjeuner*, he saw a white sports car go up the lane. Shortly afterwards, he climbed down and started to tidy up. As he was stacking prunings by his gate, the white car drove out of La Chenais, very fast, then stopped just past the mill, reversed back, and the driver got out and bribed Duval to forget he had seen his car. He gave him some story that his wife might be causing trouble. Duval says he understood such things and told him that of course he had never seen the sports car or its driver.'

'How long had it been at the mill?'

'He was very vague about the time. All he could say was, not long.'

'And he doesn't know who the driver was?'

William shook his head.

'How do you know he hasn't told you everything?'

'An honest man wouldn't have taken the money I put on the table. I was sure then that there'd be something suspect about his evidence.'

Darina was impressed. 'How did you persuade him to tell you about the other car?'

'Accused him of taking bribes, said that you and Terri were witnesses to the five hundred francs and unless he came clean I would tell the French police. Finally he folded and gave me the rest of his information.'

'Can you be sure that was all?'

'I think so.'

'And the French police know about the first two cars?'

William nodded.

'But not the white sports car?'

'Not unless they've found out from some other source.'

'What are you going to do now?'

'We're going to visit Helen and see if she can identify any of the cars.'

'She won't say anything that might incriminate Stephen.'

'It's that sports car I'm most interested in.'

Darina felt excitement shiver through her body. 'You think its driver was the murderer?'

'Let's say there are some very pertinent questions he needs to answer.'

Darina slipped her arm through his and gave it a squeeze. 'I think you're marvellous.'

William unlocked the car and helped her in.

'Do you really think Helen will know who it was?'

'I think she knows a great deal more than she has so far

told anyone. Let's see if we can get under her guard.'

'My, but you're in masterful mood today, my lover!'

He gave her a sideways glance. 'Are you suggesting I'm hustling?'

'Far from it. Men who know what they're about always turn me on.'

'Stop that or I'll take you straight back and we'll forget all about solving murders.'

'Then your friend Mike will win all the points and I won't be able to help Helen.' She gave him a wicked look. 'We said we wanted a honeymoon with a difference.'

William looked into her laughing eyes, planted a very quick kiss on the tip of her nose and started the engine. 'Right, then, let's see what we can get out of your little friend.'

Chapter Fifteen

The big wooden door of La Chenais swung open as Darina wielded the heavy knocker.

From inside came the sound of Terri's voice arguing with Stephen. Nobody came to the door. Darina and William stepped through the entrance into the open-plan living room.

Helen was once again sitting huddled on the sofa and crying.

Stephen was pacing up and down the room, his hands jammed into his pockets.

Terri was sitting on the other sofa, a long *baguette* in front of her. She sawed off a thick slice. 'Your mum's a lost cause, Steve. I tell you, she'll be at it again in a wink.' She dug a knife into a small pot on the table and spread a dark paste over the piece of bread she'd just cut.

'You know nothing about my mother,' Stephen said furiously.

'Dad says – not my real dad, Nick, my stepdad – well, he says people are either monogamous or polygamous.'

'Big words for a little girl,' Stephen sneered, flinging himself on to the sofa beside his mother.

Terri calmly bit into the piece of bread she'd prepared. 'Be like that, Steve, it doesn't bother me. You're not the only person with education.'

'You – educated!'

'Three A levels *and* one was in English.' She finished the piece of bread and started preparing another for herself. Darina made to move into the room but William put a hand on her arm to hold her where she was. Terri looked up, must have seen them but made no comment. Stephen and Helen were facing the other way and were far too intent on themselves to have noticed Darina and William enter. 'Anyway, my stepdad's monogamous and so's Mum. My real dad's monogamous too. Nobody exists for him but Jules. Mum says he was like that with her, too, in the beginning.' Terri paused and eyed the fresh slice of bread, hesitated for a moment then loaded her knife with more spread. 'But your mum's polygamous. She's just got to have men. Like a rabbit. At her age, it's disgusting.'

Helen moaned a protest and clutched at Stephen's hand. 'It's not like that, don't listen to her, darling.'

He held her comfortingly. 'I know, Mum. She doesn't know what she's talking about.'

'Oh, no?' Terri spoke with her mouth full of French bread. 'Weren't you telling me all about the dreadful boyfriends your mum had? How you had to keep rescuing her?'

'Stephen!' Helen protested.

Terri looked consideringly at the last piece of bread in her fingers before popping it into her mouth. 'You know, Helen, I thought this stuff was too odd but it definitely grows on you. It looks like Marmite but tastes quite different. Olives, you said?'

'Tapenade,' said Helen automatically. 'Puréed black olives with garlic, anchovies and olive oil.'

'Well, it's OK stuff. Like that olive oil we had next door. I mean, whoever heard of eating bread spread with oil but

178

it was the gear. Hi, you two, come and have some of this.'
Terri waved her knife at Darina and William.

They came forward and Darina bent and kissed Helen.
'How are you?' she asked. She could have answered her
own question with 'Bloody awful.' Helen's skin sagged and
had gone the shade and texture of overworked pastry. Dark
circles under her eyes ate into her cheekbones and her
mouth was tight and thin. Her appearance hadn't been
helped by make-up, not at all like Helen.

'What have you come here for?'

'Stephen!' Helen roused herself to protest. 'Darina's
my friend.'

'Friends say they've arrived, not skulk at the back of the
room picking up fag-ends.' He hadn't bothered to rise.

'Got something to hide, have you?' Terri put in, stuffing
yet another piece of bread into her mouth. She held out a
slice to Darina. 'Try this, it's great.'

'Thanks, but I know how good it is.'

Terri shrugged. 'Suit yourself,' she said, and started on
that piece as well.

William sat himself down on the sofa beside her and
looked across at Helen. 'We can't help if you don't tell us
the truth,' he said.

Helen moaned slightly and clutched again at Stephen.

'Don't worry, Mum. I won't let them bully you.'

Darina perched on the table in front of Helen and looked
her in the eye. 'You went into Nice to meet someone, didn't
you? Someone you were having an affair with.'

Helen closed her eyes.

'The police must know that. You can't have spent the
time shopping, not for clothes, not over the luncheon
period.'

Another little moan.

'It can't matter to Bernard now if you tell us,' William

179

said. chewing absent-mindedly on a tapenade-loaded piece of bread Terri had slipped into his hand.

Stephen looked at Helen, his eyes worried and very kind. 'Don't you see, Mum, whoever you met could give you an alibi.'

Another little moan.

'Helen, darling,' said Darina gently, 'you can't worry about his position or what'll happen if others know, not now.'

Helen opened her eyes and looked at Darina. 'It's not that,' she gulped. 'He . . . he was late.'

'You mean . . .' Darina glanced at her husband.

'You think *he* could have murdered Bernard?' he asked bluntly.

'No!' Helen wailed. 'He couldn't, I'm sure! But what if the police think he could? They already suspect me, I know that. I couldn't bear it if they started to put him through it as well. I couldn't!' She burst out in a paroxysm of noisy weeping and buried her head in Stephen's shoulder. He patted it awkwardly, his eyes exasperated.

Terri halted her systematic eating. 'Would he own a white sports car, this lover of yours?' she enquired baldly.

Helen lifted a bleary face in astonishment. 'How did you know?'

'I wouldn't be too sure he didn't murder Bernard. He came up to the mill just about noon the day Bernard was killed.'

'You should have told me you spoke French,' William said.

Terri gave him a contemptuous look. 'Just because I'm fat people assume I'm ignorant.' She hacked yet another piece of bread off the nearly exhausted loaf, added more tapenade, offered it to Darina, who again refused, then began eating it with great delicacy.

180

Helen sat staring at her.

'Look, Helen,' Darina said, 'you can't protect this man, whoever he is. Jacques Duval saw the car come to the mill just before lunchtime. The police will soon find out who owns it – there can't be many cars like that around here. It's much better if he goes to them first.'

Helen shuddered but she had stopped crying. Her blue eyes, bleary and inflamed with weeping, looked at Darina.

'Of course,' said Terri, leaning back against the sofa, her arms crossed over her jutting breasts, 'her lover could be a woman – how would that fit into the equation?' She glanced at each of them with an air of innocent enquiry.

Stephen leapt up. 'You interfering little . . .' he failed to find the right word. 'What do *you* know about anything?'

Darina clutched more tightly at Helen's hands. 'Come on,' she urged. 'Don't you see you've got to tell us?'

'Mummy's boy doesn't like that idea, then?' suggested Terri softly, her eyes looking squarely at Stephen.

'You're sick,' he said disgustedly. He fell back on to the sofa and put his arm round his mother. 'Anyway, I know it's not a woman. I saw them together.'

There was a frightened moan from Helen.

'So, who is it?' asked William matter-of-factly.

Helen dug a frantic hand into Stephen's free arm. 'Don't, darling! Don't tell him!'

He hugged her closer to him and looked across at William. 'I don't know who he is. I saw them together at Saint-Cézaire, a little place in the hills to the west of Grasse. I was checking it out as a possible location, we want somewhere off the main track with a good view and I'd been told it had a marvellous little terrace looking clear across to Draguignon, plus a good restaurant or two.'

'Thanks for taking me,' said Terri.

'I did ask you to come, but you said you wanted a day

off. Grab some thoughts, you said. Don't say I didn't offer.'

'OK, OK, so I didn't want to spend every minute with you. But I wouldn't have minded the view.'

'Where did you see Helen?' asked Darina.

'On a little public terrace overlooking a precipice. As soon as I saw it, I knew it would be perfect for us – lovely old houses, tall, geranium-decorated, been there since way before the revolution, old stone street, marvellous old wall and this just fantastic view! You'd think the twentieth century had never happened! Mountains and trees, the river far below and all that sky . . .' Stephen paused a moment, then went on hurriedly. 'Anyway, I was taking photographs for reference, and had sort of hidden myself between two houses for a particular angle, when Mum comes along with a man.' He looked apologetically at her. 'I didn't mean to spy on you, in fact I was just about to say hello when you went into a clinch. It was as though you didn't see the view at all,' he added with a note of disgust. 'Just like you to ignore something like that for something you could get anywhere.'

He looked back at William. 'They were only there for a few minutes. I thought about following them but there didn't seem an awful lot of point.'

'So you have no idea who the man was?'

'No, but Bernard knew him.'

'Bernard?' Helen cried. 'You told Bernard about him?'

'What a cad,' said Terri.

Stephen flushed an unpleasant brick red. 'I told you I'd dealt with Bernard. He wasn't going to hang around if he knew Mum had gone off him. All I had to do was tell him what I'd seen.'

Terri looked at him with a curious little smile flickering around her mouth. 'Which you did the day he was killed.' It was a statement of fact.

He nodded.

'Oh, Stephen, how could you?'

'Mum, to get rid of that creep I'd have done anything. He was no good for you and you'd realized it – that was why you were having it off with this other fellow.'

'Stephen, you could have ruined everything!' Helen wailed, moving away from her son. 'What did Bernard say?'

Her son shuffled his feet. 'He was madder than a mutt with fleas. He was already in a foul mood before I told him anything. In fact, he'd said I'd been hanging around making a nuisance of myself for long enough.' Stephen's smooth face acquired a look of deep resentment. 'I told him that was between you and me and then he said it was nothing of the sort, that the farm and everything in it belonged to him and he was going to see he was master in his own house.' Darina and William exchanged a glance. 'So that's when I told him.' A satisfied smile curled itself round Stephen's pliant mouth. 'He was furious, said he was going to sort the son of a bitch out and that you were going to find out what was what.' He looked up. 'Actually, I got a bit worried then, I never knew Bernard could get so angry.'

'Oh, God!' cried Helen.

'You say he recognized the man from your description?' asked William.

Stephen nodded.

'I think you'd better give us that description.'

Helen rose from the sofa and stood in front of her son. Drawing her small body up, she managed to generate an impression of power. 'If you dare to say one word more, Stephen, I'm never going to speak to you again.'

'Mum! I only wanted to help you. You could never have been happy with that pseud. You know it!'

'That's enough, Stephen, you don't know what you're talking about.'

'That's telling him,' said Terri, *sotto voce*, sitting on the sofa watching the exchanges like an umpire on the sidelines.

'And you keep out of this!' Stephen turned on her in fury.

She flung up her hands. '*Pax, pax!*'

'Stephen, you said you'd take me to Nice, to see that lawyer.' Helen picked up her handbag from the counter that divided the kitchen area from the living room. Fishing out a lipstick and mirrored compact, she attempted to repair some of the damage to her face.

Stephen looked miserably from his mother towards William. 'Right,' he said at last. He felt in his pocket and brought out a set of car keys.

Helen replaced her make-up and snapped the bag shut. Without a farewell she led the way out of the room.

Darina watched helplessly as the door closed behind them. There was no gainsaying Helen in that mood.

'We'll be off, too.' William stood up. He looked down at Terri. 'It's been interesting meeting you.'

She looked back at him, a wealth of understanding in the small hazel eyes that could have belonged to some animal wise in field lore. 'Any time,' Terri said amiably. She sat and watched them leave.

'Do you think it was Björn that Stephen saw and described to Bernard?' asked William as he turned the car round.

'At the very least, he has to be a possibility.'

'Jackpot question. Whoever it is, did he murder Bernard?'

'His was the last car Duval saw visit the mill.'

'But someone could have gone up there after Duval went in for his meal.'

'Isn't that the sort of thing you need forensic information for? Time of death, and all that?'

'Time of death is difficult to pinpoint exactly. You won't

find any pathologist willing to risk giving more than an approximate assessment. Too many variables. There will be at least an hour, maybe more, in which it could have occurred.'

They drove for a while in silence.

'Strange all those visitors that morning,' Darina eventually said.

William gave a little shrug to his shoulders. 'That's the way it goes sometimes. Don't see anyone for days then the world descends on you.'

'Were they all surprise visits, do you think?'

'Who knows?'

By the time they got back to the apartment, it was late afternoon.

'If he's not too involved with the French police, I thought we might ask Mike round tonight,' William said as they entered.

While he telephoned, Darina went into the kitchen to check what there was for a snack supper.

A few minutes later her husband joined her with an expression compounded of delight and apprehension. 'Mike and his side-kick are off to try and talk to Robert Bright. *Grâce à mon oncle*, he wants me to go with them. Thinks I can introduce the right city names to oil their path.'

'Ah,' said Darina.

'Do you mind very much?'

She laughed. 'Go and play with your chums. As long as you give me a blow-by-blow account when you get back.'

'I'll try and bring Mike and Chris with me, then you'll get the full story.'

'Are you going to tell them about what we learned this afternoon?'

'I think not. Not, that is, until we know rather more. I must go, darling, they'll be waiting for me.'

William gave her a quick hug and disappeared.

Darina surveyed the contents of the fridge. Another trip to the little shopping centre was called for.

Half an hour later, clutching several plastic bags and a loaf of French bread, Darina left the shops to return to the apartment. Then she stopped in the middle of the pavement.

Over the other side of the road was Maura. As Darina watched, she opened her handbag, took out a set of car keys and opened the door of a low, white Jaguar.

Chapter Sixteen

'Maura!' Darina called. She hefted up her shopping bags and dashed across the road.

Maura stood poised with the car door open looking harassed and wary.

'Did you try our bell? I'm sorry we were out, come up and have a drink.'

'Darling, what a lovely idea! Normally I'd say yes but today I'm in a bit of a rush.'

'Not that much of a rush, surely? Come on, it'd be so nice to have a real old gossip. William's gone to meet a chum and I'm all on my own.'

'On honeymoon!' Maura's manner warmed. 'Aren't men awful?' She glanced at her wristwatch. 'OK. What's half an hour here or there? Roland can wait for his supper.' She slammed the car door shut and locked it. 'Give me some of those bags. What have you been doing, buying up Antibes?'

'Just one or two things for supper. William could be bringing a couple of friends back.'

'Get him to take you out, that's the least he can do.'

'I don't mind cooking, really I don't. That's the most super car. Is it yours? I'd kill for a car like that.' Darina hoped Maura didn't think the remark sounded as odd as it did to herself.

'Know what you mean – driving it makes me feel really sexy. It's the biggest turn on since Harold Robbins.' She gave a small, guttural laugh and slipped the hand that wasn't holding a plastic bag through Darina's arm. 'I'm really glad you saw me, it's a long time since I've been able to have a proper chat. You can't really talk with men, can you? They never want to hear what you feel about things – things other than themselves, I mean – and if I told Roland driving a car made me feel sexy, he'd either assume it was a hint that had to be taken up or go into a sulk at the suggestion anything other than him could turn me on.'

'Where is he?'

'God knows. Roland has perfected the art of disappearing without saying what he's doing. He dropped me off here and said he'd be back for a meal at eight. Not a word about where he was going.'

'Eight?' Darina let them into the apartment. 'Then we've got lots of time for a good gossip.'

Maura followed her into the kitchen and sighed. 'There was so much I was going to do, wash my hair, do my best to cook a decent meal, glam myself up. Living with Roland means never letting yourself go.'

Maura had let herself go that day, that was for sure. There was a run in her tights. The blood-red varnish on the finger-nails that were emptying out the contents of the plastic bag was chipped. Her make-up had been put on too hurriedly, there was more eyeshadow on one eye than the other and under the fleshy jaw-bone was a thick streak of foundation. She was right about her hair needing a wash, too.

Darina pushed the shopping to one side, opened the fridge and took out a bottle of wine. 'What would you like? I'm opening this, or there's gin, whisky, rum, you name it. We've been left plentifully supplied with booze.'

'Oh, a whisky, please. Never mind about the journey home, I need a pick-me-up.'

They settled down with their drinks.

'To hell with men.' Maura gave the toast.

'To hell with some men,' Darina said.

'I'll drink to that.' And she did, deeply. After she came up for air, Maura said, 'Whoever invented love has a lot to answer for.' She considered the remark for a moment then added, 'Sex keeps the human race going quite nicely. Why couldn't it have stopped at that?'

'Spill it out,' invited Darina. 'Tell me all.'

Maura held out her glass. 'Another one first, please.' She got it.

Taking a sip rather than a gulp from the newly charged glass she contemplated its depths. 'Roland', she said slowly and distinctly, 'is the rat they named that television rodent after.'

Darina looked sympathetic.

'Roland is the most selfish, the most creatively cruel man ever born. If there was a prize for the man women most love to hate, Roland would take it in spades.'

'And the fact you haven't walked out on him only means one thing?'

'Which only proves how stupid I am.' Maura slipped from aggression to dolefulness.

'Cheer up, things can't be as bad as all that.'

'Can't they? Even if they aren't, they will be. Probably sooner than I think.'

'Where did you two meet?'

'In Peter Jones, trying out mattresses. Don't laugh, it's true! After we'd finished bouncing about on the beds, he asked me to have lunch with him. And, well, he didn't get back to his office that afternoon.' She sighed heavily. 'In those days work could take second place to other activities.'

'How long ago was that?'

Another heavy sigh. 'Several aeons ... yesterday ... what does it matter? I've blown it, that's all.' Maura drank more of her whisky. 'What about you, how did you manage to land the wicked William?'

'I was lucky, he actually wanted to get married.'

'He wanted to get married, Jules's John wanted to get married, why can't Roland want to get married?'

'Does it really matter so much?' Darina asked gently.

'Does being solvent matter? Does a designer label matter? Does making the grade in anything matter?' Another huge sigh, another quick gulp of whisky. 'I wouldn't actually mind so much if only he wasn't so blatantly unfaithful. Does he think I don't notice someone else's scent clinging to his collar like scum round the edge of the bath? Lipstick on his boxer shorts? I know I don't do the laundry but I at least *sort* it. Does he think I'm the kind of slut who mixes fragiles in with the heavy stuff? Don't answer that.'

Darina hadn't been going to. 'Has Roland ever been married?'

'God, yes. Read the book, seen the film, worn the T-shirt. Somewhere stuck in a bloody great mansion in the Home Counties, happily enjoying her Valentino wardrobe, bridge lunches, charity suppers and mammoth alimony is ex-Mrs Tait. The one and only Mrs Tait, according to Roland. Says he's never going to get himself involved in that scene again. She took him up shit creek without a parachute. Sorry, that's more mixed than Roland's drinks. Anyway, she sounds to have been a bitch of the first water who took him for as much as she could get. No children, thank heavens. The step-parent bit would be enough to put even me off. Come to think of it, perhaps I'd have been more careful about what I was getting into if there had been. Roland would be a lousy father, though. No real interest in anyone but himself and out of sight is out of mind as far as he's concerned. You can't treat children like that, can you? They need to know you're there for them, even if you're not.'

Darina thought fleetingly of Terri.

'Roland is strictly for Roland.' Maura gazed moodily at her drink. 'The ironic thing is, when we started coming down here, I thought we were getting away from the artificial life. France is where real living is at, I thought. Back to basics – I suppose on any basis that's yesterday's message by now but at the time I thought that's what we were getting into. Goodbye to entertaining to impress, goodbye to the frenetic social whirl, hello simple living, hello being together, just us. God, what an idiot I was, the South of France mayn't match Paris but it gives the London scene a run for its money.'

Maura was gazing into an empty glass again.

Darina refilled it. 'When did the trouble start?'

'Start? Did it ever really stop?' Maura sipped away at the newly filled glass. 'No, I must be fair. It's only this last trip that things have got really bad. I can always cope with the odd one-night-stand – it's when they become regular that it gets to me. I tell myself, hang in there, old girl, he'll get bored, he always does. You make him comfortable, I tell myself, he likes how I handle things. And he just *loves* my uppercrust relatives.' A bitter little smile twisted her mouth.

After a moment she added, 'Sometimes I think I'm an amalgam of all the female figures who devote themselves to men: secretary, mother, mistress, housekeeper, chauffeur – that's me, all of them in one big bundle. The economy, family size, without the family.' Maura sniffed, and a stray tear splashed down her cashmere sweater.

191

'So perhaps this one, too, will vanish, like the others,' offered Darina. She disappeared into the kitchen and found a spicy Arles sausage amongst her shopping and quickly sliced it. Picking up one of the *baguettes* she'd bought, she took it all into the living room.

Maura watched Darina pile sausage slices on a piece of French bread. She took it without comment, started to nibble in a lacklustre way then suddenly wolfed it down. 'Food is my absolute downfall,' she said, after the second slice. 'Comfort eating – I know all about it but no matter how many times it's explained to me, it's what I need, what I have to have. The only time I'm thin is when Roland's nice to me.'

'You're fine, you're half the size I am.'

'But you're tall, you can carry the weight.'

'You're hardly short.'

'Remember what Roland said yesterday?'

'About small packages?'

'That's what he really likes in a woman, a nice, petite little package. Someone he can tuck under his arm and overlook when he wants. Someone . . .'

'And who is this someone?' asked Darina, fed up with waiting for the right moment to get Maura to introduce Helen's name.

Maura reached for the *baguette*, broke herself off another piece and started piling slices of sausage on it. 'This is the really humiliating part of it all. She's a nothing! Great little body and no mind. Bet she's dynamite in the sack but she sure doesn't have conversation. He must be out of his mind if he thinks he could stick five days with her on the trot let alone five years. That's how long we've been together, would you believe it? Five bloody years and it looks as though he wants to throw it all away for that social climbing fortune hunter.'

For the first time an element of doubt entered Darina's mind. Helen had many faults but she could never be called a social climber. Nor, though she loved what money could bring her, was she a fortune hunter.

'Have I met this woman?'

Maura turned surprised eyes on her. 'I shouldn't think so. I had to ask them both to luncheon the other day but they had the grace to refuse. Roland might have been able to cope with a man he'd cuckolded but I sure as hell couldn't have faced her with her sweet smiles, pretty face and vacant brain.'

'You mean?' Darina was bemused.

'Lila Bright!'

Darina had poured Maura into a taxi just before William returned home – without the other two detectives.

'There's a meeting with the French tonight, comparing notes,' he explained. 'They're really trying to wrap this case up quickly.'

'And they don't want you interfering?'

'Only when I can be of use, like this afternoon. Have you got anything to eat? I know I shouldn't be hungry but I am.'

Darina got him a drink, sat him down with what was left of the bread and sausage then went into the kitchen. She'd bought vegetables for *crudités* but there had been no time to make more garlic mayonnaise.

She got out the apartment's powerful liquidizer, fixed the thick glass goblet over the sharp blades, added an egg, salt and some peeled cloves of garlic, fitted the cover over the top, switched the machine on and watched the heavy blades emulsify the garlic and egg. As she always did when using a liquidizer, she thought of her friend who had accidentally switched on her machine while pushing down a recalcitrant piece of food. Pain darted through Darina as she remembered her friend's description of the way her finger had been mangled. It was time this inconvenient memory ceased arriving the moment a liquidizer appeared.

It didn't take long to pour in the oil and make the mayonnaise, nor to cut up the vegetables. She arranged everything on a plate, took it through and placed it in front of William. 'Tell me all about the Brights,' she said as he stuck a stick of carrot into the golden emulsion.

'He's a pretty pathetic figure. They're living in an apartment about the size of this.' He glanced around the living room with its dining area. No more than six could be accommodated with any comfort. 'On one of the walls is a water colour of their previous house. It made Roland Tait's look like some peasant hovel.' William's eyes looked sad. 'I met Sir Robert a couple of years ago at a party Geoffrey and Honor gave. He was a tremendous personality, had the sort of charisma that draws both men and women. And now he sits in an armchair in baggy trousers complaining.'

'Complaining he's not in his big house?'

'Complaining the central heating's not warm enough, complaining about the noise from the street, complaining his shoes hurt.'

'His shoes?'

'But he doesn't complain nearly as loudly as his wife.'

'Ah, Lila!'

'Yes, Lila.'

'And what's Lila like?'

'A two times girl – too thin, too blonde, too young and too bad-tempered.'

'Not giving aid and comfort to her man, then?'

'I imagine all the friends who told him he was an idiot to marry her are now biting back the words "I told you so", or perhaps not bothering with the biting back bit.'

'What about him and Bernard?'

William helped himself to a stick of celery loaded with the garlic mayonnaise then licked his fingers. 'He was quite open about it all. Said that Bernard had ruined the last years of his life, he was a crook and a bastard and he'd got everything he deserved. He even said he would have been quite happy to despatch him himself.'

'Had he gone to see him?'

'Yes, on the morning of Bernard's death. He never hesitated over telling us. Came right out with it. Said John Rickwood had had a meeting with Bernard a couple of days before. John had apparently agreed to tackle him on behalf of all Bernard's members down here. Bright said they'd all agreed they weren't going to pay unless Bernard accepted some responsibility for their losses and chipped in with a major contribution.'

'I can imagine what Bernard said to that!'

'Right! Bright said Bernard had added the fact that he was suffering along with everybody else and they could sue him until hell froze over but that wouldn't produce money from an empty coffer. Bright told us he didn't believe Bernard had no money and he thought he would see what he could do. He went up to have a chat with him – that was how he put it.'

'And what happened?'

'Bernard repeated exactly what he'd said to Rickwood.'

'Where and when did they have their little chat?'

'Bright claimed it was at the farm, that he didn't go near the mill. He said he arrived about eleven fifteen and that Barrington Smythe pushed him out after about fifteen minutes, saying he couldn't help, that if Bright hadn't wanted to play with the big boys, he shouldn't have joined the game and he had work to do in the mill. The final insult, said Bright, was when Barrington Smythe told him he was now working as a labourer to keep body and soul together.'

'Meaning the oil mill, I suppose. It's hardly on a par with road digging!'

'Quite. Mind you, what Sir Robert called Bernard during our talk was nothing to the expletives his wife produced.'

'The lovely Lila.'

'As you say, the lovely Lila.'

'And Sir Robert left when Bernard told him to go?'

'That's what he says.'

'All that could fit in with what Duval told us. I take it Sir Robert has a large black car?'

William nodded. 'A diesel Peugeot.'

'How fond of the lovely Lila do you think he is?'

William cast a shrewd glance at his wife. 'I think she's all he's got left at the moment. And I think he's beginning to realize that he won't have her for too long.'

'Another blight to lay at Bernard's door?'

'What are you getting at?'

Darina told him about her encounter with Maura.

'Let me get this straight. You're saying she was driving a white Jaguar but that Roland is having it off with *Lila*?'

'You can't be half as surprised as I was. When I saw that white Jaguar, I would have bet anything that Roland was the mystery man in Helen's life. It all fitted in. Helen had gone off to meet Roland in Nice – he'd said he was in Cannes so no one would put two and two together – Stephen returns from wherever it is he set off for first thing and drops his little bombshell on Bernard. Bernard recognizes Helen's friend as Roland. Stephen leaves to find the rest of his locations, Bernard rings up Roland, either catching him before he set off or reaching him on a car phone. He tells him to get over there. Roland decides he'd better have things out, turns up, gets in a fight and bumps Bernard off. Then he goes off to his lunch with Helen, turning up late.'

'Lovely theory.'

'Except that it now turns out that Roland's little bit on the side is Lila Bright, not Helen, after all.'

'And he could hardly turn up at lunch with bloodstains and oil all over his clothes.'

'Yes, that's another drawback. If he had to get to Nice from La Chenais he wouldn't have had time to slip back for a change of clothes, even if he could have avoided awkward questions from Maura. No,' Darina admitted, 'as a theory it has a lot going against it.'

'I can throw another little spanner in the works as well. The Swedish car wasn't Stephen's.'

'What do you mean?'

'I mean in return for easing the questioning of Sir Robert Bright, I got Mike to fill me in on the progress of the investigation so far.'

'And?'

'Bernard died by drowning in oil. The blow on the back of his head was probably enough to knock him out, but there are no signs he was held in that pail by force. Time of death could have been anything from about eleven to twelve thirty but more likely to have been around eleven forty-five to twelve. The most helpful evidence they've had so far is Duval's account of the cars going up to La Chenais that morning. And not only did Garnier get the car details out of him but he did a good job of getting him to identify exactly what sort of cars they were.

'The big black one was almost certainly Sir Robert's Peugeot. But the Swedish car that was like one his son's friend had wasn't a Volvo at all, it was a silver grey Saab. And Stephen's statement to the police said he'd dropped

Terri off in Antibes then he'd returned to the farm as he'd forgotten his camera. He arrived just after Bernard returned from Tourettes, a little after eleven; no doubt this was when Duval was dealing with his delivery. According to the statement, Stephen said Bernard wasn't in too good a temper but he'd been quite civil. Stephen claimed he hadn't stopped to chat as he was anxious to get on with his research.'

'A very different story from the one he told us today.'

'Yes.'

'Which do you believe?'

'I think this afternoon's statement. It had the ring of truth about it and I've told Garnier and Mike everything he said. They're reporting that to the examining magistrate.'

'If Bernard was right in his claim to Stephen that the farm was his, surely his name will be on the deeds?'

William shook his head. 'You're forgetting about Lloyd's. I'm certain Bernard's whole aim would have been to salt money away that couldn't be traced to him.'

'He must have trusted Helen.'

'I don't see Bernard as being quite that trusting. I would imagine he got her to sign some sort of document before handing over the money.'

'Could that have been what Helen was looking for in the chest? Not Bernard's will at all?'

'If she could have got rid of that, there would be nothing to prove the farm and everything in it wasn't hers.' William looked at Darina. 'Could she have got rid of it?'

Darina thought back. 'Her suit jacket was all awry, she could have had something stuffed inside it. She wouldn't let me help her up at all. She could certainly have torn paper up and flushed it down the loo while she was in the bathroom, she locked the door on me.' Darina swore softly. 'All in front of my eyes, as well. What a dummy!'

198

'Hardly the sort of thing you'd be on the look-out for.'

'But if that's what happened, it means that Helen is now in sole possession of La Chenais and able to share it with anyone she wants!'

'So identifying the man Stephen saw her with is a priority. I think we should have another chat with your friend Helen. In fact, if it wasn't that I really don't think she could have forced Bernard's fingers into that cutting machine, I'd say she was the prime suspect herself.'

Several things suddenly clicked into place for Darina. 'Suppose,' she said slowly, 'suppose a piece of stone had accidentally entered the machine along with the olives. And suppose Bernard had stopped it and opened up the guard and was fishing about inside, trying to get the stone out. And suppose whilst he was doing that, someone switched the machine back on?'

A large blob of mayonnaise dripped off a piece of celery unnoticed as William stared at his wife. 'Of course! How could I be so stupid? Honeymooning has interfered with my thought processes. Why hasn't it interfered with yours?'

'Because I've been absorbing some of your brains? But would a woman have been able to wield whatever it was Bernard was hit with? Mike give you any details on that, incidentally?'

'The ubiquitous blunt instrument, according to the pathologist. Something smooth, possibly wooden, certainly curved. No identifying characteristics. It would be more difficult for a woman to strike the sort of blow that would have knocked Bernard out so that he drowned in that oil but certainly not impossible. Which means that all the women could be possible suspects.'

Darina's brief excitement was draining away. 'I still don't believe that Helen could have done it.'

'We need to talk to her, though – you must see that.'

She nodded. 'Well, the best way to get anything out of her is over a good meal.'

'Then we'll take her out, I don't want you tied to the kitchen again. Let's ring her up and see if she's free tomorrow.'

Darina went to the telephone. Helen answered, sounding depressed and weary but speedily cheered up at the suggestion of lunch. Darina said they'd collect her at one o'clock, thanked her for an offer to book somewhere but said William would do that.

That arranged, Darina and William went back to considering such other evidence as they had.

'Have the police got anywhere on finding the driver of the Saab?'

'Garnier and Mike are making the rounds of the suspects tomorrow, including Björn Björnson,' said William.

'If Roland really is out of the running, I go back to him as Helen's most likely lover. He is, after all, known as a womanizer.'

'I think Björn's going to have produce his financial consultant and work hard at proving he was with him over the critical period. Incidentally, I asked Mike to make sure they called on him during your second sitting.'

'Oh, yes?'

'I thought you might like a chance to check those locked cupboards.'

'And how am I supposed to do that?'

'You could take the keys from the cupboards in this apartment, there's a nice little selection, or you might be able to find the right key somewhere in the studio.'

Darina looked at him dubiously. 'I'll try but don't hold out too much hope – picking locks is not my forte. What do you expect to find inside there?'

200

William shrugged his shoulders. 'No idea, you were the one who raised my curiosity.'

'I've dug my own grave, in other words. Thanks a bundle! Did you learn anything else from Mike?'

'Not much. They haven't come up with any real clues. Whoever killed Bernard had his wits about him. They could only pick up bits of fingerprints from the electric switch and the only ones found on the chopping machine are, they think, Bernard's. That's going by the fact that the same ones are all over the house, his aren't on any files and, of course, they weren't able to take them from the body. There's no trace of the weapon that was used to hit him over the head and so far the French police haven't found anything significant in the mill that can throw any light on the crime or its perpetrator.'

'According to the time of death, Stephen and Sir Robert are in the frame along with the driver of the Saab car?'

'Who is the police's prime suspect. Personally, my money is on whoever was in the white sports car.'

'Did the police get the make?'

William gave a small smile. 'They didn't get the news of that out of Duval.'

'And you haven't told them about it yet?'

'Do you know, there didn't seem to be an opportunity. I don't suppose it'll do us any good. The chances of our finding which white sports car it was are not high.' He gave a small sigh. 'I shall ring Mike in the morning and spill the beans.'

'You could wait a little longer.'

'What do you mean?' His eyes were suddenly alert. 'Why are you looking so smug? Don't tell me you've found another one?'

'I finally got out of Maura that the car belonged to Roland not her and I went on and on about how marvellous it looked and I bet there wasn't another white sports car down here, let alone a Jaguar. Not a Jaguar, she said, but a white MG. And guess who it belongs to?'

'Björn?'

'Anthea Pemberton.'

Chapter Seventeen

Björn started his morning session full of confidence. Lovely women were a delight to sculpt and he was more than pleased with the progress he had made on Darina's head.

Despite her good bone structure, she wasn't the easiest of subjects. Her face reflected her thoughts and moods; it was constantly changing, revealing first one side of her character then another and another and another. It was fascinating to watch but complicated the task of capturing her. He didn't want to miss this volatility of expression. Then there was the directness of her grey eyes with their ability to focus on a person to the exclusion of all else. Very little, he felt, would escape those eyes.

Björn picked up his sculpting tool and a small ball of damp clay. He smiled at Darina. 'How goes the honeymoon, eh?'

He hardly heard much of what she said, his mind was absorbed in the technicalities of transmitting his vision of her through his hands into the clay head before him. His eyes took in the rapid change of expression, his ear heard the way the cadences of her voice varied but he couldn't have repeated a word of her conversation. In a little while, when he had been totally absorbed into the sculpting process, then he would be able to discuss anything with her. For the moment, he had to concentrate on obliterating all extraneous thought.

Usually it was not difficult. Today, however, the magic was taking longer to work.

Darina had stopped talking, there was a questioning expression on her face, she was waiting for some answer from him.

'Just keep talking,' he said. He shot her a mischievous little smile, 'Tell me how your husband has been keeping you happy since we last met.'

That set her off again, her fine eyebrows arching in delicious incredulity, her wide mouth smiling. A woman at ease with herself and totally delighted with her situation.

Björn attended to the working of her mouth, lifting the corners so that the clay head looked as amused as the girl before him.

As the clay became alive beneath his fingers, so, at last, the matter that had so preoccupied him dissolved from his consciousness and he could afford to turn part of his attention to what his sitter was saying.

'And that must be one of her pieces in your living room, on that lovely modern side-table. Are you a friend?'

'A friend?' His mind wasn't working quickly enough to pick up what she was talking about. He cursed silently, he was usually sharper than this.

She laughed, a delightful gurgle. 'You haven't been listening, have you? Well, I'm sure you have more than enough to occupy yourself with trying to capture my unlovely mug. My contribution should be to rattle on, provide verbal wallpaper, not ask you questions. Or why don't you put on that state-of-the-art sound system I can see in the corner? I'm very happy to listen to music, as long as it isn't too modern or too pop.'

'No, I'm paying attention now, I promise. Now it's fine if you ask questions, now I can even manage to answer. The stereo is for when I'm on my own. With my sitters I like to talk. What is this piece you mentioned?'

'That lovely big bowl with the swirly grey and blue glaze. It is one of Anthea Pemberton's, isn't it?'

That jolted him. He held the scalpel steadily against the right cheekbone and relaid the clay he'd smudged. Then added a smear more clay and smothered that out as well.

'Yes, you're right, it is. She's an excellent potter, don't you think?'

'Oh, I do. I bought one of her jugs from that shop in Tourettes, in the main square. I met her while we were choosing cheese and wine for a picnic the other day.' Her face clouded. 'The day William and I found Bernard's body actually.' Then her expression underwent one of its chameleon changes. 'But let's not talk about that today, we're trying to put that behind us.'

Just why he couldn't quite believe her, Björn would have found it difficult to explain.

'I loved Anthea's work. She said she wasn't an artist but I think she is, don't you?'

'Anthea has no confidence in her abilities as a creative artist, she looks on herself as an artisan, a craftsman, her skills merely technical.'

'You agree?'

'Please, don't move your head like that, keep it steady. Good, that's lovely. No, I don't agree. Anthea is just as much a creative artist as I am. Perhaps more. I interpret what is before me, she creates the shape, then her colours and her glazes are inspired by that shape.'

'You talk as though you know her.'

Oh, the penetrating quality of those eyes. Björn moved the turntable and twisted the head, altering his position so that, for a moment, the clay head came between him and the live girl.

'Yes, I know Anthea. I sometimes go along on the

evening of one of her art courses to talk with the aspiring sculptors, you know?'

'It seems to be such a small circle here, everybody appears to know everybody.'

'Rather it is a case of various circles that touch at different points.'

'And Anthea doesn't belong to the circle that holds Roland Tait, John Rickwood and you?' Again her head was held slightly to one side, a determinedly amused smile on the relaxed mouth.

His sense of unease deepened. 'No, she moves with a different set.'

'Bernard and Helen's?'

Björn gave a negligent little wave with the scalpel. 'I'm afraid I don't know.'

'That morning in Tourettes, we saw her with Bernard in the little bar by the square. We were having a coffee. She seemed very upset.'

Björn said nothing.

'She could have been the last person to see Bernard, apart from his murderer, that is.'

It gave Björn a nasty feeling to hear her say the word murderer. Yet he supposed it was the only accurate one to use.

'Of course, we had to tell the police we'd seen them together. I hope she hasn't been too troubled by them?'

Björn made some vague, non-involving comment. Anthea had indeed been interrogated by the police. She had rung him afterwards, hysterical and terrified. He had calmed her down, told her if she stuck to her story that Bernard had wanted an affair and the meeting in Tourettes was to tell him he hadn't a chance with her, that he had been very angry and left in a temper, that she had then gone home and worked in her studio, they would have to work hard to prove any different.

Eventually she had regained some of her composure.

Björn sighed. Anthea was now a definite problem. Everything had been going so smoothly until Bernard started interfering. And now he was doing it again. Alive or dead, Bernard never stopped causing problems.

There was a knock on the studio door.

'Yes?' called Björn irritably. Marie usually knew better than to interrupt him while he was working.

The door opened and the local woman who had looked after him ever since he settled in the area entered. She looked upset, her olive skin flushed and dark eyes disturbed. '*Monsieur, l'inspecteur de police demande à parler.*'

'But I've already told them...' He broke off as he realized he was talking English and Marie couldn't understand what he was saying. He put down his tool and his clay with a mixture of exasperation and apprehension. '*Je vais le voir immédiatement,*' he said to Marie. Then to Darina, 'I'm sorry, I can't think what the police want now but I'd better go and see. Do you mind waiting a few minutes?'

She shook her head. 'I'll be fine, I can brush up my French with some of your *Paris Match.*' She picked up one of the magazines.

Björn followed Marie back to the house refusing to think about what the police could want.

There he found Garnier, another French policeman and two Englishmen. He was introduced to Inspector Mike Parker and Sergeant Chris Spring, liaising with the French police on the murder of Bernard Barrington Smythe. They wanted to ask him some questions. Björn felt a lightening

207

of his heart, the English side of Bernard's life held few fears for him.

'What can I do for you, gentlemen? Can I offer you some coffee, perhaps?'

They looked grateful. Marie was instructed to bring it through to the main room and to take a cup through to his sitter in the studio. 'I am working, you see, gentlemen, so I hope you won't have to take up too much time.'

They were polite, said it would only take a few minutes and sat where he indicated. Björn settled back in one of the big leather armchairs and tried to look helpful.

At first all went smoothly. Once again he was asked about his relations with Bernard, when he'd been approached about becoming a member of Lloyd's, a Name, what his profit and loss had been since then. He minimized his involvement as far as he could but they had done their homework and seemed to have worked out a figure that wasn't too far off his actual losses.

Mike, the burly English inspector, paused at this point as though he could hardly believe how much was involved. Then, 'You must have been very upset with Mr Barrington Smythe?'

Björn shrugged his shoulders. 'It was explained to me what the risks were when I became a member. These things go in cycles – Lloyd's has been through bad times before. As long as I can weather this period, the good times will come again.'

'And you can "weather" these losses?'

Again he shrugged. '*On espère*, one hopes, inspector, one hopes. Perhaps I have to sell this house but I hope not.' He heard the equilibrium in his voice with a certain amazement. 'I am lucky, my work is much in demand, my actual needs are not many. I have no expensive wife, no demanding infants, I do not live, how do you call it?, on the pig's back.'

'High on the hog, sir, I think is what you mean,' said Mike Parker, after a bemused moment or two.

It seemed that they accepted this for they went on to question again what his movements had been on the day of Bernard's death.

'As I told *l'inspecteur*,' Björn nodded towards Garnier, sitting quietly in the background, listening intently to the English exchanges, 'first thing in the morning I was in my studio. Then, about ten thirty, my friend John Rickwood came round. He is trying to help me sort out my financial situation, because of my losses with Lloyd's, you know? He is such an excellent businessman. We had lunch together, a light salad, he is vegetarian and I try not to eat much when working, it slows my metabolism. He left about two thirty and after that I went back to the studio and worked some more.'

'And you were working on what, sir?'

For a moment Björn was thrown, the French hadn't thought they needed to bother about this question.

'A commission, a head of a child – I did her father some years ago.'

'But she wasn't sitting for you?'

'No, it was the final work I had to do before the mould was made for the casting in bronze.'

'And the head is where?'

'At this actual moment, being cast. At least, I hope very much that is where it is.'

'And the name and telephone number of the foundry?'

Björn got up and went across to his desk, walking steadily. He was more than a little perturbed that so much additional effort was being put into his part in their investigation. He found the address of the foundry, wrote

209

it down on a piece of paper and handed it over to the English inspector.

'Thank you, sir. Now, there's just one other thing and then we can leave you in peace.'

Björn threw them a questioning look, his fingers drumming a silent rhythm on the arm of the chair.

'Can you please show us your car?'

The request shook him even more. 'My car?' Björn queried.

Mike Parker gave him quick smile. 'Yes, sir, if you wouldn't mind.' He sounded as though it was a minor matter but quite obviously he was going to insist.

It would look odd if he refused and, after all, why should he?

Björn led them out of the house and opened up the garage where sat his pride and joy, the 2000E Saab he had bought last year, after Bernard had assured him losses from Lloyd's were now a thing of the past and he could look forward to good profits. He'd done a considerable amount of research, spoken to lots of people about their car experiences and was now delighted with his purchase.

'Represents quite a bit of bacon, I'd have thought,' said Mike Parker, sucking his teeth thoughtfully.

'I do a lot of driving, Inspector, not only in Provence but to Germany, Switzerland, England, for my work, you see.'

'Yes, sir, I think I do. Would you mind driving it out for us?'

A cold little feeling beginning to gather at the pit of his stomach, Björn did as they requested.

'You keep it well, I see? Beautifully polished and clean.'

'I have a man comes once a week to see to the garden, he always does the car also.' He felt they were waiting for something more. 'I like all my things in good condition. Everything in its place. So I arranged he should always clean my car, then it never gets in a mess.'

'Does a good job.' All the policemen were inspecting the Saab as thoroughly as though they were interested in buying it. Doors were opened, the bonnet raised, wheels scrutinized, boot looked at. 'Well, thank you, sir, I think that's all we need for the moment.'

'How is the investigation going, Inspector?'

'We seem to be making a certain amount of progress. That's about all I can say. You understand, sir?'

Björn said nothing.

They saluted him and left.

Thoughtfully, Björn went back through the house and across the garden to the studio.

Darina was sitting on the sofa frowning over *Paris Match*. She looked up and smiled as Björn came in. 'I should have brought my dictionary. I feel such a fool – I can't even understand all the captions to the photographs!'

Her voice was light and amused. Why, then, did he have the impression that there was an inner tension about her that hadn't been there before the interruption to their session?

'Did you deal with the police satisfactorily?'

'Oh, yes, they didn't want anything much. I suppose with these investigations they need to keep going over the same ground.' He went back to his turntable and the waiting head.

'William says it's the way to get results. Tedious but painstaking examination of every tiny detail until discrepancies emerge and odd little things start to form themselves into a pattern.'

'He must lead an interesting life.' Björn removed from the clay head the damp cloth he had placed over it when he'd been summoned to the police. But he wasn't at all concerned with William Pigram's life as a detective. He was only giving half of his attention to the head as well. Picking up his piece of clay, working it with his fingers, his eyes were taking in every detail of his studio. There was something wrong, something so slight he couldn't immediately identify what it was.

Then he had it. One of the little handles of the floor cupboards was out of line.

The handles were like little fobs, hinged and hanging. They should all be in the same position, pointing down to the ground. One was up, as though someone had been trying to open the cupboard and had carelessly not returned it to its proper alignment, or hadn't had time.

As he talked easily and continued working, Björn shifted his position so he could take in every detail of the studio.

The little desk area was also ever so slightly different. Someone had been looking for something and, perhaps in a hurry, hadn't ensured things were exactly as they had been. The difference was so subtle someone less particular about how things were ordered than Björn probably wouldn't have noticed. The drawer beneath the work surface wasn't placed exactly inside its frame. The lacquer box on top that held pencils and those odd little items that had to be housed somewhere was not precisely square to the wall. The books on the shelf above didn't have their position matched each to the other as exactly as they should.

It was as if someone had been looking for something.

Björn looked back at his lovely sitter. Her eyes were as clear and innocent as before, her manner as engagingly open.

Well, she had had a frustrating time, of that he was sure. The key to the cupboards was on a ring in his pocket and without it there was no way she could have opened them.

What worried him was why she should have wanted to.

Then he pushed the puzzle to the back of his mind, together with the unease left after the police had departed, and once again concentrated on establishing the mood necessary for effective work.

And he found that the head he had thought was progressing so well had become unsatisfactory. There was a facet of his sitter he had entirely failed to capture.

He encouraged Darina to talk about food.

'Isn't it all rubbish?' he interrupted her enthusiastic account of shopping in Antibes. 'French food isn't so markedly better than food elsewhere, surely?'

He watched her give serious consideration to this and continued to work on the head, making subtle changes.

'I don't think it's the actual food that's different. We can get a wider variety of ingredients in England these days than you can in France, and often the quality is as good. But it's their attitude. Food is important to the French at every level. To the English it's only important to some and the pretentious way a few of them talk about it is enough to put off many more. Fewer and fewer of us learn how to cook, how to produce something that tastes good however little it has cost. It used to be something taught by our mothers, now we learn reheating by microwave.'

'And you really think that that is important?'

Darina's brow wrinkled and Björn thought that this quality of hers of considering a comment instead of giving a gut reaction was both engaging and dangerous. 'Yes, I think it is. We are what we eat. I truly believe that.'

'Jules Rickwood does too. She gets too serious about food, all that vegetarianism and purity of diet. Now she is pregnant I am sure she will be more tedious than ever.'

Darina gave another of her engaging grins. 'Anybody getting too serious about anything is tedious, don't you think? Did you ever hear Bernard going on about his plans for making La Chenais the centre of Provence oil?'

213

Why bring up Bernard now? 'What a bore he could be,' Björn said lightly.

'And yet he had charm. He must have. Helen isn't someone to waste herself on anyone.'

Björn wasn't going to comment on that.

He laid down his little scalpel and looked at the head. 'Not much more to be done now. You can robe yourself, I have finished my need for you to sit.'

Buttoning her shirt, Darina came over. 'Can I look?'

He watched while she surveyed the clay representation of herself, a wary expression on her face.

Did she see it? The enigmatic quality that underlay the amusement in the eyes and around the mouth? Darina was much prettier than the Mona Lisa but Björn flattered himself that his head of her now raised as many questions as da Vinci's masterpiece had over the centuries.

'And?' he asked her.

'I think you've made me much more beautiful than I am but, yes, I can recognize myself.'

'William will be pleased?'

'Delighted. Can he see it now? He's picking me up in a few minutes.'

'Of course. He's paying, after all.'

After William and Darina had left, both delighted, Björn sat down in his chair and looked across at Anthea's bowl standing on the side-table. Apprehension tightened his shoulder muscles and acid bit into the lining of his stomach. He thought for a few moments then rose and went and found Marie. A little careful questioning elicited the information that Mrs Pigram hadn't been reading the magazine when she took the coffee through. She had been looking at the clay heads on the shelf above the cupboards. She had asked Marie something about them but because it had been in English, Marie hadn't understood and Mrs Pigram had laughed and apologized for her lack of French.

How dangerous could Darina be? Björn went back to the living room, sat at his desk and picked up the telephone. The first thing was to warn John Rickwood. After that he would need to give serious thought to the best way of dealing with this beautiful, interfering cook.

Chapter Eighteen

'Well?' asked William as they drove away.

'Well, what?'

'Did you manage to open the cupboards, stoopid?'

'No,' she said sadly. 'They've got dear little locks, nothing like those on the cupboards in our apartment, and I couldn't find the key, or keys. And while I was looking, Björn's cleaning lady came in with coffee. She nearly scared the living daylights out of me.'

'Did she twig what you were doing?'

'I don't think so. I heard the rattle of the door handle before she came in and pretended to be looking at those heads above the cupboards. Did you meet up with Mike and Garnier and did they tell you what sort of car Björn drives?'

'Yes and yes. Guess?'

'A Saab?'

'Spot on. Garnier was starting to rub his hands, convinced the case was more or less wrapped up.'

'But Björn told us he spent the morning with his financial adviser.'

'And he's holding to that. Garnier's gung-ho to blow that alibi to destruction. He didn't like it a little bit when I broke the news of the white sports car.'

'Thereby demoting Björn as prime suspect?'

'Exactly! And it's going to make their questioning of Roland a lot more interesting when they find out about his Jaguar.'

'You didn't tell them?'

'Wicked, wasn't it? But I thought they would have much more fun discovering that little bit of information for themselves.'

'I wonder if Maura will tell them about Anthea Pemberton's white MG?'

'I wonder.' William glanced at Darina. 'There's one more thing. Can you guess who Björn's financial adviser is?'

She shook her head.

'John Rickwood.'

'Really?' She thought for a moment. 'I suppose it isn't so surprising. They were very chummy at that lunch. Though at one point I thought for a moment that John could be jealous of Jules's friendship with Björn. Apparently they knew each other before she and John met.'

'How well?'

'How well, indeed. Given Björn's reputation and the fact they were both single at the time, it's hard not to assume the obvious. But I bet that whatever fires were lit are well and truly out now. John's not the sort of man to be friendly with someone his wife showed that sort of interest in.'

'Yes, and she's not the sort of girl who flirts, even in the most innocent of ways. Well, here's another little tit-bit of information for you. While I was being filled in on Björn's car and alibi, Garnier had a call on his mobile phone. He'd asked for a computer search through the last six months' driving offences to see if any Saabs driven by familiar names came up.'

'And?'

William paused for maximum effect. 'Two weeks ago John Rickwood was fined for speeding in his Saab.'

218

'Wow! So there are two suspects, both with grievances against Bernard. Not only that, they're giving each other an alibi.'

'I thought you'd like it.'

Darina's mind was working at top speed. 'Do we know just how much money Jules has lost at Lloyd's?'

'According to Mike's calculations, she lost some two hundred thousand pounds before she married John.'

'Heavens!'

'By all accounts, it should have wiped her out but Rickwood then provided a guarantee to enable her to continue her membership.'

'And since then?'

'Probably another fifty thousand.'

'Which she says she's not going to pay.'

'In any case, Rickwood is apparently well able to provide her with the funds to meet her liabilities.'

'Not much motive for murder there, then?'

'I wouldn't have thought so. It's hard to know why Rickwood would want to provide Björnson with one or need one himself.'

'Maybe Jules asked him to help Björn. John mightn't like it but I think there's a good chance he'd do it.'

'Help his wife's old flame?' William looked doubtful.

'He's besotted with her and he likes Björn. If he believes Björn's innocent and needs help, he might do it.' William looked far from convinced but there was no time to discuss the matter further, they had reached La Chenais.

Helen was waiting for them, alone.

'Stephen and Terri out?' Darina kissed her friend and thought how much better she was looking this morning, make-up in place and wearing a smart dress and jacket. Was lunch out enough to improve her morale?

'They're trying to finish Steve's location hunting.'

'Made up their row then?'

'Oh, William, it's as if they enjoy having spats, they're always at it. I really can't see what he sees in her, she's so fat! And no charm at all!'

'But bags of character,' said Darina. 'And she seems to understand him pretty well.'

'And they do say fat girls are good in bed,' William added cheerfully. 'Now, are we ready? We don't want to run the risk of losing our table.'

As they set off from the farm Darina asked, 'How are things going?'

Helen shrugged. 'I try and tell myself I'm coping but it's like emerging from an anaesthetic – I can't do anything without something hurting. And it's such hell having to cope with the funeral.'

'You're having it here?'

'Yes, less trouble all round. But Bernard's ex is trying to insist it should be in London.'

'Tell her to organize a memorial service if she's that concerned,' suggested William.

Helen gave an hysterical giggle. 'Can you imagine the knives that'd come out? It really annoys me, the way she thinks she's got rights over what happens. Bernard and I were as good as married.'

It was the opportunity Darina had been waiting for. 'Why didn't you make it official?'

There was silence in the car.

Then, 'Neither of us felt we really wanted to embark on another marriage,' said Helen.

Darina remembered something Helen had said several years ago when she'd been complaining about the lack of a man in her life. 'I mean, Darina, you know how competitive the cookery world is. I may be doing all right at the moment, but who's to say how long it's going to last?

There are new people coming along all the time and it's a constant battle to stay on top, keep up with the latest developments, second-guess public taste, search out new ideas. I just get so tired of it all sometimes. A well-heeled husband would be a life-saver.'

Then she had found Bernard, to all outward appearances very well-heeled indeed. Why not clinch the relationship? Had it been Bernard who refused? Or Helen?

'We're going to Mougins?' Helen asked as William took the turning.

'Is that all right?'

'Of course, you know it's wonderful just to get out of the house. Which restaurant?'

She sounded anxious and when William told her the name, she said nothing.

'You have to walk from here,' said William as he parked in the municipal car park. 'It's the nearest we can leave the car. At least it's a fine day.'

They walked up a long flight of steps into the picturesque little town. There were several restaurants but William led them confidently up the hill until they arrived at the one he'd chosen.

They received a warm welcome and were led to a table in a conservatory made of canvas where they could look over a lawn and admire the spring blossom.

'So nice to see Madame again so soon,' said the women in charge as she handed them menus.

'I always love coming here,' Helen said with a touch of bravado.

William looked up. 'I'm sorry, I should have asked you to suggest somewhere new but this place has happy memories for me and I wanted to share it with Darina.'

Helen sighed and said nothing.

Their apperitifs arrived. 'A Kir Royale for a royal

221

occasion,' said William, raising his glass of champagne with crème de cassis. 'Lucky man that I am to have two lovely ladies to lunch with.'

Under his warmly appreciative gaze, Helen began to relax. 'It's so wonderful to get away from La Chenais. I can't tell you what the last few days have been like. Bernard's terrible ex-wife on the telephone, Steve veering between treating me like eggshells and telling me I'm better off without Bernard, and all the dreadful formalities to try and organize. The French police have been absolutely no help at all, positively *convinced* I murdered Bernard, and the English lot are no better, wanting to know all about Lloyd's and his business, as if I knew anything! I keep on telling them that the insurance world is a closed book to me, I wouldn't know whether to fry, bake or boil it.' She looked at them with an air that managed to combine helplessness and bravery with an attractive appeal to their chivalrous instincts.

Darina gritted her teeth and plunged in. 'Helen, darling, if we're to be able to help you, really help, I mean, you've got to come clean.'

'What do you mean?' Helen looked at them both with an expression of injured innocence.

'You know exactly what I mean. Who is the man you've been meeting here? It's no use trying to pretend you don't know what I'm talking about.'

A mutinous look came over Helen's face. She said nothing.

'Look, don't you realize what a difficult situation you're in? Your only chance of any sort of alibi for the time of Bernard's death is to tell the police exactly where you were from the time you left La Chenais in the morning until you returned and found us there. Otherwise they're going to continue thinking that somehow you slipped back and killed him.'

Helen's eyes filled with tears. 'I loved Bernard. Why should I want him dead?'

Darina took firm hold of her patience. 'Helen, you admitted to us that you met another man for lunch that day. I'm sure you were very fond of Bernard but that's not the same as wanting to spend the rest of your life with him.'

Helen started to fiddle with the cutlery.

William entered the fray. 'Could you convince the police that you produced all the money for buying La Chenais, restoring it and purchasing all that new mill equipment?'

Helen dropped a knife on the floor. William bent and picked it up, placed it by the side of the table then covered her hand with his. 'We're on your side, you know, you've got to believe that.'

She looked at him, her blue eyes hazy with tears, her lower lip trembling.

'If you think the police have been unhelpful so far, you have no idea how they can get when they really start investigating someone,' Darina said persuasively. 'They'll look at all your accounts, demand exact details of where the money came from, make you produce records and receipts. Whatever arrangement was between you and Bernard, I am sure it was all perfectly legal, at any rate as far as you were concerned. You'll only be in trouble if you try to hide things.'

Helen looked doubtful.

Darina persisted. 'You met Bernard, you were attracted to him. He fell heavily for you, pursued you, persuaded you he could be the man for you. Then he made you this offer you couldn't refuse. You'd go together to France and he'd provide the funds for you to buy a property. You'd just had a very successful television series, everyone would believe it was your profits that had paid for the house and everything else. You and Bernard would live together but, just in case the Lloyd's situation meant he was asked for large sums of money, you wouldn't get married. Then the house and the mill and the oil business would all be yours and he wouldn't have to give any of it up to meet his liabilities. It must have seemed a marvellous idea.' Darina's voice was warm and persuasive.

Helen's expression was bemused.

'And at first it was all wonderful,' Darina continued. 'You enjoyed being with Bernard, having a man around who knew his way about, who could provide you with lots of nice things, who appreciated your food and thought you were absolutely wonderful. Then things started to go wrong. You met . . . now, darling, this is where you have to come clean and tell us who you met.'

Helen continued to sit mute.

'Just because he's got a white sports car and was late for your lunch doesn't mean he killed Bernard.'

'Who else could it have been?' Helen whispered.

'I don't know,' Darina said gently. 'But I gather Anthea Pemberton drives a white MG and she met Bernard in the morning not long before he was killed. We saw them together and it looked as though they were having quite a row.'

Helen's eyes narrowed. 'Bernard made an absolute idiot of himself over that woman!'

'Tell us about it,' Darina invited her.

The waiter chose that moment to arrive with their first course. Helen hardly seemed to notice the interruption. 'We met her at some charity do, about a year ago. I liked her at first. She seemed so delighted to meet me, told me how much she enjoyed my books and how often she cooked my recipes. So I invited her over for a meal.' Helen appeared to notice her plate of scallops in filo pastry for the first time. 'Oh, doesn't this look good! That saffron sauce smells divine! Well, Anthea came bringing me a lovely little jug. Of course, that gave her the perfect entrée into telling us all about her pottery and the courses she runs.'

Helen paused to eat some of her food. 'Later she flattered Bernard by asking him for some help with her accounts. That was after she'd asked us to come and have dinner with one of her courses, saying the artists would love to meet me and, of course, Bernard. I wondered a bit why he was keen to go. But Bernard always loved meeting new people, I think it was because he used to need new Names for his business and he couldn't get out of the habit.

'It was quite a fun evening.' Helen preened herself a little. 'They were a mixed bunch but nearly all of them seemed to have heard of me and some actually had one or two of my books at home, all due to that television series, of course. So I asked her to another meal and we complimented her on the courses and said what a job it must be for her to run them on her own. And then it all came out. How she'd been persuaded by some man to set them up. She'd sold a house in England to provide the capital. Then the chap had run off with some American heiress who came to one of the courses. Leaving Anthea all alone.'

Helen looked just the tiniest bit smug. 'Anthea said she's always wondered what Kevin, that was the chap's name, had seen in her – apparently he was rather a dish. Well, he was only after her money! Which she hung on to like mad. No fool, Anthea.'

Helen reached for another piece of bread to wipe up the sauce from her empty plate. 'At that stage I felt rather sorry for her and it was I who persuaded Bernard to help her with her accounting.'

She looked straight at Darina. 'I don't know who was the bigger idiot, me or Bernard.'

'You mean Anthea was after him?'

'Well, of course she was, abandoned like that. Wouldn't you be after the first red-blooded male to come along, never mind that he belonged to somebody else,' she added.

Darina ignored this. 'When did you find out they were having an affair?'

'Oh, I wouldn't grace it with the name of affair! She was due here one evening. She rang and said her car had broken down so, of course, Bernard says he'll go and fetch and take her back. We all had rather a lot to drink, it was a nasty night and I tried to persuade Anthea to stay.' Helen's mouth twisted angrily. 'No chance! She was *so* apologetic, said she had so much to do the next day before the course arrived, and couldn't she phone for a taxi? Bernard wouldn't hear of that. I didn't see him again for five hours! And then he tried to fob me off with some story about flooding and not wanting to disturb me by phoning to explain he was going to be late. I nearly threw him out there and then.'

There was silence for a moment before Darina said hurriedly, 'It sounds as though Bernard made a bit of a fool of himself.'

'I'll say! After I'd told him just what I thought of his behaviour, he was grovelling all over the place. Said it was because he'd had too much to drink, that she didn't mean anything to him. I was the one he loved and it would break his heart if I couldn't forget this "moment of madness" I think he had the nerve to describe it as.'

'You forgave him?'

'Yes, William. Well, he was so pathetic I didn't have the heart to do anything else.'

Not to mention the fact that your financial fortunes were tied up with him, thought Darina. 'Had you met this other man by then?'

For the first time Helen looked guilty. 'I knew him years

ago, in another life. In fact, he was the reason I left James, my first husband. We were going to get married.'

'So what happened?'

The waiter removed their plates.

Helen drank more wine. 'I think it was our careers, we were both working so hard. That and the children. They needed security and he couldn't offer any at that stage, he was still building up his business. My books weren't earning much and James kept begging me to return. So I did the decent thing and went back,' Helen said righteously.

'But it didn't last anyway?' commented Darina.

'I tried, I really tried but James couldn't forget – he was always suspecting me of being with some other man and in the end I thought, well, why not? Sheeps and lambs and all that.'

'With the man you'd gone off with?' asked William.

Helen shook her head. 'I couldn't bear to see him again after I left. He was my great love. We were just fantastic together and he made every man after that seem nothing.'

More food arrived and Helen gazed at her red mullet with fresh orange chutney in delight. 'Oh, isn't this divine? Don't you love the food here? Cut me off from great cooking and I'd die!'

'So, when did you meet this man again?' prompted William.

Helen finished a mouthful of fish then said, 'It must have been about three months ago, just before Bernard's little fling with Anthea. It seemed like a miracle. We went to a large luncheon party and there he was, across a crowded room.'

'Your eyes met?'

'Don't be like that, Darina! You can't imagine what it was like!' Helen looked at her friend with the eyes of an injured deer.

Darina felt guilty. Who was she to censure Helen? If this

man really had been the love of her life, it would explain so much about her conduct afterwards, the constant looking for a replacement and never finding him; the desire for some sort of emotional as well as financial security.

'I'm sorry,' she said gently. 'Tell me the full story.'

Helen gave a bleak little smile. 'There isn't too much to tell, really. We met and it was as if the years in between just didn't exist any more, for both of us. He asked me to meet him for lunch.'

'Here?'

'Not that time, that first time we went to Bruno's, in Lorgues. Marvellous restaurant, you must go there, the food's just divine. And there were other restaurants, like the one at Saint-Cézaire where Stephen saw us.' She sighed a deep, dreamy sigh. 'I can remember exactly what we ate at each one.'

'And afterwards?'

Helen's gaze dropped once again. 'He said we needed to be sure before we upset people. He was involved with someone else, you see.'

That didn't sound like Björn.

'So you embarked on an affair?'

'Darling, you make it sound so blunt, so sordid. It wasn't like that!'

'Why didn't you grab the opportunity of Bernard's "little fling" with Anthea to say it was all over?'

'I . . . I couldn't. Everything was so complicated.' Helen gazed miserably at the remains of her fish.

'Had you signed some sort of agreement?' asked William gently. 'So that even though the house and mill were in your name, Bernard could insist on your giving them to him if you broke up?'

'I worked hard to get everything together here, bloody hard!' Helen burst out. 'And it wasn't as though I hadn't

228

had expenses! Not to mention looking after Bernard better than he'd ever been looked after in his life before. I deserved some sort of consideration! Anyway, he'd have had difficulty making that piece of paper stick in a court of law, and if he had, everything would have gone down the Lloyd's chute.'

'Sounds as though you had him over a barrel,' commented William. 'Why not send him packing?'

'I didn't want to burn my boats,' Helen sulked. 'It's expensive down here, eating in places like this, and there's no point in living like a pauper.'

'You mean this love of your life wasn't prepared to commit himself?'

'He said he needed time to disentangle himself and we shouldn't rush things anyway.'

Excuses, excuses, thought Darina, catching William's eye. 'So, the day of the murder, you told Bernard you were going to Nice but actually you came here?'

Helen nodded. She looked exhausted. 'I went down to Antibes first and tried to find a new dress. I didn't like anything I saw and I was late getting here. I thought he'd be waiting but it was half an hour before he turned up.' Helen's eyes glittered. 'All he would say was that something had held him up and I wasn't to jump down his throat when he was a few minutes late. A few minutes! I couldn't understand it. He behaved as though I was the one who should apologize. He ordered an enormous brandy before he'd even kiss me or look at the menu. And drank at least half of it as soon as it came. I . . . I got quite cross.' Helen blinked rapidly.

'And have you seen Roland since?'

'No, Darina . . . Oh,' she added as she realized what she'd done. 'You knew all the time! That's not fair.'

'No, I promise you, I didn't. But he does drive a white

229

Jaguar. Maura, though, is convinced he's having an affair with Lila Bright.'

'Lila!' Helen spat the name out. 'She's history!'

'So Maura has grounds for her suspicions?'

'Roland told me about her himself. She made a dead set at him, just about the time her husband had to sell up. Roland said he was flattered and that she needed a shoulder to cry on, she was undergoing such a terrible strain. Honestly, men are such fools! The only strain Lila undergoes is the weight of her false eyelashes. As soon as he realized she intended becoming the next Mrs Tait, he was off.'

'I'm not surprised. From what I've heard, she can't match Maura for style or background or be able to make Roland as comfortable,' Darina said without compunction.

Helen looked uneasy.

William took her hand. 'So now you have La Chenais unencumbered, as you might say. All yours with no Bernard to interfere.'

'Don't be like that! I was very fond of Bernard, honestly. But there was another side to him.'

'What do you mean, Helen, what sort of side?' asked Darina.

'There was a really mean streak to Bernard. He loved digging the knife in and sometimes he could sound really threatening.'

'Threatening? In what way?'

Helen looked away from the table. 'Oh, I don't know,' she said vaguely.

'Come on, Helen, something must have happened for you to say that.'

Helen brought her attention back to Darina. For a moment it was as though she was weighing the consequences of saying anything more. Finally she gave a tiny shrug and said, 'I suppose it didn't really mean anything. I overheard him on the telephone about a week or so ago. I came back from shopping earlier than expected and as I came in he was saying something like, "And remember I can always ruin you." ' Helen's eyes went blank and she shivered. 'It was the way he said it – there was something really evil in his voice. Then he realized I was there and he added in a jokey kind of way, "as the actress said to the bishop", and put down the telephone.'

'But you don't know who he was talking to?' asked William.

She shook her head. 'I thought it must be somebody connected with Lloyd's. It's been quite dreadful, all these people complaining about all their losses and Bernard afraid he's going to have to be declared bankrupt. I tell you, I've been quite worn out by it all.'

Darina had been unable to taste anything of her meal for some time. She felt Helen couldn't have been nearly so taken aback by Bernard's attitude as she was by her friend's. Helen had never been like this in Somerset. Was it because their meetings then had concentrated on food?

'Do you think he could have been trying to blackmail somebody?'

'Blackmail, William?' Helen's eyes were round with astonishment. 'Bernard couldn't be *blackmailing* anybody, that's so dirty!'

'Threats aren't very nice,' said Darina. She looked at Helen closely, at the transparent quality of the soft purple shadows under her eyes, the lines of strain. 'Tell me, who do you think killed Bernard?'

Helen closed her eyes briefly and a pulse beat rapidly in her throat.

'You do believe it's Roland, don't you? That's why you're so worried and upset. But why? If Roland wouldn't ditch

231

Maura and ask you to leave Bernard, why should he want to kill him?'

Helen's eyes became enormous. She burst out, 'I've got to tell you, I think I'll go mad if I don't tell someone. I can't sleep, I have nightmares during the day.' She gulped, then said, 'Roland told me it looked as though he might be bankrupt himself if he couldn't get hold of sufficient cash to cover his current Lloyd's losses.'

'How much does he need?'

'Half a million.'

William whistled. 'Still, with his City connections, it should be possible to raise that.'

Helen shook her head. 'He says he's been to that well too often and his credit is exhausted. He asked me if I could help. He said we didn't owe Bernard a thing, in fact everything Bernard had given me should by rights be his, but that he would only treat it as a loan,' Helen added hurriedly.

'Is the farm and everything worth that much? And could you use it to raise the cash that quickly?' asked Darina.

Helen looked sly. 'I told him I wouldn't have to. That if he really thought what Bernard had was his, I could hand him half a million, a whole million in fact, without any trouble.'

Chapter Nineteen

Darina drew her breath in sharply. 'What do you mean, a whole million?'

'Just after we came here, Bernard showed me some bits of paper that he said were worth that much. They were his insurance for the future, he said, and nobody must know about them, otherwise they'd be taken away. What was it he called them?'

'Bearer bonds?' offered William.

'That's right, he said they were as good as money.'

'And you've got them?' Darina said in disbelief. 'Surely he would have placed them in a bank deposit box?'

Helen shook her head. 'He had a hidden safe built in La Chenais. Brought over a specialist from England to do it. He kept the key on his watch chain, he was never parted from it. At night-time he slept with the chain round his wrist.'

Back to Darina came a sudden picture of Helen flinging herself down beside Bernard's body, wrenching open his overalls and feeling inside. 'You took it off his body!'

'I had to!' Helen cried. 'I needed that money. And the document I signed saying Bernard had paid for the house and it was actually his.'

'That's what you rushed upstairs to do! When I came into

your bedroom, you'd already taken them out of the safe!'

Helen shook her head. 'The bonds were better hidden there than anywhere else. But I did take out the document and I was going through the chest to see if he'd taken a photocopy and left that amongst his papers. I told you I was looking for his will because I couldn't think of anything else. I knew it made me look mercenary but that was better than you finding out the truth!'

Now that Helen had admitted everything, she couldn't stop talking. The remainder of the meal involved Darina and William listening to an outpouring of her growing disillusionment with Bernard and the miracle of meeting Roland again and finding he still cared for her as much as she did for him.

'All I want now', she said as they drank coffee, 'is for us to be together. I long for all this to be over so that I can start to be really happy.' She gazed into the distance. 'It will be for the first time in my life.'

Darina had never felt less in tune with her friend. Helen finally appeared to realize all was not well between them, a resentful expression appeared on her face and conversation grew more and more difficult. It was symptomatic of Helen's preoccupation with herself that she made little attempt to chat to the chef when he came round. But even Darina found it hard to pay the food the compliments it deserved, let alone discuss the dishes the way she would normally have done.

'Well, it's back to sorting out Bernard's things,' said Helen dispiritedly when they returned to La Chenais. 'Those that the police have left me, that is. I suppose you're off somewhere exciting now?'

'We thought we'd pop into the Escoffier museum at Cagnes-sur-Mer. Darina wants to see the menus he did during the siege of Paris, when they plundered the zoo for meat.'

'Don't listen to him, Helen, it's the only thing that made him the slightest bit interested in going to it. I thought I couldn't come down here without paying my respects to the great man.'

'Escoffier didn't have much to do with the siege of Paris. He was appointed *chef de cuisine* at the headquarters of the Rhine army at Metz,' said Helen snappishly. 'But, yes, I think there's at least one siege menu at the museum.' She remembered her manners. 'Thanks for taking me out to lunch, it was wonderful to get away from here for a bit.'

'I can't believe it,' Darina said as William turned the car on to the main road. 'She honestly seems to think she can put all this behind her and she and Roland can go off with Bernard's money and everything will be happy ever after.'

'Her grip on reality is seriously shaky.'

'But I still don't believe she had anything to do with Bernard's murder.'

'It'll probably be possible to check if what she told us about her movements that morning was the truth. I don't see any dress-shop assistant in Antibes forgetting Helen, and certainly the restaurant will be able to confirm the time she arrived. If it all pans out, then she's in the clear.'

'I knew it was Roland. He's just her type, attractive, sophisticated—'

'Rich, at least at first sight.'

'Cynical man!'

'Well, that's all Bernard had going for him.'

'Oh, he wasn't particularly attractive at first sight but small men often have charisma.'

'Remember Napoleon?'

'Exactly! And maybe money can act as an aphrodisiac.'

'Its loss is usually pretty sobering.'

'Yes, if Roland really is facing ruin, he must be devastated. Though one would never guess it. What a cool customer! Cool enough, do you think, to have murdered

Bernard and then turned up for lunch with Helen?'

'He'd have had to do something about his clothes. Apart from that, yes, I think he probably is capable of murder. He strikes me as totally ruthless when he has to be. However, I honestly don't know if he killed Bernard. We're going to have to get Duval to identify that white sports car.'

Darina gave a little grimace. 'What a shame we had to hear all those unpleasant details over lunch. That food looked wonderful and I couldn't taste a thing.'

'Well, I, for one, won't have to eat again for a week.'

Darina managed a smile. 'That's what you've said before and hunger seems to re-establish itself remarkably quickly.'

'Not this time,' swore William.

His resolution was to be put to the test remarkably quickly. Darina soon realized the Escoffier museum wasn't holding his attention and she made sure their progress round it was swift.

Returning to their apartment block, they found a note in the letter box to say the *concierge* had a delivery for them.

It proved to be a cardboard box from a local *pâtisserie*. Inside were two delicious-looking small chocolate cakes oozing black jam and granules of chocolate. Chocolate *ganache* covered the top of each together with curls of chocolate.

'How wonderful!' Darina exclaimed. She looked for a card but failed to find one. 'Who are they from?'

The *concierge* said she'd found them sitting outside her door with a label addressed to Monsieur and Madame Pigram, together with the apartment number. She'd assumed they'd ordered them themselves.

'Now we'll have to ring round everybody and find out,' Darina said as they took the box back to the apartment. 'At least we can count Helen out, she certainly wouldn't have sent us anything like this.'

'Probably a thank-you from Roland, for the lunch the other day.'

'Or even Maura, for listening to her woes.'

'It's a very kind thought but I wish they hadn't chosen today to send them. Even thinking of eating chocolate cakes makes my stomach queasy.'

'They'll last until tomorrow. You'll be well able to face them then. Oh, look, there's your chum, Mike Parker. Let him in, darling, while I call for the lift.'

William went and opened the glass front door. 'Come to report progress?' he asked as they rejoined Darina.

'Thought you'd like to be kept up to date. We've had quite a productive day.' The burly detective looked elated.

'A cup of coffee?' offered Darina.

'You bet, and if you had a biscuit or two I wouldn't say no – we've had no lunch.'

'I don't believe it, a Frenchman skipping a meal!'

'I couldn't credit it either,' said Mike gloomily. 'I was sure Garnier would whip us off to a nice little café and stuff us full. Not a bit. He says lunch is the best time to catch people and keeps us going. If it wasn't that he'd been called off to a meeting, we'd still be at it. As it is, I sent young Chris back to fill up reports and peeled off here just in case you'd discovered anything new.'

'You're lucky, we've just come back from a most interesting lunch with Helen Mansard.' William took his colleague through to the living room while Darina searched her fridge for food.

There wasn't a great deal but she found a hunk of Camembert and a piece of *baguette* left over from breakfast, together with some of the raw vegetables and garlic mayonnaise. She put it all on a tray, added the coffee she'd made, then looked at the *pâtisserie* box. The chocolate cakes did look delicious, just the sort of thing William loved and she was by no means averse to. But they were being really spoilt with food, one way and another.

She got another plate and put the little *gâteaux* on it. Maybe William would change his mind when he saw Mike eating.

Mike was complaining about Garnier's nose-to-the-grindstone way of conducting an investigation as Darina entered the living room. His face lit up as she unloaded her tray on to the table.

'All bits and pieces, I'm afraid, but it may keep the wolf from the door.'

'You're a doll.'

William let him eat for a few minutes then he could contain his impatience no longer. 'So, what have you got to tell us?'

'First, anything from you?'

'Well, Darina didn't manage to get Björn's cupboards open.'

'Look, I told you, I don't want to know anything about that! As far as I'm concerned, any search without a warrant is illegal and nothing to do with me.'

'Come off it, Mike. The copper who hasn't stretched a point to advance an investigation hasn't been born. Now, come on, give us what you've got.'

Mike sighed, drank some more of the coffee and loaded a piece of bread with cheese. 'OK, but I'm going to expect a blow by blow account of the Mansard encounter afterwards.'

'You got it.'

The detective collected his thoughts, the rugged ridges in his face deepening with concentration. 'We filled you in on the two Saab owners, right? And that Rickwood and Björnson are providing each other with alibis?'

'What about Jules Rickwood?'

'The wife? She wasn't feeling well that day and, according to both her and that butler fellow, she spent most of the day in bed. Apparently that was why the husband went round to Björnson, so she could rest undisturbed.'

'Well,' said William, 'somehow Rickwood has never looked a real possibility for the frame. As you said, he appears to be well able to pick up his wife's Lloyd's losses.'

'Yet doesn't it strike you as a little odd that both he and Björnson own cars identical to one seen going up to the farm that morning and that they are giving each other alibis?'

'Certainly a coincidence.'

'I'm sure there's something we don't know. Maybe Rickwood had a grudge against Barrington Smythe we know nothing about. Maybe Barrington Smythe had something on him.'

'Remember what Helen said, darling,' Darina interpolated. She turned to Mike. 'Helen said she heard Bernard on the phone one day saying to someone, "Remember I can ruin you." Could he have been speaking to John?'

'The only meeting between the two we've heard about happened after that,' objected William. 'On the other hand, that doesn't mean they didn't meet earlier. I prefer, though, your theory that Rickwood for some reason is giving Björnson an alibi. Underneath all that Scandinavian charm are some very deep channels.'

'Rickwood struck me as being someone with reserves of character,' said Mike, scooping up mayonnaise with a piece of celery.

'He's certainly got those. His wife told us he survived a crash in the depths of Canada that killed his partner,' said Darina. Then she and William looked at each other. For what seemed an age neither spoke.

Then, 'Just suppose Rickwood didn't devotedly nurse his injured partner in the crash,' said William.

'But actually did him in, perhaps to gain control of the company they ran,' suggested Darina excitedly.

'And somehow Bernard found out about it,' added William. 'That would be quite something to use to threaten him.'

'To make him drop any action on behalf of the Lloyd's members, you mean?' William nodded.

Mike looked dubious. 'How long ago did you say this aeroplane accident was?'

Darina thought. 'It must be well over thirty years ago. Jules said she wasn't born and I would have said she was in her early thirties.'

'You're not suggesting he got away with murder for all those years and then Barrington Smythe suddenly ups and says he knows all about it?'

'Sounds improbable,' agreed William.

'It would make a plausible reason for assisting Björnson to murder Barrington Smythe, though. Just suppose Rickwood did do in his partner, how would Barrington Smythe know about it?'

Darina remembered the chest Helen had been searching when she came up to her bedroom. She saw once again the pile of papers on the floor. Remembered picking them up and placing them back in the chest, on top of some photographs. 'Jules said John was rescued by an army expedition. I've seen a snapshot of Bernard in army uniform – he would have been just about old enough for military service. Suppose he was a member of the expedition that found John?'

'But if there was evidence that the partner had been murdered, surely all the expedition would have known? Some action would have been taken.'

'The more one thinks about it, the more unlikely it all sounds,' agreed William. 'After all, would he recognize Rickwood after thirty years?'

'Remember he's missing the tops of two fingers. That would be quite an identification feature. And once you've murdered one person, it's much easier to kill someone else.'

'It's worth checking out,' Mike said thoughtfully.

'Couldn't you ask your brother-in-law, the Brigadier, to look into it?' Darina asked William.

'No need for that, we have our channels of communication with the army.' Mike wrote a note down on a piece of paper. 'Just give me as many details as you can remember of the incident and I'll get a fax off tonight.'

Between them William and Darina filled in the story for Mike. 'Jules said all the papers were full of the rescue at the time,' said Darina. 'He was someone back from the grave.'

'Anything else from your hectic activity?' asked William when Mike had finished making notes.

'Well, we've been following up your information about the white sports car. We haven't been able to get hold of Duval today – gone to visit some relation or other in Marseilles, apparently – but we hope to bring him in tomorrow and find out exactly what sort of car it was. We've discovered that Tait has a white Jaguar which he keeps out here, plus a Range Rover that goes back and forth.'

'What statement did he give you on his movements the day of Barrington Smythe's death?' asked William.

Mike got out a notebook and flipped back through the pages. 'He wanted to look at some property he was thinking of buying for an investment but never got to the estate agent as his car had a flat tyre and it took him for ever to change the wheel.'

'He told us something like that when he and Maura came

to lunch. But it's not much of an alibi,' said Darina, thinking it would stretch even the fertile imagination of a man like Roland to turn a puncture into an incident involving several hours.

'According to him, it took him several hours to sort it all out.'

'And he expects you to believe that?'

'I know, but he made it sound reasonably plausible. Couldn't move the nuts on the wheel. Had to walk several miles to find a telephone to phone a garage only to find it needed a phone card and he hadn't got one.'

'What about his mobile phone?' asked William looking enjoyably sceptical.

'Says the battery was out of order. Then, when he finally managed to walk to somewhere he could buy a card and find another telephone, the garage was closed for lunch. So he walked all the way back to his car and, he claims, finally managed to move the nuts and change the wheel himself. We contacted the garage where he said he took the puncture to be mended and that part of the story certainly checks out. He produced it at about three thirty and he collected it the next morning. Both occasions he was in a white Jaguar. So far we haven't been able to check any of the other details.'

'We can tell you exactly where he was, Mike.' William proceeded to give the details of his and Darina's lunch with Helen.

'That puts him firmly in the frame,' said Mike, making more notes. 'Garnier is going to be livid he failed to get any of this from La Mansard.'

'It's not looking good for Tait,' agreed William.

'Not looking good! His was the last car Duval saw going up to La Chenais that morning. He needed money and, if what Mrs Mansard says is true, by murdering Barrington

Smythe he could get his hands on a million pounds, not to mention a valuable property. *And* he gives us an elaborately false alibi. It all fits perfectly.'

'We only have Helen's word that he needs money that badly,' said Darina. 'And there are one or two details that don't quite fit in.'

'Such as?' Mike eyed the plate with the chocolate cakes and took one.

'From the timings given us by Duval and Helen, it looks as though Roland must have gone straight from the farm to the restaurant in Mougins. Yet if he killed Bernard he must have needed to change. He'd have looked pretty odd turning up at the restaurant with blood- and oil-stained clothes, yet, unless he had a change of clothes in the boot of his car, he would have had to – there wasn't time to go home for more and it would have been far too dangerous to stop at a shop.'

'You're assuming that the murder was an impulse, not premeditated,' said Mike. 'Why shouldn't Tait have planned it and been prepared with a change of clothes? Then, for an alibi, he deliberately punctures his tyre after the lunch with Mrs Mansard.'

'Wasn't it pretty reckless, though, to be seen out lunching with Helen in such a well-known restaurant?' objected Darina. 'If anyone found out about it, goodbye alibi.'

'If he had killed Bernard, he would have been under extreme stress,' said William. 'His mind may not have been working quite as coolly as usual.'

'Helen did say he seemed very odd when he arrived at the restaurant.'

'I've got to get back to Garnier and fill him in.' Mike looked at his watch. 'The meeting wasn't supposed to take long and there are a lot of lines to be followed here. However promising Tait looks, I don't think we can afford to ignore the Pemberton woman, quite apart from continuing to hammer away at the Björnson/Rickwood alibi.' He looked down at the table. 'Oh dear, I seem to have eaten both your chocolate cakes. I don't suppose you'll ever forgive me!'

'You've saved us from ourselves,' William assured him gravely. 'And your need was undoubtedly greater than ours.'

He saw him out of the apartment.

'Do you think Roland could be the killer?' asked Darina as William returned.

'I think if Duval identifies the white sports car he saw as a Jaguar, the picture's looking pretty black for him.'

'And if it turns out to have been an MG?'

'Then Anthea Pemberton has a number of questions to answer.'

'Why don't we go and put some of them to her now?'

'Now?' William looked at Darina.

'Yes, before Mike and his lot get their claws into her. Come on, it'll only take half an hour or so and she's bound to be home.'

William grabbed his leather jacket, Darina her quilted one and they took the lift down to the garage.

Chapter Twenty

Antibes rush-hour was in full swing and it took them much longer than half an hour to make their way up to the outskirts of Vence.

They found the house without difficulty. It was built of stone, three storeys high, its windows equipped with heavy shutters, the roof steeply pitched. Darina got out of their car and looked at the dark shrubs encroaching on the house. 'These give me the shivers, they seem to be wanting to take over. I'd cut the lot right back, let in more of the Provençal sun.'

There was a garage off to one side of the property. It had a window and Darina and William went and looked through it. Pressing their faces against the glass, they could just make out a white MG of considerable age.

William led the way up stone steps to the front door and rang a large brass bell that clanged noisily on the quiet air.

For several minutes nothing happened, then the door creaked open and Anthea stood there.

She looked listless and apathetic. Her print dress hung as though she'd recently lost weight, her long nose was pinched, and shadowed eyes stared out of her face. 'Oh, it's you,' was all she said.

'We were in the area and thought we'd see if you'd like

to come out for a drink,' offered Darina with spurious enthusiasm. 'You haven't got a course on, I hope?'

Anthea shook her head and pulled at a strand of hair. Then she stood back and opened the door wider. 'Why don't you come in? I've got lots of wine.'

'We don't want to impose on you.' William stepped nimbly over the threshold.

'I've been dying to tell you I bought one of your jugs after we met in Tourettes. It's going to be a lovely souvenir of our honeymoon,' said Darina, following them both into the house.

Anthea led them straight through to the kitchen. 'I live in here when the courses aren't on, except when I'm in my studio.' She stopped in the middle of the room. 'Did you really buy one of my jugs?'

Darina nodded. 'Quite a large one, with a lovely grey and blue glaze.' She gave a small laugh. 'I think I'll have to carry it on to the plane if we're to get it home in one piece.'

Anthea's depressed mouth lifted at the corners and for a brief moment she looked almost pretty. 'I'll get the wine,' she said.

'You have a lot of admirers,' Darina went on as the girl placed three wine glasses on the large scrubbed pine table and opened the fridge door. 'Björn Björnson is another – he was telling me all about you this morning.'

There was a crash and Anthea looked up, stricken. Broken on the tiles was a bottle of white wine, glass scattered all around, pale liquid splashed around her feet. 'Oh, I'm so sorry, I don't know what happened. The bottle must have been slippery.'

'Where's your pan and brush?' Darina asked, as William bent and started picking up the larger pieces of glass. 'No, don't move – your shoes look so light the glass could cut

246

through them – just tell me where they're kept.'

A few moments later it was all cleared up, Darina and William were sitting at the kitchen table and Anthea had found another bottle of wine and given it to William to open.

'I'm so sorry,' she said again. 'Everything seems to be going wrong for me these days.' She collapsed into a chair. Darina thought that if she'd been a teddy bear, stuffing would be escaping from worn seams.

'Helen told us you'd lost your partner,' she said encouragingly as William filled the three glasses with one of the local white wines.

Anthea rotated the glass on the table between her fingers. 'Kevin was no loss,' she said at last.

'Weren't you running the courses with him?' offered William.

'You mean I ran them and he swaggered about making everybody think how wonderful he was,' Anthea said with deep bitterness. 'I should have seen him for what he was as soon as we met.'

'Where was that?'

'At a similar sort of set-up in Devon. I'd been invited along as a guest potter and he was in charge of the painting side.'

'Is he a good painter?'

'He thinks so!'

'What do you think?'

Anthea appeared to treat this question seriously. Her full lower lip was sucked in and two small white front teeth bit into it as she considered her response. 'He has great colour values and he's a good draughtsman,' she said at last. 'His trouble is he has no real creativity but he can copy anything.' She laughed briefly, harshly. 'He'd make a good forger and maybe that's what he'll come to in the end,

247

when Miss America dumps him, as she's bound to when she discovers all he's really interested in is Kevin Dalton. I just hope someone's tying up all her money for her.'

'Did he get at yours?' William asked gently.

Anthea drank some of her wine. 'Thank heavens Mother's lawyer took care he couldn't. Kevin wanted the house to be in both our names and for us to have a joint bank account. I was so crazy about him I'd have agreed to anything.' She looked at her guests, her eyes painfully honest. 'It was the first time anyone had said they were in love with me. He dazzled me, I thought he was wonderful.' She looked around the kitchen. 'I used to have lots of photographs of him but I got rid of them all after he left. Tore them up and then made a bonfire of the pieces. Burnt them ceremonially on this table in one of my bowls. Then I broke the bowl and buried the pieces in the garden. But I forgot about the press cuttings.' She levered herself out of the chair and disappeared. A few minutes later she was back, carrying a well-filled scrapbook. 'Kevin was so good at getting the press to write about the courses, and him, of course. This woman came out and stayed with us.' Anthea opened the book and showed a double page spread torn from some glossy magazine. It was headlined: *Art en Vacances*. 'We got a lot of bookings after this appeared.' She turned the book so Darina could see. 'That's Kevin and me.'

The full-colour picture showed a tall man in his mid-thirties, his arm round an Anthea younger by several years than the one who sat at the table. His face was open and self-admiring, his clothes flamboyant, his abundant fair hair drawn back in a pony-tail. He was laughing into the camera. Anthea was gazing up at him, adoration making her long face attractive.

It struck Darina that what Anthea required from life was

someone to need her. This highly unsatisfactory Kevin had made her feel wanted. So did the people who came on her courses. Maybe, in some way, Bernard had too. She looked from the vibrant girl on the page to the washed-out woman sitting at the kitchen table.

It was as if Anthea had been drained of every life-giving force. Darina remembered how she had been when they had seen her in the café with Bernard. Angry, yes, maybe even full of hate, but vibrating, energy sparking off her. Now the only real indication she'd given so far that someone was still inside her was that moment she had dropped the bottle of wine. Then, for an instant, some indefinable emotion had blazed out of the dark holes that were her eyes.

'This must have been quite a coup,' said William.

'It filled our courses for almost a whole year. I still get the odd enquiry referring to it.'

'When's your next course?' he asked.

'Easter.'

'Are you full then?'

'About half.' Her voice was dull, devoid of concern. But there'd been no hesitation in her replies, her brain was in full working order however exhausted her body.

'We'd like to help you, if we can, Anthea,' William was saying now.

Once again something leapt into the deeply shadowed dark eyes. 'Why do you think I need help?' A croak in her voice betrayed nervousness.

'We saw you with Bernard in Tourettes that morning, just before he was killed,' Darina said, leaning forward and taking hold of one of Anthea's hands. It lay limp in hers, limp and cold, so cold it was hard to believe warm blood reached any part of it. 'After we found Bernard's body, we had to tell the police everything we knew about his

249

movements.' She paused a moment before adding, 'Including the fact that you seemed to be having an argument. If you could tell us what it was about, maybe we can help sort things out.'

There was no response from Anthea. For a brief moment Darina thought of Terri, of how scornfully she would have reacted to any such proposal. Get lost, she would have said. How on earth could telling you anything help me?

'I suppose Helen has told you about me . . . about me and Bernard,' Anthea said listlessly at last, disengaging her hand. She drank more wine. 'I never intended anything to happen between us.' Her tone was invested with a touch of passion. 'It wasn't like that at all.'

'What was it like?' Darina hoped Anthea wasn't going to lose her momentum again.

'He was a friend. I . . . I haven't had many friends. Bernie did my accounts, he sorted out things, I mean things with the French, like the new electricity meter I needed and the time I had a car accident and they were trying to tell me it was all my fault. If the insurance hadn't paid, I'd never have been able to afford to have had the car repaired. Bernie got it all organized.' Anthea sat swivelling her wine glass around in her hands. 'He worried about me.' She looked up with appeal in her eyes. 'He told me that. Said he worried about me.'

'So when did things change between you?' Darina asked. William was sitting back in his chair, quietly drinking his wine and leaving this bit to her.

Anthea gave a little shrug. 'Helen was getting so ratty with him. Nothing he did seemed right, she was always making snide remarks. Like how he was hardly God's gift to women.' She raised her eyes from contemplating her glass. 'That's so cruel! As though Bernard could help that he wasn't tall and desperately attractive. I mean, that's nothing if the person inside isn't attractive, is it? Like Kevin. He was attractive and didn't he know it! But inside he was mean and grasping and thought of nobody but himself. Bernard wasn't like that at all.' Another little pause.

'When I first met them, Bernard and Helen, I thought what a lovely couple they were. She seemed warm and generous, always happy to see you. He adored her and she was like a child with a puppy, always pulling its ears and stroking it, you know?'

'And then it changed?'

'Not all at once, sort of gradually. I began to find it wasn't nearly as nice to be with them. And Bernard started coming over here, to look over my accounts and sometimes just to chat. It was as though he needed to get out of the house. But then the olive harvest began and he was busy with the mill.' She fiddled with the glass again. 'I . . . I missed him.' Then life came to her face as she said, 'But we met in the evenings, I'd go over there for a meal, or they'd come here.'

'Were things any better between Bernard and Helen?'

She shook her head. 'Helen didn't seem to be as annoyed by him as before but it was awful the way Bernard was always trying so hard to be nice to her. Then he was fascinated by the olive business and Helen wasn't really interested.'

'She must have been!' protested Darina. 'She loves olive oil.'

'She may like the oil, but she was bored to tears by the trees and the picking and milling.'

'Bernard must have been upset she couldn't share his interest,' commented Darina.

'I think that's why he liked seeing me so much.' There was a ghost of a glow about Anthea now, a reflection, as if in an ancient silvered mirror, of a former excitement. 'I loved hearing him talk about olives, about the trees and the fruit. You know olives aren't native to this region? The Romans brought them here and they thrived. Provence isn't really French at all. Did you know Nice was once an Italian state? So much of its food is Mediterranean, peppers and aubergines, pasta and, of course, the oil. Do you know it's practically impossible to kill an olive tree?'

'I thought bad frosts killed them. Didn't they have an awful one in the middle fifties?'

'Lots were practically wiped out and many trees were cut down but they started growing again from the roots. Bernard said that's what happens. The roots are so strong that if the trunk is killed or just cut down, they keep throwing up new shoots. But it takes years before a new olive tree will fruit. Bernard said it was like raising children. You spend years caring for them, protecting and feeding them.' Anthea's eyes started to fill with tears. 'Once they start producing, though, they go on and on, returning value for all you have given them.'

'Doesn't sound too much like any children I know,' commented William drily.

But Darina's attention was riveted on Anthea and the tears that were now running faster and faster down her cheeks. Silent, hopeless tears that she made no effort to wipe away, escaping from her eyes like a basin with a running tap whose overflow had been blocked. 'You're pregnant!' she said, as light dawned.

'No!' Anthea wailed. 'Not now!'

'You mean?'

Anthea felt in a pocket, produced a handkerchief and tried to staunch the flow. 'It was only that one night! All those years with Kevin and I never got pregnant.'

'You mean you wanted to?'

'I thought it would keep us together. He was good with

252

children, he liked them. But nothing happened. Then, just that one night!' She dabbed hopelessly at her eyes.

Darina placed a hand on hers. 'Tell us about it.'

Anthea gave a great gulp and looked down at the hand. 'I suppose I'd better tell you. Helen's probably given you her version anyway.' She dabbed again at her eyes and this time seemed to have some effect. 'My wretched car was on the blink again and Bernard fetched me. Which was really good of him because it's half an hour each way. When he arrived he told me that Helen was in a foul mood and he was really glad I was coming. And she was. Snapping at me and treating Bernard like dirt. Finally Bernard told her if she didn't improve, he'd be off – he was tired of living with a shrew.'

'And what did Helen say?'

'She snapped back that he could do what he liked, she was fed up with both him and his bloody oil mill.' Anthea gave a small, bleak smile. 'So he said he would remove himself immediately and he'd expect her to make other arrangements. What he meant by that, I have no idea. Then he grabbed me and said he was driving me home now. I – I was terrified. He'd been drinking a lot and the road here isn't precisely straight. He could hardly get the key into the BMW's door. So I took it from him and told him I was going to drive.' She sniffed determinedly and said, 'Well, I don't have to paint in all the numbers for you, do I? I certainly wouldn't have let him drive back even if he'd wanted to. But at first all he wanted was more to drink. And to tell me how fond of me he was and that Helen was going to get her comeuppance.'

'Did he explain how?'

Anthea looked at William as though she'd forgotten he was there. 'I thought it was just one of those things you say. Anyway, he soon saw I wasn't interested in hearing

253

about Helen and, well, we woke up in bed together.' More tears started to roll down her face 'And he'd been so sweet to me and so bitchy about Helen I thought we really had a future together.'

'So what happened?'

Anthea looked at William with the eyes of someone drowning. 'I should have known by how odd he was that morning. Hardly said anything to me and disappeared back to Helen as soon as he was dressed. I thought maybe he was hung over and waited for him to return or ring me, or something.'

'Nothing?' asked Darina.

'Not a bloody word!' She got angry. 'He made me feel used! As though I was no better than a whore! After we'd been such friends.'

'Did you ring him?'

She sniffed, managing to make it sound both defensive and self-mocking. 'What do you think? Helen answered, every time. At first I pretended nothing had happened, asked when they were coming over to have a meal with me. Helen more or less accused me of trying to make off with Bernard. Made it sound as though everything was fine with them until I came along. She told me Bernard had confessed everything and she'd forgiven him – as though he was the only one who'd done anything wrong. Finally I realized it was hopeless, another of life's nasty little jokes on me, best forgotten.'

'But then you discovered you were pregnant?'

Anthea gave another sniff. 'I wasn't going to try ringing again, so I wrote him a letter.'

'Did you tell him you were having a baby?'

'No, I just said I had to see him. When I didn't get an answer, I went along to the mill – that afternoon you were both there. Later that evening Bernard did finally ring me and we arranged to meet in Tourettes. I think by then I knew it was hopeless but I just wanted him to tell me that himself. Everything was so awful!' Tears cascaded down her face.

'What did he say when you told him?'

'He was furious, said I should have taken precautions, as though it was all *my* fault! It was quite obvious he had no intention of looking after me or acknowledging the child.'

'And that was when you decided you couldn't have the baby?'

Anthea nodded. 'I'd already discussed the possibility with my doctor. I'm so regular that when I was overdue, I knew, I just knew I was pregnant, and eventually he confirmed it. So after that meeting with Bernard, I went and told him I wanted an abortion. It's so easy here, they've developed some sort of pill. You just go along and take it, stay in the clinic for the rest of the day until it's all over and then go home. I had it done yesterday.'

No wonder she looked so washed-out and hopeless. 'Not on your own, I hope?' asked Darina.

Anthea shook her head. 'Björn took me and brought me home. He ...' Anthea gulped then said, '... he's been awfully kind, a real friend.'

'You seem very close,' Darina said slowly.

Anthea coloured a painful red. 'He's just a friend. I know he has this dreadful reputation with women,' she hurried on, 'but he isn't really like that. Not with me, anyway,' she added.

'And he knows about you and Bernard?' William inserted the question.

'I had to tell someone and he knew just how miserable I was. It was even worse than when Kevin left.'

Darina thought how close they must be. There was something odd here. How had Björn, sophisticated, worldly, mixing with the rich and socially adept, become friends with this forlorn little soul?

'No doubt you both enjoy talking about working with clay,' Darina said, putting as much understanding into her voice as she could.

Anthea suddenly downed the remainder of her wine. 'What must you think of me, pouring all this out on you? I'm sorry. You must come again when I'm more myself.' She stood up hurriedly, picked up the now empty bottle from the table and carried it over to the sink. Opening the cupboard door, she deposited it in the waste bin with a determined clunk then looked pointedly at the clock on the wall, now showing nearly seven.

There was no mistaking her message.

Darina and William rose. 'We'll give you a ring in a day or two to see how you are,' Darina said. She found no difficulty in being sympathetic towards Anthea. Life seemed to have treated her with more than a little harshness. No wonder she had looked so bitter and full of hate as Bernard had left the bar that morning.

Chapter Twenty-One

'I can understand Bernard being in such a tizz when he left her that morning,' said William as he started the car. 'One night's nooky and he stood to lose all he'd organized over here, and found himself a prospective father as well. I'm surprised Anthea wasn't a murder victim herself.'

'Don't you think she got a raw deal as well?'

'Should have known what she was on about.'

'That's pretty tough. Bernard and Helen weren't married and if what she says is true, it wasn't looking as though their relationship was going to last.'

'Can we believe what she says is true?'

'About Bernard, I think so. But I don't think she's being quite straight about her relationship with Björn Björnson.'

'What do you think is going on there?'

'I don't think. I can't imagine she was having an affair with him as well as Bernard.'

'She certainly doesn't strike me as the sort of female Björnson would be interested in. But then I would have said that about Bernard as well, so where does that leave us?'

'Could he be a silent partner in her courses?'

'Wouldn't have thought so. He'd be unlikely to get much of a return on any money he invested.'

Darina couldn't think of anything else to suggest, and neither could William.

'Shall we go out for a meal?' he asked as they approached their apartment.

'Not after that lunch. Why don't I call in at the shops and get a bottle of that excellent-looking *soupe de poissons* from the *épicerie*?'

'Ideal. Then we can have a cosy evening together. See if you can get some *rouille* as well. Fish soup without that spicy mayonnaise on top is like steak and kidney without the kidney. Oh, and don't forget a *baguette* as well if they've got one left.'

'You'll be lucky.' Darina picked up her bag from the back seat. 'Let me out here and I can do the shopping while you put the car away.'

There was only one customer ahead of her at the *épicerie* but she took her time at the cash desk and Darina was afraid William would think she'd got lost. She almost expected to see him coming to find out what was happening.

The fact that he hadn't was explained by the sound of voices as she opened the apartment door.

She dropped her shopping in the kitchen and went through to the living room.

In the chair by the balcony window was Roland Tait.

He broke off what he was saying and rose as she came in. 'Forgive me for disturbing you like this, Darina, but I had to come.'

'Helen rang Roland and told him we knew all about their lunch,' said William, rising also. 'Can I get you a drink?'

On the table between him and Roland were two glasses of whisky. After all the wine, both with lunch and at Anthea's, Darina couldn't face more alcohol. 'A mineral water, please, with ice and lemon.'

'Roland was saying he'd hoped they could keep their –

what was the word you used? Relationship? Yes, that was it – keep their relationship a secret,' William said as he organized the drink for her.

'How long did you hope to keep it secret?' Darina asked.

Roland bristled. 'It was only a little fling,' he said. 'Nothing to disturb anyone.'

'A little fling?' Darina ejaculated. 'Tell Helen that!'

'Come on, darling! Women always inflate these things beyond their true worth,' said William.

Darina looked at him sharply and he returned her gaze with a bland smile. 'I think the way you chaps stick together is disgusting.'

'Roland, explain to this wife of mine how we men operate.'

'Yes, Roland, do try.' Darina sat back with a cordial smile, hiding her delight that she and William were operating as a team.

Roland glanced uneasily from one to the other. 'Helen's a lovely woman,' he said aggressively. 'No doubt she told you we knew each other many years ago.'

'And that she left her husband for you,' said Darina pleasantly.

'Now, now, darling, let the man tell the story his way.' William topped up Roland's whisky, adding a splash of water to the glass.

Roland drank deeply, then sat thinking about things. His hosts waited patiently. 'Helen is the sexiest woman I know,' he started and his voice had changed. This wasn't a man trying to spin a cobweb of half-truths and lies – this was the truth, as he saw it. 'She can make my engine motor with a flick of her hip. Those months before she left her husband, sex-wise, were the most exciting of my life. God, I spent my time in a ferment, trying to organize her into bed. What with her husband, her children, her work, not to mention the small fact that I was building a career for myself and needed to be hustling in the City, not chasing her round some sleazy hotel bedroom, things have never been so complicated.' He looked up from the drink, his eyes stark and full of a weird excitement. 'But, Jesus, I was alive! Even when I wasn't with her, I could smell her on my hands, and my fingers could feel her skin. I heard her laugh in my ears, felt her hair brushing my naked shoulders. I'd be in the throes of some complicated financial deal and suddenly I'd be so horny I'd have to leave the room. I tell you, my life was going to pot and I didn't care.' He fell silent again.

'And then Helen left her husband,' prompted Darina.

Roland roused himself to continue. 'And that's when it all fell apart. She and the kids came to live with me. I had a flat in one of the first warehouse buildings to be converted on the docks. All open-plan and plain brickwork. It was never intended for children. Those two were everywhere, fighting, crying, crawling, their toys turning the floor into a minefield. Helen's cooking overflowed the kitchen area and I'd come back from a hard day stirring the City's money pots to find every surface not taken over by homework or some comic was covered with chapattis or naan bred – she was into Indian food at that stage and the bedroom was buried in the typescript she was churning out for a book on it, my trouser press had been thrown out to give room for a table for her typewriter.

'And all that magnificent sex disappeared. She'd be harassed, driven out of her mind by those wretched kids, trying to work and look after them, James ringing her up every day to beg her to come back, and by the fact that she had to hike miles to a decent food shop and she couldn't find daytime babysitters. That meant she couldn't get to any of the press dos she said kept her sane and in the swim. By the time she'd got the kids into bed and reheated something she'd cooked during the day, both of us would be too tired to do anything more but fall into bed and sleep. Where all the energy of the previous months had gone, I'll never know. And whereas before I'd been putting together deals as though I was some magic Superglue, now everything I touched fell apart.' The two deep lines running either side of Roland's mouth strengthened until they became crevasses. His hand drummed at the table, a soundless rhythm repeated over and over that was maddening in its inevitability.

'So you told her to leave, that it was all over?' asked William dispassionately.

Roland gave him a smile of grim amusement. 'I came back one day screwing up my courage to do just that, knowing that I wouldn't, any more than I had the previous day or the one before that, that when I started, she'd look at me with those enormous eyes and I'd fall apart and she'd swear the kids would grow up, she would clean up. Did you know she's the worst housewife in the world? She can cook up a storm but as for keeping anything clean or seeing the clothes are washed and the odd button sewn on, forget it! I was doing more household chores than she was. Anyway, I realized something was odd as I put the key in the door but it was only when I opened it that it hit me, the place was quiet – no screaming kids, no Helen shouting at them to stuff it, no radio blaring out threatening the walls. They'd gone. The toy obstacle course, the food decorating the bookcases, the wet washing on the radiators, the cooking in the kitchen, all gone. I went into the bedroom and there was no paperwork and no typewriter. I went back into the main room and sitting on the Italian glass and chrome side-table I was always so terrified the kids were going to slam into and break during one of their fights was a note. In it, Helen said she was returning to James, she'd always love me but she thought it was better for everybody.'

Roland slumped down in the chair.

'What did you do?' asked Darina, trying to imagine Helen with her life disintegrating around her. Then she compared Helen's situation with Anthea's. At least Helen had had someone else to fall back on.

'I had a huge whisky and made a note to book a cleaning company in the morning to come and turn the place out.' Roland seemed to realize she was expecting something more from him and added, 'I couldn't feel anything but the most enormous relief. It was as though some madness had been removed from my blood.'

'You didn't contact her, then?'

'I wrote to her. Said I admired her courage, that she'd done the right thing and she would always be the most wonderful memory.'

'And then you got on with your life.'

'I got married, to a sexy socialite with a great ass, an address book filled with the movers and the shakers, and a talent for entertaining. My life rocked back on to the rails and I got on with building my career.'

'When did the marriage fall apart?' enquired William, leaning back in his chair with his arms behind his head, listening to Roland with all the attention of a high-price ticket holder at the hottest show in town.

Roland shrugged his shoulders. 'It was all a long time ago. Familiarity bred contempt on both sides, she got bored with grinding edges off the rough diamond, I went off her ass.'

'Did you marry again?'

'Too expensive, chum. Caroline took me for everything she could. After that I reckoned I'd do better freelancing.'

'Until Maura came along?'

'Maura and I have a loose sort of arrangement that suits us both.' Something in Roland's eyes shifted and Darina knew he was by no means blind to Maura's needs.

'And you never had any contact with Helen?'

'From the day she walked out of that Docklands flat to one evening several months ago, nary a word.'

'So meeting her down here was a bit of a shock?'

'Bill, lad, it was like opening the door on some treasure trove you'd locked up years ago and forgotten. Except when you looked at those jewels again, you knew something in you had compared them with every other jewel that had come along. And for some reason you'd refused to recognize that the others were wanting.'

Poor Maura, thought Darina. 'So it was serious, after all,' she said.

Roland's hands got busy with his drink and he avoided meeting her eyes. 'Look,' he said at last, his face serious, a piece of hair falling boyishly over his forehead, 'our affair was over twenty years ago. For a time after we met up again here, it was as if I'd recaptured all the adrenaline and energy of my late twenties. I'd have done anything to get her back into bed as often as possible.' He made a small sweeping gesture with his hand. 'But no effort was necessary. She fell off the tree like a ripe peach.'

'You weren't worried about Maura or Bernard finding out?'

Roland gave a Gallic shrug. 'Maura knows the score by now. And I owed Bernard no favours, not after what he'd done to me with Lloyd's.'

Darina waited for William to pick up on that but for the moment he seemed disinclined to distract Roland from his relationship with Helen. Instead he asked, 'When did history start repeating itself?'

Roland shifted in the chair; his immaculately clad legs in

their checked trousers crossed and recrossed themselves but he said nothing.

'Helen began to suggest you made things more permanent, that now there weren't children to complicate matters and both of you had secure careers, you could make life perfect by living together?' Darina suggested.

'She didn't understand.' Roland leant forward earnestly, an expression of transparent honesty on his face. 'She couldn't see that what we had together was terrific sex but nothing else. She's too selfish, she could never manage life the way Maura does.'

It struck Darina that Helen and Roland were perfect partners for each other, that no one deserved to be landed with either of them the way Bernard and Maura had been.

'And what about the money that Helen was offering you to help with all your Lloyd's losses?' she asked, furious with him and uncaring that it mightn't be the right time to bring this up.

'Money?' he asked innocently.

'She has a property which must be quite valuable, not to mention the bearer bonds.'

'Look, I don't know what she's been telling you but let me say this . . .' his face became ever more transparently frank, 'Helen likes to think there's something she can bring me. She thinks we failed last time because there wasn't enough money, that if she'd been able to engage someone to look after the kids, we'd still be together. Well, I can't disillusion her, can I? I can't tell her she's still a slut and I'd go mad if we lived together. As for money, I admit I've lost a packet at Lloyd's but I'm not that desperate and, even if I was, property can take for ever to raise cash on. It's sweet of her to want to help but it could take months to sell the farm.'

'But not so the bearer bonds.' William's voice had

acquired a cutting edge that made Roland look at him closely.

'I don't know anything about any bearer bonds.' He gave a little laugh that contained a sneer. 'I know Helen's never been able to hold on to money. When she left James, she was full of the publishing advance she was due. But nearly the whole of that had to go to the bank to pay off an overdraft and keep the manager off her back. She hasn't changed. One of the first things she said to me after we met down here was that she was desperate to finish her current book because she needed the next tranche of her advance.'

'So she never mentioned bearer bonds to you?' asked William slowly.

'How many times have I to tell you? Look, if anyone offered me anything like that, do you think I'd refuse? Cash, particularly at this time, is always useful.'

'Even when it comes with Helen attached?' offered Darina.

His wry smile admitted she had a point there.

'So how are you managing your Lloyd's losses?' William enquired pointedly.

'My dear old chap, I know my way around, I'm credit worthy. There are always sources I can call on.'

He looked confident as he said it and raised the whisky glass to his lips in a gesture that carried something of a flourish.

Darina found she was very angry. So angry she could hardly speak.

William shot her a warning look. Leave this to me, it said, don't blow it. 'Now that's something that women don't understand,' he said to Roland. 'They see money in terms of how much is in or not in their bank account. And, like Helen, a letter from the manager complaining about their overdraft reduces them to quivering jelly. Whereas, at your level, the more you owe the bank, the more you have them at your mercy.'

'Too right, Bill.' Roland's legs scissored across themselves again and he settled himself more comfortably into his chair.

'I can see that for some of Bernard's members, the losses could be catastrophic. Those retired, like Sir Robert, for instance, or a widow with no resources. But for a high player in the financial markets such as yourself, perhaps it would be nothing more than a momentary setback.'

Roland remained silent but a small smile played around his mouth and his eyes snapped agreement.

'So was it perhaps galling that Helen should think you needed her to come to your aid?'

'Do you know, I hadn't looked on it like that.' Roland leaned forward with an air of spontaneous discovery. 'But you're right, Bill, you're right!' He turned to Darina with a hint of apology in his voice. 'It was sweet of her to want to help, of course it was. But there was nothing she could do. I didn't need her.'

Darina couldn't bring herself to smile back at him so she got up, went into the kitchen, found some cocktail biscuits, emptied them into a small glass bowl, brought them back and placed the bowl on the table in front of Roland.

He helped himself to a handful automatically, his eyes narrowed. Darina could imagine him sitting just like that while he weighed up the viability of a dodgy deal that was being offered to him.

'Did Helen tell you your car was seen going up to the farm that morning?' William added.

'That morning?' Roland seemed to come to a decision. He looked confidingly at William, his eyes wide with an innocent openness that could have belonged to an altar boy carrying out his sacred functions with an old-age pensioner's savings in his back pocket beneath the shining white surplice. 'Look, I'll be absolutely frank with you – with you both,' he encompassed Darina in his open gaze. 'As Englishmen together in a foreign country. Then perhaps you can advise me what to do.' His voice lowered confidentially. 'I was due to meet Helen for lunch. I hadn't decided to tell her it was over but the thought was definitely on my mind. I knew what we had together wasn't going to lead anywhere, and it would only be fair to Helen to make that clear. Apart from that, I couldn't carry on being such a shit to Maura.

'I was working on some papers in my study when Bernard rang and demanded I come up to the farm. I guessed immediately that he'd found out about Helen and me and I had half a mind to say I couldn't but then I thought, damn it, I'd go and tell him he had nothing to worry about and then finish with Helen at lunchtime.'

Darina tried to visualize Roland reassuring Bernard, the man he held responsible for losing him large sums of money, that he had no designs on Helen – and failed.

Roland cleared his throat and continued. 'So I went up to the farm.'

'What time was this?' asked William.

'Time?' For a moment Roland was thrown. 'Oh, I suppose somewhere around twelve twenty. I was supposed to meet Helen at twelve thirty at Mougins. I knew I was going to be a little late but, well,' he gave an engaging little laugh, 'if she was pissed off with me, it was going to make breaking off our little affair that much easier, wasn't it?'

'So, you drove up to the farm.' William repeated his words. 'Was anyone else there?'

'Not that I could see. That ropy old Citroën Bernard drives around when he can't get hold of Helen's BMW was there but that was all. No one answered the door but Bernard would hardly have gone out, not after summoning me the way he had, so I went round to the mill.'

Roland suddenly put down his glass and covered his face with his hands. 'God, I wish I hadn't. I wish I'd never gone near the farm. I never want to see anything like that again.' His hands dropped down and his face was seared with the nearest Darina had yet seen to genuine emotion from him. 'Bernard was there all right. His head was stuck in a pail of oil and his hands looked as though the medieval torturers had been at him.' He looked at Darina. 'God knows I'd wished every evil on him ever since I realized what the Lloyd's situation was, but never that.'

'What did you do then?' asked William.

Roland swung round to meet his gaze. 'Got back in my car and high-tailed it down the lane as though the hounds of hell were after me. Whatever had happened in that mill I wanted no part of.'

'Except that when you realized Duval had seen you and your highly recognizable car, you stopped and offered him a large sum to forget you'd been anywhere near there.' William made it a statement rather than a question.

'Isn't that what you would have done?' Roland asked.

Chapter Twenty-Two

'Do you believe him?' Darina asked William after they had said goodbye to Roland. He had left perky and confident, swearing he had told Helen at their lunch it would be better if they didn't see each other again.

'Which particular part of his story did you have in mind?'

'The bit when he said that Bernard was dead when he arrived at the mill.'

'On balance, probably, yes.'

'But you doubt other aspects of what he said?'

'Don't you?'

'If I have to choose between either his or Helen's version of their affair, I think my instincts are with Helen. I'm not blind to her faults. I know she exaggerates, that she lives in pretty much of a mess and muddle, can't manage money, and that she's always been ambitious. I also think she can blind herself to certain aspects of any relationship.'

'If you accept all that, you must be able to accept Roland's version of events.'

'Except I don't think she'd lie about the money side.'

'Ah, yes, the bearer bonds.'

'I think he's lying to protect himself. I think he's desperate for money and that he'd even accept Helen if she could produce it.'

269

'The question is, did he kill to get his hands on those bonds? Did he go up to the farm with a blunt instrument and a change of clothing in his car and despatch the miller? Then go off to meet his mistress who was also the mistress of the man he'd just murdered? If so, he's a very cool customer!'

'Helen said he was upset, not at all himself.'

'Hmm.' William thought about it for a while. 'At least we now know for certain whose the white sports car was Duval saw going up to the farm.'

'And Roland's story bears out Stephen's story.'

'As to that, Stephen said he didn't know who Helen's companion was. If he and his sister lived with Roland for several months, wouldn't he have recognized him?'

'Come on, they were little more than babies. Something like two and three years old.'

'Ah, I didn't realize they were that young. So that could all tie in. And I suppose Bernard would recognize a description of Roland from Stephen?'

'Maybe he was already suspicious of Roland. Anthea said it was obvious that things between Bernard and Helen were pretty rocky.'

'OK. Still, even given all that, I don't see why Roland would obey a summons from Bernard unless he wanted to do him some damage.' Before Darina could respond, William had another thought. 'Unless, of course, Bernard threatened to tell Maura. That might have had him up there like a shot.'

'You mean, even with Helen waving a million pounds' worth of bearer bonds under his nose, Roland didn't want to risk losing Maura?'

'She makes him supremely comfortable, provides him with a classy background, and he finds her physically attractive. I wouldn't put it past him to reckon he could

270

borrow the money off Helen and still manage to keep Maura. There's only one thing that puzzles me.'

Darina smiled. 'What Maura sees in Roland?'

'Precisely.'

'He really is very attractive, I'm afraid, and some women just seem to go for shits.' She gave a brief sigh for the fallibility of her sex. 'Back with Bernard, though, the one time I felt Roland really was telling us the truth was when he described how he found Bernard's body at the mill. It was exactly how I felt when I first saw him there.'

'Except you hauled him out of the pail and Roland left him there.'

'Perhaps if I'd realized I could be top of any list of suspects, I'd have skedaddled too.'

William looked unconvinced. 'Well, let's for the moment assume you are right and that Roland did not kill Bernard. Who's your candidate for murderer instead?'

'The most obvious suspect has to be whoever was in the Saab that Duval saw going up the drive before the white sports car.'

'Rickwood or Björnson?'

'How long do you think it will take to get an answer from the army to Mike's fax?'

'At least twenty-four hours, I would think. Someone will have to do some checking among some pretty dusty records. I don't think there's much more we can do until then.'

'So what's your suggestion for tomorrow?'

'Why don't we drive into Italy?'

'Italy?'

'It wouldn't take us long, we could enjoy an Italian lunch.'

'And buy some Parmesan cheese and perhaps some *prosciutto*.'

'I hear the whisky's pretty cheap there too.'

'I think that sounds a wonderful plan.'

271

The next day was overcast but the rain looked like holding off and William and Darina saw no reason to alter their programme.

'Björn told me of a nice little place to visit in Italy that has a good restaurant for lunch,' Darina said as they passed Nice airport, having elected for Route National Sept rather than the motorway, at least until after Monte Carlo.

'Let's try it!'

Darina screwed round in her seat to get the map out of the back of the car and took another look at the airport. 'It's incredible it's not much more than a week since we landed here. I'd forgotten just how close it is. No wonder Roland and the Rickwoods find they can commute backwards and forwards so easily, and how easy it must be for Björn to get anywhere in the world.'

'Not the sort of existence I'd care for, though,' said William.

'Not down on the coast, no. It's like a luxurious rat cage. But up in the hills, there's a life that goes back to Roman times. Some of the locals there follow traditional occupations almost as though nothing has changed. Think of Duval and his oil mill. I can understand Björn and Roland and Bernard wanting to defend their homes there.'

'Hmm,' said William.

Italy seemed scruffier and less prosperous than France. Ventimiglia, the border town, looked from the main road to be everything that border towns so often are, bustling and shabby, with an air of impermanence. Beyond, however, the countryside took on Italian charm, displaying old stone towns, many perched on hills that might have strayed from some Renaissance painting.

Darina guided them to the village that Björn had talked about, crowded round the peak of yet another picturesque hill. They explored narrow streets edged with terraced stone houses and finally found the recommended restaurant, tucked away in a back street. Friendly, almost deserted, its décor unthreatening, Darina and William sank thankfully on to the high-backed chairs in the dim dining room.

'Am I being ungrateful, finding this a relief after all the bustle round Antibes?' asked Darina, deciding on pasta with mussels followed by wild boar. She put down the menu and studied an old print decorating plaster walls brushed with the patina of age.

'Ah, hankering after the Seychelles?'

'Certainly not! How boring that would have been!' Darina gave William's hand a squeeze and was disconcerted to find his attention diverted elsewhere.

'Good heavens!' he said.

Darina turned and saw Jules Rickwood entering the restaurant, dressed in a casual outfit that shrieked Italian chic: navy pleated skirt with white polka dots topped by a striped cardigan over a simple little top. Handing her carefully down the couple of steps was her husband.

They saw Darina and William in the same instant and just for a moment Darina thought they looked as though they would like to disappear. But it was too late.

They had no option but to come over. 'Well, well, fancy meeting you here!' said John.

'Would it be an intrusion if we asked to join you?' suggested Jules in her soft voice. An underlying tension in the tones caught Darina's attention. Now that she looked at Jules properly, she saw dark shadows under her eyes and a look of strain on her face that hadn't been there before.

John, too, looked like a man who had escaped from an unpleasant situation, only to find himself stuck in one that might be worse.

Darina's initial disappointment that their Italian idyll had been broken was swept away.

'Please, we would love it,' she said, as William rose and

pulled out a chair for Jules. 'I've been feeling guilty that we never rang to apologize for running out on you that evening,' she added as Jules sat down.

Jules summoned up another smile. 'I was just so embarrassed. I'm the one who should have rung and apologized. That terrible scene!'

'It was unforgivable,' agreed John as he pulled up another chair. 'Theresa has this uncanny ability to drive one to the edge of screaming insensibility. I really don't know how she does it.'

As he sat down, Darina searched for some sort of likeness to his daughter and finally decided Terri had inherited the squareness of his forehead and the directness of his eyes. Yet, even as his met hers, their glance moved away.

The waiter arrived to take the Rickwoods' orders. John, after a brief glance at the wine list, ordered a bottle of Italian Chardonnay and Jules said, 'They have the most marvellous wild mushroom risotto here, that's why I insisted John bring me.' She ordered it for both of them, declining anything beforehand. 'How on earth did you two find it?'

'Björn mentioned it.'

'Björn?' Dismay tinged her voice.

Why dismay? Darina wondered if it was because she and John weren't going to be alone. But they could easily have exchanged a few words and then gone to another table. Just how well did she know the Swede?

'Ah, yes, Björn told me you had commissioned him to do a head of Darina,' John said to William. 'I was so pleased to hear that. Robert Bright cancelling the one of Lila he'd asked Björn to do was a blow. Poor Björn needs all the funds he can scrape together at the moment. And you will be very pleased with the result,' he added hastily.

Darina caught the furious glance Jules gave her husband

274

under her lowered lashes. Was she possessive about Björn or worried that they were skirting too close to alibis for the time of Bernard's death?

'But I gather you have been advising him and the other Names down here that were managed by Bernard Barrington Smythe to sue rather than pay their debts, isn't that so?' William's tone was conversational but his eyes were watchful.

Jules stopped snapping her breadstick into tiny pieces. 'Bernard defrauded his Names! He owed us – what was it you said, darling? – "due care and attention"? Yes, that was it, due care and attention. Instead, he gambled away our capital.'

'He must have lost everything himself,' commented her husband. 'If he hadn't died, I would have expected him to have to declare bankruptcy.'

'Which wouldn't have worried him at all.' Jules started on another breadstick. 'Not in that nice house with Helen, starting up another profitable business.'

'Did you know him well?' asked Darina.

Jules gave a little shrug of her shoulders. 'I used to meet him sometimes when I came down here. He was fun and he knew everyone. When I inherited from Daddy and he suggested I became a Name, it seemed a good idea.'

'I gather you found his body.' John turned to William. 'What a terrible shock for you. On your honeymoon as well!'

'It was poor Darina that actually found him. As you say, dreadful. I wish it had been me and she hadn't had to come into such close contact with the reality. I'm afraid I'm quite used to violent death.'

'Of course, you're a policeman.' John made it sound as though he had forgotten that fact.

Food arrived for Darina and William and the Rickwoods insisted they began.

'How well did you know him?' William asked John, as he twined long ribbons of tagliatelle round his fork.

'Bernard? Not at all. I met him just once, when I went up to the farm to try and get him to contribute towards his syndicate's losses.'

'With any success?'

'None, William. He was scathing. Said he was wiped out and that losses were a hazard everyone was warned of before they joined.'

'It sounds something of a fraught meeting,' Darina suggested.

'I've handled much worse,' John said briefly.

'With Jules's capital at stake, it must be a worrying time for you,' William commented.

A shrug of the shoulders. 'I won't pretend it isn't a lot of money but we can weather its loss. I've told Jules she isn't to let it bother her. Even if we have to pay first and sue later, we won't suffer.' He gave his wife a look that was the visual equivalent of wrapping a soft shawl around shoulders that needed warmth.

'John is a very successful businessman,' Jules said with a touch of complacency.

'And I understand you have been advising Björn on his position? That, in fact, you were with him the morning Bernard was killed?'

'William, surely you aren't part of the investigating team?' John said lightly but with a touch of steel in his voice.

Darina was watching Jules. Was the look she darted at William frightened?

At that moment the plates of risotto arrived and the tension was lost.

'I'm afraid old habits die hard,' said William, after the Rickwoods had begun to eat and he and Darina had been served with their main course.

'And that includes being kept informed of suspects and their movements, it seems.' Again there was that touch of steel in John's voice. Darina could understand his success in business. This man wouldn't let much stand in his way.

'Oh, can't we forget about poor Bernard and his terrible death?' pleaded Jules. 'Isn't it enough that the police came round picking over our movements that day like second-hand clothes dealers? We came here to try and get away from everything.'

'I apologize.' William turned quickly to her. 'It's unforgivable of me. Tell us, instead, about this place. You've been here before, you said?'

Darina listened to Jules describing earlier visits, giving details of the twelfth-century castle and fourteenth- and fifteenth-century houses with only half an ear. She was aware of William's frustration at being so close to one of his main suspects yet unable to pursue questioning any further without being totally out of line. Even more strongly, though, she was aware of John Rickwood's total concentration on his wife. Of the slight smile that came to his mouth as he gradually relaxed, the light in his eyes as they rested on her now animated face.

The rest of lunch passed in civilized chat on matters Italian, including a good place to buy Parmesan in Ventimiglia.

After the meal, the two couples walked back to their cars, both parked in the same public space.

'Nice car, that,' said William as John Rickwood unlocked the door of his grey Saab.

'Isn't it? I've been very pleased with it. And being diesel, it's very economic in France.' John held the door open for his wife and helped her into the passenger seat.

'Do you ever get to drive it?' Darina asked Jules.

She glanced up, laughing. 'I'm allowed to spell him on long trips.'

Darina could see William was dying to ask more about the car but, as if the other man sensed his desire, John slipped into the driver's seat and started the engine. Then he leaned across his wife to say a quick goodbye before reversing out of the parking space and accelerating away.

Darina slipped her arm through William's as they went over to their little hired car. 'What a frustrating encounter!'

'Wasn't it just? Except that his reaction to my attempted questioning was as revealing as any answer could have been.'

'You think he's got something to hide?'

'From today's evidence, I'd say definitely.'

Back in their apartment, William went straight to the telephone. 'Let's find out if Mike has heard anything back from the army on Rickwood's rescue. Where's that official number he gave me?'

'Won't he have finished for the day?'

'Come on, in the middle of an investigation?'

'I know you go on working till all hours but do the French?'

William didn't answer. He was busy with his pocket diary.

Darina took her coat off and then placed the cheese she'd bought in the fridge. Finishing that job, she found William standing in the kitchen doorway.

'What's happened? You look as though World War Three has broken out.'

'Mike Parker was taken to hospital yesterday with cyanide poisoning.'

'Cyanide? You can't be serious!'

'Apparently Mike's sharing a hotel room with Chris. Shortly after he was with us, he complained of a headache and stomach pains and went up to bed. Chris checked him a little later and found he was in a terrible state, hyperventilating, vomiting and with convulsions. He called for an ambulance. The doctor smelt almonds on Mike's breath and diagnosed cyanide poisoning. If it gets recognized soon enough, there are effective antidotes and they reckon he's going to be all right now but it was touch and go for a time and if he hadn't received treatment so promptly, Chris says it's doubtful if he would have pulled through.'

Darina's knees went weak and she sat down on the kitchen stool. 'But how? I mean, cyanide's not the sort of thing you ingest accidentally.'

William came and leant against the sink, his arms crossed over his chest, his shoulders hunched, his face full of worry. 'Mike had nothing to eat or drink after he left here. Cyanide is a quick-acting poison but the delay in the symptoms appearing suggests, according to the medics, that he ate some sort of plant. There are a number that contain cyanogenic glycosides in varying amounts.'

'Of course there are!' Darina exclaimed, memory suddenly yielding information she had forgotten about. 'I looked into dangerous plants at one time, after that awful experience when I got involved in death by poisonous mushroom, you remember? Apricot kernels contain cyanide, they can be lethal, and there are other seeds and even foliage. Do they know what Mike ate?'

William shook his head. 'The dreadful thing is, though, it had to be something he had here. You remember how he complained he hadn't eaten for hours and was starving?'

'And he didn't eat anything after he left?'

'Nary a thing. Certainly he didn't start picking bits of

279

shrubs or plants to chomp on. It couldn't, in other words, have been accidental.'

'But I only gave him left-overs of food we'd eaten ourselves.'

Then Darina looked at William and the same thought hit him. 'Except, of course, those little chocolate cakes.' Silence built between them. 'Darling, that's scary,' Darina said at last. She had a vision of William and herself struck down, alone in this apartment, not knowing who to call, perhaps without the strength to make a telephone call anyway and hoping that whatever it was would clear their systems and go away.

If they'd eaten those little cakes, they'd almost certainly be dead by now.

'Scary isn't the word for it. Not only have we nearly killed Mike but I feel sick when I think it could have happened to you.'

'And to you!'

He grinned weakly. 'I was too full of lunch to want to touch a cream *gâteau*, ever! But you're always game for something else to eat.'

Yes. If Mike hadn't eaten them first, Darina thought she might well have succumbed to the lure of the rich chocolate treat.

'Do we still have the box those cakes came in?'

Darina opened the door to the cupboard underneath the sink and investigated the contents of the waste bin. 'This is it,' she said, dragging out a soggy cardboard box. William placed it gingerly on the work top.

Darina went back to rootling around the waste bin. 'Here's the bit of paper with our names on it.' She straightened up holding an even soggier bit of paper and placed it next to the remains of the box.

'Looks as though the label could have been torn from

an envelope, perhaps a business one, the quality is too ordinary for personal notepaper. And our names are written in capitals. If we can find something to compare the writing with, an expert *might* be able to make an identification.'

'Doesn't sound too promising. But there's the name of the shop on the cake box,' Darina said. 'I think that's the little *boulangerie–pâtisserie* in the shopping precinct below.'

'Get your coat, quickly. And can we find something to put this in?' William indicated the remains of the box.

Darina found a plastic bag and slid the soggy cardboard inside.

At the little shopping centre, the French were making their last purchases of the day.

William made for the *boulangerie*.

Madame, trim, neat and seemingly as fresh as when she started her long day, asked if she could help. There were only one or two loaves left on the slatted shelves behind the counter but numerous pastries were still lined up on the glass shelves of the counter unit itself. Among the éclairs, the flaky pastries and the golden pear tarts, Darina could see a number of individual *gâteaux forêts noires* that looked remarkably like the ones she had seen Mike eat the previous evening. And yet not quite. She tried to wrench her memory back to the cakes she had placed in front of poor Mike.

William reached for the remains of the battered cardboard box.

Madame looked at it and agreed that it had indeed come from her establishment.

Following the ensuing conversation with some difficulty, Darina gathered that William was explaining that he and his new wife (Darina smiled at the proprietress with as much charm as she could muster) had been sent a present of two *gâteaux comme ça*, he pointed at the little cakes and, it was so annoying, the card had got lost and they didn't know who to thank. Could Madame perhaps describe someone who had bought two such cakes yesterday?

Madame thought briefly then shrugged her shoulders. She was desolate, but to remember one purchase among the many her shop serviced every day was impossible. *Impossible*, she repeated the word with a spread of her chubby little hands and a shake of her carefully coiffed ginger hair.

Was there an assistant, asked William, who might possibly have served the kind friend of theirs who'd purchased the *gâteaux*?

'Sophie!' yelled Madame with an astonishing volume.

A slim girl appeared from the back regions. '*Oui, Mama.*'

A rapid exchange of French ensued before Madame turned back to William and regretted that Sophie had been unable to remember serving anyone two gateaux *forêts noires* the previous day.

William thanked Madame for her help and turned to go, but Darina stepped forward and asked for two of the chocolate cakes. Madame showed no emotion but obligingly took a piece of flat cardboard, folded and slotted in the cunningly cut edges to form a box, added a doily in the bottom then placed the two *gâteaux* inside, brought the lid down on top, tied it with paper tape and handed it over with a warm smile. Darina opened her purse and brought out a fifty franc note, hoping that that would cover the cost; translating numbers from French to English always defeated her.

Pocketing the change and picking up the box, she followed William out of the shop, trying to ignore the curious glances of the couple of customers waiting to be served.

'It was always a long shot,' observed William. 'But it's a blow none the less.' His nostrils were pinched and the muscles around his eyes were tight. He was walking quickly back to their apartment block without waiting to see if she was keeping up, his shoulders still hunched. Darina realized with a shock how used she had become in the last week to a relaxed William. Now he was as twitchy as at home when involved in a testing case.

William swerved away from the front door to their block and went instead towards the *concierge*'s apartment, in the next-door block.

Again Darina struggled to understand his rapid French and the *concierge*'s replies to his questions. She couldn't keep up with it all but it seemed that the *concierge* could offer no more help than the proprietress of the *boulangerie*. She had gone out in the afternoon to sort out a problem with one of the garages and had returned to find the box sitting outside her door. That was all she knew.

William's shoulders slumped in a dispirited way. Darina felt for him. She could imagine just how much he wanted to be able to present Garnier with some concrete evidence as to where the chocolate cakes had come from.

Back in the apartment, Darina placed her box on the dining table. She undid the string, lifted the lid of the box and looked at the pieces of chocolate cake sitting on their doily. Then she dashed into the kitchen and once again went through the contents of the waste bin.

She found what she was looking for and waved it at William, who had followed her. 'Look, darling! It's different!'

In Darina's hand were the remains of a white doily. She took it back into the living room and placed it on the table by the box. The cakes she had just bought had been placed on one made from gold foil. 'And these aren't quite the same as yesterday's. There's chocolate *ganache* and *dragées* round the sides, see? The others just had it on top.'

William studied the contents of the box. 'You're sure?'

'Of course,' Darina said impatiently. 'Food's my business, remember?'

'So you're suggesting that the cakes weren't bought downstairs?'

'It would have taken a little time to doctor them, wouldn't it? I should think they had seeds added, they would have mixed in nicely with the black cherry jam. It's not the season for seeds but some shrubs hang on to theirs for ages. I can think of one or two with the right properties that could be growing around here.'

William poked a cautious finger at one of the chocolate *gâteaux*.

Darina continued. 'But no one's going to sit in a car sticking seeds into cakes with people passing to and fro. The possibility of somebody noticing and remembering would be far too great. So the cakes were prepared somewhere else and brought here. Something quite different was bought at our *pâtisserie*, then the *gâteaux* lifted on their doily and switched with whatever was in the box. Slip aside the tape and it wouldn't have taken a moment. No wonder Madame couldn't remember anyone buying those particular ones. But maybe someone noticed the box being placed on the *concierge*'s doorstep.'

'Garnier would certainly do a door-to-door inquiry. But we're dealing with someone who thinks of every possibility. I'm willing to bet we won't find anyone remembering anything significant. Even checking every *pâtisserie* around Antibes is unlikely to yield much – lots must use a doily like this.' He flicked at the limp lacy circle, creased, crumpled and stained with smears of chocolate.

'They might have been bought in a supermarket.'

'In that case, even if we managed to identify which one, it would be unlikely to help us.' William flung himself down in a chair, his expression now more worried than ever. 'It all adds up to a killer who is clever as well as ruthless and appears to consider us a threat.'

'But we aren't even part of the official investigation.'

'Something has alerted them. We must have said something to someone.'

'We've talked to nearly everyone we know is connected with the case.'

'Including a long lunch with Helen immediately before the cakes appeared.'

'She wouldn't have had time to organize them.'

'No? She did ask us if we were going straight back, remember? And she might well have specialist knowledge. It would be interesting to check her shrubs to see what she had available.'

'You've really got it in for her, haven't you?'

'I can't say she appeals to me, especially after what we heard over lunch, but personal feelings don't come into it. I'm looking at motive, means and opportunity. She had all of those.'

'Aren't there others who should be considered in the same way?'

'OK, let's consider who else we've been talking to. What about Björn? What did you say to him during your last session?'

'Björn?' Darina thought back. 'Nothing really important, nothing to do with the case, anyway.'

William looked at her for a long moment. 'Could he have realized you were trying to open his cupboards?'

Darina considered carefully. 'I didn't touch anything much and I think I left everything as it was. I couldn't open them anyway.'

'If he thought you'd tried, and he had something to hide, he might have been scared into action.'

Darina shivered. 'But he's got an alibi for Bernard's murder. John Rickwood.'

'There's no proof that they were at Björn's all the time they say they were. They could be in it together – Björn because of his Lloyd's losses and John because of his wife's.'

'But you keep saying that's not a strong enough motive for John.'

'Maybe he's just furnishing Björn with an alibi. If that's his only involvement, it's unlikely John would feel threatened enough to want to poison us. Anyway, we haven't talked to him so we couldn't have made him suspicious.'

'Unless . . .' Darina said thoughtfully.

'Unless what?'

'Terri. She was with us when you were questioning Duval. Could she have thought of her father when he mentioned a Swedish car?'

'She could have told him we were digging around. If he's really got something to hide, perhaps he might think we were better out of the way.'

'Has there been any response to the fax Mike sent to the army?'

'Damn, I never got round to asking, I was too shocked by the news of his poisoning. I'll ring back now.'

Five minutes later William put down the phone again. He looked dispirited. 'Chris says they've had a long fax back. The gist of it is that, according to the report made after the exercise when Rickwood's plane was found, his partner died of natural causes. There was a doctor in the army party and he examined the body and it was his opinion that internal injuries sustained at the time of the crash were responsible for his death. His examination wasn't helped by the fact that a bear had mauled the body about but the attack had clearly been after death and there was sufficient evidence left for the doctor to be in no doubt.' He went and helped himself to a whisky and water.

Darina declined the offer of one herself. 'Trust the army to be careful to cover every contingency! Was Bernard on the exercise?'

'No, his name is not among the party members.'

'A promising theory down the plug-hole, then.'

'We'd better look at the others again. There are problems with them, though. Is the trouble Björnson's in at Lloyd's really a strong enough motive for premeditated murder? And if he did line Rickwood up as an alibi, that's what it would mean. I can imagine him killing him in a rage but planning it all ahead is something else.'

'Of course,' said Darina slowly, 'if you concentrate on the blood and oil angle, the most obvious candidate has to be Helen. She had a whole wardrobe of alternative outfits on the spot. She could have come back before her lunch, killed Bernard, changed and driven to the restaurant. She could have dumped the stained clothes anywhere on the way.'

'Ah, so you're admitting her as a suspect at last, are you?'

'I'm just considering all the possibilities. But if the Saab driver is innocent, why doesn't he come forward and say, yes, I saw Bernard that morning and left him alive and well in his mill.'

'When it would make him a prime suspect? I think we need another talk with Helen. You game for a visit to the farm in the morning?'

'If it will help get to the bottom of all this, I'm game for anything.' Darina helped herself to a glass of wine and came and sat beside William. 'You know,' she said slowly, 'I thought this part of the world was wonderful when we first arrived. I loved the sun and the food. Provence has always meant olive oil and lush fruit and vegetables to me, simple things that are full of gutsy flavour. I expected to find life down here was like that too. Instead money seems to motivate most people and losing large sums is treated like grievous bodily harm. Bernard's schemes for making olive oil, the essence of pure, natural health, now seem almost obscene.'

'Didn't I hear somewhere that in classical times olive oil was venerated, used for religious ceremony as well as food? Well, to some, money is a religion. Perhaps it seemed natural to him.'

'Pig, you shouldn't joke about these things!'

'Darling, I never joke about the causes of crime. There are certain, deeply held beliefs that, once challenged, can push some people to terrible lengths, even to murder. Money is one of them. Maybe, years ago, olive oil was another.'

Darina sighed. 'Why do people have to offend nature and make everything so complicated?'

'I've no answer to that,' William said. He drained his glass and set it down with a determined finality on the table. 'Let's do something really decadent this evening, something we would never normally do.'

'I know!' Darina gave him a grin of deep complicity. 'Let's go to that casino in San Juan and gamble away the housekeeping money.'

Her husband stood up. 'You never cease to amaze me. Come on, glam yourself up and we'll think of a lucky number.'

Chapter Twenty-Three

Lady luck visits those who don't woo her. William and Darina left the casino late that night considerably richer than they had arrived, feeling just a little guilty. Decadence had proved highly enjoyable. 'Perhaps it's as well we aren't staying here long,' said Darina the next morning. 'I could get hooked on living dangerously.'

'Don't worry, a few words with Helen and you'll have your feet on the ground again,' her husband said. 'We won't ring, better to surprise her.'

A little later they stood waiting outside the front door of the farm.

No one answered their knock. 'We'd better check the mill,' said William.

Darina followed him with reluctance, the ghost of Bernard rising before her. She almost couldn't bring herself to enter. Against her will, she found her eyes inexorably seeking out the machinery, the white tiles, the huge stainless steel pails, her mind flinching from the memory of what had been there on her last visit. But it was all right, no gobbets of blood defaced the spotless surface of the tiles. And the machinery was silent, the pails empty.

Helen was at the other end of the mill. Dressed in old jeans and a baggy sweatshirt, she appeared to be cleaning out a cupboard. Another memory rose in Darina's mind, of Bernard unlocking the big wooden door and taking out a bottle of oil for Anthea.

On a trestle table arranged by the cupboard was a jumble of bottles and tins.

Helen looked round as they entered. 'Hello,' she said in surprise, 'I wasn't expecting to see you again so soon.' Her expression was wary. Then she came across and kissed Darina. 'You put me to shame, I haven't rung yet to thank you for that delicious lunch.'

'Our pleasure,' said William easily. 'What are you doing? Stock-taking?' He picked up one of the tins, adorned with the same paper label as the flagon-shaped bottles, a striking design of olive fruit and leaves. '*Huile à La Chenais, Provence,*' he read out. 'Aren't you Alpes Maritimes here, not Provence?

'The whole region is known as Provence,' Helen said airily. 'And I thought Alpes Maritimes didn't have at all the same ring.' She looked at the collection on the table. 'I've put the place up for sale. I can't live here any more and . . .' she hesitated for a moment then added, '. . . and I may need the money in a hurry.'

Did she, wondered Darina, still have hopes of Roland? Was Helen's account of their affair more accurate than his? Only one thing was certain, that Roland couldn't be trusted in any direction and Helen herself was unreliable. Just how far would she go to keep him?

Darina took off her cream jacket and hung it carefully on one of the machines. 'If you pass out the bottles, we can put them on the table.'

Helen looked at her smart cinnamon trousers and cream chenille top. 'They're very dusty,' she said doubtfully.

'Come on, what are friends for? If we help, it'll be done in no time. Is this your entire stock?'

'No.' Helen sighed. 'There are hundreds of litres still up there.' She gestured to the three green-painted tanks that lay along the top of the cupboards. At the end of the run was a pipe leading down to a tap. 'Lots of people come with their own bottles – we charge less for that. These were filled for local outlets as well as for sale from here. Bernard had only just got going with his marketing. He had great plans for a shop in one of the other buildings. He wanted to sell not only oil but souvenirs and other olive products, like soap and the olives themselves prepared in different flavourings. Did you know you can't eat a green olive straight from the tree? They need immersing in brine to remove bitter glucosides. There are all sorts of herbs and aromatics that can be added. I've been experimenting with a whole range of different recipes, and preserving black olives as well.' Helen's brief enthusiasm died. 'Well, I suppose I can use it all in an article or a book some time.' She reached back into the cupboard and brought out some more bottles.

Darina arranged them across the table in lines of five and William started tidying the ones already there so that counting would be easy.

For once Helen seemed to be less than her usual talkative self and for a little while they worked in silence.

'How's Stephen doing with his location hunting?' asked Darina after a bit.

Helen looked gloomy. 'He says he's nearly finished, which means that he'll be leaving. Still, I shan't be sorry to get rid of that dreadful Terri. The sight of her by an open fridge door gorging herself on Pont l'Évêque is enough to give me a nervous breakdown.'

'Has she had any more meetings with her father?'

'And that's another thing. When I try to be sympathetic, ask about her family and all that, she snaps my head off. I told her how difficult it was for me when James got married again. That sanctimonious Pru, always telling the children they needed a stable home, as though she and James were horses!' Helen gave a strangled gurgle of laughter. 'She's so boring they could have used her to drive through the Channel Tunnel. You'd have thought that would have made Terri realize I knew what she was having to cope with, I mean with Jules as a step-mum and a half-sister or -brother to look forward to.'

'You know the Rickwoods, then?' asked William.

'Slightly. Bernard persuaded Jules that becoming a member of Lloyds would not only make her richer but give her social cachet as well.' Helen paused from passing out bottles of olive oil and straightened her back with a slight groan. 'Jules likes social cachet. Bernard introduced us when we first bought La Chenais, two years ago. She angled for the contract to do it up but she was far too expensive. Then we heard she'd got engaged to a captain of industry. By then Bernard was on the verge of retiring and his comment was, pity she couldn't have done it earlier, when he'd have had a chance to enrol whoever it was in his agency. Typical Bernard!' Helen dived back into the cupboard, reaching into its depths to bring out the bottles from the back.

'When did you meet the captain of industry?' asked William, making slight adjustments to the arrangement on the table.

Helen emerged with an armful of bottles of which Darina carefully relieved her one by one. 'By the time they arrived down here in the New Year, Bernard had been declared *persona non grata*. But Jules had heard about the mill and she turns up one afternoon. Can you beat it? Tries to tell us she didn't know it was ours. Claimed she never knew our address and said she'd just heard the oil was wonderful. Do you know how loopy she is about the food she eats?

'She asks for a guided tour then calmly tells Bernard she's not going to cough up her Lloyd's losses, after he'd given her a free bottle! I hope it choked her,' Helen added viciously. 'They were eating at the same restaurant as us the following week. I asked her how she liked the oil and she looked through me as though I wasn't there, wouldn't even introduce us to her husband.'

'But John Rickwood came to see Bernard, didn't he? On behalf of the Lloyd's members down here?' William asked.

Helen nodded. 'A couple of days before Bernard was killed. I'd gone shopping but he told me all about it afterwards.' She sighed and straightened her back again. 'That sort of thing really annoyed Bernard. He was always going on about how everyone was delighted when their Lloyd's profits came through but they weren't prepared to accept the downside. After all, it wasn't as though he hadn't suffered losses along with the rest. Why else do you think he was bothering with all this?' Helen waved an arm that encompassed the rows of oil bottles, the machinery and other equipment in the mill.

'Come off it, Helen,' said William, with a touch of exasperation. 'The amount of money Bernard poured into equipping this place means it'll be years before you make a profit on the oil.'

She met his eyes for a moment, then gave an angry little shrug and plunged back into the cupboard. 'Bernard said,' her voice emerged muffled, 'if we could get the right outlets, we'd soon be making a good income from the olives.' She emerged from the cupboard with a set of cardboard boxes. 'Put these with the others, they're ready for mailing.'

Darina opened a box and found it contained one of the half-litre flagons, well protected with packing. She disinterred and placed it with the others. 'Do you have much mail-order business?'

'Haven't sent one yet,' Helen said cheerfully. 'But

Bernard was sure that as soon as word started getting around, we'd be sending bottles everywhere.'

'Wouldn't it be more sensible to send the tins?' asked William, opening another box and taking out the flagon it contained.

'They were a late development. We were going to major on them for the next season, get them properly printed and the right size of box.' Helen gave a deep sigh. 'Bernard was so full of plans.'

For a moment Darina could believe she was truly mourning Bernard. Then she thought that even if Helen had fallen out of love with him, she could still miss him and his cruel end must have shaken her. Unless, of course, she'd been responsible for that end. Could her friend actually have turned on that chopping machine that had reduced his fingers to bloody stumps?

Darina couldn't believe it. Even with all Helen's childish insensitivity and self-centredness, she couldn't be a murderer, especially such a cruel one.

'What have we got here?' exclaimed William suddenly. He'd been taking each bottle of oil out of its cardboard box and placing it on the table. Now he'd found a box that contained not a flagon but something else wrapped in protective bubble plastic.

'I don't know what that can be,' declared Helen, pushing stray strands of hair off her face.

'Have we got all the boxes out?' asked William, as he started to unwrap the protective plastic.

She nodded. 'Every last son of a bitch. The cupboard is bare. We had twenty of those bottles ready in boxes and I counted them as I took them out, I wanted to see if any had actually been mailed. But they were all there. Good heavens!' she added as William revealed what had been wrapped up in the box.

He placed it on the table on the last little clear area, where it stood beside the bottles, their oil gleaming gold through the clear glass.

They all stood and stared as though refusing to accept the evidence of their eyes.

It was a china figurine. To be more precise, there were two figures, beautifully moulded and painted. After a moment's shocked appraisal, Darina realized she could identify each of them. Sir Robert Bright's features were unmistakable, as were Margaret Thatcher's, even though their expressions were unfamiliar and their naked bodies had never before been seen in public. Especially in such a compromising position.

'That's obscene,' said Helen in awe.

'And witty,' added William. He lifted the figurine and turned it around so they could study it from all angles. Everything about it was lewd, from the moulding of the bodies, copulating in one of the less well-known positions, to the abandoned lust on the faces. And yet the piece was saved from being merely obscene by an indefinable air of humour. Not only by that, either. Such was the skill of the modeller, the figurine was a miniature work of art.

William turned it over. On Mrs Thatcher's bottom, in minute letters it said: *L'Amour No.* 2, 3/200.

'What does that mean?' asked a bewildered Helen.

'I think,' said William judiciously, 'that this is number two in a series of poses, maybe with the same protagonists in different positions, maybe with two other people, and that this model is the third in a limited edition of two hundred.' He opened another box. This contained a bottle of oil, which he added to those already on the table. There was one last box to check.

This one contained not oil but a second bubble-wrapped package.

295

Darina held her breath as William carefully unwrapped then placed it on the table beside the first.

Gérard Depardieu and the Princess Royal were having a right royal time and looking as though they were enjoying every minute of it.

After a moment's awed silence, William turned the piece upside down and they could all see, on the princess's left hip, the tiny legend: *L'Amour no. 5, 10/200.*

'So now we know there are at least five different poses in the series,' said William, replacing it beside the first.

'But where did Bernard get it? I mean, he must have hidden it there, it couldn't have been anybody else.' Helen was still bewildered.

'I'm not sure how to say this, Helen,' said William, his voice without expression, 'but it looks as though Bernard was forming a collection of . . . how shall I put it?'

'If you're suggesting he liked porn, forget it!'

'Men quite often hide these things, you know. And I don't mean hide them under the bed but pretend they don't exist.'

Helen shook her head vehemently. 'Not Bernard. We had a discussion about girly magazines and that sort of thing once and he said none of that was any fun on your own. He liked company.'

William looked by no means convinced.

'Do you mean, darling, that there are people who collect things like, like . . .' Darina hesitated, then waved at the statuettes, 'like these?'

'Oh, there's a thriving market. I would say these are very definitely collectors' items. The fact that they are limited editions says that, if nothing else. I would imagine they command quite a high price.'

'But where do people buy something like that? Isn't it illegal?'

'Only if they're sent through the post. At least, that's the position in England. And the purveyors of these items are almost certainly sending them through the post as I imagine the bulk of their business is done through mail order. Discreet ads, placed in suitable magazines, recognizable to those in the market for such things.'

Helen shuddered. 'If making and selling them isn't against the law, it should be. I mean, using real people like that. And Margaret Thatcher!'

Darina gazed at the statuettes with even more interest. 'You mean it could be like collecting Royal Copenhagen annual plates?'

'Something like that, except the owners of these little figures probably don't display them in the china cabinet but hide them away. They either gloat over them in private or show them to very special friends.'

'I tell you,' Helen reiterated stubbornly, 'Bernard wasn't like that.'

Darina found herself studying the figurines more and more closely. She picked up the first and turned it around, examining the way the heads were moulded and the line of the bodies. She was conscious of William looking at her with amusement. Helen had ostentatiously started counting the bottles of olive oil.

At last Darina put the figurine back on the trestle table and said, 'I think I know who made these.'

'You mean?'

'Yes, darling, I think it's Björn's work. Robert Bright's head, apart from his expression, is almost identical to the one in Björn's studio. You remember I said that he was very talented at modelling figures as well? I've looked at the ones he's got in his studio long enough to be almost certain he did these. Either him or somebody who works in exactly the same way.'

'Well, well, well. Do you think these are what he keeps in those cupboards?'

'Could be. And I would place a fairly large bet that they get fired in Anthea's kiln.' Darina looked up at William. 'They would make a perfect partnership.'

'And Anthea could have given these two to Bernard.'

'A love token you mean?' Helen's voice was scornful. 'If that's the sort of thing she's into, no wonder she upset Bernard so.'

'But maybe if Bernard knew she was involved with something like this, he upset her,' countered William. 'Perhaps by suggesting he was going to spread the news.' He looked at his watch. 'I don't know if Garnier is still in his office but I must try and get hold of him. This is something the examining magistrate needs to know. Helen, can I use your phone?'

She was intrigued now. 'Of course, use the mobile.' She reached for where it was sitting on the corner of the table and handed it to him. Then took Darina into the house to make coffee.

'Does William really think Anthea could have murdered Bernard?' Helen asked as she filled a kettle.

'Difficult to say,' Darina replied, leaning against one of the working surfaces.

'And what about Björn? Mightn't he want to kill Bernard as well?'

'Depends whether Bernard knew he was involved.' Darina said. It was the question she had been asking herself.

William emerged from the mill and waved to Darina through the window to come outside. With a word of apology to Helen, she went and joined him in the courtyard.

'What's happening now?'

'I've spoken to Garnier.' William had an air of suppressed excitement. 'Mike's going to be OK but he needs time to recover and the French, very reluctantly, have decided to ask me to join the team, purely temporarily, on the basis that by the time they've got somebody else out from London and properly briefed them, Mike could be well enough to resume his duties. Garnier's already spoken to London.' William's dark-flecked grey eyes were sparkling with delight.

'Oh, darling, I'm so pleased!'

'Are you really?' He looked at her a trifle ruefully.

'Of course I am! It's the best thing that could happen. Have you told Garnier about the figurines?'

William nodded.

'Do you really think they could have provided a motive for murder?'

'If you're right about Björn Björnson modelling them,' he said, 'then I think Bernard could have destroyed his reputation as a serious sculptor. I don't know how much they're making out of these.' William lifted up the two boxes he was carrying, plastic bubble wrapping emerging from their tops, 'But I would doubt it's matching his earnings from his heads.'

'But what about his alibi? What about the fact that he and John Rickwood insist they spent most of that morning together? Does that mean Anthea killed Bernard?'

'I don't know. I would think she got into this with Björn because she needed the money. She's one of the few people we've met who doesn't seem to be a member of Lloyd's but the recession can't have done her courses any good and losing the charismatic Kevin, with his ability to get the press writing about them, can't have helped either.'

Darina perched herself on the table where they'd had lunch with Helen and Bernard in what now seemed a dim and distant past. Only the sun now warming her back was the same. 'If it wasn't for Bernard, I'd have said she was involved with Björn sexually. She seems to me someone who's starving for love and there must be some basis for his reputation for making it with any woman he meets.'

'We've only her word about Bernard,' said William slowly. 'Perhaps Bernard misread some signals and made a fool of himself and Helen got hold of the wrong end of the stick. Perhaps it has been Björn all along and Anthea's been leading us up the garden path.'

Darina stared at him, her mind racing with the possible implications.

'Both Björn and Anthea have a lot of questions to answer. Garnier's arranging for them to be brought in and he's sending a car for me. That means you'll be able to keep ours and be independent.' William gave her a quick kiss on the mouth that was over as soon as it started. 'Come on, we'd better go back to Helen.'

Darina followed her husband into the house. She could be pleased for William and his delight in being officially involved in the case but it did seem that she was now going to be cut off from both the investigation and her husband.

Chapter Twenty-Four

While they waited for the French police car to arrive, William questioned Helen.

Nothing much came out. She was convinced Bernard had had the hots for Anthea and that the girl had made a dead set at him. She knew nothing about the statuettes but repeated her assertion that Bernard would have had no interest in collecting that sort of art work. She knew Björn but he was not a particular friend and she had no idea how close he and Anthea were. She looked at William. 'You're going to suggest Bernard was blackmailing whoever made that obscene piece, aren't you? Well, Anthea never has two pennies to rub together and Björn owes all that money to Lloyd's. He wouldn't get anything out of either of them and he'd know it!'

How interesting, Darina thought, studying her friend, that Helen hadn't denied the possibility Bernard might want to blackmail someone, as she had the suggestion he might be interested in collecting pornographic material.

'They could be raking in sizeable sums from producing works like these.' William placed his hand on the cardboard boxes that now stood on the big low table in front of where he sat on one of the sofas. 'Money which will be stashed away quietly somewhere.'

There came the sound of a car drawing up outside and a moment later a knock on the front door.

Helen firmly asserted her rights by opening it.

On the doorstep stood Chris Spring, looking rumpled and careworn.

'How's Mike?' asked Darina immediately.

He gave her an anxious smile, said, 'Getting better, the Froggie doctors say,' and went over to William. 'Ready, Gov? Oh, I brought you a copy of that fax. Mike said you were to have one when it came in.' He handed over an envelope.

'Bully for him,' said William, looking surprised. He took it and reached for his jacket, lying on the sofa beside him. 'You did a good job getting here,' he said, shrugging the jacket on. 'Thanks for bringing this.' He slipped the envelope into his inner pocket.

'We've got a French driver. Don't think I'd be let loose with one of their cars on these roads, do you?' Chris sounded as though there was little love lost between him and the French officials he was having to deal with. 'Be bloody glad when Mike's back. I may speak the lingo but understanding the Frog mentality is beyond me, I can tell you.'

'We'll battle with them together.' William put a hand on the sergeant's shoulder and gently shepherded him towards the door.

Just before they disappeared, William turned and gave his wife a happy smile. 'Look after yourself, I'll give you a ring later.'

'Well!' said Helen as the door closed behind them. 'I thought you were meant to be on honeymoon. Talk about deserting the bride!' She poured Darina out more coffee. 'But, then, he's been sniffing around ever since you found poor Bernard's body, hasn't he?' She eyed Darina sardonically. 'And you've been showing just as much interest. All that talk about helping me, you just want to play detective. And now you've been abandoned while the boys go off to play together.' She looked by no means displeased. 'I always said you can't trust men.'

'Helen, you've never said anything of the kind!'

'Not to you, maybe. But all my life men have let me down.'

'You seem to have done quite well out of Bernard,' Darina couldn't resist saying. She looked round the carefully furnished room. 'All this is now yours, presumably without question.'

'And don't think for one moment I haven't earned it,' Helen snapped. 'Keeping Bernard interested was as difficult as creating a genuinely new dish. Frankly Darina, even if Roland hadn't come along, I don't know how long I could have kept it up. Perhaps it's as well Bernard died when he did.' As Darina looked at her in dismay, Helen stretched her small body and rose in one lithe movement from the sofa, her full mouth smiling inscrutably. 'How about I show you the bearer bonds?'

'Sure!' With a sense of anticipation, Darina realized that she had only half believed in their existence. 'The police didn't find them?'

'Police!' Helen was scornful. 'They don't have a clue about looking for anything. Didn't find those figurines, did they?'

She had a point there. Darina wondered if they had given the cupboard anything more than a quick once-over to see if anybody had hidden a blunt instrument there. Or had they opened a couple of boxes and then assumed all the rest were the same?

'Hello, your policeman husband isn't too careful, either. He dropped that envelope he was given.' Helen swooped towards the door but Darina was before her.

'I'll give it back to him later,' she said, picking it up. 'He knows what's inside it anyway.' But she drew the piece of paper out of the envelope all the same.

'Ah, little Miss Nosy! Well, go ahead, I'm all for us girls freelancing. We've got to look after our interests. Let me know when you're ready to see my little secret.' Helen leant against the sofa-back looking both irritated and curious.

'I'm sorry.' Darina stuffed the fax into her trouser pocket. 'You know I'm dying to see your bonds.'

With a strong sense of disappointment, Darina followed Helen upstairs. The fax hadn't contained much more than William had reported after his telephone conversation the previous night. There was a copy of part of the army report plus the names of the officers and men involved. The commanding officer had been Captain Allison, his number two, Lieutenant Warburton. The doctor had been called Sheldon, there'd been two non-commissioned officers, Sergeant Rose and Corporal Harvey, and three privates, Smith, Harrington and Dobie. None of the names meant anything to her.

Helen bounced happily up the stairs. Darina wondered if her good spirits meant Roland had been in touch again. Maybe asked her if she could really come up with sufficient funds to get him out of trouble?

In Helen's bedroom, the room that had been hers and Bernard's, the pile of papers was no longer on the floor, the chest was neatly closed. Apart from that, however, there was considerably more mess than when Darina had seen it before. Clothes hung over chair-backs and lay in piles on the floor. There were dirty mugs on a bedside table and the chest. The bed was unmade. Bottles of make-up and nail varnish littered various surfaces, open books had their places kept by being put face down, their spines strained.

Among brand-new cookery books were a couple of novels, paperbacks of the more lurid type. On one of the bedside tables, jostling a bulging Filofax and a pile of letters, were two bottles of pills and a couple of used glasses.

Helen picked up a key from the bedside table and headed across the room. It had an attractively rustic look, the short walls and steeply sloping ceiling framed by beams, with joints secured by large wooden pegs, one blunt and one sharp end poking out either side. Presumably because a bathroom had been fitted into the end of the bedroom, the gap between the last set of beams and the dividing wall was much smaller than the others.

Helen crouched down, grabbed the wooden peg that joined the two beams and twisted it. The short piece of wall between the low ceiling, upright beam and bathroom wall sprang open a small amount. She smiled triumphantly at Darina, pulled the secret door towards her and revealed a safe. She inserted the key she'd picked up, twirled a combination lock, and within seconds it was open.

'I'm surprised Bernard trusted you with the code.' Darina was sitting on the chest, watching her.

'Bernard, my dear, trusted me with *everything*.' Helen gleamed with satisfaction. 'I think it went back to his humble beginnings.' She looked up from the safe. 'He wasn't public school and all that, you know. He clawed his way up – he used to say it was through bullshit and bravado. His father was a fish wholesaler, had a stall in Billingsgate, but it was his mother who held the financial strings. His father handed all the money over to her.' She gave a small, neat smile.

'But Bernard wasn't so trusting he didn't safeguard his interests by getting you to sign that document you told us about.' It was a statement of fact.

Helen shrugged. 'He was a businessman, after all. What

if I had died suddenly? He certainly didn't want Stephen and Sasha inheriting it all. And I couldn't have willed it to him. We'd have to have been married for French law to have allowed that.'

'So it was a legal document?'

'Witnessed by a notary.' Helen turned back to the open safe and took out a slim sheaf of papers. 'There are various securities here. Some Bernard was ready to cash in. "A sop for the wolves at Lloyd's," he told me. But not the bearer bonds. He said nobody knew about them.' Helen frowned as she flipped through the papers she'd taken out.

Had Bernard trusted Helen because of his parents' relationship or because he'd had a reckless streak? Bernard had been a bit of a showman, something of a gambler. A blackmailer as well?

A groan issued from Helen. She dropped the papers she'd been holding, plunged a hand back into the safe and felt around its recess. Then she returned her attention to the papers, pushing them around on the floor so that they were laid out individually. 'They've got to be here, they've just got to be,' she moaned. 'I checked them only the other day.'

Darina came across and started picking up the pieces of paper one by one, carefully checking that nothing was stuck together. Each of them was identified as a share certificate belonging to a particular company. Each was marked with the name of Bernard Barrington Smythe. Darina had no idea what a bearer bond looked like but of one thing she was certain, it wouldn't carry the name of the holder.

'Are you sure there isn't anything else in the safe?' she asked finally.

Helen had been watching her like a child convinced its mother can reveal a lost treasure after all its own searchings have proved fruitless. Now her face crumpled. 'No, there's nothing!' she wailed.

'And you're sure they were in there?'

'I told you, I checked them the day before yesterday.' Distress was giving way to temper.

'So who else knows about the safe?' Darina would have been willing to lay a pretty large bet on the answer.

'Only Steve.' As Darina said nothing, Helen rushed on, 'He was worried about me. He wanted to know I was going to be all right without Bernard.'

'Helen, you can't make me believe Stephen wasn't overjoyed Bernard was out of your life. He'd have done anything to separate you two.'

'No, you've got it all wrong. He was blaming himself for telling Bernard about Roland. He said he didn't think Roland was serious about me.'

That had the ring of truth about it if nothing else did. 'And he asked how much money you had?'

Helen's gaze dropped to the little pile of share certificates. 'Something like that,' she mumbled.

'So you took him up here and opened the safe, no doubt telling him the combination at the same time, showing him bonds to the tune of a million pounds that anyone could cash and then left the key on your bedside table.'

'Darina, Steve's my son! And I didn't tell him the combination.' An uneasy look fought its way through her self-justification. 'At least, I may have mentioned Bernard chose his old London telephone number. But he couldn't know what that was,' she added hurrriedly.

'Oh, no?' asked Darina with a certain amount of acid. She left the little pile of certificates on the floor and went across to the bedside table, picked up the Filofax and flipped through the address section. She turned one of the 'B' pages so Helen could see. 'Bernard's London telephone number? Right?'

Helen slumped back against the beam running up the wall. 'Oh, God,' she moaned. 'He's taken them.' She scrambled up from the floor and headed out of the room.

Darina followed her into another bedroom. Both male and female clothes lay strewn about this one. Darina recognized Terri's Renaissance leggings trailing off the seat of a chair.

'Looks as though they're still here,' she commented.

Helen paid no attention but went over to a small cupboard on tall legs that did service as a bedside table and opened the little drawer at the top. 'Thank God,' she breathed. She held up a passport. 'He must still be here.'

'Is Terri's there as well?'

Before Helen could answer, the front door slammed and Stephen's voice called, 'Mum? Mum?' Heavy steps pounded up the stairs. Both women went out to meet him.

Stephen was out of breath and his expression had been shocked out of its normal complacency. In fact, he looked terrified.

'What have you done with them?' demanded Helen.

If there'd been any doubt before, the guilty shifting of his eyes was sufficient proof.

Helen grasped her son by the arms and shook him, her small frame powerful in her distress. 'How could you? How could you, Steve? I trusted you!' She collapsed back against the wall with a wail.

Stephen flushed.

Helen drew herself up like a trapeze artist ready to leap across a void. 'Give them back, Stephen. Give those bonds back to me now.' Her voice was imperious and she held out a demanding hand.

Stephen thrust his hands into his pockets. 'I haven't got them.' The words came out through gritted teeth.

Panic filled Helen's voice. 'You must have them. You're the only one who knew about the safe and the combination.'

Darina intervened. 'I don't think he means he didn't take

them, I think he means he hasn't got them now – that's it, isn't it, Stephen? Has Terri taken them?'

Stephen sagged against the wall. 'We were in a traffic jam in Antibes, on our way to see the last house on my list.' He looked moodily down at his trainers, scuffing the heel of one against the toe of the other. 'You know what a funny mood she was in before we left? Well, she got worse. I couldn't say anything right and finally she started complaining about me being a mummy's boy, how I couldn't do anything without running to you first.' He looked at Helen with challenge in his eyes. 'I told her you needed looking after and she said, "Huh!" in that scornful way she has. I told her I'd taken a million pounds from you and she said I could pull the other one. So I brought them out and showed her. The next thing I know, she's snatched them and is out of the car. I tried to go after her.' His expression was despairing. 'She just stood there in the middle of Boulevard Wilson and held them up above her head and said if I came any nearer, she'd tear them into pieces. You know what she's like, she's capable of anything. And then the traffic began to move and everyone started hooting and I couldn't think what else to do.'

'So you came back to Mummy!' Helen's voice shook with a mixture of scorn and distress. 'Why the hell did you take them in the first place?'

'I didn't want you to give them to Roland.'

'You thought you should have them?'

Stephen flushed. 'I just didn't want you to give them to Roland,' he repeated stubbornly.

'Well,' Helen said nastily, 'if you want me to speak to you again, you'd better get them back from Terri.'

Chapter Twenty-Five

Terri stuffed the stiff pieces of paper into her emerald satin knapsack, thrust her arms through its straps then shrugged it comfortably on to her shoulders and started threading her way through the traffic up the hill.

She wasn't worried Stephen would follow her. By the time he'd managed to turn his car round, she'd have disappeared down one of the side roads. Of course, if he was bright, he would be waiting for her by the entrance to her father's villa on the Cap.

She didn't think he was that bright. Brilliant director, of course; give him a play, or even just a scene, and he could plot the whole thing, motivation, audience awareness, atmosphere, how to convey the heart of the matter economically and artistically to achieve maximum effect.

Give Stephen a real-life situation with real people and he was lost, hopelessly lost.

Look at how he behaved with that mother of his! Anyone with any sense could see she didn't really care twopence about her children; Helen Mansard only cared about her career and men, in that order.

Terri turned left and followed the road as it wound past a school. Navigating by instinct, she had a reasonably clear idea of the layout of Antibes from the map she'd used to direct Stephen the times he'd driven her to the villa. Her short, fat legs, clad today in the zebra-patterned leggings under a long, black sweater topped by the emerald satin jacket, moved quickly and efficiently.

She puffed her way up to the top of a small hill and paused, catching a glimpse of sparkling sea over to her right and again to her left. Yes, she knew exactly where the Cap was.

When would Stephen realize he had to get out from under his mother and start living his own life?

The thing was, he had definite possibilities. He could go places, if only he'd shape up a bit. She could make sure he did. He needed someone like her to keep him pointed in the right direction.

Would he realize that, after what she'd done to him?

For a moment Terri came to a full stop. Should she return and give him back the bonds? But he'd only hand them over to Helen and the thought of what she would do with them made Terri continue.

Once among the winding Cap roads, she took several wrong turnings. It was not easy in that rarefied area to find people to ask the way and it was late morning by the time she finally arrived at the villa.

The gates were closed. Terri looked at the small video camera poised above the electronic bleeper, gave an automatic hitch to her knapsack, and pushed the button.

'*Oui*?' came the supercilious voice of that poncy butler. Oh, how Jules must love him!

'Terri Rickwood,' she announced, keeping her voice level with some difficulty. The sod could see who she was, why didn't he just open the gates? Then she realized what name she'd given him and felt a mirthless laugh rise within her.

The gates clicked open and Terri marched through.

The butler stood waiting for her at the front door.

'Monsieur and Madame are in the salon,' he announced in faultless English.

'*Va-t-en!*'

Henri's professional carapace was too well polished for the idiomatic insult to penetrate. Without a flicker, he led her across the marble hall and Terri had to follow with as much dignity as she could muster. She couldn't help but admire the panache with which he opened the double doors and announced her name.

Her father and Jules were sitting by the window, Jules once again engaged on her dreary embroidery, her father with one of his endless reports in his hand. Terri thought he looked older and somehow rather worn. For the first time in her life she recognized that he wasn't always going to be there for her to rail against and resent for not being what she hungered for in a father. The realization made her catch her breath.

'Terri, darling, how lovely to see you again.' Jules rose and came forward with outstretched hand. As so often before, Terri wondered exactly why she resented this woman so much. Why, when she tried so hard to be a friend and never attempted to usurp Terri's mother? She couldn't be jealous, could she?

Jealous of her father's all-consuming passion for Jules? The way he looked at her, cared for her, put her first in all things?

Terri thrust the thought away and allowed Jules to kiss her on the forehead.

Her father came up, gave Terri a peck on the cheek, then disengaged himself.

'Have you come for lunch?' enquired Jules.

Terri could see her mentally preparing to ring for Henri and hand out instructions for another place to be laid at the table.

She slipped off her knapsack, set it on a marble table, undid the buckle and pulled out the bearer bonds. 'These are for you, Dad.'

He looked at them in astonishment. 'Where on earth did these come from?'

'Bernard squirrelled them away. They're part of his ill-gotten gains.' Terri stood her ground squarely and spoke with authority.

Her father's expression grew bewildered. 'Why are you giving them to me? If they really are Bernard's, they should be sent to the Committee at Lloyd's so they can be applied against his liabilities.'

'Dad!' Terri said in exasperation. 'All I've heard since I came down here is how Bernard did the dirty on all the people he put into Lloyd's, like Jules.' She turned towards her stepmother and hesitated as she saw the look on her face. It reminded Terri of the time she'd been busted with a load of cannabis. Jules had had just that look as she sat in court with Terri's father, mother and stepfather. Terri ignored her. 'Well, these will pay her losses. You can divide the rest between some of Bernard's other victims.'

'Is this so that your father can give you the money for your shop?' Jules sounded like a schoolmistress.

That finished Terri. 'Do you seriously think all I consider is myself?' she yelled. 'That I've done this for me? When it's probably cost me my future happiness?' That was pitching it a bit strong but Terri felt so mad. She turned to her father. 'You believe me, Dad, don't you?' He looked at her in amazement. 'Helen shouldn't have the money, not when Stephen says she's going to give it to a boyfriend.' Terri regarded her father anxiously. Why did he look so sad?

'Stephen. I suppose that's this boyfriend of yours?' he grated out.

Was that all he'd taken in?

There came the sound of the doorbell. 'Interfering with a luncheon party, am I? No wonder you were so concerned I might want a meal.'

Jules flinched. 'Terri, you know you're always welcome.'

The double doors were thrust open. Stephen and his mother entered in a constipated rush. Helen's hair was falling down, Stephen had eyes for no one but Terri. 'There she is!' He started across the acres of Aubusson. Helen moaned his name and tried to keep up with him.

Following them more quietly was Darina Pigram and behind her came Henri. 'Monsieur, Madame,' he stuttered, his composure quite gone. 'I apologize. It appears the gate didn't quite shut itself after Miss Rickwood. I will have it seen to.' He retreated from a situation beyond his control.

Stephen reached Terri and her father and snatched the bearer bonds. 'Those belong to my mother!' he shouted. For a moment the look he turned on Terri made her think she'd gone too far. 'You little thief!' he spat at her.

'Not nearly as big a thief as you,' she retorted.

'Terri, you don't understand,' Helen wailed. 'Steve was trying to protect me.'

She was wearing the same dingy jeans and sweatshirt she'd had on that morning, her only make-up was lipstick and that was half eaten off. At least Jules always cared about how she looked. 'Steve's just like you, out for himself,' Terri told her. 'Neither of you has any right to the bonds.'

'They were in my mother's safe and as far as I'm concerned they're hers.' Stephen handed the certificates to Helen, who clutched them as though they were all that stood between her and destitution.

Terri sniffed disdainfully. 'If you think you can enjoy that money after I've finished telling everybody about it, good luck!'

Helen moaned, an involuntary sound that belonged to an upset child. Her small, round body was rigid with tension. She gazed at each of the company in turn, her eyes imploring them to understand. Then, with a supreme effort, she thrust the creased and battered certificates at John Rickwood. 'Terri's right, they aren't mine.'

Terri let out her breath and felt her face break into a huge smile. She could have flung her arms around Helen and kissed her. Instead she grabbed Stephen's hand. 'Your mum's all right,' she whispered to him. After a startled look at her, he pulled his hand away but Terri had seen his eyes and knew he was actually relieved with the outcome. They'd be all right, she knew it.

'I don't think that's a good idea.' Darina Pigram came forward and neatly whisked away the certificates. 'I'm sorry,' she said to Helen, 'I know you mean well but John isn't the right person to hold them.'

'Why not?' Jules's voice, harsh as Terri had never heard it before, broke into the assembly.

'The police will be here in a few minutes. They will explain.'

For the first time in her life, Terri felt truly frightened. It was not just the thought of police but the look in Darina's eyes. The kindness and laughter usually there had gone and they were very cold. She also seemed taller than ever.

'Take me home, Steve,' Helen said. 'I can't cope with more police.'

He glanced towards Darina.

'I think that would be best,' she said. 'I'll be in touch later.'

Stephen put an arm round his mother and began to guide her from the salon. Half-way to the double doors, he turned back towards Terri. 'Are you coming with us?'

A tiny exultant feeling danced in her heart but it did

nothing to dispel the coldness in her stomach. She shook her head. 'I can't leave here yet, Steve.'

He seemed to understand and turned back to his mother. Helen appeared to have exhausted all her strength; she almost tottered and had to grab at Stephen's arm to steady herself. Terri found the stray locks of hair hanging down from her head and the way her shoulders hunched themselves infinitely pathetic. It was a relief when the doors closed behind them.

'Do we have to wait for the police?' asked John Rickwood. 'You obviously know what they're going to say.'

'It would be best,' Darina replied. 'They won't be long.' Her tall figure was straight and stern.

Fear sat under Terri's rib-cage like cold porridge.

Her father's face was drawn – before her eyes he aged ten years. He turned to Jules. 'Why don't you go and rest, my darling?'

Her stepmother's face was pale and set but, in her way, she looked as implacable as Darina. 'I'm staying here,' she said, and sat down in the chair by the window, holding herself together like a parcel with dodgy string.

Terri plonked herself down on one of the uncomfortable upright sofas at the edge of the room. She desperately needed something to eat. Only food could help her now. But Jules was not one for delicious little tit-bits before lunch. On the table by the window were two glasses of wine but there was nothing to accompany them.

'Why don't we all sit?' her father suggested in a resigned way. He waved at a chair and Darina lowered herself into it. He took his usual chair and the four of them sat in uncomfortable silence.

Then Jules said in the social voice that always grated on Terri's ears, 'I suppose there's no reason why we shouldn't talk like civilized people?' But the doorbell spared them whatever innocuous subject she might feel was suitable.

There was a faint sigh from her father and Jules clutched at the arms of her chair.

The butler had recovered his aplomb. Despite herself, Terri had to admire the way he managed to express, without overt discourtesy, his distaste at having the police in the villa.

There were only two of them. A Frenchman called Garnier and Darina's husband, William.

The sight of William Pigram's tall figure should have been a comfort to Terri. But he, too, had gone all cold and serious.

It was Garnier who spoke first, in French, explaining that his English colleague had very kindly agreed to join the investigation into Bernard Barrington Smythe's murder following the unfortunate collapse of Inspector Parker from food poisoning. Inspector Pigram had come across evidence that morning that had opened up the investigation and it was Inspector Pigram who would explain what had brought them to the villa to speak with Monsieur Rickwood. But, he added, glancing round the salon at the three women sitting there, perhaps Monsieur would like to take them into another room?

Terri's father stood up. His French, she knew, was not as good as hers but it was adequate. 'I quite agree,' he said in English. 'We'll go into the study.'

'No!' Jules said in the same harsh voice, 'I insist on hearing whatever it is.'

Garnier looked at Jules and shrugged his shoulders. '*Eh bien*,' he said, found himself a chair to sit in and left the floor to his English counterpart.

William Pigram took up station in front of the windows and the view of sweeping lawns and blue, blue

Mediterranean sea, and Terri realized the uncomfortable sofa she was sitting on gave her a perfect view of everyone in the room.

'During the investigation into the murder of Bernard Barrington Smythe, police attention has become focused on the driver of a Saab car seen driving to La Chenais at around the time the victim was killed.'

He didn't sound like William Pigram at all – his voice was frighteningly official.

'We have found two owners of almost identical Saab cars among our list of suspects,' the official voice continued. 'You, sir, and Mr Björnson.'

'As I explained to your colleague,' John Rickwood said quietly, 'Björn and I spent that morning together, going through his financial situation.'

'That was the statement you gave us.' The way he said this was not reassuring. 'However, this morning we have had a most interesting conversation with Mr Björnson.'

'If he says I didn't spend the morning with him, he's lying!'

'Björn Björnson has not retracted his statement,' William said steadily, unmoved by the outburst, 'but he is refusing to answer questions and has sent for a lawyer. That, in itself, tells its own story.'

Terri's father looked relieved. Jules's face was pale and set.

'Until this morning we felt you were furnishing Björnson with an alibi rather than the other way about. Your wife's losses through her membership of Lloyd's didn't seem a sufficient motive for murder.'

'What happened to change your mind, Inspector?'

Terri could almost believe her father was in complete command of the situation, he spoke so naturally.

'This morning we were able to study the report filed by

319

the army expedition that found you in Labrador after your air crash.'

'I fail to see that that can have any bearing on this unfortunate matter.' Once again his voice was level and unstrained.

'For a while we agreed with you. It was my wife,' the Inspector glanced in Darina's direction and for a moment the reassuringly warm side of William Pigram surfaced, 'it was my wife who recognized what the rest of us missed. Earlier she and I had discussed the possibility that Bernard Barrington Smythe, as a national serviceman, had been a member of the party that rescued you and learned something you would be prepared to kill to keep secret.'

John Rickwood laughed. 'You're not suggesting I murdered poor Philip, are you? That there was some sort of cover-up which Bernard was threatening to expose?' Terri started to relax. It was going to be all right, after all. Then she saw how white Jules had gone.

'Why did I tell you that story?' Jules asked despairingly, then clamped her lips shut as though she had said too much already.

William ignored her. 'Yes, we did think that was the most likely possibility,' he said. 'But the army report made it clear your partner had died as a result of injuries sustained in the crash. Not only that, Barrington Smythe was not among the names of the expedition. However, while we were bringing in and questioning Björnson as a result of the discovery of other evidence, my wife . . . but let her tell this part.' William turned to Darina.

She had been listening intently to everything that had been said. When her husband handed her the floor, she gave a slight shake of her head, as though she would prefer him to continue. But he remained waiting for her to speak and finally she leaned forward slightly and addressed John

Rickwood. 'It was the list of expedition names that first caught my attention. We had been looking for Barrington Smythe and it wasn't there. But there was a Smith and Helen had told me that Bernard's parents were from the East End of London, that he was a self-made man, and I thought how much more likely it was he had been born Smith rather than Barrington Smythe. While Helen and Steve were trying to work out what Terri intended to do with the bonds she'd taken, I took another look at the expedition report. It mentioned that a bear had mauled the body of your partner.' Darina stopped and her expression became terribly sad. 'I had a vision of someone stranded alone and injured in a desperate place, his partner dead. He had snow to melt for water but nothing to eat and starvation stared him in the face. Until he realized that a source of life-giving protein was right beside him.'

Terri found she could hardly breathe. She felt sick, so sick she brought a hand up to her mouth.

'Did a bear actually come along afterwards, or was that part of the cover-up story?' Darina looked straight at John Rickwood.

His face was ghastly, somehow the skin seemed to have shrunk, to have moulded itself to the cheek and jaw-bones like a death's head. But his voice remained as level as before. 'That was the ironic thing. There was a bear. I'd crawled into the wreck of the plane for the night as I always did, leaving the fire damped down, and then I heard this snuffling. The torch batteries had long gone but there was enough of a moon that I could see this lurching, swaying figure over where Philip—' he swallowed hard and for the first time his voice faltered '—over where the remains of Philip's body were. I found the gun we always carried and shot it.' He closed his eyes. 'If only that damned animal had come along a few days earlier, I wouldn't have been

321

forced to . . . to do what I had to do.' He cast an agonized look over at Jules. She looked carved out of ice. 'I hope you can forgive me, my darling, I had to tell the truth.' Jules said nothing, not an eyelid on that cold face flickered and there was a long silence before he added, 'I've never eaten meat since.'

'And the expedition?' asked William matter-of-factly.

Terri lowered the hand from her mouth, her stomach now under control. For the first time in her life she was filled with an uncomplicated love for her father. Now she knew what he had gone through, she felt she could forgive him anything.

John Rickwood sighed. 'Nothing was ever said but I knew from the way attitudes suddenly changed towards me, that the expedition had realized but some sort of decision seemed to have been taken not to mention the matter. The commanding officer, what was his name? Flashman? No, Allison, that was it. He was so terribly . . . *English*! I was far too weak to try and persuade him how desperate my situation had been and, anyway, that unacknowledged conspiracy of silence was too inhibiting. When we got back to civilization and I thanked Allison and his men, I made a last effort to bring the subject up and he looked me straight in the eye and said, "English honour, that's what we must remember." And I understood the truth was impossible.'

'And Barrington Smythe?' asked William Pigram. He was also seated now and Terri saw he was taking notes.

Her father gave a deep sigh. 'I'd forgotten them all until that morning I went to see him about the Lloyd's mess. We had run into Barrington Smythe and Helen shortly before, at some restaurant. Jules was so mad at him over the Lloyd's mess, she refused to introduce us and I'd assumed that was why he'd looked at me so oddly. Then when I turned up at his place, he could hardly wait to tell me he'd remembered where we'd met! Out it all came, the crash, his part in the expedition, what he knew about me.'

John Rickwood sat back in his chair and looked out of the window. 'I remembered them all then: Allison, so stiff and correct on the surface, so disgusted and embarrassed beneath; his second-in-command, unable to meet my eyes after they discovered what I'd done; the supercilious doctor, even Smith, the bouncy little private, so eager to play his part and the one member of that expedition who hadn't treated me as a pariah. That morning, it's incredible to think it was only a few days ago, it was almost a relief that something I had had to keep buried inside me for so long could be talked about.'

'You didn't try to tell him he'd mistaken you?' asked William.

Terri watched her father shake his head. 'Not many people have lost the first two joints of their fingers the way I have.' He held up the maimed hand. 'And my name isn't that usual. No, even when I realized that he was intent on making me force his members to abandon legal action and pay up without protest, there was no way I could have convinced him I wasn't the cannibal he'd helped rescue.'

There came a sound between a sigh and a groan and Jules slipped to the floor in a dead faint.

Darina was out of her chair in an instant but John Rickwood reached his wife first and crouched beside her, cradling her head in his arms. Terri remained where she was. In her experience, people were always too ready to form a crowd round someone who needed space and air. William helped her father get Jules on to a sofa and Darina asked where she could get some water.

'I'll go.' John Rickwood disappeared from the room and was back in minutes, followed by Henri bearing a silver tray with a cut-glass jug of water and a matching tumbler.

'May I also suggest brandy?' said the butler.

'She wouldn't drink it – she's pregnant.' Terri's father reached for the water and gently raised Jules's head.

Jules groaned; her eyelids fluttered, then her eyes opened – and looked straight into her husband's. She gave a small cry and pressed herself back into the sofa. 'Don't . . . don't . . .' She turned away from him, half burying her face in the cushions. 'Can't forgive . . . can't forget . . . people would never forget . . .' Then she turned to face him again and her voice rose in a demented shriek, 'Cannibal . . . cannibal . . . how could you?'

Terri saw her father draw back, his face a stony mask, as Jules broke into a passion of weeping. Then he put the glass on a table and placed a hand on her shoulder, paying no attention to the way it flinched beneath his touch. 'Darling,' he said, 'I understand, believe me I understand. You've got to be brave now. I shall have to go with the police and tell them everything, how I killed Bernard to stop him telling the world about the crash and how I persuaded Björn to say I was with him the whole time.'

Jules looked very small and vulnerable as her eyes searched his face. He took her hands in his, gave an exclamation and started gently rubbing them. 'You're so cold, my darling. You must go to bed and look after yourself. Remember the child.'

She pulled her hands away and placed them underneath her armpits but her eyes never left his face. 'You'll come back?' she said in a whisper. It was impossible to tell whether it was a plea or a question. Or, if it was a question, what she wanted as the answer.

'You'll be told what's happening, I promise.' He looked up at William, who gave him a nod.

Terri watched her father as he rose to his feet. 'I'm ready

to go with you and answer all your questions,' he said to Garnier. He looked at Darina. 'Will you look after my wife?'

'Of course I will,' said Darina.

Then he looked at Terri. She rose from the sofa and went towards him. 'I'll be here, Dad. You can rely on me.'

His eyes looked into hers as though she truly was his daughter. But he said, 'I want you to go home. I shan't be able to handle things here if I'm worried about you. Henri will take you to the airport and put you on a plane. Have you got your passport with you?'

Terri nodded. She always carried that.

'Don't worry about your things – that boy can take them back. Use the housekeeping funds for her flight, Henri. Madame will replace them.'

The butler had been standing a little apart, watching the proceedings with a gently detached air that failed to conceal a burning curiosity. 'Certainly, sir,' he said.

'Telephone her mother to meet her – the number's in the book under Arden.'

Henri dipped his head in acknowledgement.

Terri said nothing. She didn't want her father any more worried than he was. She was, however, making her own plans.

Chapter Twenty-Six

Darina helped a limp Jules into bed. Henri had taken one of Jules's arms round his shoulder, helping support her up the stairs, and shown the way into a room on the right of the landing, but he appeared to consider anything further concerning a half-fainting pregnant woman was not within his scope of duties.

Darina unzipped Jules's dress and removed her shoes, letting the limp body sink back on to the enormous bed. Then she managed to pull off the quilted chintz cover and slip Jules's legs underneath the bedclothes. 'Can I get you anything?' she asked, folding up the coverlet and placing it on the buttoned chair that stood by an antique Regency sofa table equipped with a Sheraton mirror and a battery of expensive cosmetics.

The girl's eyes, puzzled and anxious, looked back at her. 'What's going to happen to John?'

'I expect the police will question him until they are satisfied he has told them everything about how Bernard died and . . .' She hesitated, wondering whether to mention the poisoning attempt. The girl had enough to cope with at the moment, she decided. 'And they know exactly what happened.'

'Will he be arrested?'

'Since he's admitted to the killing, I should think he probably will be. Shall I ask Henri to call a doctor? He could give you a sedative so you can sleep.'

'I don't like taking things and I feel quite sleepy anyway,' Jules murmured, closing her eyes. 'When I wake up I'll see about a lawyer.'

Darina stood looking at the dark lashes that swept her cheeks. What a shock she had had! Witnessing Jules's revulsion and instinctive rejection of her husband, she could almost understand John Rickwood's desperate bid to prevent his secret getting out. Cannibalism, the last of the taboos. For some people, it was worse than murder. In Holy Communion bread and wine are consumed as the flesh and blood of Christ but nothing can change human flesh into the staff of life. A person can be *in extremis*, as John was, and still not be forgiven for breaking that unwritten rule that is burnt into the human psyche: thou shalt not eat the flesh of one of thy brethren. Had he told his first wife? Was that why their marriage had broken up? Was he convinced it would poison the relationship between him and his second wife? Perhaps deny him his unborn child?

Darina moved over to the windows. She pulled the curtain cords and shut out the view of gracious gardens, sparkling sea and dancing yachts, and moved on to the next, which opened on to a small balcony with a flight of stairs to the garden. How splendidly Terri had reacted to her father's confession. Even after he'd admitted to murder she hadn't flinched.

Jules now appeared to be asleep. Darina slipped out of the room, quietly closed the door and went down the stairs.

John Rickwood was waiting in the hall with William and Garnier. Behind them stood the butler and Terri.

John looked up at her. 'How is she?'

'Fine. She's asleep.'

'Will you stay with her until Henri returns from the airport? I wouldn't like her to wake and find she's alone.'

'Of course I will, but don't you have a maidservant as well?'

'Maidservant?'

Henri stepped forward. 'I think Madame means Odile, the cook.' He looked at his watch. 'She is here now but will be leaving shortly. She is off this evening as Monsieur and Madame were to dine out. I will ask her to set a luncheon tray for Madame Pigram and something for Madame when she wakes together with a light supper.'

Garnier held out his hand to Darina. '*Mes félicitations, Madame, vous êtes extraordinaire.*' He gave a slight bow and she had to take it as a compliment. 'Monsieur,' he said politely to John Rickwood, and indicated the front door.

William lagged behind to give Darina a quick kiss. 'You were brilliant, darling.'

'I thought you wouldn't be able to persuade Garnier after I called you from Helen's. I was so relieved when you did turn up.'

'After you'd demonstrated your amazing deductive powers, it was all plain sailing.'

'Will you be long?'

He gave a helpless shrug. 'Who can tell? You know what a time questioning can take.'

Darina did indeed; the checking and rechecking that had to be carried out, the testing of the witness's story against known facts, the search for discrepancies.

William left and Henri closed the door behind him. 'I will collect my coat and some car keys, then I will drive Mam'selle to the airport. Does Mam'selle wish to ring her mother in England first?'

'No, Mam'selle doesn't,' Terri stated belligerently. But,

surprisingly, she made no attempt to persuade him not to take her.

'Would you like me to ring your mother?' Darina asked while they waited for Henri to reappear.

'Thanks, but no thanks.' Terri grinned at her.

'Just what have you in mind?'

'If you don't know, you can't be blamed.'

'Dreadful girl. I suppose you intend getting back to Stephen somehow. I don't know why you didn't go with him and Helen.'

'I had to be here,' Terri said simply.

Henri came back into the hall buttoning a smart reefer coat over his black jacket and grey striped trousers. He held a set of car keys. 'I have taken the liberty of setting the answer machine on the telephone so that Madame will not be inconvenienced by having to respond to any call,' he announced to Darina. 'And if Madame wishes for anything before I return, she will find the kitchen through there. She is to make herself at home.'

Where, she wondered, had Henri learned his perfect English?

She followed them out of the house and round to the garage. On an impulse, she reached for Terri and gave her a kiss, 'Be careful and—' she glanced towards Henri, now aiming the car tag at the garage door, '—*au revoir*,' she whispered.

Henri stood by the open garage, hesitated, then came up to Darina. 'Perhaps Madame should know that when Monsieur went to Monsieur Björnson's that day, he took the Peugeot.'

On the right of the garage stood the grey Saab, on the left a small, four-door Peugeot. It was this car that Henri now drove out, and he opened one of the back doors for Terri.

Terri ignored it. 'Nah, I'll sit in the front with you, Henri.'

She yanked the door open and plumped herself heavily in the seat. For a moment he looked disconcerted, then, accepting the inevitable, regained the driver's seat and set off. By the time they were half-way down the drive, the garage door had shut itself and the villa gates had opened. Darina stood and watched while the car drove through and, almost immediately, the gates swung to again. But they hadn't quite shut. That was how Helen and Stephen had been able to gain access so quickly.

Darina moved to return to the house, then was struck by a thought and went over to where the shrubs grew in thick profusion around the house. Maybe there was another odd end she could tie up for William.

Half-way through her search, Odile came out of the house, took a bicycle from the garage and, with a polite *au revoir* to Darina, rode down the drive.

It occurred to Darina that lunch and supper would be very scratch if the time Odile had spent on them was anything to go by. Then she returned to her scrutiny of the shrubs. She finally found what she thought could have been responsible for Mike's collapse – a laurel with long, shiny leaves. Still adhering to some of the branches, among new, young growth, were a few wrinkled purple-black berries.

She tore off a small branch. The slightest of noises, no more than an indrawn breath, made her look up. She was below the balcony that led off Jules Rickwood's bedroom and caught the swirl of a white *négligé* disappearing through the door.

Darina's mind moved into top gear. Henri's parting remark fused with several other thoughts and the result suddenly floated up from her subconscious like a surfacing dolphin.

Placing the branch on a convenient window sill, she walked quickly into the house and upstairs.

Jules was in bed, the covers drawn up to her chin. She

looked wan and vulnerable. Darina ignored her and walked over to the mirrored cupboards that lined the walls. Opening door after door she started rifling through the rows of designer clothes.

Jules raised herself on her pillows. 'What are you doing?' Her voice was sharp and far from vulnerable.

'Looking for the clothes you wore when you killed Bernard,' announced Darina calmly.

Jules sat back on her pillows, her expression confident and sly.

Darina came and stood at the foot of the bed, leaving the cupboard doors open. She looked down at the lovely girl. 'But I won't find any bloodstained clothes, will I? You're much too clever for that. That's one of the things John liked about you, wasn't it, your intelligence?'

Jules gave a charming little pout. 'The first time we met he said he hated talking to females who were all looks and no sense.'

'And when you found out how rich he was, you decided he was your best chance to achieve the lifestyle you wanted.' Darina dug her hands deep into her trouser pockets. 'Your membership of Lloyd's may have brought you status but it was eating away your precious capital and you had to wait three years before you could escape from the trap you were caught in. By then, you could be wiped out. Even intact, the money you'd inherited from your father wasn't enough to sustain the sort of life you wanted, was it?'

Jules's gaze wandered away from Darina and fastened itself on the view from the window. It was as though she'd cut herself off from what was being said.

'Appearances have always been important to you, haven't they? You try to convince people it's purity you want, organic food, the best olive oil – how much of it is actually true? Did you really not know Bernard was responsible for La Chenais oil? Or did you want to check out the latest organic fashion and reckoned that was a way round your declared determination not to speak to him again? Are you a vegetarian because you believe it's politically correct?'

'The very thought of eating animals is anathema to me,' Jules said dreamily.

'In that case it must indeed have been a shock when your husband confessed to you that in order to keep alive he had been reduced to eating the flesh of another human. Instead of being the brave hero, he was a social pariah. What would people say, what would people think when they knew? You'd never be able to remain his wife. And being Mrs John Rickwood was important to you. How humiliating to have to be the divorced wife of a disgraced man. And who knew how the truth might affect his business? It could crash and take all your dreams with it. Your hard-won security was suddenly threatened. You had one chance – to get rid of the only other person who knew the truth.'

Jules returned her dreamy gaze to Darina. 'I heard John was a cannibal for the first time today,' she said.

'No. John told you as soon as he came back from his meeting with Bernard. He wouldn't have risked you hearing it from Bernard first. This morning, when he apologized for telling the truth, it was because he knew you didn't want anyone else to know. But then you collapsed. We thought it was because you were hearing the news of his cannibalism for the first time. John must have known there had to be some other reason. "Can't forgive, can't forget, people would never forget," you said, when you came round. Were you preparing to excuse yourself for killing the person who was going to expose John unless he recommended everyone pay up? Which you knew he'd never do and, anyway, you certainly weren't prepared to cover any more losses.'

Jules slid lower in the bed, once again pulling the covers up to her chin. She lay huddled under their protection as though trying to get warm, looking at Darina through half-closed eyes.

'But then you heard your husband admit to killing Bernard. You realized that he was taking on responsibility for the crime himself, that he wanted to save you. Miraculously, you were going to escape the consequences of your crime. But you forgot one thing.'

Jules's eyelids snapped open.

'You forgot your attempt to get rid of William and me. What made you think we were a danger? You might as well tell me, I'm sure you haven't told your husband anything about it and as soon as the police realize he knows nothing of any poisoned *gâteaux forêts noires*, it's not going to take them long to come to the right conclusion, particularly when they question Henri about the cars and hear that John wasn't driving the Saab that day – that it remained conveniently in the garage. How easy for you to slip down from this balcony and drive off without Henri realizing you weren't still up in your bedroom. No doubt you locked your door but he doesn't like you, does he? You knew that, when you said you didn't want to be disturbed, you would be left alone.'

Jules's eyes became slits. 'You think you're so clever, don't you? Björn warned me you were clever. "Very observant," he said. He rang after your last session with him. He's very observant as well. He'd noticed that John drove the Peugeot to him that morning. But why that should have led him to think I was in danger, I don't know.' For a moment she looked puzzled. 'But I knew I couldn't take the risk. If you were that clever, it was easier to get rid of you both.'

'After all, you'd killed once, why not again?'

Jules gave a little giggle. 'It gets quite easy. I was going to shoot Bernard with this.' She suddenly threw back the bedcovers and revealed a shotgun pointing at Darina.

Darina went very still.

'I'll say I thought you were a burglar – several houses round here have been done recently. I'll say I brought the gun up here because I was nervous, I hadn't realized you were still in the house. Charles Steinbaum is a keen shot, he left several guns for John to use. John wouldn't upset me like that, he hasn't hunted since we became engaged. But I knew where the key to the gun case was.

'When I decided I had to kill Bernard, I thought it would make the perfect weapon: the police can't identify shot, it's not like a bullet. So I rang Bernard and told him I wanted a chat with him on our own. I said I'd only come if no one else was around.' She gave a mocking little laugh. 'He was delighted. He thought I wanted to bargain with him, that he could get some money out of me. He said Helen was going out for the day and Stephen and Terri wouldn't be around. Then I suggested to Björn he get John to discuss his financial situation since John's very clever with money. Björn'll do anything for me. We were very close at one time. We only split up because he's determined not to get married – he says it would interfere with his career. I told John I needed a day in bed.'

Jules lay relaxed against the pillows, carefully holding the gun pointed at Darina. 'I knocked at La Chenais just to check there wasn't anyone else around. No one came and so I slipped off my clothes and pulled on a bin liner. Not very chic—' she giggled '—but very practical. I thought there might be quite a bit of blood, you see, shooting him at close quarters. And I know just how clever the forensic boys are these days. So, in my plastic dress and no shoes, I went quietly along to the mill with my little shotgun, like the farmer after the rabbit, bang, bang, bang. The door was open and I looked in and there was Bernard, bending over that chopping machine, his hands right in it. He'd shown me all the switches when he took me round that time, so I just flicked the right one on.'

This was a girl who could slip over the edge of sanity at any moment. Darina remained very still. 'What a shock for him.'

'Wasn't I clever? The noise he made! It was pure animal in agony!' She gave a shiver that was sheer excitement, her eyes fever bright. 'Then he came at me, his bloody fingers reaching out like freshly butchered meat.' She swallowed. 'He was coming so fast, I never imagined anyone could move that fast. I didn't have time to aim, so I swiped at him.' In the throes of re-creating the drama, Jules forgot about Darina and started to swing the gun. It was only for a fraction of a second, but Darina had seen her opportunity, leapt on to the bed and grabbed for the gun.

For a moment the two of them grappled for possession. Then Jules's finger pulled one of the triggers. The explosion in the confines of the room deafened Darina and she felt as though her ear drums had exploded. So confused were her senses, she had no idea whether she had been hit or not. Unable to assess the situation, she acted on instinct, jammed down her hip on the gun and forced the stock into Jules's body.

Jules cried out as the wood bit cruelly into her chest.

At the same time the door to the bedroom burst open and Terri and Henri were suddenly there.

'Watch it, she's got a gun,' gasped Darina, as though they couldn't have heard the shot as they came up the stairs. But even as she spoke, Jules managed to pull the second trigger – again came a shattering explosion and one of the mirrored doors disintegrated in a shower of silvered glass and wooden splinters.

'I've got her,' Terri screeched, scrambling on to the pillow above Jules's head. She forced a knee on to each of her shoulders and anchored her to the bed, Jules flinging her head from side to side in a frustrated attempt to free herself.

Henri forced his hands underneath Darina's body and got hold of Jules's arms. 'I think she's safe now, Madame,' he said.

Slowly Darina raised herself and grabbed the gun. Both barrels had been discharged but she didn't trust Jules not to use it as she had on Bernard, swinging the stock with murderous rage.

Jules was spitting anger, her eyes flickering rapidly, trying to look in all directions at once, her body squirming and flailing under the restraining force of Terri and the butler.

The room was a shambles. The first shot had blasted its way through the bottles on the dressing table, the little mirror and a window. Broken glass was everywhere and stray pellets had scarred the walls.

Ignoring the chaos, Darina opened drawers until she found a collection of tights. With some difficulty she managed to tie Jules's legs together then, with the help of the others, Jules's arms behind her.

'Quite a little parcel, Madame,' said Henri with satisfaction.

'Tell me,' said Darina, panting after all her efforts, 'where did you learn your English and how did Mrs Rickwood so annoy you?'

'Eton, Madam. My mother was French, my father English. Unfortunately, he was a gambler, lost all his money and killed himself in a car crash before I finished my schooling. I was left with no qualifications and an appreciation of how to live in a style I could no longer afford. It seemed sensible to become a butler. I have been happy to assist a number of excellent employers appreciate the benefits that can be bought with money and to help them acquire a style that has nothing to do with it. As for Mrs Rickwood,' he looked down at the hapless Jules, still struggling on the bed, 'she's a cheapskate and jumped-up nobody with no idea how to treat servants. Now, will you call the police, Madam, or shall I?'

'I will,' said Darina faintly.

Chapter Twenty-Seven

'What brought you and Henri back?' Darina asked Terri while they were waiting for the police. They'd left the butler keeping guard over Jules while they went downstairs for Darina to ring through to Garnier.

'As soon as we were out of the gate, I asked him what he meant about my father not driving the Saab. And he got the way he does, you know, all snooty and high-falutin, saying it was nothing for little girls to worry about. So when we came to a stop at traffic lights, I tried to pinch the key out of the lock but it wouldn't come. Henri slapped my hand and I got so mad I tore my T-shirt from top to bottom.' Terri opened her emerald bomber jacket to reveal the two pieces held together with a safety pin. 'And I told him that unless he came clean, I'd scream and scream and make people think he was abducting me.' She grinned. 'He got really shirty then and told me there was no need to go to such lengths. Then I remembered William saying how the police had zeroed in on a Saab car visiting Bernard about the time he was killed. So I asked Henri what Jules had been up to and he told me she'd spent the day in bed. Then he added that her room had a balcony with a stairway leading down to the garden. Of course, it was quite clear to me then that Jules had killed Bernard. I always knew she was no good.' Terri sounded quite gleeful. 'I told Henri we must go back, that we couldn't leave you alone in the house with her. You know, until I said that, I really don't think he'd thought you were in any danger. Even then it took a full minute, with us still heading towards Nice and me screaming at him, for him to realize. And then it took us ages to find somewhere to turn round and come back. When we heard that shot, I thought for sure you were dead.'

'There was a moment when I wasn't at all sure I was still in one piece,' confessed Darina. 'I take it you had already thought out that T-shirt trick to get Henri to take you to La Chenais.'

Terri grinned and said nothing.

It wasn't long before William and Garnier arrived.

'Where's Dad?' asked Terri.

'Still at the station,' said William. 'Don't look so worried, Terri. He'll be all right and he's not the only one there, the examining magistrate is still talking to Björn Björnson and Anthea Pemberton – there are a number of details that have to be tied up.' He turned to Darina. 'I've been so worried, are you really all right?'

'Fine, the odd bruise but nothing more.'

'You could have been killed! I'll never forgive myself for not realizing that Rickwood was shielding her and I'll never forgive him for putting you in such jeopardy.'

'I'm sure he had no idea how far she'd go, darling. Remember, he knew nothing about the poisoning attempt on us. As far as he was aware, Bernard was her only target.'

'How could he live with her and not realize what she was like?'

'Quite easily,' said Terri cheerfully. 'I've seen her lots of times and never realized. I knew I didn't like her but if all the people we didn't like were murderers, the world would be full of them, wouldn't it?'

It seemed to take ages for all the formalities to be concluded. Jules was taken away. Darina underwent endless questioning before her statement could be prepared. When she was finally free to go, she found John Rickwood was being released at the same time.

He looked a broken man, crushed by all that had happened over the last few days. 'Terri is waiting for you at the villa,' Darina told him.

For a moment he seemed unable to take in the meaning of her words, then he sighed. 'I've never been much of a father to her. I've only just understood how little I've given her.'

'You've time ahead,' Darina said gently. 'She's a staunch soul.'

William appeared and told him a car had been arranged to take him back.

'Will you be all right?' Darina asked. 'Would you like us to come with you?'

He shook his head. 'I'll be fine. I'll get Terri to stay with me tonight and tomorrow I'll take her up to her boyfriend. Perhaps we can get something sorted out about her future.'

Darina watched him leave and wondered about the future of his unborn child.

'Come on, my darling, time we went home,' said William.

'What about Anthea and Björn?' asked Darina, as he started the car she'd driven first to the Rickwood villa then the police station.

'Much as we thought. They've got a very nice little business going with the *L'Amour* series. They swear there's nothing between them. Personally, I think Anthea was telling us the truth about her relationship with Bernard. He was trying to blackmail them, by the way.'

'And Anthea actually thought he might stand by her pregnancy?'

341

'She says she was sure when he knew the truth, he'd give up trying to get money out of them. Until she met him in that bar in Tourettes.'

'Poor Anthea, life has been very unfair to her. And John really was with Björn the morning Bernard was killed?'

William nodded. 'So it seems. Björn refused to answer questions when it looked as though Jules was about to step into the frame. I think he was really very fond of her at one time.'

'And who's now got the bearer bonds?'

'Garnier's put them in their safe. Eventually they'll go back to Bernard's syndicate and be set against the losses. They'll alleviate the situation for the Names slightly. John thinks they have a good case for negligence and is going to advise they sue the underwriters. The Committee may in the end decide to help pay their losses. At the very least, it should postpone settlement day.'

'I wonder how long it's going to take for Helen to get over Roland?'

'Do you know, I don't think I care?'

William parked the car in the apartment garage and they took the lift up to their honeymoon home.

'What would you like to eat?' asked Darina, opening a cupboard and frowning at a packet of pasta. 'There's a bit of ham in the fridge. I could cook some tagliatelle and make a sauce from chopped ham, *crème fraîche* and some green peppercorns?'

'You're not going to cook a thing,' announced William, coming up behind her and slipping his arms around her waist. He gently kissed the back of her neck, exposed by the plait running up the back of her head. 'I thought we could have a quick shower, change and go out for a meal. It's time we got on with enjoying a proper honeymoon.'

'You mean, no more murder investigations?'

'I mean for the rest of the time we're in Antibes, we enjoy the sun, the food and each other. If the phone rings, we don't answer. If we see anyone we know while we're out, we disappear. I don't intend to share one little bit of you with anyone else.'

'Darling, you say the nicest things.' Darina turned and placed her arms behind his head. It was soon quite obvious that neither of them had forgotten what a honeymoon was meant to be for.

A selection of bestsellers from Headline

All Headline books are available at your local bookshop or newsagent, or can be ordered direct from the publisher. Just tick the titles you want and fill in the form below. Prices and availability subject to change without notice.

Headline Book Publishing, Cash Sales Department, Bookpoint, 39 Milton Park, Abingdon, OXON, OX14 4TD, UK. If you have a credit card you may order by telephone – 01235 400400.

Please enclose a cheque or postal order made payable to Bookpoint Ltd to the value of the cover price and allow the following for postage and packing:

UK & BFPO: £1.00 for the first book, 50p for the second book and 30p for each additional book ordered up to a maximum charge of £3.00.

OVERSEAS & EIRE: £2.00 for the first book, £1.00 for the second book and 50p for each additional book.

Name ....

Address ....

....

....

If you would prefer to pay by credit card, please complete:
Please debit my Visa/Access/Diner's Card/American Express (delete as applicable) card no:

Signature .... Expiry Date ....